I0831382

THE MAN IN THE IRON MASK

VOLUME ONE OF TWO

The Man in the Iron Mask

Dumas, Alexandre 1802 – 1870

First Published as a serial between 1847 - 1850
First Published in English in 1858 by G. Routledge & Co. by an anonymous translator.

Text set in 18 point Helvetica.
Chapter headings set in Helvetica Neue.

ISBN: 978-1-83412-393-6 Volume One
ISBN: 978-1-83412-394-3 Volume Two

THE MAN IN THE IRON MASK

VOLUME ONE OF TWO

ALEXANDRE DUMAS

GRAND TYPE CLASSICS

CONTENTS

The Man in the Iron Mask

VOLUME TWO

CHAPTER ONE

The Prisoner

SINCE ARAMIS'S singular transformation into a confessor of the order, Baisemeaux was no longer the same man. Up to that period, the place which Aramis had held in the worthy governor's estimation was that of a prelate whom he respected and a friend to whom he owed a debt of gratitude; but now he felt himself an inferior, and that Aramis was his master. He himself lighted a lantern, summoned a turnkey, and said, returning to Aramis, "I am at your orders, monseigneur." Aramis merely nodded his head, as much as to say, "Very good"; and signed to him with his hand to lead the way. Baisemeaux advanced, and Aramis followed him. It was a calm and lovely starlit night; the steps of three men resounded on the flags of the terraces, and the clinking of the keys hanging from the jailer's girdle made itself heard up to the stories of the towers, as if to remind the prisoners that the liberty of earth was a luxury beyond their reach. It might have been said that the alteration effected in Baisemeaux extended even to the prisoners. The turnkey, the same who, on Aramis's first arrival had shown himself so inquisitive and curious, was now not only silent, but impassible. He held his head down, and seemed afraid to keep his ears open. In this wise they reached the basement of the Bertaudiere, the two first stories of which were mounted silently and somewhat slowly; for Baisemeaux, though far from disobeying, was far from exhibiting any eagerness to obey. On arriving at the door, Baisemeaux showed a disposition to enter the prisoner's chamber; but Aramis, stopping him on the threshold, said, "The rules do not allow the governor to hear the prisoner's confession."

Baisemeaux bowed, and made way for Aramis, who took the lantern and entered; and then signed to them to close the door behind him. For an instant he remained standing, listening whether Baisemeaux and the turnkey had retired; but as soon as he was assured by the sound of their descending footsteps that they had left the tower, he put the lantern on the table and gazed around. On a bed of green serge, similar in all respect to the other beds in the Bastile, save that it was newer, and under curtains half-drawn, reposed a young man, to whom we have already once before introduced Aramis. According to custom, the prisoner was without a light. At the hour of curfew, he was bound to extinguish his lamp, and we perceive how much he was favored, in being allowed to keep it burning even till then. Near the bed a large leathern armchair, with twisted legs, sustained his clothes. A little table – without pens, books, paper, or ink – stood neglected in sadness near the window; while several plates, still unemptied, showed that the prisoner had scarcely touched his evening meal. Aramis saw that the young man was stretched upon his bed, his face half concealed by his arms. The arrival of a visitor did not caused any change of position; either he was waiting in expectation, or was asleep. Aramis lighted the candle from the lantern, pushed back the armchair, and approached the bed with an evident mixture of interest and respect. The young man raised his head. "What is it?" said he.

"You desired a confessor?" replied Aramis.

"Yes."

"Because you were ill?"

"Yes."

"Very ill?"

The young man gave Aramis a piercing glance, and answered, "I thank you." After a moment's silence, "I have seen you before," he continued. Aramis bowed.

Doubtless the scrutiny the prisoner had just made of the cold, crafty, and imperious character stamped upon the features of the bishop of Vannes was little reassuring to one in his situation, for he added, "I am better."

"And so?" said Aramis.

"Why, then – being better, I have no longer the same need of a confessor, I think."

"Not even of the hair-cloth, which the note you found in your bread informed you of?"

The young man started; but before he had either assented or denied, Aramis continued, "Not even of the ecclesiastic from whom you were to hear an important revelation?"

"If it be so," said the young man, sinking

again on his pillow, "it is different; I am listening."

Aramis then looked at him more closely, and was struck with the easy majesty of his mien, one which can never be acquired unless Heaven has implanted it in the blood or heart. "Sit down, monsieur," said the prisoner.

Aramis bowed and obeyed. "How does the Bastile agree with you?" asked the bishop.

"Very well."

"You do not suffer?"

"No."

"You have nothing to regret?"

"Nothing."

"Not even your liberty?"

"What do you call liberty, monsieur?" asked the prisoner, with the tone of a man who is preparing for a struggle.

"I call liberty, the flowers, the air, light, the stars, the happiness of going whithersoever the sinewy limbs of one-and-twenty chance to wish to carry you."

The young man smiled, whether in resignation or contempt, it was difficult to tell. "Look," said he, "I have in that Japanese vase two roses gathered yesterday evening in the bud from the governor's garden; this morning they have blown and spread their vermilion chalice beneath my gaze; with every opening petal they unfold the treasures of their perfumes, filling my chamber with a fragrance that embalms it. Look now on these two roses; even among roses these are beautiful, and the rose is the most beautiful of flowers. Why, then, do you bid me desire other flowers when I possess the loveliest of all?"

Aramis gazed at the young man in surprise.

"If **flowers** constitute liberty," sadly resumed the captive, "I am free, for I possess them."

"But the air!" cried Aramis; "air is so necessary to life!"

"Well, monsieur," returned the prisoner; "draw near to the window; it is open. Between high heaven and earth the wind whirls on its waftages of hail and lightning, exhales its torrid mist or breathes in gentle breezes. It caresses my face. When mounted on the back of this armchair, with my arm around the bars of the window to sustain myself, I fancy I am swimming the wide expanse before me." The countenance of Aramis darkened as the young man continued: "Light I have! what is better than light? I have the sun, a friend who comes to visit me every day without the permission of the governor or the jailer's company. He comes in at the window, and traces in my room a square the shape of the window, which lights up the hangings of my bed and floods the very floor. This luminous square increases from ten o'clock till midday, and decreases from one till three slowly, as if, having hastened to my presence, it sorrowed at bidding me farewell. When its last ray disappears I have enjoyed its presence for five hours. Is not that sufficient? I have been told that there are unhappy beings who dig in quarries, and laborers who toil in mines, who never behold it at all." Aramis wiped the drops from his brow. "As to the stars which are so delightful to view," continued the young man, "they all resemble each other save in size and brilliancy. I am a favored mortal, for if you had not lighted that candle you would have been able to see the beautiful stars which I was gazing at from my couch before your arrival, whose silvery rays were stealing through my brain."

Aramis lowered his head; he felt himself overwhelmed with the bitter flow of that sinister philosophy which is the religion of the captive.

"So much, then, for the flowers, the air, the daylight, and the stars," tranquilly continued the young man; "there remains but exercise. Do I not walk all day in the governor's garden if it is fine – here if it rains? in the fresh air if it is warm; in perfect warmth, thanks to my winter stove, if it be cold? Ah! monsieur, do you fancy," continued the prisoner, not without bitterness, "that men have not done everything for me that a man can hope for or desire?"

"Men!" said Aramis; "be it so; but it seems to me you are forgetting Heaven."

"Indeed I have forgotten Heaven," murmured the prisoner, with emotion; "but why do you mention it? Of what use is it to talk to a prisoner of Heaven?"

Aramis looked steadily at this singular youth, who possessed the resignation of a martyr with the smile of an atheist. "Is not Heaven in everything?" he murmured in a reproachful tone.

"Say rather, at the end of everything," answered the prisoner, firmly.

"Be it so," said Aramis; "but let us return to our starting-point."

"I ask nothing better," returned the young man.

"I am your confessor."

"Yes."

"Well, then, you ought, as a penitent, to

tell me the truth."

"My whole desire is to tell it you."

"Every prisoner has committed some crime for which he has been imprisoned. What crime, then, have you committed?"

"You asked me the same question the first time you saw me," returned the prisoner.

"And then, as now you evaded giving me an answer."

"And what reason have you for thinking that I shall now reply to you?"

"Because this time I am your confessor."

"Then if you wish me to tell what crime I have committed, explain to me in what a crime consists. For as my conscience does not accuse me, I aver that I am not a criminal."

"We are often criminals in the sight of the great of the earth, not alone for having ourselves committed crimes, but because we know that crimes have been committed."

The prisoner manifested the deepest attention.

"Yes, I understand you," he said, after a pause; "yes, you are right, monsieur; it is very possible that, in such a light, I am a criminal in the eyes of the great of the earth."

"Ah! then you know something," said Aramis, who thought he had pierced not merely through a defect in the harness, but through the joints of it.

"No, I am not aware of anything," replied the young man; "but sometimes I think – and I say to myself – "

"What do you say to yourself?"

"That if I were to think but a little more deeply I should either go mad or I should divine a great deal."

"And then – and then?" said Aramis, impatiently.

"Then I leave off."

"You leave off?"

"Yes; my head becomes confused and my ideas melancholy; I feel **ennui** overtaking me; I wish – "

"What?"

"I don't know; but I do not like to give myself up to longing for things which I do not possess, when I am so happy with what I have."

"You are afraid of death?" said Aramis, with a slight uneasiness.

"Yes," said the young man, smiling.

Aramis felt the chill of that smile, and shuddered. "Oh, as you fear death, you know more about matters than you say," he cried.

"And you," returned the prisoner, "who bade me to ask to see you; you, who, when I did ask to see you, came here promising a world of confidence; how is it that, nevertheless, it is you who are silent, leaving it for me to speak? Since, then, we both wear masks, either let us both retain them or put them aside together."

Aramis felt the force and justice of the remark, saying to himself, "This is no ordinary man; I must be cautious. – Are you ambitious?" said he suddenly to the prisoner, aloud, without preparing him for the alteration.

"What do you mean by ambitious?" replied the youth.

"Ambition," replied Aramis, "is the feeling which prompts a man to desire more – much more – than he possesses."

"I said that I was contented, monsieur; but, perhaps, I deceive myself. I am ignorant of the nature of ambition; but it is not impossible I may have some. Tell me your mind; that is all I ask."

"An ambitious man," said Aramis, "is one who covets that which is beyond his station."

"I covet nothing beyond my station," said the young man, with an assurance of manner which for the second time made the bishop of Vannes tremble.

He was silent. But to look at the kindling eye, the knitted brow, and the reflective attitude of the captive, it was evident that he expected something more than silence, – a silence which Aramis now broke. "You lied the first time I saw you," said he.

"Lied!" cried the young man, starting up

on his couch, with such a tone in his voice, and such a lightning in his eyes, that Aramis recoiled, in spite of himself.

"I **should** say," returned Aramis, bowing, "you concealed from me what you knew of your infancy."

"A man's secrets are his own, monsieur," retorted the prisoner, "and not at the mercy of the first chance-comer."

"True," said Aramis, bowing still lower than before, "'Tis true; pardon me, but to-day do I still occupy the place of a chance-comer? I beseech you to reply, monseigneur."

This title slightly disturbed the prisoner; but nevertheless he did not appear astonished that it was given him. "I do not know you, monsieur," said he.

"Oh, but if I dared, I would take your hand and kiss it!"

The young man seemed as if he were going to give Aramis his hand; but the light which beamed in his eyes faded away, and he coldly and distrustfully withdrew his hand again. "Kiss the hand of a prisoner," he said, shaking his head, "to what purpose?"

"Why did you tell me," said Aramis, "that you were happy here? Why, that you aspired to nothing? Why, in a word, by thus speaking, do you prevent me from being frank in my turn?"

The same light shone a third time in the young man's eyes, but died ineffectually away as before.

"You distrust me," said Aramis.

"And why say you so, monsieur?"

"Oh, for a very simple reason; if you know what you ought to know, you ought to mistrust everybody."

"Then do not be astonished that I am mistrustful, since you suspect me of knowing what I do not know."

Aramis was struck with admiration at this energetic resistance. "Oh, monseigneur! you drive me to despair," said he, striking the armchair with his fist.

"And, on my part, I do not comprehend

you, monsieur."

"Well, then, try to understand me." The prisoner looked fixedly at Aramis.

"Sometimes it seems to me," said the latter, "that I have before me the man whom I seek, and then – "

"And then your man disappears, – is it not so?" said the prisoner, smiling. "So much the better."

Aramis rose. "Certainly," said he; "I have nothing further to say to a man who mistrusts me as you do."

"And I, monsieur," said the prisoner, in the same tone, "have nothing to say to a man who will not understand that a prisoner ought to be mistrustful of everybody."

"Even of his old friends," said Aramis. "Oh, monseigneur, you are **too** prudent!"

"Of my old friends? – you one of my old friends, – you?"

"Do you no longer remember," said Aramis, "that you once saw, in the village where your early years were spent – "

"Do you know the name of the village?" asked the prisoner.

"Noisy-le-Sec, monseigneur," answered Aramis, firmly.

"Go on," said the young man, with an immovable aspect.

"Stay, monseigneur," said Aramis; "if you are positively resolved to carry on this game, let us break off. I am here to tell you many things, 'tis true; but you must allow me to see that, on your side, you have a desire to know them. Before revealing the important matters I still withhold, be assured I am in need of some encouragement, if not candor; a little sympathy, if not confidence. But you keep yourself intrenched in a pretended which paralyzes me. Oh, not for the reason you think; for, ignorant as you may be, or indifferent as you feign to be, you are none the less what you are, monseigneur, and there is nothing – nothing, mark me! which can cause you not to be so."

"I promise you," replied the prisoner,

"to hear you without impatience. Only it appears to me that I have a right to repeat the question I have already asked, 'Who **are** you?'"

"Do you remember, fifteen or eighteen years ago, seeing at Noisy-le-Sec a cavalier, accompanied by a lady in black silk, with flame-colored ribbons in her hair?"

"Yes," said the young man; "I once asked the name of this cavalier, and they told me that he called himself the Abbe d'Herblay. I was astonished that the abbe had so warlike an air, and they replied that there was nothing singular in that, seeing that he was one of Louis XIII.'s musketeers."

"Well," said Aramis, "that musketeer and abbe, afterwards bishop of Vannes, is your confessor now."

"I know it; I recognized you."

"Then, monseigneur, if you know that, I must further add a fact of which you are ignorant – that if the king were to know this evening of the presence of this musketeer, this abbe, this bishop, this confessor, **here** – he, who has risked everything to visit you, to-morrow would behold the steely glitter of the executioner's axe in a dungeon more gloomy, more obscure than yours."

While listening to these words, delivered with emphasis, the young man had raised himself on his couch, and was now gazing more and more eagerly at Aramis.

The result of his scrutiny was that he appeared to derive some confidence from it. "Yes," he murmured, "I remember perfectly. The woman of whom you speak came once with you, and twice afterwards with another." He hesitated.

"With another, who came to see you every month – is it not so, monseigneur?"

"Yes."

"Do you know who this lady was?"

The light seemed ready to flash from the prisoner's eyes. "I am aware that she was one of the ladies of the court," he said.

"You remember that lady well, do you not?"

"Oh, my recollection can hardly be very confused on this head," said the young prisoner. "I saw that lady once with a gentleman about forty-five years old. I saw her once with you, and with the lady dressed in black. I have seen her twice since then with the same person. These four people, with my master, and old Perronnette, my jailer, and the governor of the prison, are the only persons with whom I have ever spoken, and, indeed, almost the only persons I have ever seen."

"Then you were in prison?"

"If I am a prisoner here, then I was comparatively free, although in a very narrow sense – a house I never quitted, a garden surrounded with walls I could not climb, these constituted my residence, but you know it, as you have been there. In a word, being accustomed to live within these bounds, I never cared to leave them. And so you will understand, monsieur, that having never seen anything of the world, I have nothing left to care for; and therefore, if you relate anything, you will be obliged to explain each item to me as you go along."

"And I will do so," said Aramis, bowing; "for it is my duty, monseigneur."

"Well, then, begin by telling me who was my tutor."

"A worthy and, above all, an honorable gentleman, monseigneur; fit guide for both body and soul. Had you ever any reason to complain of him?"

"Oh, no; quite the contrary. But this gentleman of yours often used to tell me that my father and mother were dead. Did he deceive me, or did he speak the truth?"

"He was compelled to comply with the orders given him."

"Then he lied?"

"In one respect. Your father is dead."

"And my mother?"

"She is dead **for you**."

"But then she lives for others, does she not?"

"Yes."

"And I – and I, then" (the young man looked sharply at Aramis) "am compelled to live in the obscurity of a prison?"

"Alas! I fear so."

"And that because my presence in the world would lead to the revelation of a great secret?"

"Certainly, a very great secret."

"My enemy must indeed be powerful, to be able to shut up in the Bastile a child such as I then was."

"He is."

"More powerful than my mother, then?"

"And why do you ask that?"

"Because my mother would have taken my part."

Aramis hesitated. "Yes, monseigneur; more powerful than your mother."

"Seeing, then, that my nurse and preceptor were carried off, and that I, also, was separated from them – either they were, or I am, very dangerous to my enemy?"

"Yes; but you are alluding to a peril from which he freed himself, by causing the nurse and preceptor to disappear," answered Aramis, quietly.

"Disappear!" cried the prisoner, "how did they disappear?"

"In a very sure way," answered Aramis – "they are dead."

The young man turned pale, and passed his hand tremblingly over his face. "Poison?" he asked.

"Poison."

The prisoner reflected a moment. "My enemy must indeed have been very cruel, or hard beset by necessity, to assassinate those two innocent people, my sole support; for the worthy gentleman and the poor nurse had never harmed a living being."

"In your family, monseigneur, necessity is stern. And so it is necessity which compels me, to my great regret, to tell you that this gentleman and the unhappy lady have been assassinated."

"Oh, you tell me nothing I am not aware of," said the prisoner, knitting his brows.

"How?"

"I suspected it."

"Why?"

"I will tell you."

At this moment the young man, supporting himself on his two elbows, drew close to Aramis's face, with such an expression of dignity, of self-command and of defiance even, that the bishop felt the electricity of enthusiasm strike in devouring flashes from that great heart of his, into his brain of adamant.

"Speak, monseigneur. I have already told you that by conversing with you I endanger my life. Little value as it has, I implore you to accept it as the ransom of your own."

"Well," resumed the young man, "this is why I suspected they had killed my nurse and my preceptor – "

"Whom you used to call your father?"

"Yes; whom I called my father, but whose

son I well knew I was not."

"Who caused you to suppose so?"

"Just as you, monsieur, are too respectful for a friend, he was also too respectful for a father."

"I, however," said Aramis, "have no intention to disguise myself."

The young man nodded assent and continued: "Undoubtedly, I was not destined to perpetual seclusion," said the prisoner; "and that which makes me believe so, above all, now, is the care that was taken to render me as accomplished a cavalier as possible. The gentleman attached to my person taught me everything he knew himself – mathematics, a little geometry, astronomy, fencing and riding. Every morning I went through military exercises, and practiced on horseback. Well, one morning during the summer, it being very hot, I went to sleep in the hall. Nothing, up to that period, except the respect paid me, had enlightened me, or even roused my suspicions. I lived as children, as birds, as plants, as the air and the sun do. I had just turned my fifteenth year – "

"This, then, is eight years ago?"

"Yes, nearly; but I have ceased to reckon time."

"Excuse me; but what did your tutor tell you, to encourage you to work?"

"He used to say that a man was bound to make for himself, in the world, that fortune which Heaven had refused him at his birth. He added that, being a poor, obscure orphan, I had no one but myself to look to; and that nobody either did, or ever would, take any interest in me. I was, then, in the hall I have spoken of, asleep from fatigue with long fencing. My preceptor was in his room on the first floor, just over me. Suddenly I heard him exclaim, and then he called: 'Perronnette! Perronnette!' It was my nurse whom he called."

"Yes, I know it," said Aramis. "Continue, monseigneur."

"Very likely she was in the garden; for my preceptor came hastily downstairs. I rose, anxious at seeing him anxious. He opened the garden-door, still crying out, 'Perronnette! Perronnette!' The windows of the hall looked into the court; the shutters were closed; but through a chink in them I saw my tutor draw near a large well, which was almost directly under the windows of his study. He stooped over the brim, looked into the well, and again cried out, and made wild and affrighted gestures. Where I was, I could not only see, but hear – and see and hear I did."

"Go on, I pray you," said Aramis.

"Dame Perronnette came running up, hearing the governor's cries. He went to meet her, took her by the arm, and drew her quickly towards the edge; after which, as they both bent over it together, 'Look, look,' cried he, 'what a misfortune!'

"'Calm yourself, calm yourself,' said Perronnette; 'what is the matter?'

"'The letter!' he exclaimed; 'do you see that

letter?' pointing to the bottom of the well.

"'What letter?' she cried.

"'The letter you see down there; the last letter from the queen.'

"At this word I trembled. My tutor – he who passed for my father, he who was continually recommending me modesty and humility – in correspondence with the queen!

"'The queen's last letter!' cried Perronnette, without showing more astonishment than at seeing this letter at the bottom of the well; 'but how came it there?'

"'A chance, Dame Perronnette – a singular chance. I was entering my room, and on opening the door, the window, too, being open, a puff of air came suddenly and carried off this paper – this letter of her majesty's; I darted after it, and gained the window just in time to see it flutter a moment in the breeze and disappear down the well.'

"'Well,' said Dame Perronnette; 'and if the letter has fallen into the well, 'tis all the same as if it was burnt; and as the queen burns all her letters every time she comes – '

"And so you see this lady who came every month was the queen," said the prisoner.

"'Doubtless, doubtless,' continued the old gentleman; 'but this letter contained instructions – how can I follow them?'

"'Write immediately to her; give her a plain account of the accident, and the queen will no doubt write you another letter in place of this.'

"'Oh! the queen would never believe the story,' said the good gentleman, shaking his head; 'she will imagine that I want to keep this letter instead of giving it up like the rest, so as to have a hold over her. She is so distrustful, and M. de Mazarin so – Yon devil of an Italian is capable of having us poisoned at the first breath of suspicion.'"

Aramis almost imperceptibly smiled.

"'You know, Dame Perronnette, they are both so suspicious in all that concerns Philippe.'

"Philippe was the name they gave me,"

said the prisoner.

"'Well, 'tis no use hesitating,' said Dame Perronnette, 'somebody must go down the well.'

"'Of course; so that the person who goes down may read the paper as he is coming up.'

"'But let us choose some villager who cannot read, and then you will be at ease.'

"'Granted; but will not any one who descends guess that a paper must be important for which we risk a man's life? However, you have given me an idea, Dame Perronnette; somebody shall go down the well, but that somebody shall be myself.'

"But at this notion Dame Perronnette lamented and cried in such a manner, and so implored the old nobleman, with tears in her eyes, that he promised her to obtain a ladder long enough to reach down, while she went in search of some stout-hearted youth, whom she was to persuade that a jewel had fallen into the well, and that this jewel was wrapped in a paper. 'And as paper,' remarked my preceptor, 'naturally unfolds in water, the young man would not be surprised at finding nothing, after all, but the letter wide open.'

"'But perhaps the writing will be already effaced by that time,' said Dame Perronnette.

"'No consequence, provided we secure the letter. On returning it to the queen, she will see at once that we have not betrayed her; and consequently, as we shall not rouse the distrust of Mazarin, we shall have nothing to fear from him.'

"Having come to this resolution, they parted. I pushed back the shutter, and, seeing that my tutor was about to re-enter, I threw myself on my couch, in a confusion of brain caused by all I had just heard. My governor opened the door a few moments after, and thinking I was asleep gently closed it again. As soon as ever it was shut, I rose, and, listening, heard the sound of retiring footsteps. Then I returned to the shutters, and saw my tutor and Dame

Perronnette go out together. I was alone in the house. They had hardly closed the gate before I sprang from the window and ran to the well. Then, just as my governor had leaned over, so leaned I. Something white and luminous glistened in the green and quivering silence of the water. The brilliant disk fascinated and allured me; my eyes became fixed, and I could hardly breathe. The well seemed to draw me downwards with its slimy mouth and icy breath; and I thought I read, at the bottom of the water, characters of fire traced upon the letter the queen had touched. Then, scarcely knowing what I was about, and urged on by one of those instinctive impulses which drive men to destruction, I lowered the cord from the windlass of the well to within about three feet of the water, leaving the bucket dangling, at the same time taking infinite pains not to disturb that coveted letter, which was beginning to change its white tint for the hue of chrysoprase, – proof enough that it was sinking, – and then, with the rope weltering in my hands, slid down into the abyss. When I saw myself hanging over the dark pool, when I saw the sky lessening above my head, a cold shudder came over me, a chill fear got the better of me, I was seized with giddiness, and the hair rose on my head; but my strong will still reigned supreme over all the terror and disquietude. I gained the water, and at once plunged into it, holding on by one hand, while I immersed the other and seized the dear letter, which, alas! came in two in my grasp. I concealed the two fragments in my body-coat, and, helping myself with my feet against the sides of the pit, and clinging on with my hands, agile and vigorous as I was, and, above all, pressed for time, I regained the brink, drenching it as I touched it with the water that streamed off me. I was no sooner out of the well with my prize, than I rushed into the sunlight, and took refuge in a kind of shrubbery at the bottom of the garden. As I entered my hiding-place, the bell which resounded when the great gate was opened, rang. It was my preceptor come back again. I had but just time. I calculated that it would take ten minutes before he would gain my place of concealment, even if, guessing where I was, he came straight to it; and twenty if he were obliged to look for me. But this was time enough to allow me to read the cherished letter, whose fragments I hastened to unite again. The writing was already fading, but I managed to decipher it all.

"And will you tell me what you read therein, monseigneur?" asked Aramis, deeply interested.

"Quite enough, monsieur, to see that my tutor was a man of noble rank, and that Perronnette, without being a lady of quality, was far better than a servant; and also to perceived that I must myself be high-born, since the queen, Anne of Austria, and

Mazarin, the prime minister, commended me so earnestly to their care." Here the young man paused, quite overcome.

"And what happened?" asked Aramis.

"It happened, monsieur," answered he, "that the workmen they had summoned found nothing in the well, after the closest search; that my governor perceived that the brink was all watery; that I was not so dried by the sun as to prevent Dame Perronnette spying that my garments were moist; and, lastly, that I was seized with a violent fever, owing to the chill and the excitement of my discovery, an attack of delirium supervening, during which I related the whole adventure; so that, guided by my avowal, my governor found the pieces of the queen's letter inside the bolster where I had concealed them."

"Ah!" said Aramis, "now I understand."

"Beyond this, all is conjecture. Doubtless the unfortunate lady and gentleman, not daring to keep the occurrence secret, wrote of all this to the queen and sent back the torn letter."

"After which," said Aramis, "you were arrested and removed to the Bastile."

"As you see."

"Your two attendants disappeared?"

"Alas!"

"Let us not take up our time with the dead, but see what can be done with the living. You told me you were resigned."

"I repeat it."

"Without any desire for freedom?"

"As I told you."

"Without ambition, sorrow, or thought?"

The young man made no answer.

"Well," asked Aramis, "why are you silent?"

"I think I have spoken enough," answered the prisoner, "and that now it is your turn. I am weary."

Aramis gathered himself up, and a shade of deep solemnity spread itself over his countenance. It was evident that he had reached the crisis in the part he had come to the prison to play. "One question," said

Aramis.

"What is it? speak."

"In the house you inhabited there were neither looking-glasses nor mirrors?"

"What are those two words, and what is their meaning?" asked the young man; "I have no sort of knowledge of them."

"They designate two pieces of furniture which reflect objects; so that, for instance, you may see in them your own lineaments, as you see mine now, with the naked eye."

"No; there was neither a glass nor a mirror in the house," answered the young man.

Aramis looked round him. "Nor is there anything of the kind here, either," he said; "they have again taken the same precaution."

"To what end?"

"You will know directly. Now, you have told me that you were instructed in mathematics, astronomy, fencing, and riding; but you have not said a word about history."

"My tutor sometimes related to me the principal deeds of the king, St. Louis, King

Francis I., and King Henry IV."

"Is that all?"

"Very nearly."

"This also was done by design, then; just as they deprived you of mirrors, which reflect the present, so they left you in ignorance of history, which reflects the past. Since your imprisonment, books have been forbidden you; so that you are unacquainted with a number of facts, by means of which you would be able to reconstruct the shattered mansion of your recollections and your hopes."

"It is true," said the young man.

"Listen, then; I will in a few words tell you what has passed in France during the last twenty-three or twenty-four years; that is, from the probable date of your birth; in a word, from the time that interests you."

"Say on." And the young man resumed his serious and attentive attitude.

"Do you know who was the son of Henry IV.?"

"At least I know who his successor was."

"How?"

"By means of a coin dated 1610, which bears the effigy of Henry IV.; and another of 1612, bearing that of Louis XIII. So I presumed that, there being only two years between the two dates, Louis was Henry's successor."

"Then," said Aramis, "you know that the last reigning monarch was Louis XIII.?"

"I do," answered the youth, slightly reddening.

"Well, he was a prince full of noble ideas and great projects, always, alas! deferred by the trouble of the times and the dread struggle that his minister Richelieu had to maintain against the great nobles of France. The king himself was of a feeble character, and died young and unhappy."

"I know it."

"He had been long anxious about having a heir; a care which weighs heavily on princes, who desire to leave behind them more than one pledge that their best thoughts and works will be continued."

"Did the king, then, die childless?" asked the prisoner, smiling.

"No, but he was long without one, and for a long while thought he should be the last of his race. This idea had reduced him to the depths of despair, when suddenly, his wife, Anne of Austria – "

The prisoner trembled.

"Did you know," said Aramis, "that Louis XIII.'s wife was called Anne of Austria?"

"Continue," said the young man, without replying to the question.

"When suddenly," resumed Aramis, "the queen announced an interesting event. There was great joy at the intelligence, and all prayed for her happy delivery. On the 5th of September, 1638, she gave birth to a son."

Here Aramis looked at his companion, and thought he observed him turning pale. "You are about to hear," said Aramis, "an account which few indeed could now avouch; for it refers to a secret which they imagined buried with the dead, entombed in the abyss of the confessional."

"And you will tell me this secret?" broke in the youth.

"Oh!" said Aramis, with unmistakable emphasis, "I do not know that I ought to risk this secret by intrusting it to one who has no desire to quit the Bastile."

"I hear you, monsieur."

"The queen, then, gave birth to a son. But while the court was rejoicing over the event, when the king had shown the new-born child to the nobility and people, and was sitting gayly down to table, to celebrate the event, the queen, who was alone in her room, was again taken ill and gave birth to a second son."

"Oh!" said the prisoner, betraying a better acquaintance with affairs than he had owned to, "I thought that Monsieur was only born in – "

Aramis raised his finger; "Permit me to

continue," he said.

The prisoner sighed impatiently, and paused.

"Yes," said Aramis, "the queen had a second son, whom Dame Perronnette, the midwife, received in her arms."

"Dame Perronnette!" murmured the young man.

"They ran at once to the banqueting-room, and whispered to the king what had happened; he rose and quitted the table. But this time it was no longer happiness that his face expressed, but something akin to terror. The birth of twins changed into bitterness the joy to which that of an only son had given rise, seeing that in France (a fact you are assuredly ignorant of) it is the oldest of the king's sons who succeeds his father."

"I know it."

"And that the doctors and jurists assert that there is ground for doubting whether the son that first makes his appearance is the elder by the law of heaven and of nature."

The prisoner uttered a smothered cry, and became whiter than the coverlet under which he hid himself.

"Now you understand," pursued Aramis, "that the king, who with so much pleasure saw himself repeated in one, was in despair about two; fearing that the second might dispute the first's claim to seniority, which had been recognized only two hours before; and so this second son, relying on party interests and caprices, might one day sow discord and engender civil war throughout the kingdom; by these means destroying the very dynasty he should have strengthened."

"Oh, I understand! – I understand!" murmured the young man.

"Well," continued Aramis; "this is what they relate, what they declare; this is why one of the queen's two sons, shamefully parted from his brother, shamefully sequestered, is buried in profound obscurity; this is why that second son has disappeared, and so completely, that not a soul in France, save his mother, is aware of his existence."

"Yes! his mother, who has cast him off," cried the prisoner in a tone of despair.

"Except, also," Aramis went on, "the lady in the black dress; and, finally, excepting – "

"Excepting yourself – is it not? You who come and relate all this; you, who rouse in my soul curiosity, hatred, ambition, and, perhaps, even the thirst of vengeance; except you, monsieur, who, if you are the man to whom I expect, whom the note I have received applies to, whom, in short, Heaven ought to send me, must possess about you – "

"What?" asked Aramis.

"A portrait of the king, Louis XIV., who at this moment reigns upon the throne of France."

"Here is the portrait," replied the bishop, handing the prisoner a miniature in enamel, on which Louis was depicted life-like, with a handsome, lofty mien. The prisoner eagerly seized the portrait, and gazed at it with devouring eyes.

"And now, monseigneur," said Aramis, "here is a mirror." Aramis left the prisoner time to recover his ideas.

"So high! – so high!" murmured the young man, eagerly comparing the likeness of Louis with his own countenance reflected in the glass.

"What do you think of it?" at length said Aramis.

"I think that I am lost," replied the captive; "the king will never set me free."

"And I – I demand to know," added the bishop, fixing his piercing eyes significantly upon the prisoner, "I demand to know which of these two is king; the one this miniature portrays, or whom the glass reflects?"

"The king, monsieur," sadly replied the young man, "is he who is on the throne, who is not in prison; and who, on the other hand, can cause others to be entombed there. Royalty means power; and you behold how powerless I am."

"Monseigneur," answered Aramis, with a respect he had not yet manifested, "the king, mark me, will, if you desire it, be the one that, quitting his dungeon, shall maintain himself upon the throne, on which his friends will place him."

"Tempt me not, monsieur," broke in the prisoner bitterly.

"Be not weak, monseigneur," persisted Aramis; "I have brought you all the proofs of your birth; consult them; satisfy yourself that you are a king's son; it is for **us** to act."

"No, no; it is impossible."

"Unless, indeed," resumed the bishop ironically, "it be the destiny of your race, that the brothers excluded from the throne should be always princes void of courage and honesty, as was your uncle, M. Gaston d'Orleans, who ten times conspired against his brother Louis XIII."

"What!" cried the prince, astonished; "my uncle Gaston 'conspired against his brother'; conspired to dethrone him?"

"Exactly, monseigneur; for no other reason. I tell you the truth."

"And he had friends – devoted friends?"

"As much so as I am to you."

"And, after all, what did he do? – Failed!"

"He failed, I admit; but always through his own fault; and, for the sake of purchasing – not his life – for the life of the king's brother is sacred and inviolable – but his liberty, he sacrificed the lives of all his friends, one after another. And so, at this day, he is a very blot on history, the detestation of a hundred noble families in this kingdom."

"I understand, monsieur; either by weakness or treachery, my uncle slew his friends."

"By weakness; which, in princes, is always treachery."

"And cannot a man fail, then, from incapacity and ignorance? Do you really believe it possible that a poor captive such as I, brought up, not only at a distance from the court, but even from the world – do you believe it possible that such a one could assist those of his friends who should attempt to serve him?" And as Aramis was about to reply, the young man suddenly cried out, with a violence which betrayed the temper of his blood, "We are speaking of friends; but how can I have any friends – I, whom no one knows; and have neither liberty, money, nor influence, to gain any?"

"I fancy I had the honor to offer myself to your royal highness."

"Oh, do not style me so, monsieur; 'tis either treachery or cruelty. Bid me not think of aught beyond these prison-walls, which so grimly confine me; let me again love, or, at least, submit to my slavery and my obscurity."

"Monseigneur, monseigneur; if you again utter these desperate words – if, after having received proof of your high birth, you still remain poor-spirited in body and soul, I will comply with your desire, I will depart, and renounce forever the service of a master, to whom so eagerly I came to devote my assistance and my life!"

"Monsieur," cried the prince, "would it not have been better for you to have reflected, before telling me all that you have done, that you have broken my heart forever?"

"And so I desire to do, monseigneur."

"To talk to me about power, grandeur, eye, and to prate of thrones! Is a prison the fit place? You wish to make me believe in splendor, and we are lying lost in night; you boast of glory, and we are smothering our words in the curtains of this miserable bed; you give me glimpses of power absolute whilst I hear the footsteps of the every-watchful jailer in the corridor – that step which, after all, makes you tremble more than it does me. To render me somewhat less incredulous, free me from the Bastile; let me breathe the fresh air; give me my spurs and trusty sword, then we shall begin to understand each other."

"It is precisely my intention to give you all this, monseigneur, and more; only, do you desire it?"

"A word more," said the prince. "I know there are guards in every gallery, bolts to every door, cannon and soldiery at every barrier. How will you overcome the sentries – spike the guns? How will you break through the bolts and bars?"

"Monseigneur, – how did you get the note which announced my arrival to you?"

"You can bribe a jailer for such a thing as a note."

"If we can corrupt one turnkey, we can corrupt ten."

"Well; I admit that it may be possible to release a poor captive from the Bastile; possible so to conceal him that the king's people shall not again ensnare him; possible, in some unknown retreat, to sustain the unhappy wretch in some suitable manner."

"Monseigneur!" said Aramis, smiling.

"I admit that, whoever would do this much

for me, would seem more than mortal in my eyes; but as you tell me I am a prince, brother of the king, how can you restore me the rank and power which my mother and my brother have deprived me of? And as, to effect this, I must pass a life of war and hatred, how can you cause me to prevail in those combats – render me invulnerable by my enemies? Ah! monsieur, reflect on all this; place me, to-morrow, in some dark cavern at a mountain's base; yield me the delight of hearing in freedom sounds of the river, plain and valley, of beholding in freedom the sun of the blue heavens, or the stormy sky, and it is enough. Promise me no more than this, for, indeed, more you cannot give, and it would be a crime to deceive me, since you call yourself my friend."

Aramis waited in silence. "Monseigneur," he resumed, after a moment's reflection, "I admire the firm, sound sense which dictates your words; I am happy to have discovered my monarch's mind."

"Again, again! oh, God! for mercy's sake," cried the prince, pressing his icy hands upon his clammy brow, "do not play with me! I have no need to be a king to be the happiest of men."

"But I, monseigneur, wish you to be a king for the good of humanity."

"Ah!" said the prince, with fresh distrust inspired by the word; "ah! with what, then, has humanity to reproach my brother?"

"I forgot to say, monseigneur, that if you would allow me to guide you, and if you consent to become the most powerful monarch in Christendom, you will have promoted the interests of all the friends whom I devote to the success of your cause, and these friends are numerous."

"Numerous?"

"Less numerous than powerful, monseigneur."

"Explain yourself."

"It is impossible; I will explain, I swear

before Heaven, on that day that I see you sitting on the throne of France."

"But my brother?"

"You shall decree his fate. Do you pity him?"

"Him, who leaves me to perish in a dungeon? No, no. For him I have no pity!"

"So much the better."

"He might have himself come to this prison, have taken me by the hand, and have said, 'My brother, Heaven created us to love, not to contend with one another. I come to you. A barbarous prejudice has condemned you to pass your days in obscurity, far from mankind, deprived of every joy. I will make you sit down beside me; I will buckle round your waist our father's sword. Will you take advantage of this reconciliation to put down or restrain me? Will you employ that sword to spill my blood?' 'Oh! never,' I would have replied to him, 'I look on you as my preserver, I will respect you as my master. You give me far more than Heaven bestowed; for through you I possess liberty and the privilege of loving and being loved in this world.'"

"And you would have kept your word, monseigneur?"

"On my life! While now – now that I have guilty ones to punish – "

"In what manner, monseigneur?"

"What do you say as to the resemblance that Heaven has given me to my brother?"

"I say that there was in that likeness a providential instruction which the king ought to have heeded; I say that your mother committed a crime in rendering those different in happiness and fortune whom nature created so startlingly alike, of her own flesh, and I conclude that the object of punishment should be only to restore the equilibrium."

"By which you mean – "

"That if I restore you to your place on your brother's throne, he shall take yours in prison."

"Alas! there's such infinity of suffering in prison, especially it would be so for one who has drunk so deeply of the cup of enjoyment."

"Your royal highness will always be free to act as you may desire; and if it seems good to you, after punishment, you will have it in your power to pardon."

"Good. And now, are you aware of one thing, monsieur?"

"Tell me, my prince."

"It is that I will hear nothing further from you till I am clear of the Bastile."

"I was going to say to your highness that I should only have the pleasure of seeing you once again."

"And when?"

"The day when my prince leaves these gloomy walls."

"Heavens! how will you give me notice of it?"

"By myself coming to fetch you."

"Yourself?"

"My prince, do not leave this chamber save with me, or if in my absence you are compelled to do so, remember that I am not concerned in it."

"And so I am not to speak a word of this to any one whatever, save to you?"

"Save only to me." Aramis bowed very low. The prince offered his hand.

"Monsieur," he said, in a tone that issued from his heart, "one word more, my last. If you have sought me for my destruction; if you are only a tool in the hands of my enemies; if from our conference, in which you have sounded the depths of my mind, anything worse than captivity result, that is to say, if death befall me, still receive my blessing, for you will have ended my troubles and given me repose from the tormenting fever that has preyed on me for eight long, weary years."

"Monseigneur, wait the results ere you judge me," said Aramis.

"I say that, in such a case, I bless and forgive you. If, on the other hand, you are come to restore me to that position in the sunshine of fortune and glory to which I was destined by Heaven; if by your means

I am enabled to live in the memory of man, and confer luster on my race by deeds of valor, or by solid benefits bestowed upon my people; if, from my present depths of sorrow, aided by your generous hand, I raise myself to the very height of honor, then to you, whom I thank with blessings, to you will I offer half my power and my glory: though you would still be but partly recompensed, and your share must always remain incomplete, since I could not divide with you the happiness received at your hands."

"Monseigneur," replied Aramis, moved by the pallor and excitement of the young man, "the nobleness of your heart fills me with joy and admiration. It is not you who will have to thank me, but rather the nation whom you will render happy, the posterity whose name you will make glorious. Yes; I shall indeed have bestowed upon you more than life, I shall have given you immortality."

The prince offered his hand to Aramis,

who sank upon his knee and kissed it.

"It is the first act of homage paid to our future king," said he. "When I see you again, I shall say, 'Good day, sire.'"

"Till then," said the young man, pressing his wan and wasted fingers over his heart, – "till then, no more dreams, no more strain on my life – my heart would break! Oh, monsieur, how small is my prison – how low the window – how narrow are the doors! To think that so much pride, splendor, and happiness, should be able to enter in and to remain here!"

"Your royal highness makes me proud," said Aramis, "since you infer it is I who brought all this." And he rapped immediately on the door. The jailer came to open it with Baisemeaux, who, devoured by fear and uneasiness, was beginning, in spite of himself, to listen at the door. Happily, neither of the speakers had forgotten to smother his voice, even in the most passionate outbreaks.

"What a confessor!" said the governor,

forcing a laugh; "who would believe that a compulsory recluse, a man as though in the very jaws of death, could have committed crimes so numerous, and so long to tell of?"

Aramis made no reply. He was eager to leave the Bastile, where the secret which overwhelmed him seemed to double the weight of the walls. As soon as they reached Baisemeaux's quarters, "Let us proceed to business, my dear governor," said Aramis.

"Alas!" replied Baisemeaux.

"You have to ask me for my receipt for one hundred and fifty thousand livres," said the bishop.

"And to pay over the first third of the sum," added the poor governor, with a sigh, taking three steps towards his iron strong-box.

"Here is the receipt," said Aramis.

"And here is the money," returned Baisemeaux, with a threefold sigh.

"The order instructed me only to give a receipt; it said nothing about receiving the money," rejoined Aramis. "Adieu, monsieur le governeur!"

And he departed, leaving Baisemeaux almost more than stifled with joy and surprise at this regal present so liberally bestowed by the confessor extraordinary to the Bastile.

CHAPTER TWO

How Mouston had become Fatter without giving Porthos Notice thereof, and of the Troubles which Consequently Befell that Worthy Gentleman

SINCE THE DEPARTURE OF Athos for Blois, Porthos and D'Artagnan were seldom together. One was occupied with harassing duties for the king, the other had been making many purchases of furniture which he intended to forward to his estate, and by aid of which he hoped to establish in his various residences something of the courtly luxury he had witnessed in all its dazzling brightness in his majesty's society. D'Artagnan, ever faithful, one morning during an interval of service thought about Porthos, and being uneasy at not having heard anything of him for a fortnight, directed his steps towards his hotel, and pounced upon him just as he was getting up. The worthy baron had a pensive – nay, more than pensive – melancholy air. He was sitting on his bed, only half-dressed, and with legs dangling over the edge, contemplating a host of garments, which with their fringes, lace, embroidery, and slashes of ill-assorted hues, were strewed all over the floor. Porthos, sad and reflective as La Fontaine's hare, did not observe D'Artagnan's entrance, which was, moreover, screened at this moment by

M. Mouston, whose personal corpulency, quite enough at any time to hide one man from another, was effectually doubled by a scarlet coat which the intendant was holding up for his master's inspection, by the sleeves, that he might the better see it all over. D'Artagnan stopped at the threshold and looked in at the pensive Porthos and then, as the sight of the innumerable garments strewing the floor caused mighty sighs to heave the bosom of that excellent gentleman, D'Artagnan thought it time to put an end to these dismal reflections, and coughed by way of announcing himself.

"Ah!" exclaimed Porthos, whose countenance brightened with joy; "ah! ah! Here is D'Artagnan. I shall then get hold of an idea!"

At these words Mouston, doubting what was going on behind him, got out of the way, smiling kindly at the friend of his master, who thus found himself freed from the material obstacle which had prevented his reaching

D'Artagnan. Porthos made his sturdy knees crack again in rising, and crossing the room in two strides, found himself face to face with his friend, whom he folded to his breast with a force of affection that seemed to increase with every day. "Ah!" he repeated, "you are always welcome, dear friend; but just now you are more welcome than ever."

"But you seem to have the megrims here!" exclaimed D'Artagnan.

Porthos replied by a look expressive of dejection. "Well, then, tell me all about it, Porthos, my friend, unless it is a secret."

"In the first place," returned Porthos, "you know I have no secrets from you. This, then, is what saddens me."

"Wait a minute, Porthos; let me first get rid of all this litter of satin and velvet!"

"Oh, never mind," said Porthos, contemptuously; "it is all trash."

"Trash, Porthos! Cloth at twenty-five livres an ell! gorgeous satin! regal velvet!"

"Then you think these clothes are – "

"Splendid, Porthos, splendid! I'll wager that you alone in France have so many; and suppose you never had any more made, and were to live to be a hundred years of age, which wouldn't astonish me in the very least, you could still wear a new dress the day of your death, without being obliged to see the nose of a single tailor from now till then."

Porthos shook his head.

"Come, my friend," said D'Artagnan, "this unnatural melancholy in you frightens me. My dear Porthos, pray get it out, then. And the sooner the better."

"Yes, my friend, so I will: if, indeed, it is possible."

"Perhaps you have received bad news from Bracieux?"

"No: they have felled the wood, and it has yielded a third more than the estimate."

"Then there has been a falling-off in the pools of Pierrefonds?"

"No, my friend: they have been fished, and there is enough left to stock all the pools in the neighborhood."

"Perhaps your estate at Vallon has been destroyed by an earthquake?"

"No, my friend; on the contrary, the ground was struck with lightning a hundred paces from the chateau, and a fountain sprung up in a place entirely destitute of water."

"What in the world **is** the matter, then?"

"The fact is, I have received an invitation for the **fete** at Vaux," said Porthos, with a lugubrious expression.

"Well! do you complain of that? The king has caused a hundred mortal heart-burnings among the courtiers by refusing invitations. And so, my dear friend, you are really going to Vaux?"

"Indeed I am!"

"You will see a magnificent sight."

"Alas! I doubt it, though."

"Everything that is grand in France will be brought together there!"

"Ah!" cried Porthos, tearing out a lock of hair in his despair.

"Eh! good heavens, are you ill?" cried D'Artagnan.

"I am as firm as the Pont-Neuf! It isn't that."

"But what is it, then?"

"'Tis that I have no clothes!"

D'Artagnan stood petrified. "No clothes! Porthos, no clothes!" he cried, "when I see at least fifty suits on the floor."

"Fifty, truly; but not one which fits me!"

"What? not one that fits you? But are you not measured, then, when you give an order?"

"To be sure he is," answered Mouston; "but unfortunately **I** have gotten stouter!"

"What! **you** stouter!"

"So much so that I am now bigger than the baron. Would you believe it, monsieur?"

"**Parbleu!** it seems to me that is quite evident."

"Do you see, stupid?" said Porthos, "that is quite evident!"

"Be still, my dear Porthos," resumed D'Artagnan, becoming slightly impatient, "I don't understand why your clothes should not fit you, because Mouston has grown stouter."

"I am going to explain it," said Porthos. "You remember having related to me the story of the Roman general Antony, who had always seven wild boars kept roasting, each cooked up to a different point; so that he might be able to have his dinner at any time of the day he chose to ask for it. Well, then, I resolved, as at any time I might be invited to court to spend a week, I resolved to have always seven suits ready for the occasion."

"Capitally reasoned, Porthos – only a man must have a fortune like yours to gratify such whims. Without counting the time lost in being measured, the fashions are always changing."

"That is exactly the point," said Porthos, "in regard to which I flattered myself I had hit on a very ingenious device."

"Tell me what it is; for I don't doubt your

genius."

"You remember what Mouston once was, then?"

"Yes; when he used to call himself Mousqueton."

"And you remember, too, the period when he began to grow fatter?"

"No, not exactly. I beg your pardon, my good Mouston."

"Oh! you are not in fault, monsieur," said Mouston, graciously. "You were in Paris, and as for us, we were at Pierrefonds."

"Well, well, my dear Porthos; there was a time when Mouston began to grow fat. Is that what you wished to say?"

"Yes, my friend; and I greatly rejoice over the period."

"Indeed, I believe you do," exclaimed D'Artagnan.

"You understand," continued Porthos, "what a world of trouble it spared for me."

"No, I don't – by any means."

"Look here, my friend. In the first place,

as you have said, to be measured is a loss of time, even though it occur only once a fortnight. And then, one may be travelling; and then you wish to have seven suits always with you. In short, I have a horror of letting any one take my measure. Confound it! either one is a nobleman or not. To be scrutinized and scanned by a fellow who completely analyzes you, by inch and line – 'tis degrading! Here, they find you too hollow; there, too prominent. They recognize your strong and weak points. See, now, when we leave the measurer's hands, we are like those strongholds whose angles and different thicknesses have been ascertained by a spy."

"In truth, my dear Porthos, you possess ideas entirely original."

"Ah! you see when a man is an engineer – "

"And has fortified Belle-Isle – 'tis natural, my friend."

"Well, I had an idea, which would doubtless have proved a good one, but for Mouston's carelessness."

D'Artagnan glanced at Mouston, who replied by a slight movement of his body, as if to say, "You will see whether I am at all to blame in all this."

"I congratulated myself, then," resumed Porthos, "at seeing Mouston get fat; and I did all I could, by means of substantial feeding, to make him stout – always in the hope that he would come to equal myself in girth, and could then be measured in my stead."

"Ah!" cried D'Artagnan. "I see – that spared you both time and humiliation."

"Consider my joy when, after a year and a half's judicious feeding – for I used to feed him up myself – the fellow – "

"Oh! I lent a good hand myself, monsieur," said Mouston, humbly.

"That's true. Consider my joy when, one morning, I perceived Mouston was obliged to squeeze in, as I once did myself, to get through the little secret door that those fools of architects had made in the chamber of the late Madame du Vallon, in the chateau of Pierrefonds. And, by the way, about that door, my friend, I should like to ask you, who know everything, why these wretches of architects, who ought to have the compasses run into them, just to remind them, came to make doorways through which nobody but thin people can pass?"

"Oh, those doors," answered D'Artagnan, "were meant for gallants, and they have generally slight and slender figures."

"Madame du Vallon had no gallant!" answered Porthos, majestically.

"Perfectly true, my friend," resumed D'Artagnan; "but the architects were probably making their calculations on a basis of the probability of your marrying again."

"Ah! that is possible," said Porthos. "And now I have received an explanation of how it is that doorways are made too narrow, let us return to the subject of Mouston's fatness. But see how the two things apply to each other. I have always noticed that people's ideas run parallel. And so, observe this phenomenon, D'Artagnan. I was talking to you of Mouston, who is fat, and it led us on to Madame du Vallon – "

"Who was thin?"

"Hum! Is it not marvelous?"

"My dear friend, a **savant** of my acquaintance, M. Costar, has made the same observation as you have, and he calls the process by some Greek name which I forget."

"What! my remark is not then original?" cried Porthos, astounded. "I thought I was the discoverer."

"My friend, the fact was known before Aristotle's days – that is to say, nearly two thousand years ago."

"Well, well, 'tis no less true," said Porthos, delighted at the idea of having jumped to a conclusion so closely in agreement with the greatest sages of antiquity.

"Wonderfully – but suppose we return to

Mouston. It seems to me, we have left him fattening under our very eyes."

"Yes, monsieur," said Mouston.

"Well," said Porthos, "Mouston fattened so well, that he gratified all my hopes, by reaching my standard; a fact of which I was well able to convince myself, by seeing the rascal, one day, in a waistcoat of mine, which he had turned into a coat – a waistcoat, the mere embroidery of which was worth a hundred pistoles."

"'Twas only to try it on, monsieur," said Mouston.

"From that moment I determined to put Mouston in communication with my tailors, and to have him measured instead of myself."

"A capital idea, Porthos; but Mouston is a foot and a half shorter than you."

"Exactly! They measured him down to the ground, and the end of the skirt came just below my knee."

"What a marvelous man you are, Porthos! Such a thing could happen only to you."

"Ah! yes; pay your compliments; you have ample grounds to go upon. It was exactly at that time – that is to say, nearly two years and a half ago – that I set out for Belle-Isle, instructing Mouston (so as always to have, in every event, a pattern of every fashion) to have a coat made for himself every month."

"And did Mouston neglect complying with your instructions? Ah! that was anything but right, Mouston."

"No, monsieur, quite the contrary; quite the contrary!"

"No, he never forgot to have his coats made; but he forgot to inform me that he had got stouter!"

"But it was not my fault, monsieur! your tailor never told me."

"And this to such an extent, monsieur," continued Porthos, "that the fellow in two years has gained eighteen inches in girth, and so my last dozen coats are all too large, from a foot to a foot and a half."

"But the rest; those which were made

when you were of the same size?"

"They are no longer the fashion, my dear friend. Were I to put them on, I should look like a fresh arrival from Siam; and as though I had been two years away from court."

"I understand your difficulty. You have how many new suits? nine? thirty-six? and yet not one to wear. Well, you must have a thirty-seventh made, and give the thirty-six to Mouston."

"Ah! monsieur!" said Mouston, with a gratified air. "The truth is, that monsieur has always been very generous to me."

"Do you mean to insinuate that I hadn't that idea, or that I was deterred by the expense? But it wants only two days to the **fete**; I received the invitation yesterday; made Mouston post hither with my wardrobe, and only this morning discovered my misfortune; and from now till the day after to-morrow, there isn't a single fashionable tailor who will undertake to make me a suit."

"That is to say, one covered all over with

gold, isn't it?"

"I wish it so! undoubtedly, all over."

"Oh, we shall manage it. You won't leave for three days. The invitations are for Wednesday, and this is only Sunday morning."

"'Tis true; but Aramis has strongly advised me to be at Vaux twenty-four hours beforehand."

"How, Aramis?"

"Yes, it was Aramis who brought me the invitation."

"Ah! to be sure, I see. You are invited on the part of M. Fouquet?"

"By no means! by the king, dear friend. The letter bears the following as large as life: 'M. le Baron du Vallon is informed that the king has condescended to place him on the invitation list – '"

"Very good; but you leave with M. Fouquet?"

"And when I think," cried Porthos, stamping on the floor, "when I think I shall have no clothes, I am ready to burst with rage! I should like to strangle somebody or smash something!"

"Neither strangle anybody nor smash anything, Porthos; I will manage it all; put on one of your thirty-six suits, and come with me to a tailor."

"Pooh! my agent has seen them all this morning."

"Even M. Percerin?"

"Who is M. Percerin?"

"Oh! only the king's tailor!"

"Oh, ah, yes," said Porthos, who wished to appear to know the king's tailor, but now heard his name mentioned for the first time; "to M. Percerin's, by Jove! I was afraid he would be too busy."

"Doubtless he will be; but be at ease, Porthos; he will do for me what he wouldn't do for another. Only you must allow yourself to be measured!"

"Ah!" said Porthos, with a sigh, "'Tis vexatious, but what would you have me do?"

"Do? As others do; as the king does."

"What! do they measure the king, too? does he put up with it?"

"The king is a beau, my good friend, and so are you, too, whatever you may say about it."

Porthos smiled triumphantly. "Let us go to the king's tailor," he said; "and since he measures the king, I think, by my faith, I may do worse than allow him to measure **me!**"

CHAPTER THREE

Who Messire Jean Percerin was

THE KING'S TAILOR, Messire Jean Percerin, occupied a rather large house in the Rue St. Honore, near the Rue de l'Arbre Sec. He was a man of great taste in elegant stuffs, embroideries, and velvets, being hereditary tailor to the king. The preferment of his house reached as far back as the time of Charles IX.; from whose reign dated, as we know, fancy in **bravery** difficult enough to gratify. The Percerin of that period was a Huguenot, like Ambrose Pare, and had been spared by the Queen of Navarre, the beautiful Margot, as they used to write and say, too, in those days; because, in sooth, he was the only one who could make for her those wonderful riding-habits which she so loved to wear, seeing that they were marvelously well suited to hide certain anatomical defects, which the Queen of Navarre used very studiously to conceal. Percerin being saved, made, out of gratitude, some beautiful black bodices, very inexpensively indeed, for Queen Catherine, who ended by being pleased at the preservation of a Huguenot people, on whom she had long looked with detestation. But Percerin was a very prudent man; and having heard it said that there was no more dangerous sign for a Protestant than to be smiled up on by Catherine, and having observed that her smiles were more frequent than usual, he speedily turned Catholic with all his family; and having thus become irreproachable, attained the lofty position of master tailor to the Crown of France. Under Henry III., gay king as he was, this position was as grand as the height of one of the loftiest peaks of the Cordilleras. Now Percerin had been a clever man all his life, and by way of keeping up his reputation beyond the grave, took very good care not to make a bad death of it, and so contrived to die very skillfully; and that at the very moment he felt his powers of invention declining. He left a son and a daughter, both worthy of the name they were called upon to bear; the son, a cutter as unerring and exact as the square rule; the daughter, apt at embroidery, and at designing ornaments. The marriage of Henry IV. and Marie de Medlcl, and the exquisite court-mourning for the afore-mentioned queen, together with a few words let fall by M. de Bassompiere, king of the **beaux** of the period, made the fortune of the second generation of Percerins. M. Concino Concini, and his wife Galligai, who subsequently shone at the French court, sought to Italianize the fashion, and introduced some Florentine tailors; but Percerin, touched to the quick in his patriotism and his self-esteem, entirely defeated these foreigners, and that so well that Concino was the first to give up his compatriots, and held the French tailor in such esteem that he would never employ any other, and thus wore a doublet of his on the very day that Vitry blew out his brains with a pistol at the Pont du Louvre.

And so it was a doublet issuing from M. Percerin's workshop, which the Parisians rejoiced in hacking into so many pieces with the living human body it contained. Notwithstanding the favor Concino Concini had shown Percerin, the king, Louis XIII., had the generosity to bear no malice to his tailor, and to retain him in his service. At the time that Louis the Just afforded this great example of equity, Percerin had brought up two sons, one of whom made his **debut** at the marriage of Anne of Austria, invented that admirable Spanish costume, in which Richelieu danced a saraband, made the costumes for the tragedy of “Mirame,” and stitched on to Buckingham’s mantle those famous pearls which were destined to be scattered about the pavements of the Louvre. A man becomes easily notable who has made the dresses of a Duke of Buckingham, a M. de Cinq-Mars, a Mademoiselle Ninon, a M. de Beaufort, and a Marion de Lorme. And thus Percerin the third had attained the summit of his glory when his father died. This same Percerin III., old, famous and wealthy, yet further dressed Louis XIV.; and having no son, which was a great cause of sorrow to him, seeing that with himself his dynasty would end, he had brought up several hopeful pupils. He possessed a carriage, a country house, men-servants the tallest in Paris; and by special authority from Louis XIV., a pack of hounds. He worked for MM. de Lyonne and Letellier, under a sort of patronage; but politic man as he was, and versed in state secrets, he never succeeded in fitting M. Colbert. This is beyond explanation; it is a matter for guessing or for intuition. Great geniuses of every kind live on unseen, intangible ideas; they act without themselves knowing why. The great Percerin (for, contrary to the rule of dynasties, it was, above all, the last of the Percerins who deserved the name of Great), the great Percerin was inspired when he cut a robe for the queen, or a coat for the king; he could mount a mantle for Monsieur, the clock of a stocking for Madame; but, in spite of his supreme talent, he could never hit off anything approaching a creditable fit for M. Colbert. "That man," he used often to say, "is beyond my art; my needle can never dot him down." We need scarcely say that Percerin was M. Fouquet's tailor, and that the superintendent highly esteemed him.

M. Percerin was nearly eighty years old, nevertheless still fresh, and at the same time so dry, the courtiers used to say, that he was positively brittle. His renown and his fortune were great enough for M. le Prince, that king of fops, to take his arm when talking over the fashions; and for those least eager to pay never to dare to leave their accounts in arrear with him; for Master Percerin would for the first time make clothes upon credit, but the second never, unless paid for the former order.

It is easy to see at once that a tailor of such renown, instead of running after customers, made difficulties about obliging any fresh ones. And so Percerin declined to fit **bourgeois**, or those who had but recently obtained patents of nobility. A story used to circulate that even M. de Mazarin, in exchange for Percerin supplying him with a full suit of ceremonial vestments as cardinal, one fine day slipped letters of nobility into his pocket.

It was to the house of this grand llama of tailors that D'Artagnan took the despairing Porthos; who, as they were going along, said to his friend, "Take care, my good D'Artagnan, not to compromise the dignity of a man such as I am with the arrogance of this Percerin, who will, I expect, be very impertinent; for I give you notice, my friend, that if he is wanting in respect I will infallibly chastise him."

"Presented by me," replied D'Artagnan, "you have nothing to fear, even though you were what you are not."

"Ah! 'tis because – "

"What? Have you anything against Percerin, Porthos?"

"I think that I once sent Mouston to a fellow of that name."

"And then?"

"The fellow refused to supply me."

"Oh, a misunderstanding, no doubt, which it will be now exceedingly easy to set right. Mouston must have made a mistake."

"Perhaps."

"He has confused the names."

"Possibly. That rascal Mouston never can remember names."

"I will take it all upon myself."

"Very good."

"Stop the carriage, Porthos; here we are."

"Here! how here? We are at the Halles; and you told me the house was at the corner of the Rue de l'Arbre Sec."

"'Tis true, but look."

"Well, I do look, and I see – "

"What?"

"**Pardieu!** that we are at the Halles!"

"You do not, I suppose, want our horses to clamber up on the roof of the carriage in front of us?"

"No."

"Nor the carriage in front of us to mount on top of the one in front of it. Nor that the second should be driven over the roofs of the thirty or forty others which have arrived before us."

"No, you are right, indeed. What a number of people! And what are they all about?"

"'Tis very simple. They are waiting their turn."

"Bah! Have the comedians of the Hotel de Bourgogne shifted their quarters?"

"No; their turn to obtain an entrance to M. Percerin's house."

"And we are going to wait too?"

"Oh, we shall show ourselves prompter and not so proud."

"What are we to do, then?"

"Get down, pass through the footmen and lackeys, and enter the tailor's house, which I will answer for our doing, if you go first."

"Come along, then," said Porthos.

They accordingly alighted and made their way on foot towards the establishment. The cause of the confusion was that M. Percerin's doors were closed, while a servant, standing before them, was explaining to the illustrious customers of the illustrious tailor that just then M. Percerin could not receive anybody. It was bruited about outside still, on the authority of what the great lackey had told some great noble whom he favored, in confidence, that M. Percerin was engaged on five costumes for the king, and that, owing to the urgency of the case, he was meditating in his office on the ornaments, colors, and cut of these five suits. Some, contented with this reason, went away again, contented to repeat the tale to others, but others, more tenacious, insisted on having the doors opened, and among these last three Blue Ribbons, intended to take parts in a ballet, which would inevitably fail unless the said three had their costumes shaped by the very hand of the great Percerin himself. D'Artagnan, pushing on Porthos, who scattered the groups of people right and left, succeeded in gaining the counter, behind which the journeyman tailors were doing their best to answer queries. (We forgot to mention that at the door they wanted to put off Porthos like the rest, but D'Artagnan, showing himself, pronounced merely these words, “The king’s order,” and was let in with his friend.) The poor fellows had enough to do, and did their best, to reply to the demands of the customers in the absence of their master, leaving off drawing a stitch to knit a sentence; and when wounded pride, or disappointed expectation, brought down upon them too cutting a rebuke, he who was attacked made a dive and disappeared under the counter. The line of discontented lords formed a truly remarkable picture. Our captain of musketeers, a man of sure and rapid observation, took it all in at a glance; and having run over the groups, his eye rested on a man in front of him. This man, seated upon a stool, scarcely showed his head above the counter that sheltered him. He was about forty years of age, with a melancholy aspect, pale face, and soft luminous eyes. He was looking at D’Artagnan and the rest, with his chin resting upon his hand, like a calm and inquiring amateur. Only on perceiving, and doubtless recognizing, our captain, he pulled his hat down over his eyes. It was this action, perhaps, that attracted D'Artagnan's attention. If so, the gentleman who had pulled down his hat produced an effect entirely different from what he had desired. In other respects his costume was plain, and his hair evenly cut enough for customers, who were not close observers, to take him for a mere tailor's apprentice, perched behind the board, and carefully stitching cloth or velvet. Nevertheless, this man held up his head too often to be very productively employed with his fingers. D'Artagnan was not deceived, – not he; and he saw at once that if this man was working at anything, it certainly was not at velvet.

"Eh!" said he, addressing this man, "and so you have become a tailor's boy, Monsieur Moliere!"

"Hush, M. d'Artagnan!" replied the man, softly, "you will make them recognize me."

"Well, and what harm?"

"The fact is, there is no harm, but – "

"You were going to say there is no good in doing it either, is it not so?"

"Alas! no; for I was occupied in examining some excellent figures."

"Go on – go on, Monsieur Moliere. I quite understand the interest you take in the plates – I will not disturb your studies."

"Thank you."

"But on one condition; that you tell me where M. Percerin really is."

"Oh! willingly; in his own room. Only – "

"Only that one can't enter it?"

"Unapproachable."

"For everybody?"

"Everybody. He brought me here so that I might be at my ease to make my observations, and then he went away."

"Well, my dear Monsieur Moliere, but you will go and tell him I am here."

"I!" exclaimed Moliere, in the tone of a courageous dog, from which you snatch the bone it has legitimately gained; "I disturb myself! Ah! Monsieur d'Artagnan, how hard you are upon me!"

"If you don't go directly and tell M. Percerin that I am here, my dear Moliere," said D'Artagnan, in a low tone, "I warn you of one thing: that I won't exhibit to you the friend I have brought with me."

Moliere indicated Porthos by an imperceptible gesture, "This gentleman, is it not?"

"Yes."

Moliere fixed upon Porthos one of those looks which penetrate the minds and hearts of men. The subject doubtless appeared a very promising one, for he immediately rose and led the way into the adjoining chamber.

CHAPTER FOUR

The Patterns

DURING ALL THIS TIME the noble mob was slowly heaving away, leaving at every angle of the counter either a murmur or a menace, as the waves leave foam or scattered seaweed on the sands, when they retire with the ebbing tide. In about ten minutes Moliere reappeared, making another sign to D'Artagnan from under the hangings. The latter hurried after him, with

Porthos in the rear, and after threading a labyrinth of corridors, introduced him to M. Percerin's room. The old man, with his sleeves turned up, was gathering up in folds a piece of gold-flowered brocade, so as the better to exhibit its luster. Perceiving D'Artagnan, he put the silk aside, and came to meet him, by no means radiant with joy, and by no means courteous, but, take it altogether, in a tolerably civil manner.

"The captain of the king's musketeers will excuse me, I am sure, for I am engaged."

"Eh! yes, on the king's costumes; I know that, my dear Monsieur Percerin. You are making three, they tell me."

"Five, my dear sir, five."

"Three or five, 'tis all the same to me, my dear monsieur; and I know that you will make them most exquisitely."

"Yes, I know. Once made they will be the most beautiful in the world, I do not deny it; but that they may be the most beautiful in the word, they must first be made; and to do this, captain, I am pressed for time."

"Oh, bah! there are two days yet; 'tis much more than you require, Monsieur Percerin," said D'Artagnan, in the coolest possible manner.

Percerin raised his head with the air of a man little accustomed to be contradicted, even in his whims; but D'Artagnan did not pay the least attention to the airs which the illustrious tailor began to assume.

"My dear M. Percerin," he continued, "I bring you a customer."

"Ah! ah!" exclaimed Percerin, crossly.

"M. le Baron du Vallon de Bracieux de Pierrefonds," continued D'Artagnan. Percerin attempted a bow, which found no favor in the eyes of the terrible Porthos, who, from his first entry into the room, had been regarding the tailor askance.

"A very good friend of mine," concluded D'Artagnan.

"I will attend to monsieur," said Percerin, "but later."

"Later? but when?"

"When I have time."

"You have already told my valet as much," broke in Porthos, discontentedly.

"Very likely," said Percerin; "I am nearly always pushed for time."

"My friend," returned Porthos, sententiously, "there is always time to be found when one chooses to seek it."

Percerin turned crimson; an ominous sign indeed in old men blanched by age.

"Monsieur is quite at liberty to confer his custom elsewhere."

"Come, come, Percerin," interposed D'Artagnan, "you are not in a good temper to-day. Well, I will say one more word to you, which will bring you on your knees; monsieur is not only a friend of mine, but more, a friend of M. Fouquet's."

"Ah! ah!" exclaimed the tailor, "that is another thing." Then turning to Porthos, "Monsieur le baron is attached to the superintendent?" he inquired.

"I am attached to myself," shouted Porthos, at the very moment that the tapestry was raised to introduce a new speaker in the dialogue. Moliere was all observation, D'Artagnan laughed, Porthos swore.

"My dear Percerin," said D'Artagnan, "you will make a dress for the baron. 'Tis I who ask you."

"To you I will not say nay, captain."

"But that is not all; you will make it for him at once."

"'Tis impossible within eight days."

"That, then, is as much as to refuse, because the dress is wanted for the **fete** at Vaux."

"I repeat that it is impossible," returned the obstinate old man.

"By no means, dear Monsieur Percerin, above all if **I** ask you," said a mild voice at the door, a silvery voice which made D'Artagnan prick up his ears. It was the voice of Aramis.

"Monsieur d'Herblay!" cried the tailor.

"Aramis," murmured D'Artagnan.

"Ah! our bishop!" said Porthos.

"Good morning, D'Artagnan; good morning, Porthos; good-morning, my dear friends," said Aramis. "Come, come, M. Percerin, make the baron's dress; and I will answer for it you will gratify M. Fouquet." And he accompanied the words with a sign, which seemed to say, "Agree, and dismiss them."

It appeared that Aramis had over Master Percerin an influence superior even to D'Artagnan's, for the tailor bowed in assent, and turning round upon Porthos, said, "Go and get measured on the other side."

Porthos colored in a formidable manner. D'Artagnan saw the storm coming, and addressing Moliere, said to him, in an undertone, "You see before you, my dear monsieur, a man who considers himself disgraced, if you measure the flesh and bones that Heaven has given him; study this type for me, Master Aristophanes, and profit by it."

Moliere had no need of encouragement, and his gaze dwelt long and keenly on the Baron Porthos. "Monsieur," he said, "if you will come with me, I will make them take your measure without touching you."

"Oh!" said Porthos, "how do you make that out, my friend?"

"I say that they shall apply neither line nor rule to the seams of your dress. It is a new method we have invented for measuring people of quality, who are too sensitive to allow low-born fellows to touch them. We know some susceptible persons who will not put up with being measured, a process which, as I think, wounds the natural dignity of a man; and if perchance monsieur should be one of these – "

"**Corboeuf!** I believe I am too!"

"Well, that is a capital and most consolatory coincidence, and you shall have the benefit of our invention."

"But how in the world can it be done?"

asked Porthos, delighted.

"Monsieur," said Moliere, bowing, "if you will deign to follow me, you will see."

Aramis observed this scene with all his eyes. Perhaps he fancied from D'Artagnan's liveliness that he would leave with Porthos, so as not to lose the conclusion of a scene well begun. But, clear-sighted as he was, Aramis deceived himself. Porthos and Moliere left together: D'Artagnan remained with Percerin. Why? From curiosity, doubtless; probably to enjoy a little longer the society of his good friend Aramis. As Moliere and Porthos disappeared, D'Artagnan drew near the bishop of Vannes, a proceeding which appeared particularly to disconcert him.

"A dress for you, also, is it not, my friend?"

Aramis smiled. "No," said he.

"You will go to Vaux, however?"

"I shall go, but without a new dress. You forget, dear D'Artagnan, that a poor bishop of Vannes is not rich enough to have new dresses for every **fete**."

"Bah!" said the musketeer, laughing, "and do we write no more poems now, either?"

"Oh! D'Artagnan," exclaimed Aramis, "I have long ago given up all such tomfoolery."

"True," repeated D'Artagnan, only half convinced. As for Percerin, he was once more absorbed in contemplation of the brocades.

"Don't you perceive," said Aramis, smiling, "that we are greatly boring this good gentleman, my dear D'Artagnan?"

"Ah! ah!" murmured the musketeer, aside; "that is, I am boring you, my friend." Then aloud, "Well, then, let us leave; I have no further business here, and if you are as disengaged as I, Aramis – "

"No, not I – I wished – "

"Ah! you had something particular to say to M. Percerin? Why did you not tell me so at once?"

"Something particular, certainly," repeated Aramis, "but not for you, D'Artagnan. But, at the same time, I hope you will believe that I can never have anything so particular to say that a friend like you may not hear it."

"Oh, no, no! I am going," said D'Artagnan, imparting to his voice an evident tone of curiosity; for Aramis's annoyance, well dissembled as it was, had not a whit escaped him; and he knew that, in that impenetrable mind, every thing, even the most apparently trivial, was designed to some end; an unknown one, but an end that, from the knowledge he had of his friend's character, the musketeer felt must be important.

On his part, Aramis saw that D'Artagnan was not without suspicion, and pressed him. "Stay, by all means," he said, "this is what it is." Then turning towards the tailor, "My dear Percerin," said he, – "I am even very happy that you are here, D'Artagnan."

"Oh, indeed," exclaimed the Gascon, for the third time, even less deceived this time than before.

Percerin never moved. Aramis roused him violently, by snatching from his hands the stuff upon which he was engaged. “My dear Percerin,” said he, “I have, near hand, M. Lebrun, one of M. Fouquet’s painters.”

“Ah, very good,” thought D’Artagnan; “but why Lebrun?”

Aramis looked at D’Artagnan, who seemed to be occupied with an engraving of Mark Antony. “And you wish that I should make him a dress, similar to those of the Epicureans?” answered Percerin. And while saying this, in an absent manner, the worthy tailor endeavored to recapture his piece of brocade.

“An Epicurean’s dress?” asked D’Artagnan, in a tone of inquiry.

“I see,” said Aramis, with a most engaging smile, “it is written that our dear D’Artagnan shall know all our secrets this evening. Yes, friend, you have surely heard speak of M. Fouquet’s Epicureans, have you not?”

“Undoubtedly. Is it not a kind of poetical society, of which La Fontaine, Loret, Pelisson, and Moliere are members, and which holds its sittings at Saint-Mande?"

"Exactly so. Well, we are going to put our poets in uniform, and enroll them in a regiment for the king."

"Oh, very well, I understand; a surprise M. Fouquet is getting up for the king. Be at ease; if that is the secret about M. Lebrun, I will not mention it."

"Always agreeable, my friend. No, Monsieur Lebrun has nothing to do with this part of it; the secret which concerns him is far more important than the other."

"Then, if it is so important as all that, I prefer not to know it," said D'Artagnan, making a show of departure.

"Come in, M. Lebrun, come in," said Aramis, opening a side-door with his right hand, and holding back D'Artagnan with his left.

"I'faith, I too, am quite in the dark," quoth Percerln.

Aramis took an "opportunity," as is said in theatrical matters.

"My dear M. de Percerin," Aramis continued,

"you are making five dresses for the king, are you not? One in brocade; one in hunting-cloth; one in velvet; one in satin; and one in Florentine stuffs."

"Yes; but how – do you know all that, monseigneur?" said Percerin, astounded.

"It is all very simple, my dear monsieur; there will be a hunt, a banquet, concert, promenade and reception; these five kinds of dress are required by etiquette."

"You know everything, monseigneur!"

"And a thing or two in addition," muttered D'Artagnan.

"But," cried the tailor, in triumph, "what you do not know, monseigneur – prince of the church though you are – what nobody will know – what only the king, Mademoiselle de la Valliere, and myself do know, is the color of the materials and nature of the ornaments, and the cut, the **ensemble**, the finish of it all!"

"Well," said Aramis, "that is precisely what I have come to ask you, dear Percerin."

"Ah, bah!" exclaimed the tailor, terrified, though Aramis had pronounced these words in his softest and most honeyed tones. The request appeared, on reflection, so exaggerated, so ridiculous, so monstrous to M. Percerin that first he laughed to himself, then aloud, and finished with a shout. D'Artagnan followed his example, not because he found the matter so "very funny," but in order not to allow Aramis to cool.

"At the outset, I appear to be hazarding an absurd question, do I not?" said Aramis. "But D'Artagnan, who is incarnate wisdom itself, will tell you that I could not do otherwise than ask you this."

"Let us see," said the attentive musketeer; perceiving with his wonderful instinct that they had only been skirmishing till now, and that the hour of battle was approaching.

"Let us see," said Percerin, incredulously.

"Why, now," continued Aramis, "does M. Fouquet give the king a **fete?** – Is it not to please him?"

"Assuredly," said Percerin. D'Artagnan nodded assent.

"By delicate attentions? by some happy device? by a succession of surprises, like that of which we were talking? – the enrolment of our Epicureans."

"Admirable."

"Well, then; this is the surprise we intend. M. Lebrun here is a man who draws most excellently."

"Yes," said Percerin; "I have seen his pictures, and observed that his dresses were highly elaborated. That is why I at once agreed to make him a costume – whether to agree with those of the Epicureans, or an original one."

"My dear monsieur, we accept your offer, and shall presently avail ourselves of it; but just now, M. Lebrun is not in want of the dresses you will make for himself, but of those you are making for the king."

Percerin made a bound backwards, which D'Artagnan – calmest and most appreciative of men, did not consider overdone, so many strange and startling aspects wore the proposal which Aramis had just hazarded. "The king's dresses! Give the king's dresses to any mortal whatever! Oh! for once, monseigneur, your grace is mad!" cried the poor tailor in extremity.

"Help me now, D'Artagnan," said Aramis, more and more calm and smiling. "Help me now to persuade monsieur, for **you** understand; do you not?"

"Eh! eh! – not exactly, I declare."

"What! you do not understand that M. Fouquet wishes to afford the king the surprise of finding his portrait on his arrival at Vaux; and that the portrait, which be a striking resemblance, ought to be dressed exactly as the king will be on the day it is shown?"

"Oh! yes, yes," said the musketeer, nearly convinced, so plausible was this reasoning. "Yes, my dear Aramis, you are right; it is a happy idea. I will wager it is one of your own, Aramis."

"Well, I don't know," replied the bishop; "either mine or M. Fouquet's." Then scanning Percerin, after noticing D'Artagnan's hesitation, "Well, Monsieur Percerin," he asked, "what do you say to this?"

"I say, that – "

"That you are, doubtless, free to refuse. I know well – and I by no means count upon compelling you, my dear monsieur. I will say more, I even understand all the delicacy you feel in taking up with M. Fouquet's idea; you dread appearing to flatter the king. A noble spirit, M. Percerin, a noble spirit!" The tailor stammered. "It would, indeed, be a very pretty compliment to pay the young prince," continued Aramis; "but as the surintendant told me, 'if Percerin refuse, tell him that it will not at all lower him in my opinion, and I shall always esteem him, only – '"

"'Only?'" repeated Percerin, rather troubled.

"'Only,'" continued Aramis, "'I shall

be compelled to say to the king,' – you understand, my dear Monsieur Percerin, that these are M. Fouquet's words, – 'I shall be constrained to say to the king, "Sire, I had intended to present your majesty with your portrait, but owing to a feeling of delicacy, slightly exaggerated perhaps, although creditable, M. Percerin opposed the project."'"

"Opposed!" cried the tailor, terrified at the responsibility which would weigh upon him; "I to oppose the desire, the will of M. Fouquet when he is seeking to please the king! Oh, what a hateful word you have uttered, monseigneur. Oppose! Oh, 'tis not I who said it, Heaven have mercy on me. I call the captain of the musketeers to witness it! Is it not true, Monsieur d'Artagnan, that I have opposed nothing?"

D'Artagnan made a sign indicating that he wished to remain neutral. He felt that there was an intrigue at the bottom of it, whether comedy or tragedy; he was at his wit's end at not being able to fathom it, but in the meanwhile wished to keep clear.

But already Percerin, goaded by the idea that the king was to be told he stood in the way of a pleasant surprise, had offered Lebrun a chair, and proceeded to bring from a wardrobe four magnificent dresses, the fifth being still in the workmen's hands; and these masterpieces he successively fitted upon four lay figures, which, imported into France in the time of Concini, had been given to Percerin II. by Marshal d'Onore, after the discomfiture of the Italian tailors ruined in their competition. The painter set to work to draw and then to paint the dresses. But Aramis, who was closely watching all the phases of his toil, suddenly stopped him.

"I think you have not quite got it, my dear Lebrun," he said; "your colors will deceive you, and on canvas we shall lack that exact resemblance which is absolutely requisite. Time is necessary for attentively observing the finer shades."

"Quite true," said Percerin, "but time is wanting, and on that head, you will agree with me, monseigneur, I can do nothing."

"Then the affair will fail," said Aramis, quietly, "and that because of a want of precision in the colors."

Nevertheless Lebrun went on copying the materials and ornaments with the closest fidelity – a process which Aramis watched with ill-concealed impatience.

"What in the world, now, is the meaning of this imbroglio?" the musketeer kept saying to himself.

"That will never do," said Aramis: "M. Lebrun, close your box, and roll up your canvas."

"But, monsieur," cried the vexed painter, "the light is abominable here."

"An idea, M. Lebrun, an idea! If we had a pattern of the materials, for example, and with time, and a better light – "

"Oh, then," cried Lebrun, "I would answer for the effect."

"Good!" said D'Artagnan, "this ought to be the knotty point of the whole thing; they want a pattern of each of the materials. **Mordioux!** Will this Percerin give in now?"

Percerin, beaten from his last retreat, and duped, moreover, by the feigned good-nature of Aramis, cut out five patterns and handed them to the bishop of Vannes.

"I like this better. That is your opinion, is it not?" said Aramis to D'Artagnan.

"My dear Aramis," said D'Artagnan, "my opinion is that you are always the same."

"And, consequently, always your friend," said the bishop in a charming tone.

"Yes, yes," said D'Artagnan, aloud; then, in a low voice, "If I am your dupe, double Jesuit that you are, I will not be your accomplice; and to prevent it, 'tis time I left this place. – Adieu, Aramis," he added aloud, "adieu; I am going to rejoin Porthos."

"Then wait for me," said Aramis, pocketing the patterns, "for I have done, and shall be glad to say a parting word to our dear old friend."

Lebrun packed up his paints and brushes, Percerin put back the dresses into the closet, Aramis put his hand on his pocket to assure himself the patterns were secure, – and they all left the study.

CHAPTER FIVE

Where, Probably, Moliere Obtained his First Idea of the Bourgeois Gentilhomme

D'ARTAGNAN FOUND PORTHOS in the adjoining chamber; but no longer an irritated Porthos, or a disappointed Porthos, but Porthos radiant, blooming, fascinating, and chattering with Moliere, who was looking upon him with a species of idolatry, and as a man would who had not only never seen anything greater, but not even ever anything so great. Aramis went straight up to Porthos and offered him his white hand, which lost itself in the gigantic clasp of his old friend, – an operation which Aramis never hazarded without a certain uneasiness. But the friendly pressure having been performed not too painfully for him, the bishop of Vannes passed over to Moliere.

"Well, monsieur," said he, "will you come with me to Saint-Mande?"

"I will go anywhere you like, monseigneur," answered Moliere.

"To Saint-Mande!" cried Porthos, surprised at seeing the proud bishop of Vannes fraternizing with a journeyman tailor. "What, Aramis, are you going to take this gentleman to Saint-Mande?"

"Yes," said Aramis, smiling, "our work is pressing."

"And besides, my dear Porthos," continued D'Artagnan, "M. Moliere is not altogether what he seems."

"In what way?" asked Porthos.

"Why, this gentleman is one of M. Percerin's chief clerks, and is expected at Saint-Mande to try on the dresses which M. Fouquet has ordered for the Epicureans."

"'Tis precisely so," said Moliere.

"Yes, monsieur."

"Come, then, my dear M. Moliere," said Aramis, "that is, if you have done with M. du Vallon."

"We have finished," replied Porthos.

"And you are satisfied?" asked D'Artagnan.

"Completely so," replied Porthos.

Moliere took his leave of Porthos with much ceremony, and grasped the hand which the captain of the musketeers furtively offered him.

"Pray, monsieur," concluded Porthos, mincingly, "above all, be exact."

"You will have your dress the day after to-morrow, monsieur le baron," answered Moliere. And he left with Aramis.

Then D'Artagnan, taking Porthos's arm, "What has this tailor done for you, my dear Porthos," he asked, "that you are so pleased with him?"

"What has he done for me, my friend! done for me!" cried Porthos, enthusiastically.

"Yes, I ask you, what has he done for you?"

"My friend, he has done that which no tailor ever yet accomplished: he has taken my measure without touching me!"

"Ah, bah! tell me how he did it."

"First, then, they went, I don't know where, for a number of lay figures, of all heights and sizes, hoping there would be one to suit mine, but the largest – that of the drum-major of the Swiss guard – was two inches too short, and a half foot too narrow in the chest."

"Indeed!"

"It is exactly as I tell you, D'Artagnan; but he is a great man, or at the very least a great tailor, is this M. Moliere. He was not at all put at fault by the circumstance."

"What did he do, then?"

"Oh! it is a very simple matter. I'faith, 'tis an unheard-of thing that people should have been so stupid as not to have discovered this method from the first. What annoyance and humiliation they would have spared me!"

"Not to mention of the costumes, my dear Porthos."

"Yes, thirty dresses."

"Well, my dear Porthos, come, tell me M. Moliere's plan."

"Moliere? You call him so, do you? I shall make a point of recollecting his name."

"Yes; or Poquelin, if you prefer that."

"No; I like Moliere best. When I wish to recollect his name, I shall think of **voliere** [an aviary]; and as I have one at Pierrefonds – "

"Capital!" returned D'Artagnan. "And M. Moliere's plan?"

"'Tis this: instead of pulling me to pieces, as all these rascals do – of making me bend my back, and double my joints – all of them low and dishonorable practices – " D'Artagnan made a sign of approbation with his head. "'Monsieur,' he said to me," continued Porthos, "'a gentleman ought to measure himself. Do me the pleasure to draw near this glass;' and I drew near the glass. I must own I did not exactly understand what this good M. Voliere wanted with me."

"Moliere!"

"Ah! yes, Moliere – Moliere. And as the fear of being measured still possessed me, 'Take care,' said I to him, 'what you are going to do with me; I am very ticklish, I warn you.' But he, with his soft voice (for he is a courteous fellow, we must admit, my friend), he with his soft voice, 'Monsieur,' said he, 'that your dress may fit you well, it must be made according to your figure. Your figure is exactly reflected in this mirror. We shall take the measure of this reflection.'"

"In fact," said D'Artagnan, "you saw yourself in the glass; but where did they find one in which you could see your whole figure?"

"My good friend, it is the very glass in which

the king is used to look to see himself."

"Yes; but the king is a foot and a half shorter than you are."

"Ah! well, I know not how that may be; it is, no doubt, a cunning way of flattering the king; but the looking-glass was too large for me. 'Tis true that its height was made up of three Venetian plates of glass, placed one above another, and its breadth of three similar parallelograms in juxtaposition."

"Oh, Porthos! what excellent words you have command of. Where in the word did you acquire such a voluminous vocabulary?"

"At Belle-Isle. Aramis and I had to use such words in our strategic studies and castramentative experiments."

D'Artagnan recoiled, as though the sesquipedalian syllables had knocked the breath out of his body.

"Ah! very good. Let us return to the looking-glass, my friend."

"Then, this good M. Voliere – "

"Moliere."

"Yes – Moliere – you are right. You will see now, my dear friend, that I shall recollect his name quite well. This excellent M. Moliere set to work tracing out lines on the mirror, with a piece of Spanish chalk, following in all the make of my arms and my shoulders, all the while expounding this maxim, which I thought admirable: 'It is advisable that a dress should not incommode its wearer.'"

"In reality," said D'Artagnan, "that is an excellent maxim, which is, unfortunately, seldom carried out in practice."

"That is why I found it all the more astonishing, when he expatiated upon it."

"Ah! he expatiated?"

"**Parbleu!**"

"Let me hear his theory."

"'Seeing that,' he continued, 'one may, in awkward circumstances, or in a troublesome position, have one's doublet on one's shoulder, and not desire to take one's doublet off – '"

"True," said D'Artagnan.

"'And so,' continued M. Voliere – "

"Moliere."

"Moliere, yes. 'And so,' went on M. Moliere, 'you want to draw your sword, monsieur, and you have your doublet on your back. What do you do?'

"'I take it off,' I answered.

"'Well, no,' he replied.

"'How no?'

"'I say that the dress should be so well made, that it will in no way encumber you, even in drawing your sword.'

"'Ah, ah!'

"'Throw yourself on guard,' pursued he.

"I did it with such wondrous firmness, that two panes of glass burst out of the window.

"''Tis nothing, nothing,' said he. 'Keep your position.'

"I raised my left arm in the air, the forearm gracefully bent, the ruffle drooping, and my wrist curved, while my right arm, half extended, securely covered my wrist with the elbow, and my breast with the wrist."

"Yes," said D'Artagnan, "'Tis the true guard – the academic guard."

"You have said the very word, dear friend. In the meanwhile, Voliere – "

"Moliere."

"Hold! I should certainly, after all, prefer to call him – what did you say his other name was?"

"Poquelin."

"I prefer to call him Poquelin."

"And how will you remember this name better than the other?"

"You understand, he calls himself Poquelin, does he not?"

"Yes."

"If I were to call to mind Madame Coquenard."

"Good."

"And change **Coc** into **Poc**, **nard** into **lin**; and instead of Coquenard I shall have Poquelin."

"'Tis wonderful," cried D'Artagnan, astounded. "Go on, my friend, I am listening to you with admiration."

"This Coquelin sketched my arm on the glass."

"I beg your pardon – Poquelin."

"What did I say, then?"

"You said Coquelin."

"Ah! true. This Poquelin, then, sketched my arm on the glass; but he took his time over it; he kept looking at me a good deal. The fact is, that I must have been looking particularly handsome."

"'Does it weary you?' he asked.

"'A little,' I replied, bending a little in my hands, 'but I could hold out for an hour or so longer.'

"'No, no, I will not allow it; the willing fellows will make it a duty to support your arms, as of old, men supported those of the prophet.'

"'Very good,' I answered.

"'That will not be humiliating to you?'

"'My friend,' said I, 'there is, I think, a great difference between being supported and being measured.'"

"The distinction is full of the soundest sense," interrupted D'Artagnan.

"Then," continued Porthos, "he made a sign: two lads approached; one supported my left arm, while the other, with infinite address, supported my right."

"'Another, my man,' cried he. A third approached. 'Support monsieur by the waist,' said he. The **garcon** complied."

"So that you were at rest?" asked D'Artagnan.

"Perfectly; and Pocquenard drew me on the glass."

"Poquelin, my friend."

"Poquelin – you are right. Stay, decidedly I prefer calling him Voliere."

"Yes; and then it was over, wasn't it?"

"During that time Voliere drew me as I appeared in the mirror."

"'Twas delicate in him."

"I much like the plan; it is respectful, and keeps every one in his place."

"And there it ended?"

"Without a soul having touched me, my friend."

"Except the three **garcons** who supported you."

"Doubtless; but I have, I think, already explained to you the difference there is between supporting and measuring."

"'Tis true," answered D'Artagnan; who said afterwards to himself, "I'faith, I greatly deceive myself, or I have been the means of a good windfall to that rascal Moliere, and we shall assuredly see the scene hit off to the life in some comedy or other." Porthos smiled.

"What are you laughing at?" asked D'Artagnan.

"Must I confess? Well, I was laughing over my good fortune."

"Oh, that is true; I don't know a happier man than you. But what is this last piece of luck that has befallen you?'

"Well, my dear fellow, congratulate me."

"I desire nothing better."

"It seems that I am the first who has had his measure taken in that manner."

"Are you so sure of it?'

"Nearly so. Certain signs of intelligence which passed between Voliere and the other **garcons** showed me the fact."

"Well, my friend, that does not surprise me from Moliere," said D'Artagnan.

"Voliere, my friend."

"Oh, no, no, indeed! I am very willing to leave you to go on saying Voliere; but, as for me, I shall continued to say Moliere. Well, this, I was saying, does not surprise me, coming from Moliere, who is a very ingenious fellow, and inspired you with this grand idea."

"It will be of great use to him by and by, I am sure."

"Won't it be of use to him, indeed? I believe you, it will, and that in the highest degree; – for you see my friend Moliere is of all known tailors the man who best clothes our barons, comtes, and marquises – according to their measure."

On this observation, neither the application nor depth of which we shall discuss, D'Artagnan and Porthos quitted M. de Percerin's house and rejoined their carriages, wherein we will leave them, in order to look after Moliere and Aramis at Saint-Mande.

CHAPTER SIX

The Bee-Hive, the Bees, and the Honey

THE BISHOP OF VANNES, much annoyed at having met D'Artagnan at M. Percerin's, returned to Saint-Mande in no very good humor. Moliere, on the other hand, quite delighted at having made such a capital rough sketch, and at knowing where to find his original again, whenever he should desire to convert his sketch into a picture, Moliere arrived in the merriest of moods. All the first story of the left wing was occupied by the most celebrated Epicureans in Paris, and those on the freest footing in the house – every one in his compartment, like the bees in their cells, employed in producing the honey intended for that royal cake which M. Fouquet proposed to offer his majesty Louis XIV. during the **fete** at Vaux. Pelisson, his head leaning on his hand, was engaged in drawing out the plan of the prologue to the "Facheux," a comedy in three acts, which was to be put on the stage by Poquelin de Moliere, as D'Artagnan called him, or Coquelin de Voliere, as Porthos styled him. Loret, with all the charming innocence of a gazetteer, – the gazetteers of all ages have always been so artless! – Loret was composing an account of the **fetes** at Vaux, before those **fetes** had taken place. La Fontaine sauntered about from one to the other, a peripatetic, absent-minded, boring, unbearable dreamer, who kept buzzing and humming at everybody's elbow a thousand poetic abstractions. He so often disturbed Pelisson, that the latter, raising his head, crossly said, "At least, La Fontaine, supply me with a rhyme, since you have the run of the gardens at Parnassus."

"What rhyme do you want?" asked the **Fabler** as Madame de Sevigne used to call him.

"I want a rhyme to **lumiere**."

"**Orniere**," answered La Fontaine.

"Ah, but, my good friend, one cannot talk of **wheel-ruts** when celebrating the delights of Vaux," said Loret.

"Besides, it doesn't rhyme," answered Pelisson.

"What! doesn't rhyme!" cried La Fontaine, in surprise.

"Yes; you have an abominable habit, my friend, – a habit which will ever prevent your becoming a poet of the first order. You rhyme in a slovenly manner."

"Oh, oh, you think so, do you, Pelisson?"

"Yes, I do, indeed. Remember that a rhyme is never good so long as one can find a better."

"Then I will never write anything again save in prose," said La Fontaine, who had taken up Pelisson's reproach in earnest. "Ah! I often suspected I was nothing but a rascally poet! Yes, 'tis the very truth."

"Do not say so; your remark is too sweeping, and there is much that is good in your 'Fables.'"

"And to begin," continued La Fontaine, following up his idea, "I will go and burn a hundred verses I have just made."

"Where are your verses?"

"In my head."

"Well, if they are in your head you cannot burn them."

"True," said La Fontaine; "but if I do not burn them – "

"Well, what will happen if you do not burn them?"

"They will remain in my mind, and I shall

never forget them!"

"The deuce!" cried Loret; "what a dangerous thing! One would go mad with it!"

"The deuce! the deuce!" repeated La Fontaine; "what can I do?"

"I have discovered the way," said Moliere, who had entered just at this point of the conversation.

"What way?"

"Write them first and burn them afterwards."

"How simple! Well, I should never have discovered that. What a mind that devil of a Moliere has!" said La Fontaine. Then, striking his forehead, "Oh, thou wilt never be aught but an ass, Jean La Fontaine!" he added.

"**What** are you saying there, my friend?" broke in Moliere, approaching the poet, whose aside he had heard.

"I say I shall never be aught but an ass," answered La Fontaine, with a heavy sigh and swimming eyes. "Yes, my friend," he added, with increasing grief, "it seems that I rhyme in a slovenly manner."

"Oh, 'tis wrong to say so."

"Nay, I am a poor creature!"

"Who said so?"

"**Parbleu!** 'twas Pelisson; did you not, Pelisson?"

Pelisson, again absorbed in his work, took good care not to answer.

"But if Pelisson said you were so," cried Moliere, "Pelisson has seriously offended you."

"Do you think so?"

"Ah! I advise you, as you are a gentleman, not to leave an insult like that unpunished."

"**What!**" exclaimed La Fontaine.

"Did you ever fight?"

"Once only, with a lieutenant in the light horse."

"What wrong had he done you?"

"It seems he ran away with my wife."

"Ah, ah!" said Moliere, becoming slightly pale; but as, at La Fontaine's declaration, the others had turned round, Moliere kept upon his lips the rallying smile which had so nearly died away, and continuing to make La Fontaine speak –

"And what was the result of the duel?"

"The result was, that on the ground my opponent disarmed me, and then made an apology, promising never again to set foot in my house."

"And you considered yourself satisfied?" said Moliere.

"Not at all! on the contrary, I picked up my sword. 'I beg your pardon, monsieur,' I said, 'I have not fought you because you were my wife's friend, but because I was told I ought to fight. So, as I have never known any peace save since you made her acquaintance, do me the pleasure to continue your visits as heretofore, or **morbleu!** let us set to again.' And so," continued La Fontaine, "he was compelled to resume his friendship with madame, and I continue to be the happiest of husbands."

All burst out laughing. Moliere alone

passed his hand across his eyes. Why? Perhaps to wipe away a tear, perhaps to smother a sigh. Alas! we know that Moliere was a moralist, but he was not a philosopher. "'Tis all one," he said, returning to the topic of the conversation, "Pelisson has insulted you."

"Ah, truly! I had already forgotten it."

"And I am going to challenge him on your behalf."

"Well, you can do so, if you think it indispensable."

"I do think it indispensable, and I am going to – "

"Stay," exclaimed La Fontaine, "I want your advice."

"Upon what? this insult?"

"No; tell me really now whether **lumiere** does not rhyme with **orniere**."

"I should make them rhyme."

"Ah! I knew you would."

"And I have made a hundred thousand such rhymes in my time."

"A hundred thousand!" cried La Fontaine. "Four times as many as 'La Pucelle,' which M. Chaplain is meditating. Is it also on this subject, too, that you have composed a hundred thousand verses?"

"Listen to me, you eternally absent-minded creature," said Moliere.

"It is certain," continued La Fontaine, "that **legume**, for instance, rhymes with **posthume**."

"In the plural, above all."

"Yes, above all in the plural, seeing that then it rhymes not with three letters, but with four; as **orniere** does with **lumiere**."

"But give me **ornieres** and **lumieres** in the plural, my dear Pelisson," said La Fontaine, clapping his hand on the shoulder of his friend, whose insult he had quite forgotten, "and they will rhyme."

"Hem!" coughed Pelisson.

"Moliere says so, and Moliere is a judge of such things; he declares he has himself made a hundred thousand verses."

"Come," said Moliere, laughing, "he is off now."

"It is like **rivage**, which rhymes admirably with **herbage**. I would take my oath of it."

"But – " said Moliere.

"I tell you all this," continued La Fontaine, "because you are preparing a **divertissement** for Vaux, are you not?"

"Yes, the 'Facheux.'"

"Ah, yes, the 'Facheux;' yes, I recollect. Well, I was thinking a prologue would admirably suit your **divertissement**."

"Doubtless it would suit capitally."

"Ah! you are of my opinion?"

"So much so, that I have asked you to write this very prologue."

"You asked **me** to write it?"

"Yes, you, and on your refusal begged you to ask Pelisson, who is engaged upon it at this moment."

"Ah! that is what Pelisson is doing, then? I'faith, my dear Moliere, you are indeed often right."

"When?"

"When you call me absent-minded. It is a monstrous defect; I will cure myself of it, and do your prologue for you."

"But inasmuch as Pelisson is about it! – "

"Ah, true, miserable rascal that I am! Loret was indeed right in saying I was a poor creature."

"It was not Loret who said so, my friend."

"Well, then, whoever said so, 'tis the same to me! And so your **divertissement** is called the 'Facheux?' Well, can you make **heureux** rhyme with **facheux?**"

"If obliged, yes."

"And even with **capriceux**."

"Oh, no, no."

"It would be hazardous, and yet why so?"

"There is too great a difference in the cadences."

"I was fancying," said La Fontaine, leaving Moliere for Loret – "I was fancying – "

"What were you fancying?" said Loret, in the middle of a sentence. "Make haste."

"You are writing the prologue to the 'Facheux,' are you not?"

"No! **mordieu!** it is Pelisson."

"Ah, Pelisson," cried La Fontaine, going over to him, "I was fancying," he continued, "that the nymph of Vaux – "

"Ah, beautiful!" cried Loret. "The nymph of Vaux! thank you, La Fontaine; you have just given me the two concluding verses of my paper."

"Well, if you can rhyme so well, La Fontaine," said Pelisson, "tell me now in what way you would begin my prologue?"

"I should say, for instance, 'Oh! nymph, who – ' After 'who' I should place a verb in the second person singular of the present indicative; and should go on thus: 'this grot profound.'"

"But the verb, the verb?" asked Pelisson.

"To admire the greatest king of all kings round," continued La Fontaine.

"But the verb, the verb," obstinately insisted Pelisson. "This second person singular of the present indicative?"

"Well, then; quittest:

"Oh, nymph, who quittest now this grot profound, To admire the greatest king of all kings round."

"You would not put 'who quittest,' would you?"

"Why not?"

"'Quittest,' after 'you who'?"

"Ah! my dear fellow," exclaimed La Fontaine, "you are a shocking pedant!"

"Without counting," said Moliere, "that the second verse, 'king of all kings round,' is very weak, my dear La Fontaine."

"Then you see clearly I am nothing but a poor creature, – a shuffler, as you said."

"I never said so."

"Then, as Loret said."

"And it was not Loret either; it was Pelisson."

"Well, Pelisson was right a hundred times over. But what annoys me more than anything, my dear Moliere, is, that I fear we shall not have our Epicurean dresses."

"You expected yours, then, for the **fete?**"

"Yes, for the **fete**, and then for after the **fete**. My housekeeper told me that my own is rather faded."

"**Diable!** your housekeeper is right; rather more than faded."

"Ah, you see," resumed La Fontaine, "the fact is, I left it on the floor in my room, and my cat – "

"Well, your cat – "

"She made her nest upon it, which has rather changed its color."

Moliere burst out laughing; Pelisson and Loret followed his example. At this juncture, the bishop of Vannes appeared, with a roll of plans and parchments under his arm. As if the angel of death had chilled all gay and sprightly fancies – as if that wan form had scared away the Graces to whom Xenocrates sacrificed – silence immediately reigned through the study, and every one resumed his self-possession and his pen. Aramis distributed the notes of invitation, and thanked them in the name of M. Fouquet. "The superintendent," he said, "being kept to his room by business, could not come and see them, but begged them to send him some of the fruits of their day's work, to enable him to forget the fatigue of his labor in the night."

At these words, all settled down to work. La Fontaine placed himself at a table, and set his rapid pen an endless dance across the smooth white vellum; Pelisson made a fair copy of his prologue; Moliere contributed fifty fresh verses, with which his visit to Percerin had inspired him; Loret, an article on the marvelous **fetes** he predicted; and Aramis, laden with his booty like the king of the bees, that great black drone, decked with purple and gold, re-entered his apartment, silent and busy. But before departing, "Remember, gentlemen," said he, "we leave to-morrow evening."

"In that case, I must give notice at home," said Moliere.

"Yes; poor Moliere!" said Loret, smiling; "he loves his home."

"'**He** loves,' yes," replied Moliere, with his sad, sweet smile. "'He loves,' that does not mean, they love **him**."

"As for me," said La Fontaine, "they love me at Chateau Thierry, I am very sure."

Aramis here re-entered after a brief disappearance.

"Will any one go with me?" he asked. "I am going by Paris, after having passed a quarter of an hour with M. Fouquet. I offer my carriage."

"Good," said Moliere, "I accept it. I am in a hurry."

"I shall dine here," said Loret. "M. de Gourville has promised me some craw-fish."

"He has promised me some whitings. Find a rhyme for that, La Fontaine."

Aramis went out laughing, as only he could laugh, and Moliere followed him. They were at the bottom of the stairs, when La Fontaine opened the door, and shouted out:

"He has promised us some whitings, In return for these our writings."

The shouts of laughter reached the ears of Fouquet at the moment Aramis opened the door of the study. As to Moliere, he had undertaken to order the horses, while Aramis went to exchange a parting word with the superintendent. "Oh, how they are laughing there!" said Fouquet, with a sigh.

"Do you not laugh, monseigneur?"

"I laugh no longer now, M. d'Herblay. The **fete** is approaching; money is departing."

"Have I not told you that was my business?"

"Yes, you promised me millions."

"You shall have them the day after the king's **entree** into Vaux."

Fouquet looked closely at Aramis, and passed the back of his icy hand across his moistened brow. Aramis perceived that the superintendent either doubted him, or felt he was powerless to obtain the money. How could Fouquet suppose that a poor bishop, ex-abbe, ex-musketeer, could find any?

"Why doubt me?" said Aramis. Fouquet smiled and shook his head.

"Man of little faith!" added the bishop.

"My dear M. d'Herblay," answered Fouquet, "if I fall – "

"Well; if you 'fall'?"

"I shall, at least, fall from such a height, that I shall shatter myself in falling." Then giving himself a shake, as though to escape from himself, "Whence came you," said he, "my friend?"

"From Paris – from Percerin."

"And what have you been doing at Percerin's, for I suppose you attach no great importance to our poets' dresses?"

"No; I went to prepare a surprise."

"Surprise?"

"Yes; which you are going to give to the king."

"And will it cost much?"

"Oh! a hundred pistoles you will give

Lebrun."

"A painting? – Ah! all the better! And what is this painting to represent?"

"I will tell you; then at the same time, whatever you may say or think of it, I went to see the dresses for our poets."

"Bah! and they will be rich and elegant?"

"Splendid! There will be few great monseigneurs with so good. People will see the difference there is between the courtiers of wealth and those of friendship."

"Ever generous and grateful, dear prelate."

"In your school."

Fouquet grasped his hand. "And where are you going?" he said.

"I am off to Paris, when you shall have given a certain letter."

"For whom?"

"M. de Lyonne."

"And what do you want with Lyonne?"

"I wish to make him sign a **lettre de cachet**."

"'**Lettre de cachet!**' Do you desire to put

somebody in the Bastile?"

"On the contrary – to let somebody out."

"And who?"

"A poor devil – a youth, a lad who has been Bastiled these ten years, for two Latin verses he made against the Jesuits."

"'Two Latin verses!' and, for 'two Latin verses,' the miserable being has been in prison for ten years!"

"Yes!"

"And has committed no other crime?"

"Beyond this, he is as innocent as you or I."

"On your word?"

"On my honor!"

"And his name is – "

"Seldon."

"Yes. – But it is too bad. You knew this, and you never told me!"

"'Twas only yesterday his mother applied to me, monseigneur."

"And the woman is poor!"

"In the deepest misery."

"Heaven," said Fouquet, "sometimes

bears with such injustice on earth, that I hardly wonder there are wretches who doubt of its existence. Stay, M. d'Herblay." And Fouquet, taking a pen, wrote a few rapid lines to his colleague Lyonne. Aramis took the letter and made ready to go.

"Wait," said Fouquet. He opened his drawer, and took out ten government notes which were there, each for a thousand francs. "Stay," he said; "set the son at liberty, and give this to the mother; but, above all, do not tell her – "

"What, monseigneur?"

"That she is ten thousand livres richer than I. She would say I am but a poor superintendent! Go! and I pray that God will bless those who are mindful of his poor!"

"So also do I pray," replied Aramis, kissing Fouquet's hand.

And he went out quickly, carrying off the letter for Lyonne and the notes for Seldon's mother, and taking up Moliere, who was beginning to lose patience.

CHAPTER SEVEN

Another Supper at the Bastile

SEVEN O'CLOCK SOUNDED FROM the great clock of the Bastile, that famous clock, which, like all the accessories of the state prison, the very use of which is a torture, recalled to the prisoners' minds the destination of every hour of their punishment. The time-piece of the Bastile, adorned with figures, like most of the clocks of the period, represented St. Peter in bonds.

It was the supper hour of the unfortunate captives. The doors, grating on their enormous hinges, opened for the passage of the baskets and trays of provisions, the abundance and the delicacy of which, as M. de Baisemeaux has himself taught us, was regulated by the condition in life of the prisoner. We understand on this head the theories of M. de Baisemeaux, sovereign dispenser of gastronomic delicacies, head cook of the royal fortress, whose trays, full-laden, were ascending the steep staircases, carrying some consolation to the prisoners in the shape of honestly filled bottles of good vintages. This same hour was that of M. le gouverneur's supper also. He had a guest to-day, and the spit turned more heavily than usual. Roast partridges, flanked with quails and flanking a larded leveret; boiled fowls; hams, fried and sprinkled with white wine, **cardons** of Guipuzcoa and **la bisque ecrevisses**: these, together with soups and **hors d'oeuvres**, constituted the governor's bill of fare. Baisemeaux, seated at table, was rubbing his hands and looking at the bishop of Vannes, who, booted like a cavalier, dressed in gray and sword at side, kept talking of his hunger and testifying the liveliest impatience. M. de Baisemeaux de Montlezun was not accustomed to the unbending movements of his greatness my lord of Vannes, and this evening Aramis, becoming sprightly, volunteered confidence on confidence. The prelate had again a little touch of the musketeer about him. The bishop just trenched on the borders only of license in his style of conversation. As for M. de Baisemeaux, with the facility of vulgar people, he gave himself up entirely upon this point of his guest's freedom. "Monsieur," said he, "for indeed to-night I dare not call you monseigneur."

"By no means," said Aramis; "call me monsieur; I am booted."

"Do you know, monsieur, of whom you remind me this evening?"

"No! faith," said Aramis, taking up his glass; "but I hope I remind you of a capital guest."

"You remind me of two, monsieur. Francois, shut the window; the wind may annoy his greatness."

"And let him go," added Aramis. "The supper is completely served, and we shall eat it very well without waiters. I like exceedingly to be **tete-a-tete** when I am with a friend." Baisemeaux bowed respectfully.

"I like exceedingly," continued Aramis, "to help myself."

"Retire, Francois," cried Baisemeaux. "I was saying that your greatness puts me in mind of two persons; one very illustrious, the late cardinal, the great Cardinal de la Rochelle, who wore boots like you."

"Indeed," said Aramis; "and the other?"

"The other was a certain musketeer, very handsome, very brave, very adventurous, very fortunate, who, from being abbe, turned musketeer, and from musketeer turned abbe." Aramis condescended to smile. "From abbe," continued Baisemeaux, encouraged by Aramis's smile – "from abbe, bishop – and from bishop – "

"Ah! stay there, I beg," exclaimed Aramis.

"I have just said, monsieur, that you gave me the idea of a cardinal."

"Enough, dear M. Baisemeaux. As you said, I have on the boots of a cavalier, but I do not intend, for all that, to embroil myself with the church this evening."

"But you have wicked intentions, nevertheless, monseigneur."

"Oh, yes, wicked, I own, as everything mundane is."

"You traverse the town and the streets in disguise?"

"In disguise, as you say."

"And you still make use of your sword?"

"Yes, I should think so; but only when I am compelled. Do me the pleasure to summon Francois."

"Have you no wine there?"

"'Tis not for wine, but because it is hot here,

and the window is shut."

"I shut the windows at supper-time so as not to hear the sounds or the arrival of couriers."

"Ah, yes. You hear them when the window is open?"

"But too well, and that disturbs me. You understand?"

"Nevertheless I am suffocated. Francois." Francois entered. "Open the windows, I pray you, Master Francois," said Aramis. "You will allow him, dear M. Baisemeaux?"

"You are at home here," answered the governor. The window was opened. "Do you not think," said M. de Baisemeaux, "that you will find yourself very lonely, now M. de la Fere has returned to his household gods at Blois? He is a very old friend, is he not?"

"You know it as I do, Baisemeaux, seeing that you were in the musketeers with us."

"Bah! with my friends I reckon neither bottles of wine nor years."

"And you are right. But I do more than love

M. de la Fere, dear Baisemeaux; I venerate him."

"Well, for my part, though 'tis singular," said the governor, "I prefer M. d'Artagnan to him. There is a man for you, who drinks long and well! That kind of people allow you at least to penetrate their thoughts."

"Baisemeaux, make me tipsy to-night; let us have a merry time of it as of old, and if I have a trouble at the bottom of my heart, I promise you, you shall see it as you would a diamond at the bottom of your glass."

"Bravo!" said Baisemeaux, and he poured out a great glass of wine and drank it off at a draught, trembling with joy at the idea of being, by hook or by crook, in the secret of some high archiepiscopal misdemeanor. While he was drinking he did not see with what attention Aramis was noting the sounds in the great court. A courier came in about eight o'clock as Francois brought in the fifth bottle, and, although the courier made a great noise, Baisemeaux heard nothing.

"The devil take him," said Aramis.

"What! who?" asked Baisemeaux. "I hope 'tis neither the wine you drank nor he who is the cause of your drinking it."

"No; it is a horse, who is making noise enough in the court for a whole squadron."

"Pooh! some courier or other," replied the governor, redoubling his attention to the passing bottle. "Yes; and may the devil take him, and so quickly that we shall never hear him speak more. Hurrah! hurrah!"

"You forget me, Baisemeaux! my glass is empty," said Aramis, lifting his dazzling Venetian goblet.

"Upon my honor, you delight me. Francois, wine!" Francois entered. "Wine, fellow! and better."

"Yes, monsieur, yes; but a courier has just arrived."

"Let him go to the devil, I say."

"Yes, monsieur, but – "

"Let him leave his news at the office; we will see to it to-morrow. To-morrow, there will be time to-morrow; there will be daylight," said Baisemeaux, chanting the words.

"Ah, monsieur," grumbled the soldier Francois, in spite of himself, "monsieur."

"Take care," said Aramis, "take care!"

"Of what? dear M. d'Herblay," said Baisemeaux, half intoxicated.

"The letter which the courier brings to the governor of a fortress is sometimes an order."

"Nearly always."

"Do not orders issue from the ministers?"

"Yes, undoubtedly; but – "

"And what to these ministers do but countersign the signature of the king?"

"Perhaps you are right. Nevertheless, 'tis very tiresome when you are sitting before a good table, **tete-a-tete** with a friend – Ah! I beg your pardon, monsieur; I forgot it is I who engage you at supper, and that I speak to a future cardinal."

"Let us pass over that, dear Baisemeaux, and return to our soldier, to Francois."

"Well, and what has Francois done?"

"He has demurred!"

"He was wrong, then?"

"However, he **has** demurred, you see; 'tis because there is something extraordinary in this matter. It is very possible that it was not Francois who was wrong in demurring, but you, who are in the wrong in not listening to him."

"Wrong? I to be wrong before Francois? that seems rather hard."

"Pardon me, merely an irregularity. But I thought it my duty to make an observation which I deem important."

"Oh! perhaps you are right," stammered Baisemeaux. "The king's order is sacred; but as to orders that arrive when one is at supper, I repeat that the devil – "

"If you had said as much to the great cardinal – hem! my dear Baisemeaux, and if his order had any importance."

"I do it that I may not disturb a bishop. **Mordioux!** am I not, then, excusable?"

"Do not forget, Baisemeaux, that I have worn the soldier's coat, and I am accustomed to obedience everywhere."

"You wish, then – "

"I wish that you would do your duty, my friend; yes, at least before this soldier."

"'Tis mathematically true," exclaimed Baisemeaux. Francois still waited: "Let them send this order of the king's up to me," he repeated, recovering himself. And he added in a low tone, "Do you know what it is? I will tell you something about as interesting as this. 'Beware of fire near the powder magazine;' or, 'Look close after such and such a one, who is clever at escaping,' Ah! if you only knew, monseigneur, how many times I have been suddenly awakened from the very sweetest, deepest slumber, by messengers arriving at full gallop to tell me, or rather, bring me a slip of paper containing these words: 'Monsieur de Baisemeaux, what news?' 'Tis clear enough that those who waste their time writing such orders have never slept in the Bastile. They would know better; they have never considered the thickness of my walls, the vigilance of my officers, the number of rounds we go. But, indeed, what can you expect, monseigneur? It is their business to write and torment me when I am at rest, and to trouble me when I am happy," added Baisemeaux, bowing to Aramis. "Then let them do their business."

"And do you do yours," added the bishop, smiling.

Francois re-entered; Baisemeaux took from his hands the minister's order. He slowly undid it, and as slowly read it. Aramis pretended to be drinking, so as to be able to watch his host through the glass. Then, Baisemeaux, having read it: "What was I just saying?" he exclaimed.

"What is it?" asked the bishop.

"An order of release! There, now; excellent news indeed to disturb us!"

"Excellent news for him whom it concerns, you will at least agree, my dear governor!"

"And at eight o'clock in the evening!"

"It is charitable!"

"Oh! charity is all very well, but it is for that fellow who says he is so weary and tired, but not for me who am amusing myself," said Baisemeaux, exasperated.

"Will you lose by him, then? And is the prisoner who is to be set at liberty a good payer?"

"Oh, yes, indeed! a miserable, five-franc rat!"

"Let me see it," asked M. d'Herblay. "It is no indiscretion?"

"By no means; read it."

"There is 'Urgent,' on the paper; you have seen that, I suppose?"

"Oh, admirable! 'Urgent!' – a man who has been there ten years! It is **urgent** to set him free to-day, this very evening, at eight o'clock! – **urgent!**" And Baisemeaux, shrugging his shoulders with an air of supreme disdain, flung the order on the table and began eating again.

"They are fond of these tricks!" he said, with his mouth full; "they seize a man, some fine day, keep him under lock and key for ten years, and write to you, 'Watch this fellow well,' or 'Keep him very strictly.' And then, as soon as you are accustomed to look upon the prisoner as a dangerous man, all of a sudden, without rhyme or reason they write – 'Set him at liberty,' and actually add to their missive – 'urgent.' You will own, my lord, 'tis enough to make a man at dinner shrug his shoulders!"

"What do you expect? It is for them to write," said Aramis, "for you to execute the order."

"Good! good! execute it! Oh, patience! You must not imagine that I am a slave."

"Gracious Heaven! my very good M. Baisemeaux, who ever said so? Your independence is well known."

"Thank Heaven!"

"But your goodness of heart is also known."

"Ah! don't speak of it!"

"And your obedience to your superiors. Once a soldier, you see, Baisemeaux, always a soldier."

"And I shall directly obey; and to-morrow morning, at daybreak, the prisoner referred to shall be set free."

"To-morrow?"

"At dawn."

"Why not this evening, seeing that the **lettre de cachet** bears, both on the direction and inside, '**urgent**'?"

"Because this evening we are at supper, and our affairs are urgent, too!"

"Dear Baisemeaux, booted though I be, I feel myself a priest, and charity has higher claims upon me than hunger and thirst. This unfortunate man has suffered long enough, since you have just told me that he has been your prisoner these ten years. Abridge his suffering. His good time has come; give him the benefit quickly. God will repay you in Paradise with years of felicity."

"You wish it?"

"I entreat you."

"What! in the very middle of our repast?"

"I implore you; such an action is worth ten Benedicites."

"It shall be as you desire, only our supper will get cold."

"Oh! never heed that."

Baisemeaux leaned back to ring for Francois, and by a very natural motion turned round towards the door. The order had remained on the table; Aramis seized the opportunity when Baisemeaux was not looking to change the paper for another, folded in the same manner, which he drew swiftly from his pocket. "Francois," said the governor, "let the major come up here with the turnkeys of the Bertaudiere." Francois bowed and quitted the room, leaving the two companions alone.

CHAPTER EIGHT

The General of the Order

THERE WAS NOW A brief silence, during which Aramis never removed his eyes from Baisemeaux for a moment. The latter seemed only half decided to disturb himself thus in the middle of supper, and it was clear he was trying to invent some pretext, whether good or bad, for delay, at any rate till after dessert. And it appeared also that he had hit upon an excuse at last.

"Eh! but it is impossible!" he cried.

"How impossible?" said Aramis. "Give me a glimpse of this impossibility."

"'Tis impossible to set a prisoner at liberty at such an hour. Where can he go to, a man so unacquainted with Paris?"

"He will find a place wherever he can."

"You see, now, one might as well set a blind man free!"

"I have a carriage, and will take him wherever he wishes."

"You have an answer for everything. Francois, tell monsieur le major to go and open the cell of M. Seldon, No. 3, Bertaudiere."

"Seldon!" exclaimed Aramis, very naturally. "You said Seldon, I think?"

"I said Seldon, of course. 'Tis the name of the man they set free."

"Oh! you mean to say Marchiali?" said Aramis.

"Marchiali? oh! yes, indeed. No, no, Seldon."

"I think you are making a mistake, Monsieur Baisemeaux."

"I have read the order."

"And I also."

"And I saw 'Seldon' in letters as large as that," and Baisemeaux held up his finger.

"And I read 'Marchiali' in characters as large as this," said Aramis, also holding up two fingers.

"To the proof; let us throw a light on the matter," said Baisemeaux, confident he was right. "There is the paper, you have only to read it."

"I read 'Marchiali,'" returned Aramis, spreading out the paper. "Look."

Baisemeaux looked, and his arms dropped suddenly. "Yes, yes," he said, quite overwhelmed; "yes, Marchiali. 'Tis plainly written Marchiali! Quite true!"

"Ah! – "

"How? the man of whom we have talked so much? The man whom they are every day telling me to take such care of?"

"There is 'Marchiali,'" repeated the inflexible Aramis.

"I must own it, monseigneur. But I understand nothing about it."

"You believe your eyes, at any rate."

"To tell me very plainly there is 'Marchiali.'"

"And in a good handwriting, too."

"'Tis a wonder! I still see this order and the name of Seldon, Irishman. I see it. Ah! I even recollect that under this name there was a blot of ink."

"No, there is no ink; no, there is no blot."

"Oh! but there was, though; I know it, because I rubbed my finger – this very one – in the powder that was over the blot."

"In a word, be it how it may, dear M. Baisemeaux," said Aramis, "and whatever you may have seen, the order is signed to release Marchiali, blot or no blot."

"The order is signed to release Marchiali," replied Baisemeaux, mechanically, endeavoring to regain his courage.

"And you are going to release this prisoner.

If your heart dictates you to deliver Seldon also, I declare to you I will not oppose it the least in the world." Aramis accompanied this remark with a smile, the irony of which effectually dispelled Baisemeaux's confusion of mind, and restored his courage.

"Monseigneur," he said, "this Marchiali is the very same prisoner whom the other day a priest confessor of **our order** came to visit in so imperious and so secret a manner."

"I don't know that, monsieur," replied the bishop.

"'Tis no such long time ago, dear Monsieur d'Herblay."

"It is true. But **with us**, monsieur, it is good that the man of to-day should no longer know what the man of yesterday did."

"In any case," said Baisemeaux, "the visit of the Jesuit confessor must have given happiness to this man."

Aramis made no reply, but recommenced eating and drinking. As for Baisemeaux, no longer touching anything that was on the table, he again took up the order and examined it every way. This investigation, under ordinary circumstances, would have made the ears of the impatient Aramis burn with anger; but the bishop of Vannes did not become incensed for so little, above all, when he had murmured to himself that to do so was dangerous. "Are you going to release Marchiali?" he said. "What mellow, fragrant and delicious sherry this is, my dear governor."

"Monseigneur," replied Baisemeaux, "I shall release the prisoner Marchiali when I have summoned the courier who brought the order, and above all, when, by interrogating him, I have satisfied myself."

"The order is sealed, and the courier is ignorant of the contents. What do you want to satisfy yourself about?"

"Be it so, monseigneur; but I shall send to the ministry, and M. de Lyonne will either confirm or withdraw the order."

"What is the good of all that?" asked Aramis, coldly.

"What good?"

"Yes; what is your object, I ask?"

"The object of never deceiving oneself, monseigneur; nor being wanting in the respect which a subaltern owes to his superior officers, nor infringing the duties of a service one has accepted of one's own free will."

"Very good; you have just spoken so eloquently, that I cannot but admire you. It is true that a subaltern owes respect to his superiors; he is guilty when he deceives himself, and he should be punished if he infringed either the duties or laws of his office."

Baisemeaux looked at the bishop with astonishment.

"It follows," pursued Aramis, "that you are going to ask advice, to put your conscience at ease in the matter?"

"Yes, monseigneur."

"And if a superior officer gives you orders, you will obey?"

"Never doubt it, monseigneur."

"You know the king's signature well, M. de Baisemeaux?"

"Yes, monseigneur."

"Is it not on this order of release?"

"It is true, but it may – "

"Be forged, you mean?"

"That is evident, monseigneur."

"You are right. And that of M. de Lyonne?"

"I see it plain enough on the order; but for the same reason that the king's signature may have been forged, so also, and with even greater probability, may M. de Lyonne's."

"Your logic has the stride of a giant, M. de Baisemeaux," said Aramis; "and your reasoning is irresistible. But on what special grounds do you base your idea that these signatures are false?"

"On this: the absence of counter-signatures. Nothing checks his majesty's signature; and M. de Lyonne is not there to tell me he has signed."

"Well, Monsieur de Baisemeaux," said Aramis, bending an eagle glance on the governor, "I adopt so frankly your doubts, and your mode of clearing them up, that I will take a pen, if you will give me one."

Baisemeaux gave him a pen.

"And a sheet of white paper," added Aramis.

Baisemeaux handed him some paper.

"Now, I – I, also – I, here present – incontestably, I – am going to write an order to which I am certain you will give credence, incredulous as you are!"

Baisemeaux turned pale at this icy assurance of manner. It seemed to him that the voice of the bishop's, but just now so playful and gay, had become funereal and sad; that the wax lights changed into the tapers of a mortuary chapel, the very glasses of wine into chalices of blood.

Aramis took a pen and wrote. Baisemeaux, in terror, read over his shoulder.

"A. M. D. G.," wrote the bishop; and he drew a cross under these four letters, which signify **ad majorem Dei gloriam**, "to the greater glory of God;" and thus he continued: "It is our pleasure that the order brought to M. de Baisemeaux de Montlezun, governor, for the king, of the castle of the Bastile, be held by him good and effectual, and be immediately carried into operation."

(Signed) D'HERBLAY

"General of the Order, by the grace of God."

Baisemeaux was so profoundly astonished, that his features remained contracted, his lips parted, and his eyes fixed. He did not move an inch, nor articulate a sound. Nothing could be heard in that large chamber but the wing-whisper of a little moth, which was fluttering to its death about the candles. Aramis, without even deigning to look at the man whom he had reduced to so miserable a condition, drew from his pocket a small case of black wax; he sealed the letter, and stamped it with a seal suspended at his breast, beneath his doublet, and when the operation was concluded, presented – still in silence – the missive to M. de Baisemeaux. The latter, whose hands trembled in a manner to excite pity, turned a dull and meaningless gaze upon the letter. A last gleam of feeling played over his features, and he fell, as if thunder-struck, on a chair.

"Come, come," said Aramis, after a long silence, during which the governor of the Bastile had slowly recovered his senses, "do not lead me to believe, dear Baisemeaux, that the presence of the general of the order is as terrible as His, and that men die merely from having seen Him. Take courage, rouse yourself; give me your hand – obey."

Baisemeaux, reassured, if not satisfied, obeyed, kissed Aramis's hand, and rose. "Immediately?" he murmured.

"Oh, there is no pressing haste, my host; take your place again, and do the honors over this beautiful dessert."

"Monseigneur, I shall never recover such a shock as this; I who have laughed, who have jested with you! I who have dared to treat you on a footing of equality!"

"Say nothing about it, old comrade," replied the bishop, who perceived how strained the cord was and how dangerous it would have been to break it; "say nothing about it. Let us each live in our own way; to you, my protection and my friendship; to me, your obedience. Having exactly fulfilled these two requirements, let us live happily."

Baisemeaux reflected; he perceived, at a glance, the consequence of this withdrawal of a prisoner by means of a forged order; and, putting in the scale the guarantee offered him by the official order of the general, did not consider it of any value.

Aramis divined this. "My dear Baisemeaux," said he, "you are a simpleton. Lose this habit of reflection when I give myself the trouble to think for you."

And at another gesture he made, Baisemeaux bowed again. "How shall I set about it?" he said.

"What is the process for releasing a prisoner?"

"I have the regulations."

"Well, then, follow the regulations, my friend."

"I go with my major to the prisoner's room, and conduct him, if he is a personage of importance."

"But this Marchiali is not an important personage," said Aramis carelessly.

"I don't know," answered the governor, as if he would have said, "It is for you to instruct me."

"Then if you don't know it, I am right; so act towards Marchiali as you act towards one of obscure station."

"Good; the regulations so provide. They are to the effect that the turnkey, or one of the lower officials, shall bring the prisoner before the governor, in the office."

"Well, 'tis very wise, that; and then?"

"Then we return to the prisoner the valuables he wore at the time of his imprisonment, his clothes and papers, if the minister's orders have not otherwise dictated."

"What was the minister's order as to this Marchiali?"

"Nothing; for the unhappy man arrived here without jewels, without papers, and almost without clothes."

"See how simple, then, all is. Indeed, Baisemeaux, you make a mountain of everything. Remain here, and make them bring the prisoner to the governor's house."

Baisemeaux obeyed. He summoned his lieutenant, and gave him an order, which the latter passed on, without disturbing himself about it, to the next whom it concerned.

Half an hour afterwards they heard a gate shut in the court; it was the door to the dungeon, which had just rendered up its prey to the free air. Aramis blew out all the candles which lighted the room but one, which he left burning behind the door. This flickering glare prevented the sight from resting steadily on any object. It multiplied tenfold the changing forms and shadows of the place, by its wavering uncertainty. Steps drew near.

"Go and meet your men," said Aramis to Baisemeaux.

The governor obeyed. The sergeant and turnkeys disappeared. Baisemeaux re-entered, followed by a prisoner. Aramis had placed himself in the shade; he saw without being seen. Baisemeaux, in an agitated tone of voice, made the young man acquainted with the order which set him at liberty. The prisoner listened, without making a single gesture or saying a word.

"You will swear ('tis the regulation that requires it)," added the governor, "never to reveal anything that you have seen or heard in the Bastile."

The prisoner perceived a crucifix; he stretched out his hands and swore with his lips. "And now, monsieur, you are free. Whither do you intend going?"

The prisoner turned his head, as if looking behind him for some protection, on which he ought to rely. Then was it that Aramis came out of the shade: "I am here," he said, "to render the gentleman whatever service he may please to ask."

The prisoner slightly reddened, and, without hesitation, passed his arm through that of Aramis. "God have you in his holy keeping," he said, in a voice the firmness of which made the governor tremble as much as the form of the blessing astonished him.

Aramis, on shaking hands with Baisemeaux, said to him; "Does my order trouble you? Do you fear their finding it here, should they come to search?"

"I desire to keep it, monseigneur," said Baisemeaux. "If they found it here, it would be a certain indication I should be lost, and in that case you would be a powerful and a last auxiliary for me."

"Being your accomplice, you mean?" answered Aramis, shrugging his shoulders. "Adieu, Baisemeaux," said he.

The horses were in waiting, making each rusty spring reverberate the carriage again with their impatience. Baisemeaux accompanied the bishop to the bottom of the steps. Aramis caused his companion to mount before him, then followed, and without giving the driver any further order, "Go on," said he. The carriage rattled over the pavement of the courtyard. An officer with a torch went before the horses, and gave orders at every post to let them pass. During the time taken in opening all the barriers, Aramis barely breathed, and you might have heard his "sealed heart knock against his ribs." The prisoner, buried in a corner of the carriage, made no more sign of life than his companion. At length, a jolt more sever than the others announced to them that they had cleared the last watercourse. Behind the carriage closed the last gate, that in the Rue St. Antoine. No more walls either on the right or the left; heaven everywhere, liberty everywhere, and life everywhere. The horses, kept in check by a vigorous hand, went quietly as far as the middle of the faubourg. There they began to trot. Little by little, whether they were warming to their work, or whether they were urged, they gained in swiftness, and once past Bercy, the carriage seemed to fly, so great was the ardor of the coursers. The horses galloped thus as far as Villeneuve St. George's, where relays were waiting. Then four instead of two whirled the carriage away in the direction of Melun, and pulled up for a moment in the middle of the forest of Senart. No doubt the order had been given the postilion beforehand, for Aramis had no occasion even to make a sign.

"What is the matter?" asked the prisoner, as if waking from a long dream.

"The matter is, monseigneur," said Aramis, "that before going further, it is necessary your royal highness and I should converse."

"I will await an opportunity, monsieur," answered the young prince.

"We could not have a better, monseigneur. We are in the middle of a forest, and no one can hear us."

"The postilion?"

"The postilion of this relay is deaf and dumb, monseigneur."

"I am at your service, M. d'Herblay."

"Is it your pleasure to remain in the carriage?"

"Yes; we are comfortably seated, and I like this carriage, for it has restored me to liberty."

"Wait, monseigneur; there is yet a precaution to be taken."

"What?"

"We are here on the highway; cavaliers or carriages traveling like ourselves might pass, and seeing us stopping, deem us in some difficulty. Let us avoid offers of assistance, which would embarrass us."

"Give the postilion orders to conceal the carriage in one of the side avenues."

"'Tis exactly what I wished to do, monseigneur."

Aramis made a sign to the deaf and dumb driver of the carriage, whom he touched on the arm. The latter dismounted, took the leaders by the bridle, and led them over the velvet sward and the mossy grass of a winding alley, at the bottom of which, on this moonless night, the deep shades formed a curtain blacker than ink. This done, the man lay down on a slope near his horses, who, on either side, kept nibbling the young oak shoots.

"I am listening," said the young prince to Aramis; "but what are you doing there?"

"I am disarming myself of my pistols, of which we have no further need, monseigneur."

CHAPTER NINE

The Tempter

"MY PRINCE," said Aramis, turning in the carriage towards his companion, "weak creature as I am, so unpretending in genius, so low in the scale of intelligent beings, it has never yet happened to me to converse with a man without penetrating his thoughts through that living mask which has been thrown over our mind, in order to retain its expression. But to-night, in this darkness, in the reserve which you maintain, I can read nothing on your features, and something tells me that I shall have great difficulty in wresting from you a sincere declaration. I beseech you, then, not for love of me, for subjects should never weigh as anything in the balance which princes hold, but for love of yourself, to retain every syllable, every inflexion which, under the present most grave circumstances, will all have a sense and value as important as any every uttered in the world."

"I listen," replied the young prince, "decidedly, without either eagerly seeking or fearing anything you are about to say to me." And he buried himself still deeper in the thick cushions of the carriage, trying to deprive his companion not only of the sight of him, but even of the very idea of his presence.

Black was the darkness which fell wide and dense from the summits of the intertwining trees. The carriage, covered in by this prodigious roof, would not have received a particle of light, not even if a ray could have struggled through the wreaths of mist that were already rising in the avenue.

"Monseigneur," resumed Aramis, "you know the history of the government which to-day controls France. The king issued from an infancy imprisoned like yours, obscure as yours, and confined as yours; only, instead of ending, like yourself, this slavery in a prison, this obscurity in solitude, these straightened circumstances in concealment, he was fain to bear all these miseries, humiliations, and distresses, in full daylight, under the pitiless sun of royalty; on an elevation flooded with light, where every stain appears a blemish, every glory a stain. The king has suffered; it rankles in his mind; and he will avenge himself. He will be a bad king. I say not that he will pour out his people's blood, like Louis XI., or Charles IX.; for he has no mortal injuries to avenge; but he will devour the means and substance of his people; for he has himself undergone wrongs in his own interest and money. In the first place, then, I acquit my conscience, when I consider openly the merits and the faults of this great prince; and if I condemn him, my conscience absolves me."

Aramis paused. It was not to listen if the silence of the forest remained undisturbed, but it was to gather up his thoughts from the very bottom of his soul – to leave the thoughts he had uttered sufficient time to eat deeply into the mind of his companion.

"All that Heaven does, Heaven does well," continued the bishop of Vannes; "and I am so persuaded of it that I have long been thankful to have been chosen depositary of the secret which I have aided you to discover. To a just Providence was necessary an instrument, at once penetrating, persevering, and convinced, to accomplish a great work. I am this instrument. I possess penetration, perseverance, conviction; I govern a mysterious people, who has taken for its motto, the motto of God, '**Patiens quia oeternus**.'" The prince moved. "I divine, monseigneur, why you are raising your head, and are surprised at the people I have under my command. You did not know you were dealing with a king – oh! monseigneur, king of a people very humble, much disinherited; humble because they have no force save when creeping; disinherited, because never, almost never in this world, do my people reap the harvest they sow, nor eat the fruit they cultivate. They labor for an abstract idea; they heap together all the atoms of their power, so from a single man; and round this man, with the sweat of their labor, they create a misty halo, which his genius shall, in turn, render a glory gilded with the rays of all the crowns in Christendom. Such is the man you have beside you, monseigneur. It is to tell you that he has drawn you from the abyss for a great purpose, to raise you above the powers of the earth – above himself."[1]

The prince lightly touched Aramis's arm. "You speak to me," he said, "of that religious order whose chief you are. For me, the result of your words is, that the day you desire to hurl down the man you shall have raised, the event will be accomplished; and that you will keep under your hand your creation of yesterday."

"Undeceive yourself, monseigneur," replied the bishop. "I should not take the trouble to play this terrible game with your royal highness, if I had not a double interest in gaining it. The day you are elevated, you are elevated forever; you will overturn the footstool, as you rise, and will send it rolling so far, that not even the sight of it will ever again recall to you its right to simple gratitude."

---

1 "He is patient because he is eternal." is how the Latin translates. It is from St. Augustine. This motto was sometimes applied to the Papacy, but not to the Jesuits.

"Oh, monsieur!"

"Your movement, monseigneur, arises from an excellent disposition. I thank you. Be well assured, I aspire to more than gratitude! I am convinced that, when arrived at the summit, you will judge me still more worthy to be your friend; and then, monseigneur, we two will do such great deeds, that ages hereafter shall long speak of them."

"Tell me plainly, monsieur – tell me without disguise – what I am to-day, and what you aim at my being to-morrow."

"You are the son of King Louis XIII., brother of Louis XIV., natural and legitimate heir to the throne of France. In keeping you near him, as Monsieur has been kept – Monsieur, your younger brother – the king reserved to himself the right of being legitimate sovereign. The doctors only could dispute his legitimacy. But the doctors always prefer the king who is to the king who is not. Providence has willed that you should be persecuted; this persecution to-day consecrates you king of France. You had, then, a right to reign, seeing that it is disputed; you had a right to be proclaimed seeing that you have been concealed; and you possess royal blood, since no one has dared to shed yours, as that of your servants has been shed. Now see, then, what this Providence, which you have so often accused of having in every way thwarted you, has done for you. It has given you the features, figure, age, and voice of your brother; and the very causes of your persecution are about to become those of your triumphant restoration. To-morrow, after to-morrow – from the very first, regal phantom, living shade of Louis XIV., you will sit upon his throne, whence the will of Heaven, confided in execution to the arm of man, will have hurled him, without hope of return."

"I understand," said the prince, "my brother's blood will not be shed, then."

"You will be sole arbiter of his fate."

"The secret of which they made an evil

use against me?"

"You will employ it against him. What did he do to conceal it? He concealed you. Living image of himself, you will defeat the conspiracy of Mazarin and Anne of Austria. You, my prince, will have the same interest in concealing him, who will, as a prisoner, resemble you, as you will resemble him as a king."

"I fall back on what I was saying to you. Who will guard him?"

"Who guarded **you?**"

"You know this secret – you have made use of it with regard to myself. Who else knows it?"

"The queen-mother and Madame de Chevreuse."

"What will they do?"

"Nothing, if you choose."

"How is that?"

"How can they recognize you, if you act in such a manner that no one can recognize you?"

"'Tis true; but there are grave difficulties."

"State them, prince."

"My brother is married; I cannot take my brother's wife."

"I will cause Spain to consent to a divorce; it is in the interest of your new policy; it is human morality. All that is really noble and really useful in this world will find its account therein."

"The imprisoned king will speak."

"To whom do you think he will speak – to the walls?"

"You mean, by walls, the men in whom you put confidence."

"If need be, yes. And besides, your royal highness – "

"Besides?"

"I was going to say, that the designs of Providence do not stop on such a fair road. Every scheme of this caliber is completed by its results, like a geometrical calculation. The king, in prison, will not be for you the cause of embarrassment that you have been for the king enthroned. His soul is naturally proud and impatient; it is, moreover, disarmed and enfeebled, by being accustomed to honors, and by the license of supreme power. The same Providence which has willed that the concluding step in the geometrical calculation I have had the honor of describing to your royal highness should be your ascension to the throne, and the destruction of him who is hurtful to you, has also determined that the conquered one shall soon end both his own and your sufferings. Therefore, his soul and body have been adapted for but a brief agony. Put into prison as a private individual, left alone with your doubts, deprived of everything, you have exhibited the most sublime, enduring principle of life in withstanding all this. But your brother, a captive, forgotten, and in bonds, will not long endure the calamity; and Heaven will resume his soul at the appointed time – that is to say, soon."

At this point in Aramis's gloomy analysis,

a bird of night uttered from the depths of the forest that prolonged and plaintive cry which makes every creature tremble.

"I will exile the deposed king," said Philippe, shuddering; "'twill be more human."

"The king's good pleasure will decide the point," said Aramis. "But has the problem been well put? Have I brought out of the solution according to the wishes or the foresight of your royal highness?"

"Yes, monsieur, yes; you have forgotten nothing – except, indeed, two things."

"The first?"

"Let us speak of it at once, with the same frankness we have already conversed in. Let us speak of the causes which may bring about the ruin of all the hopes we have conceived. Let us speak of the risks we are running."

"They would be immense, infinite, terrific, insurmountable, if, as I have said, all things did not concur to render them of absolutely no account. There is no danger either for you or for me, if the constancy and intrepidity of your royal highness are equal to that perfection of resemblance to your brother which nature has bestowed upon you. I repeat it, there are no dangers, only obstacles; a word, indeed, which I find in all languages, but have always ill-understood, and, were I king, would have obliterated as useless and absurd."

"Yes, indeed, monsieur; there is a very serious obstacle, an insurmountable danger, which you are forgetting."

"Ah!" said Aramis.

"There is conscience, which cries aloud; remorse, that never dies."

"True, true," said the bishop; "there is a weakness of heart of which you remind me. You are right, too, for that, indeed, is an immense obstacle. The horse afraid of the ditch, leaps into the middle of it, and is killed! The man who trembling crosses his sword with that of another leaves loopholes whereby his enemy has him in his power."

"Have you a brother?" said the young man

to Aramis.

“I am alone in the world,” said the latter, with a hard, dry voice.

“But, surely, there is some one in the world whom you love?” added Philippe.

“No one! – Yes, I love you.”

The young man sank into so profound a silence, that the mere sound of his respiration seemed like a roaring tumult for Aramis. “Monseigneur,” he resumed, “I have not said all I had to say to your royal highness; I have not offered you all the salutary counsels and useful resources which I have at my disposal. It is useless to flash bright visions before the eyes of one who seeks and loves darkness: useless, too, is it to let the magnificence of the cannon’s roar make itself heard in the ears of one who loves repose and the quiet of the country. Monseigneur, I have your happiness spread out before me in my thoughts; listen to my words; precious they indeed are, in their import and their sense, for you who look with such tender regard upon the bright heavens, the verdant meadows, the pure air. I know a country instinct with delights of every kind, an unknown paradise, a secluded corner of the world – where alone, unfettered and unknown, in the thick covert of the woods, amidst flowers, and streams of rippling water, you will forget all the misery that human folly has so recently allotted you. Oh! listen to me, my prince. I do not jest. I have a heart, and mind, and soul, and can read your own, – aye, even to its depths. I will not take you unready for your task, in order to cast you into the crucible of my own desires, of my caprice, or my ambition. Let it be all or nothing. You are chilled and galled, sick at heart, overcome by excess of the emotions which but one hour's liberty has produced in you. For me, that is a certain and unmistakable sign that you do not wish to continue at liberty. Would you prefer a more humble life, a life more suited to your strength? Heaven is my witness, that I wish your happiness to be the result of the trial to which I have exposed you."

"Speak, speak," said the prince, with a vivacity which did not escape Aramis.

"I know," resumed the prelate, "in the Bas-Poitou, a canton, of which no one in France suspects the existence. Twenty leagues of country is immense, is it not? Twenty leagues, monseigneur, all covered with water and herbage, and reeds of the most luxuriant nature; the whole studded with islands covered with woods of the densest foliage. These large marshes, covered with reeds as with a thick mantle, sleep silently and calmly beneath the sun's soft and genial rays. A few fishermen with their families indolently pass their lives away there, with their great living-rafts of poplar and alder, the flooring formed of reeds, and the roof woven out of thick rushes. These barks, these floating-houses, are wafted to and fro by the changing winds. Whenever they touch a bank, it is but by chance; and so gently, too, that the sleeping fisherman is not awakened by the shock. Should he wish to land, it is merely because he has seen a large flight of landrails or plovers, of wild ducks, teal, widgeon, or woodchucks, which fall an easy pray to net or gun. Silver shad, eels, greedy pike, red and gray mullet, swim in shoals into his nets; he has but to choose the finest and largest, and return the others to the waters. Never yet has the food of the stranger, be he soldier or simple citizen, never has any one, indeed, penetrated into that district. The sun's rays there are soft and tempered: in plots of solid earth, whose soil is swart and fertile, grows the vine, nourishing with generous juice its purple, white, and golden grapes. Once a week, a boat is sent to deliver the bread which has been baked at an oven – the common property of all. There – like the seigneurs of early days – powerful in virtue of your dogs, your fishing-lines, your guns, and your beautiful reed-built house, would you live, rich in the produce of the chase, in plentitude of absolute secrecy. There would years of your life roll away, at the end of which, no longer recognizable, for you would have been perfectly transformed, you would have succeeded in acquiring a destiny accorded to you by Heaven. There are a thousand pistoles in this bag, monseigneur – more, far more, than sufficient to purchase the whole marsh of which I have spoken; more than enough to live there as many years as you have days to live; more than enough to constitute you the richest, the freest, and the happiest man in the country. Accept it, as I offer it you – sincerely, cheerfully. Forthwith, without a moment's pause, I will unharness two of my horses, which are attached to the carriage yonder, and they, accompanied by my servant – my deaf and dumb attendant – shall conduct you – traveling throughout the night, sleeping during the day – to the locality I have described; and I shall, at least, have the satisfaction of knowing that I have rendered to my prince the major service he himself preferred. I shall have made one human being happy; and Heaven for that will hold me in better account than if I had made one man powerful; the former task is far more difficult. And now, monseigneur, your answer to this proposition? Here is the money. Nay, do not hesitate. At Poitou, you can risk nothing, except the chance of catching the fevers prevalent there; and even of them, the so-called wizards of the country will cure you, for the sake of your pistoles. If you play the other game, you run the chance of being assassinated on a throne, strangled in a prison-cell. Upon my soul, I assure you, now I begin to compare them together, I myself should hesitate which lot I should accept."

"Monsieur," replied the young prince, "before I determine, let me alight from this carriage, walk on the ground, and consult that still voice within me, which Heaven bids us all to hearken to. Ten minutes is all I ask, and then you shall have your answer."

"As you please, monseigneur," said Aramis, bending before him with respect, so solemn and august in tone and address had sounded these strange words.

CHAPTER TEN

Crown and Tiara

ARAMIS WAS THE FIRST to descend from the carriage; he held the door open for the young man. He saw him place his foot on the mossy ground with a trembling of the whole body, and walk round the carriage with an unsteady and almost tottering step. It seemed as if the poor prisoner was unaccustomed to walk on God's earth. It was the 15th of August, about eleven o'clock at night; thick clouds, portending a tempest, overspread the heavens, and shrouded every light and prospect underneath their heavy folds. The extremities of the avenues were imperceptibly detached from the copse, by a lighter shadow of opaque gray, which, upon closer examination, became visible in the midst of the obscurity. But the fragrance which ascended from the grass, fresher and more penetrating than that which exhaled from the trees around him; the warm and balmy air which enveloped him for the first time for many years past; the ineffable enjoyment of liberty in an open country, spoke to the prince in so seductive a language, that notwithstanding the preternatural caution, we would almost say dissimulation of his character, of which we have tried to give an idea, he could not restrain his emotion, and breathed a sigh of ecstasy. Then, by degrees, he raised his aching head and inhaled the softly scented air, as it was wafted in gentle gusts to his uplifted face. Crossing his arms on his chest, as if to control this new sensation of delight, he drank in delicious draughts of that mysterious air which interpenetrates at night the loftiest forests. The sky he was contemplating, the murmuring waters, the universal freshness – was not all this reality? Was not Aramis a madman to suppose that he had aught else to dream of in this world? Those exciting pictures of country life, so free from fears and troubles, the ocean of happy days that glitters incessantly before all young imaginations, are real allurements wherewith to fascinate a poor, unhappy prisoner, worn out by prison cares, emaciated by the stifling air of the Bastile. It was the picture, it will be remembered, drawn by Aramis, when he offered the thousand pistoles he had with him in the carriage to the prince, and the enchanted Eden which the deserts of Bas-Poitou hid from the eyes of the world. Such were the reflections of Aramis as he watched, with an anxiety impossible to describe, the silent progress of the emotions of Philippe, whom he perceived gradually becoming more and more absorbed in his meditations. The young prince was offering up an inward prayer to Heaven, to be divinely guided in this trying moment, upon which his life or death depended. It was an anxious time for the bishop of Vannes, who had never before been so perplexed. His iron will, accustomed to overcome all obstacles, never finding itself inferior or vanquished on any occasion, to be foiled in so vast a project from not having foreseen the influence which a view of nature in all its luxuriance would have on the human mind! Aramis, overwhelmed by anxiety, contemplated with emotion the painful struggle that was taking place in Philippe's mind. This suspense lasted the whole ten minutes which the young man had requested. During this space of time, which appeared an eternity, Philippe continued gazing with an imploring and sorrowful look towards the heavens; Aramis did not remove the piercing glance he had fixed on Philippe. Suddenly the young man bowed his head. His thought returned to the earth, his looks perceptibly hardened, his brow contracted, his mouth assuming an expression of undaunted courage; again his looks became fixed, but this time they wore a worldly expression, hardened by covetousness, pride, and strong desire. Aramis's look immediately became as soft as it had before been gloomy. Philippe, seizing his hand in a quick, agitated manner, exclaimed:

"Lead me to where the crown of France is to be found."

"Is this your decision, monseigneur?" asked Aramis.

"It is."

"Irrevocably so?"

Philippe did not even deign to reply. He gazed earnestly at the bishop, as if to ask him if it were possible for a man to waver after having once made up his mind.

"Such looks are flashes of the hidden fire that betrays men's character," said Aramis, bowing over Philippe's hand; "you will be great, monseigneur, I will answer for that."

"Let us resume our conversation. I wished to discuss two points with you; in the first place the dangers, or the obstacles we may meet with. That point is decided. The other is the conditions you intend imposing on me. It is your turn to speak, M. d'Herblay."

"The conditions, monseigneur?"

"Doubtless. You will not allow so mere a trifle to stop me, and you will not do me the injustice to suppose that I think you have no interest in this affair. Therefore, without subterfuge or hesitation, tell me the truth – "

"I will do so, monseigneur. Once a king – "

"When will that be?"

"To-morrow evening – I mean in the night."

"Explain yourself."

"When I shall have asked your highness a

question."

"Do so."

"I sent to your highness a man in my confidence with instructions to deliver some closely written notes, carefully drawn up, which will thoroughly acquaint your highness with the different persons who compose and will compose your court."

"I perused those notes."

"Attentively?"

"I know them by heart."

"And understand them? Pardon me, but I may venture to ask that question of a poor, abandoned captive of the Bastile? In a week's time it will not be requisite to further question a mind like yours. You will then be in full possession of liberty and power."

"Interrogate me, then, and I will be a scholar representing his lesson to his master."

"We will begin with your family, monseigneur."

"My mother, Anne of Austria! all her sorrows, her painful malady. Oh! I know her

– I know her."

"Your second brother?" asked Aramis, bowing.

"To these notes," replied the prince, "you have added portraits so faithfully painted, that I am able to recognize the persons whose characters, manners, and history you have so carefully portrayed. Monsieur, my brother, is a fine, dark young man, with a pale face; he does not love his wife, Henrietta, whom I, Louis XIV., loved a little, and still flirt with, even although she made me weep on the day she wished to dismiss Mademoiselle de la Valliere from her service in disgrace."

"You will have to be careful with regard to the watchfulness of the latter," said Aramis; "she is sincerely attached to the actual king. The eyes of a woman who loves are not easily deceived."

"She is fair, has blue eyes, whose affectionate gaze reveals her identity. She halts slightly in her gait; she writes a letter every day, to which I have to send an answer by M. de Saint-Aignan."

"Do you know the latter?"

"As if I saw him, and I know the last verses he composed for me, as well as those I composed in answer to his."

"Very good. Do you know your ministers?"

"Colbert, an ugly, dark-browed man, but intelligent enough, his hair covering his forehead, a large, heavy, full head; the mortal enemy of M. Fouquet."

"As for the latter, we need not disturb ourselves about him."

"No; because necessarily you will not require me to exile him, I suppose?"

Aramis, struck with admiration at the remark, said, "You will become very great, monseigneur."

"You see," added the prince, "that I know my lesson by heart, and with Heaven's assistance, and yours afterwards, I shall seldom go wrong."

"You have still an awkward pair of eyes to

deal with, monseigneur."

"Yes, the captain of the musketeers, M. d'Artagnan, your friend."

"Yes; I can well say 'my friend.'"

"He who escorted La Valliere to Le Chaillot; he who delivered up Monk, cooped in an iron box, to Charles II.; he who so faithfully served my mother; he to whom the crown of France owes so much that it owes everything. Do you intend to ask me to exile him also?"

"Never, sire. D'Artagnan is a man to whom, at a certain given time, I will undertake to reveal everything; but be on your guard with him, for if he discovers our plot before it is revealed to him, you or I will certainly be killed or taken. He is a bold and enterprising man."

"I will think it over. Now tell me about M. Fouquet; what do you wish to be done with regard to him?"

"One moment more, I entreat you, monseigneur; and forgive me, if I seem to fail in respect to questioning you further."

"It is your duty to do so, nay, more than that, your right."

"Before we pass to M. Fouquet, I should very much regret forgetting another friend of mine."

"M. du Vallon, the Hercules of France, you mean; oh! as far as he is concerned, his interests are more than safe."

"No; it is not he whom I intended to refer to."

"The Comte de la Fere, then?"

"And his son, the son of all four of us."

"That poor boy who is dying of love for La Valliere, whom my brother so disloyally bereft him of? Be easy on that score. I shall know how to rehabilitate his happiness. Tell me only one thing, Monsieur d'Herblay; do men, when they love, forget the treachery that has been shown them? Can a man ever forgive the woman who has betrayed him? Is that a French custom, or is it one of the laws of the human heart?"

"A man who loves deeply, as deeply as

Raoul loves Mademoiselle de la Valliere, finishes by forgetting the fault or crime of the woman he loves; but I do not yet know whether Raoul will be able to forget."

"I will see after that. Have you anything further to say about your friend?"

"No; that is all."

"Well, then, now for M. Fouquet. What do you wish me to do for him?"

"To keep him on as surintendant, in the capacity in which he has hitherto acted, I entreat you."

"Be it so; but he is the first minister at present."

"Not quite so."

"A king, ignorant and embarrassed as I shall be, will, as a matter of course, require a first minister of state."

"Your majesty will require a friend."

"I have only one, and that is yourself."

"You will have many others by and by, but none so devoted, none so zealous for your glory."

"You shall be my first minister of state."

"Not immediately, monseigneur, for that would give rise to too much suspicion and astonishment."

"M. de Richelieu, the first minister of my grandmother, Marie de Medici, was simply bishop of Lucon, as you are bishop of Vannes."

"I perceive that your royal highness has studied my notes to great advantage; your amazing perspicacity overpowers me with delight."

"I am perfectly aware that M. de Richelieu, by means of the queen's protection, soon became cardinal."

"It would be better," said Aramis, bowing, "that I should not be appointed first minister until your royal highness has procured my nomination as cardinal."

"You shall be nominated before two months are past, Monsieur d'Herblay. But that is a matter of very trifling moment; you would not offend me if you were to ask more than that, and you would cause me serious regret if you were to limit yourself to that."

"In that case, I have something still further to hope for, monseigneur."

"Speak! speak!"

"M. Fouquet will not keep long at the head of affairs, he will soon get old. He is fond of pleasure, consistently, I mean, with all his labors, thanks to the youthfulness he still retains; but this protracted youth will disappear at the approach of the first serious annoyance, or at the first illness he may experience. We will spare him the annoyance, because he is an agreeable and noble-hearted man; but we cannot save him from ill-health. So it is determined. When you shall have paid all M. Fouquet's debts, and restored the finances to a sound condition, M. Fouquet will be able to remain the sovereign ruler in his little court of poets and painters, – we shall have made him rich. When that has been done, and I have become your royal highness's prime minister, I shall be able to think of my own interests and yours."

The young man looked at his interrogator.

"M. de Richelieu, of whom we were speaking just now, was very much to blame in the fixed idea he had of governing France alone, unaided. He allowed two kings, King Louis XIII. and himself, to be seated on the self-same throne, whilst he might have installed them more conveniently upon two separate and distinct thrones."

"Upon two thrones?" said the young man, thoughtfully.

"In fact," pursued Aramis, quietly, "a cardinal, prime minister of France, assisted by the favor and by the countenance of his Most Christian Majesty the King of France, a cardinal to whom the king his master lends the treasures of the state, his army, his counsel, such a man would be acting with twofold injustice in applying these mighty resources to France alone. Besides," added Aramis, "you will not be a king such as your father was, delicate in health, slow in judgment, whom all things wearied; you will be a king governing by your brain and by your sword; you will have in the government of the state no more than you will be able to manage unaided; I should only interfere with you. Besides, our friendship ought never to be, I do not say impaired, but in any degree affected, by a secret thought. I shall have given you the throne of France, you will confer on me the throne of St. Peter. Whenever your loyal, firm, and mailed hand should joined in ties of intimate association the hand of a pope such as I shall be, neither Charles V., who owned two-thirds of the habitable globe, nor Charlemagne, who possessed it entirely, will be able to reach to half your stature. I have no alliances, I have no predilections; I will not throw you into persecutions of heretics, nor will I cast you into the troubled waters of family dissension; I will simply say to you: The whole universe is our own; for me the minds of men, for you their bodies. And as I shall be the first to die, you will have my inheritance. What do you say of my plan, monseigneur?"

"I say that you render me happy and proud, for no other reason than that of having comprehended you thoroughly. Monsieur d'Herblay, you shall be cardinal, and when cardinal, my prime minister; and then you will point out to me the necessary steps to be taken to secure your election as pope, and I will take them. You can ask what guarantees from me you please."

"It is useless. Never shall I act except in such a manner that you will be the gainer; I shall never ascend the ladder of fortune, fame, or position, until I have first seen you placed upon the round of the ladder immediately above me; I shall always hold myself sufficiently aloof from you to escape incurring your jealousy, sufficiently near to sustain your personal advantage and to watch over your friendship. All the contracts in the world are easily violated because the interests included in them incline more to one side than to another. With us, however, this will never be the case; I have no need of any guarantees."

"And so – my dear brother – will disappear?"

"Simply. We will remove him from his bed by means of a plank which yields to the pressure of the finger. Having retired to rest a crowned sovereign, he will awake a captive. Alone you will rule from that moment, and you will have no interest dearer and better than that of keeping me near you."

"I believe it. There is my hand on it, Monsieur d'Herblay."

"Allow me to kneel before you, sire, most respectfully. We will embrace each other on the day we shall have upon our temples, you the crown, I the tiara."

"Still embrace me this very day also, and be, for and towards me, more than great, more than skillful, more than sublime in genius; be kind and indulgent – be my father!"

Aramis was almost overcome as he listened to his voice; he fancied he detected in his own heart an emotion hitherto unknown; but this impression was speedily removed. “His father!” he thought; “yes, his Holy Father.”

And they resumed their places in the carriage, which sped rapidly along the road leading to Vaux-le-Vicomte.

CHAPTER ELEVEN

The Chateau de Vaux-le-Vicomte

THE CHATEAU OF VAUX-le-Vicomte, situated about a league from Melun, had been built by Fouquet in 1655, at a time when there was a scarcity of money in France; Mazarin had taken all that there was, and Fouquet expended the remainder. However, as certain men have fertile, false, and useful vices, Fouquet, in scattering broadcast millions of money in the construction of this palace, had found a means of gathering, as the result of his generous profusion, three illustrious men together: Levau, the architect of the building; Lenotre, the designer of the gardens; and Lebrun, the decorator of the apartments. If the Chateau de Vaux possessed a single fault with which it could be reproached, it was its grand, pretentious character. It is even at the present day proverbial to calculate the number of acres of roofing, the restoration of which would, in our age, be the ruin of fortunes cramped and narrowed as the epoch itself. Vaux-le-Vicomte, when its magnificent gates, supported by caryatides, have been passed through, has the principal front of the main building opening upon a vast, so-called, court of honor, inclosed by deep ditches, bordered by a magnificent stone balustrade. Nothing could be more noble in appearance than the central forecourt raised upon the flight of steps, like a king upon his throne, having around it four pavilions at the angles, the immense Ionic columns of which rose majestically to the whole height of the building. The friezes ornamented with arabesques, and the pediments which crowned the pilasters, conferred richness and grace on every part of the building, while the domes which surmounted the whole added proportion and majesty. This mansion, built by a subject, bore a far greater resemblance to those royal residences which Wolsey fancied he was called upon to construct, in order to present them to his master from the fear of rendering him jealous. But if magnificence and splendor were displayed in any one particular part of this palace more than another, – if anything could be preferred to the wonderful arrangement of the interior, to the sumptuousness of the gilding, and to the profusion of the paintings and statues, it would be the park and gardens of Vaux.

The **jets d'eau**, which were regarded as wonderful in 1653, are still so, even at the present time; the cascades awakened the admiration of kings and princes; and as for the famous grotto, the theme of so many poetical effusions, the residence of that illustrious nymph of Vaux, whom Pelisson made converse with La Fontaine, we must be spared the description of all its beauties. We will do as Despreaux did, – we will enter the park, the trees of which are of eight years' growth only – that is to say, in their present position – and whose summits even yet, as they proudly tower aloft, blushingly unfold their leaves to the earliest rays of the rising sun. Lenotre had hastened the pleasure of the Maecenas of his period; all the nursery-grounds had furnished trees whose growth had been accelerated by careful culture and the richest plant-food. Every tree in the neighborhood which presented a fair appearance of beauty or stature had been taken up by its roots and transplanted to the park. Fouquet could well afford to purchase trees to ornament his park, since he had bought up three villages and their appurtenances (to use a legal word) to increase its extent. M. de Scudery said of this palace, that, for the purpose of keeping the grounds and gardens well watered, M. Fouquet had divided a river into a thousand fountains, and gathered the waters of a thousand fountains into torrents. This same Monsieur de Scudery said a great many other things in his "Clelie," about this palace of Valterre, the charms of which he describes most minutely. We should be far wiser to send our curious readers to Vaux to judge for themselves, than to refer them to "Clelie;" and yet there are as many leagues from Paris to Vaux, as there are volumes of the "Clelie."

This magnificent palace had been got ready for the reception of the greatest reigning sovereign of the time. M. Fouquet's friends had transported thither, some their actors and their dresses, others their troops of sculptors and artists; not forgetting others with their ready-mended pens, – floods of impromptus were contemplated. The cascades, somewhat rebellious nymphs though they were, poured forth their waters brighter and clearer than crystal: they scattered over the bronze triton and nereids their waves of foam, which glistened like fire in the rays of the sun. An army of servants were hurrying to and fro in squadrons in the courtyard and corridors; while Fouquet, who had only that morning arrived, walked all through the palace with a calm, observant glance, in order to give his last orders, after his intendants had inspected everything.

It was, as we have said, the 15th of August. The sun poured down its burning rays upon the heathen deities of marble and bronze: it raised the temperature of the water in the conch shells, and ripened, on the walls, those magnificent peaches, of which the king, fifty years later, spoke so regretfully, when, at Marly, on an occasion of a scarcity of the finer sorts of peaches being complained of, in the beautiful gardens there – gardens which had cost France double the amount that had been expended on Vaux – the **great king** observed to some one: “You are far too young to have eaten any of M. Fouquet’s peaches.”

Oh, fame! Oh, blazon of renown! Oh, glory of this earth! That very man whose judgment was so sound and accurate where merit was concerned – he who had swept into his coffers the inheritance of Nicholas Fouquet, who had robbed him of Lenotre and Lebrun, and had sent him to rot for the remainder of his life in one of the state prisons – merely remembered the peaches of that vanquished, crushed, forgotten enemy! It was to little purpose that Fouquet had squandered thirty millions of francs in the fountains of his gardens, in the crucibles of his sculptors, in the writing-desks of his literary friends, in the portfolios of his painters; vainly had he fancied that thereby he might be remembered. A peach – a blushing, rich-flavored fruit, nestling in the trellis work on the garden-wall, hidden beneath its long, green leaves, – this little vegetable production, that a dormouse would nibble up without a thought, was sufficient to recall to the memory of this great monarch the mournful shade of the last surintendant of France.

With a perfect reliance that Aramis had made arrangements fairly to distribute the vast number of guests throughout the palace, and that he had not omitted to attend to any of the internal regulations for their comfort, Fouquet devoted his entire attention to the **ensemble** alone. In one direction Gourville showed him the preparations which had been made for the fireworks; in another, Moliere led him over the theater; at last, after he had visited the chapel, the **salons**, and the galleries, and was again going downstairs, exhausted with fatigue, Fouquet saw Aramis on the staircase. The prelate beckoned to him. The surintendant joined his friend, and, with him, paused before a large picture scarcely finished. Applying himself, heart and soul, to his work, the painter Lebrun, covered with perspiration, stained with paint, pale from fatigue and the inspiration of genius, was putting the last finishing touches with his rapid brush. It was the portrait of the king, whom they were expecting, dressed in the court suit which Percerin had condescended to show beforehand to the bishop of Vannes. Fouquet placed himself before this portrait, which seemed to live, as one might say, in the cool freshness of its flesh, and in its warmth of color. He gazed upon it long and fixedly, estimated the prodigious labor that had been bestowed upon it, and, not being able to find any recompense sufficiently great for this Herculean effort, he passed his arm round the painter's neck and embraced him. The surintendant, by this action, had utterly ruined a suit of clothes worth a thousand pistoles, but he had satisfied, more than satisfied, Lebrun. It was a happy moment for the artist; it was an unhappy moment for M. Percerin, who was walking behind Fouquet, and was engaged in admiring, in Lebrun's painting, the suit that he had made for his majesty, a perfect **objet d'art**, as he called it, which was not to be matched except in the wardrobe of the surintendant. His distress and his exclamations were interrupted by a signal which had been given from the summit of the mansion. In the direction of Melun, in the still empty, open plain, the sentinels of Vaux had just perceived the advancing procession of the king and the queens. His majesty was entering Melun with his long train of carriages and cavaliers.

"In an hour – " said Aramis to Fouquet.

"In an hour!" replied the latter, sighing.

"And the people who ask one another what is the good of these royal **fetes!**" continued the bishop of Vannes, laughing, with his false smile.

"Alas! I, too, who am not the people, ask myself the same thing."

"I will answer you in four and twenty hours, monseigneur. Assume a cheerful countenance, for it should be a day of true rejoicing."

"Well, believe me or not, as you like, D'Herblay," said the surintendant, with a swelling heart, pointing at the **cortege** of Louis, visible in the horizon, "he certainly loves me but very little, and I do not care much more for him; but I cannot tell you how it is, that since he is approaching my house – "

"Well, what?"

"Well, since I know he is on his way here, as my guest, he is more sacred than ever for me; he is my acknowledged sovereign, and as such is very dear to me."

"Dear? yes," said Aramis, playing upon the word, as the Abbe Terray did, at a later period, with Louis XV.

"Do not laugh, D'Herblay; I feel that, if he really seemed to wish it, I could love that young man."

"You should not say that to me," returned Aramis, "but rather to M. Colbert."

"To M. Colbert!" exclaimed Fouquet. "Why so?"

"Because he would allow you a pension out of the king's privy purse, as soon as he becomes surintendant," said Aramis, preparing to leave as soon as he had dealt this last blow.

"Where are you going?" returned Fouquet, with a gloomy look.

"To my own apartment, in order to change my costume, monseigneur."

"Whereabouts are you lodging, D'Herblay?"

"In the blue room on the second story."

"The room immediately over the king's room?"

"Precisely."

"You will be subject to very great restraint there. What an idea to condemn yourself to a room where you cannot stir or move about!"

"During the night, monseigneur, I sleep or read in my bed."

"And your servants?"

"I have but one attendant with me. I find my reader quite sufficient. Adieu, monseigneur; do not overfatigue yourself; keep yourself fresh for the arrival of the king."

"We shall see you by and by, I suppose, and shall see your friend Du Vallon also?"

"He is lodging next to me, and is at this moment dressing."

And Fouquet, bowing, with a smile, passed on like a commander-in-chief who pays the different outposts a visit after the enemy has been signaled in sight.[2]

---

2 In the five-volume edition, Volume 4 ends here.

CHAPTER TWELVE

The Wine of Melun

THE KING HAD, in point of fact, entered Melun with the intention of merely passing through the city. The youthful monarch was most eagerly anxious for amusements; only twice during the journey had he been able to catch a glimpse of La Valliere, and, suspecting that his only opportunity of speaking to her would be after nightfall, in the gardens, and after the ceremonial of reception had been gone through, he had been very desirous to arrive at Vaux as early as possible. But he reckoned without his captain of the musketeers, and without M. Colbert. Like Calypso, who could not be consoled at the departure of Ulysses, our Gascon could not console himself for not having guessed why Aramis had asked Percerin to show him the king's new costumes. "There is not a doubt," he said to himself, "that my friend the bishop of Vannes had some motive in that;" and then he began to rack his brains most uselessly. D'Artagnan, so intimately acquainted with all the court intrigues, who knew the position of Fouquet better than even Fouquet himself did, had conceived the strangest fancies and suspicions at the announcement of the **fete**, which would have ruined a wealthy man, and which became impossible, utter madness even, for a man so poor as he was. And then, the presence of Aramis, who had returned from Belle-Isle, and been nominated by Monsieur Fouquet inspector-general of all the arrangements; his perseverance in mixing himself up with all the surintendant's affairs; his visits to Baisemeaux; all this suspicious singularity of conduct had excessively troubled and tormented D'Artagnan during the last two weeks.

"With men of Aramis's stamp," he said, "one is never the stronger except sword in hand. So long as Aramis continued a soldier, there was hope of getting the better of him; but since he has covered his cuirass with a stole, we are lost. But what can Aramis's object possibly be?" And D'Artagnan plunged again into deep thought. "What does it matter to me, after all," he continued, "if his only object is to overthrow M. Colbert? And what else can he be after?" And D'Artagnan rubbed his forehead – that fertile land, whence the plowshare of his nails had turned up so many and such admirable ideas in his time. He, at first, thought of talking the matter over with Colbert, but his friendship for Aramis, the oath of earlier days, bound him too strictly. He revolted at the bare idea of such a thing, and, besides, he hated the financier too cordially. Then, again, he wished to unburden his mind to the king; but yet the king would not be able to understand the suspicions which had not even a shadow of reality at their base. He resolved to address himself to Aramis, direct, the first time he met him. "I will get him," said the musketeer, "between a couple of candles, suddenly, and when he least expects it, I will place my hand upon his heart, and he will tell me – What will he tell me? Yes, he will tell me something, for **mordioux!** there is something in it, I know."

Somewhat calmer, D'Artagnan made every preparation for the journey, and took the greatest care that the military household of the king, as yet very inconsiderable in numbers, should be well officered and well disciplined in its meager and limited proportions. The result was that, through the captain's arrangements, the king, on arriving at Melun, saw himself at the head of both the musketeers and Swiss guards, as well as a picket of the French guards. It might almost have been called a small army. M. Colbert looked at the troops with great delight: he even wished they had been a third more in number.

"But why?" said the king.

"In order to show greater honor to M. Fouquet," replied Colbert.

"In order to ruin him the sooner," thought D'Artagnan.

When this little army appeared before Melun, the chief magistrates came out to meet the king, and to present him with the keys of the city, and invited him to enter the Hotel de Ville, in order to partake of the wine of honor. The king, who expected to pass through the city and to proceed to Vaux without delay, became quite red in the face from vexation.

"Who was fool enough to occasion this delay?" muttered the king, between his teeth, as the chief magistrate was in the middle of a long address.

"Not I, certainly," replied D'Artagnan, "but I believe it was M. Colbert."

Colbert, having heard his name pronounced, said, "What was M. d'Artagnan good enough to say?"

"I was good enough to remark that it was you who stopped the king's progress, so that he might taste the **vin de Brie**. Was I right?"

"Quite so, monsieur."

"In that case, then, it was you whom the king called some name or other."

"What name?"

"I hardly know; but wait a moment – idiot, I think it was – no, no, it was fool or dolt. Yes; his majesty said that the man who had thought of the **vin de Melun** was something of the sort."

D'Artagnan, after this broadside, quietly caressed his mustache; M. Colbert's large head seemed to become larger and larger than ever. D'Artagnan, seeing how ugly anger made him, did not stop half-way. The orator still went on with his speech, while the king's color was visibly increasing.

"**Mordioux!**" said the musketeer, coolly, "the king is going to have an attack of determination of blood to the head. Where the deuce did you get hold of that idea, Monsieur Colbert? You have no luck."

"Monsieur," said the financier, drawing himself up, "my zeal for the king's service inspired me with the idea."

"Bah!"

"Monsieur, Melun is a city, an excellent city, which pays well, and which it would be imprudent to displease."

"There, now! I, who do not pretend to be a financier, saw only one idea in your idea."

"What was that, monsieur?"

"That of causing a little annoyance to M. Fouquet, who is making himself quite giddy on his donjons yonder, in waiting for us."

This was a home-stroke, hard enough in all conscience. Colbert was completely thrown out of the saddle by it, and retired, thoroughly discomfited. Fortunately, the speech was now at an end; the king drank the wine which was presented to him, and then every one resumed the progress through the city. The king bit his lips in anger, for the evening was closing in, and all hope of a walk with La Valliere was at an end. In order that the whole of the king's household should enter Vaux, four hours at least were necessary, owing to the different arrangements. The king, therefore, who was boiling with impatience, hurried forward as much as possible, in order to reach it before nightfall. But, at the moment he was setting off again, other and fresh difficulties arose.

"Is not the king going to sleep at Melun?" said Colbert, in a low tone of voice, to D'Artagnan.

M. Colbert must have been badly inspired

that day, to address himself in that manner to the chief of the musketeers; for the latter guessed that the king's intention was very far from that of remaining where he was. D'Artagnan would not allow him to enter Vaux except he were well and strongly accompanied; and desired that his majesty would not enter except with all the escort. On the other hand, he felt that these delays would irritate that impatient monarch beyond measure. In what way could he possibly reconcile these difficulties? D'Artagnan took up Colbert's remark, and determined to repeated it to the king.

"Sire," he said, "M. Colbert has been asking me if your majesty does not intend to sleep at Melun."

"Sleep at Melun! What for?" exclaimed Louis XIV. "Sleep at Melun! Who, in Heaven's name, can have thought of such a thing, when M. Fouquet is expecting us this evening?"

"It was simply," replied Colbert, quickly, "the fear of causing your majesty the least delay; for, according to established etiquette, you cannot enter any place, with the exception of your own royal residences, until the soldiers' quarters have been marked out by the quartermaster, and the garrison properly distributed."

D'Artagnan listened with the greatest attention, biting his mustache to conceal his vexation; and the queens were not less interested. They were fatigued, and would have preferred to go to rest without proceeding any farther; more especially, in order to prevent the king walking about in the evening with M. de Saint-Aignan and the ladies of the court, for, if etiquette required the princesses to remain within their own rooms, the ladies of honor, as soon as they had performed the services required of them, had no restrictions placed upon them, but were at liberty to walk about as they pleased. It will easily be conjectured that all these rival interests, gathering together in vapors, necessarily produced clouds, and that the clouds were likely to be followed by a tempest. The king had no mustache to gnaw, and therefore kept biting the handle of his whip instead, with ill-concealed impatience. How could he get out of it? D'Artagnan looked as agreeable as possible, and Colbert as sulky as he could. Who was there he could get in a passion with?

"We will consult the queen," said Louis XIV., bowing to the royal ladies. And this kindness of consideration softened Maria Theresa's heart, who, being of a kind and generous disposition, when left to her own free-will, replied:

"I shall be delighted to do whatever your majesty wishes."

"How long will it take us to get to Vaux?" inquired Anne of Austria, in slow and measured accents, placing her hand upon her bosom, where the seat of her pain lay.

"An hour for your majesty's carriages," said D'Artagnan; "the roads are tolerably good."

The king looked at him. "And a quarter of an hour for the king," he hastened to add.

"We should arrive by daylight?" said Louis XIV.

"But the billeting of the king's military escort," objected Colbert, softly, "will make his majesty lose all the advantage of his speed, however quick he may be."

"Double ass that you are!" thought D'Artagnan; "if I had any interest or motive in demolishing your credit with the king, I could do it in ten minutes. If I were in the king's place," he added aloud, "I should, in going to M. Fouquet, leave my escort behind me; I should go to him as a friend; I should enter accompanied only by my captain of the guards; I should consider that I was acting more nobly, and should be invested with a still more sacred character by doing so."

Delight sparkled in the king's eyes. "That is indeed a very sensible suggestion. We will go to see a friend as friends; the gentlemen who are with the carriages can go slowly: but we who are mounted will ride on." And he rode off, accompanied by all those who were mounted. Colbert hid his ugly head behind his horse's neck.

"I shall be quits," said D'Artagnan, as he galloped along, "by getting a little talk with Aramis this evening. And then, M. Fouquet is a man of honor. **Mordioux!** I have said so, and it must be so."

And this was the way how, towards seven o'clock in the evening, without announcing his arrival by the din of trumpets, and without even his advanced guard, without out-riders or musketeers, the king presented himself before the gate of Vaux, where Fouquet, who had been informed of his royal guest's approach, had been waiting for the last half-hour, with his head uncovered, surrounded by his household and his friends.

CHAPTER THIRTEEN

Nectar and Ambrosia

M. FOUQUET HELD THE stirrup of the king, who, having dismounted, bowed most graciously, and more graciously still held out his hand to him, which Fouquet, in spite of a slight resistance on the king's part, carried respectfully to his lips. The king wished to wait in the first courtyard for the arrival of the carriages, nor had he long to wait, for the roads had been put into excellent order by the superintendent, and a stone would hardly have been found of the size of an egg the whole way from Melun to Vaux; so that the carriages, rolling along as though on a carpet, brought the ladies to Vaux, without jolting or fatigue, by eight o'clock. They were received by Madame Fouquet, and at the moment they made their appearance, a light as bright as day burst forth from every quarter, trees, vases, and marble statues. This species of enchantment lasted until their majesties had retired into the palace. All these wonders and magical effects which the chronicler has heaped up, or rather embalmed, in his recital, at the risk of rivaling the brain-born scenes of romancers; these splendors whereby night seemed vanquished and nature corrected, together with every delight and luxury combined for the satisfaction of all the senses, as well as the imagination, Fouquet did in real truth offer to his sovereign in that enchanting retreat of which no monarch could at that time boast of possessing an equal. We do not intend to describe the grand banquet, at which the royal guests were present, nor the concerts, nor the fairy-like and more than magic transformations and metamorphoses; it will be enough for our purpose to depict the countenance the king assumed, which, from being gay, soon wore a very gloomy, constrained, and irritated expression. He remembered his own residence, royal though it was, and the mean and indifferent style of luxury that prevailed there, which comprised but little more than what was merely useful for the royal wants, without being his own personal property. The large vases of the Louvre, the older furniture and plate of Henry II., of Francis I., and of Louis XI., were but historic monuments of earlier days; nothing but specimens of art, the relics of his predecessors; while with Fouquet, the value of the article was as much in the workmanship as in the article itself. Fouquet ate from a gold service, which artists in his own employ had modeled and cast for him alone. Fouquet drank wines of which the king of France did not even know the name, and drank them out of goblets each more valuable than the entire royal cellar.

What, too, was to be said of the apartments, the hangings, the pictures, the servants and officers, of every description, of his household? What of the mode of service in which etiquette was replaced by order; stiff formality by personal, unrestrained comfort; the happiness and contentment of the guest became the supreme law of all who obeyed the host? The perfect swarm of busily engaged persons moving about noiselessly; the multitude of guests, – who were, however, even less numerous than the servants who waited on them, – the myriad of exquisitely prepared dishes, of gold and silver vases; the floods of dazzling light, the masses of unknown flowers of which the hot-houses had been despoiled, redundant with luxuriance of unequaled scent and beauty; the perfect harmony of the surroundings, which, indeed, was no more than the prelude of the promised **fete**, charmed all who were there; and they testified their admiration over and over again, not by voice or gesture, but by deep silence and rapt attention, those two languages of the courtier which acknowledge the hand of no master powerful enough to restrain them.

As for the king, his eyes filled with tears; he dared not look at the queen. Anne of Austria, whose pride was superior to that of any creature breathing, overwhelmed her host by the contempt with which she treated everything handed to her. The young queen, kind-hearted by nature and curious by disposition, praised Fouquet, ate with an exceedingly good appetite, and asked the names of the strange fruits as they were placed upon the table.

Fouquet replied that he was not aware of their names. The fruits came from his own stores; he had often cultivated them himself, having an intimate acquaintance with the cultivation of exotic fruits and plants. The king felt and appreciated the delicacy of the replies, but was only the more humiliated; he thought the queen a little too familiar in her manners, and that Anne of Austria resembled Juno a little too much, in being too proud and haughty; his chief anxiety, however, was himself, that he might remain cold and distant in his behavior, bordering lightly the limits of supreme disdain or simple admiration.

But Fouquet had foreseen all this; he was, in fact, one of those men who foresee everything. The king had expressly declared that, so long as he remained under Fouquet's roof, he did not wish his own different repasts to be served in accordance with the usual etiquette, and that he would, consequently, dine with the rest of society; but by the thoughtful attention of the surintendant, the king's dinner was served up separately, if one may so express it, in the middle of the general table; the dinner, wonderful in every respect, from the dishes of which was composed, comprised everything the king liked and generally preferred to anything else. Louis had no excuse – he, indeed, who had the keenest appetite in his kingdom – for saying that he was not hungry. Nay, M. Fouquet did even better still; he certainly, in obedience to the king's expressed desire, seated himself at the table, but as soon as the soups were served, he arose and personally waited on the king, while Madame Fouquet stood behind the queen-mother's armchair. The disdain of Juno and the sulky fits of temper of Jupiter could not resist this excess of kindly feeling and polite attention. The queen ate a biscuit dipped in a glass of San-Lucar wine; and the king ate of everything, saying to M. Fouquet: “It is impossible, monsieur le surintendant, to dine better anywhere.” Whereupon the whole court began, on all sides, to devour the dishes spread before them with such enthusiasm that it looked as though a cloud of Egyptian locusts was settling down on green and growing crops.

As soon, however, as his hunger was appeased, the king became morose and overgloomed again; the more so in proportion to the satisfaction he fancied he had previously manifested, and particularly on account of the deferential manner which his courtiers had shown towards Fouquet. D’Artagnan, who ate a good deal and drank but little, without allowing it to be noticed, did not lose a single opportunity, but made a great number of observations which he turned to good profit.

When the supper was finished, the king expressed a wish not to lose the promenade. The park was illuminated; the moon, too, as if she had placed herself at the orders of the lord of Vaux, silvered the trees and lake with her own bright and quasi-phosphorescent light. The air was strangely soft and balmy; the daintily shell-gravelled walks through the thickly set avenues yielded luxuriously to the feet. The **fete** was complete in every respect, for the king, having met La Valliere in one of the winding paths of the wood, was able to press her hand and say, “I love you,” without any one overhearing him except M. d’Artagnan, who followed, and M. Fouquet, who preceded him.

The dreamy night of magical enchantments stole smoothly on. The king having requested to be shown to his room, there was immediately a movement in every direction. The queens passed to their own apartments, accompanied by them music of theorbos and lutes; the king found his musketeers awaiting him on the grand flight of steps, for M. Fouquet had brought them on from Melun and had invited them to supper. D’Artagnan’s suspicions at once disappeared. He was weary, he had supped well, and wished, for once in his life, thoroughly to enjoy a **fete** given by a man who was in every sense of the word a king. "M. Fouquet," he said, "is the man for me."

The king was conducted with the greatest ceremony to the chamber of Morpheus, of which we owe some cursory description to our readers. It was the handsomest and largest in the palace. Lebrun had painted on the vaulted ceiling the happy as well as the unhappy dreams which Morpheus inflicts on kings as well as on other men. Everything that sleep gives birth to that is lovely, its fairy scenes, its flowers and nectar, the wild voluptuousness or profound repose of the senses, had the painter elaborated on his frescoes. It was a composition as soft and pleasing in one part as dark and gloomy and terrible in another. The poisoned chalice, the glittering dagger suspended over the head of the sleeper; wizards and phantoms with terrific masks, those half-dim shadows more alarming than the approach of fire or the somber face of midnight, these, and such as these, he had made the companions of his more pleasing pictures. No sooner had the king entered his room than a cold shiver seemed to pass through him, and on Fouquet asking him the cause of it, the king replied, as pale as death:

"I am sleepy, that is all."

"Does your majesty wish for your attendants at once?"

"No; I have to talk with a few persons first," said the king. "Will you have the goodness to tell M. Colbert I wish to see him."

Fouquet bowed and left the room.

CHAPTER FOURTEEN

A Gascon, and a Gascon and a Half

D'ARTAGNAN HAD DETERMINED TO lose no time, and in fact he never was in the habit of doing so. After having inquired for Aramis, he had looked for him in every direction until he had succeeded in finding him. Besides, no sooner had the king entered Vaux, than Aramis had retired to his own room, meditating, doubtless, some new piece of gallant attention for his majesty's amusement. D'Artagnan desired the servants to announce him, and found on the second story (in a beautiful room called the Blue Chamber, on account of the color of its hangings) the bishop of Vannes in company with Porthos and several of the modern Epicureans. Aramis came forward to embrace his friend, and offered him the best seat. As it was after awhile generally remarked among those present that the musketeer was reserved, and wished for an opportunity for conversing secretly with Aramis, the Epicureans took their leave. Porthos, however, did not stir; for true it is that, having dined exceedingly well, he was fast asleep in his armchair; and the freedom of conversation therefore was not interrupted by a third person. Porthos had a deep, harmonious snore, and people might talk in the midst of its loud bass without fear of disturbing him. D'Artagnan felt that he was called upon to open the conversation.

"Well, and so we have come to Vaux," he said.

"Why, yes, D'Artagnan. And how do you like the place?"

"Very much, and I like M. Fouquet, also."

"Is he not a charming host?"

"No one could be more so."

"I am told that the king began by showing great distance of manner towards M. Fouquet, but that his majesty grew much more cordial afterwards."

"You did not notice it, then, since you say you have been told so?"

"No; I was engaged with the gentlemen who have just left the room about the theatrical performances and the tournaments which are to take place to-morrow."

"Ah, indeed! you are the comptroller-general of the **fetes** here, then?"

"You know I am a friend of all kinds of amusement where the exercise of the imagination is called into activity; I have always been a poet in one way or another."

"Yes, I remember the verses you used to write, they were charming."

"I have forgotten them, but I am delighted to read the verses of others, when those others are known by the names of Moliere, Pelisson, La Fontaine, etc."

"Do you know what idea occurred to me this evening, Aramis?"

"No; tell me what it was, for I should never be able to guess it, you have so many."

"Well, the idea occurred to me, that the true king of France is not Louis XIV."

"**What!**" said Aramis, involuntarily, looking the musketeer full in the eyes.

"No, it is Monsieur Fouquet."

Aramis breathed again, and smiled. "Ah! you are like all the rest, jealous," he said. "I would wager that it was M. Colbert who turned that pretty phrase." D'Artagnan, in order to throw Aramis off his guard, related Colbert's misadventures with regard to the **vin de Melun**.

"He comes of a mean race, does Colbert," said Aramis.

"Quite true."

"When I think, too," added the bishop, "that that fellow will be your minister within four months, and that you will serve him as blindly as you did Richelieu or Mazarin – "

"And as you serve M. Fouquet," said D'Artagnan.

"With this difference, though, that M. Fouquet is not M. Colbert."

"True, true," said D'Artagnan, as he pretended to become sad and full of reflection; and then, a moment after, he added, "Why do you tell me that M. Colbert will be minister in four months?"

"Because M. Fouquet will have ceased to be so," replied Aramis.

"He will be ruined, you mean?" said D'Artagnan.

"Completely so."

"Why does he give these **fetes**, then?" said the musketeer, in a tone so full of thoughtful consideration, and so well assumed, that the bishop was for the moment deceived by it. “Why did you not dissuade him from it?”

The latter part of the phrase was just a little too much, and Aramis’s former suspicions were again aroused. “It is done with the object of humoring the king.”

“By ruining himself?”

“Yes, by ruining himself for the king.”

“A most eccentric, one might say, sinister calculation, that.”

“Necessity, necessity, my friend.”

“I don’t see that, dear Aramis.”

“Do you not? Have you not remarked M. Colbert’s daily increasing antagonism, and that he is doing his utmost to drive the king to get rid of the superintendent?”

“One must be blind not to see it.”

“And that a cabal is already armed against M. Fouquet?”

“That is well known.”

“What likelihood is there that the king

would join a party formed against a man who will have spent everything he had to please him?"

"True, true," said D'Artagnan, slowly, hardly convinced, yet curious to broach another phase of the conversation. "There are follies, and follies," he resumed, "and I do not like those you are committing."

"What do you allude to?"

"As for the banquet, the ball, the concert, the theatricals, the tournaments, the cascades, the fireworks, the illuminations, and the presents – these are well and good, I grant; but why were not these expenses sufficient? Why was it necessary to have new liveries and costumes for your whole household?"

"You are quite right. I told M. Fouquet that myself; he replied, that if he were rich enough he would offer the king a newly erected chateau, from the vanes at the houses to the very sub-cellars; completely new inside and out; and that, as soon as the king had left, he would burn the whole building and its contents, in order that it might not be made use of by any one else."

"How completely Spanish!"

"I told him so, and he then added this: 'Whoever advises me to spare expense, I shall look upon as my enemy.'"

"It is positive madness; and that portrait, too!"

"What portrait?" said Aramis.

"That of the king, and the surprise as well."

"What surprise?"

"The surprise you seem to have in view, and on account of which you took some specimens away, when I met you at Percerin's." D'Artagnan paused. The shaft was discharged, and all he had to do was to wait and watch its effect.

"That is merely an act of graceful attention," replied Aramis.

D'Artagnan went up to his friend, took hold of both his hands, and looking him full in the eyes, said, "Aramis, do you still care for me a very little?"

"What a question to ask!"

"Very good. One favor, then. Why did you take some patterns of the king's costumes at Percerin's?"

"Come with me and ask poor Lebrun, who has been working upon them for the last two days and nights."

"Aramis, that may be truth for everybody else, but for me – "

"Upon my word, D'Artagnan, you astonish me."

"Be a little considerate. Tell me the exact truth; you would not like anything disagreeable to happen to me, would you?"

"My dear friend, you are becoming quite incomprehensible. What suspicion can you have possibly got hold of?"

"Do you believe in my instinctive feelings? Formerly you used to have faith in them. Well, then, an instinct tells me that you have some concealed project on foot."

"I – a project?"

"I am convinced of it."

"What nonsense!"

"I am not only sure of it, but I would even swear it."

"Indeed, D'Artagnan, you cause me the greatest pain. Is it likely, if I have any project in hand that I ought to keep secret from you, I should tell you about it? If I had one that I could and ought to have revealed, should I not have long ago divulged it?"

"No, Aramis, no. There are certain projects which are never revealed until the favorable opportunity arrives."

"In that case, my dear fellow," returned the bishop, laughing, "the only thing now is, that the 'opportunity' has not yet arrived."

D'Artagnan shook his head with a sorrowful expression. "Oh, friendship, friendship!" he said, "what an idle word you are! Here is a man who, if I were but to ask it, would suffer himself to be cut in pieces for my sake."

"You are right," said Aramis, nobly.

"And this man, who would shed every drop of blood in his veins for me, will not open up before me the least corner in his heart. Friendship, I repeat, is nothing but an unsubstantial shadow – a lure, like everything else in this bright, dazzling world."

"It is not thus you should speak of **our** friendship," replied the bishop, in a firm, assured voice; "for ours is not of the same nature as those of which you have been speaking."

"Look at us, Aramis; three out of the old 'four.' You are deceiving me; I suspect you; and Porthos is fast asleep. An admirable trio of friends, don't you think so? What an affecting relic of the former dear old times!"

"I can only tell you one thing, D'Artagnan, and I swear it on the Bible: I love you just as I used to do. If I ever suspect you, it is on account of others, and not on account of either of us. In everything I may do, and should happen to succeed in, you will find your fourth. Will you promise me the same favor?"

"If I am not mistaken, Aramis, your words – at the moment you pronounce them – are full of generous feeling."

"Such a thing is very possible."

"You are conspiring against M. Colbert. If that be all, **mordioux**, tell me so at once. I have the instrument in my own hand, and will pull out the tooth easily enough."

Aramis could not conceal a smile of disdain that flitted over his haughty features. "And supposing that I were conspiring against Colbert, what harm would there be in **that?**"

"No, no; that would be too trifling a matter for you to take in hand, and it was not on that account you asked Percerin for those patterns of the king's costumes. Oh! Aramis, we are not enemies, remember – we are brothers. Tell me what you wish to undertake, and, upon the word of a D'Artagnan, if I cannot help you, I will swear to remain neuter."

"I am undertaking nothing," said Aramis.

"Aramis, a voice within me speaks and

seems to trickle forth a rill of light within my darkness: it is a voice that has never yet deceived me. It is the king you are conspiring against."

"The king?" exclaimed the bishop, pretending to be annoyed.

"Your face will not convince me; the king, I repeat."

"Will you help me?" said Aramis, smiling ironically.

"Aramis, I will do more than help you – I will do more than remain neuter – I will save you."

"You are mad, D'Artagnan."

"I am the wiser of the two, in this matter."

"You to suspect me of wishing to assassinate the king!"

"Who spoke of such a thing?" smiled the musketeer.

"Well, let us understand one another. I do not see what any one can do to a legitimate king as ours is, if he does not assassinate him." D'Artagnan did not say a word. "Besides, you have your guards and your musketeers here," said the bishop.

"True."

"You are not in M. Fouquet's house, but in your own."

"True; but in spite of that, Aramis, grant me, for pity's sake, one single word of a true friend."

"A true friend's word is ever truth itself. If I think of touching, even with my finger, the son of Anne of Austria, the true king of this realm of France – if I have not the firm intention of prostrating myself before his throne – if in every idea I may entertain to-morrow, here at Vaux, will not be the most glorious day my king ever enjoyed – may Heaven's lightning blast me where I stand!" Aramis had pronounced these words with his face turned towards the alcove of his own bedroom, where D'Artagnan, seated with his back towards the alcove, could not suspect that any one was lying concealed. The earnestness of his words, the studied slowness with which he pronounced them, the solemnity of his oath, gave the musketeer the most complete satisfaction. He took hold of both Aramis's hands, and shook them cordially. Aramis had endured reproaches without turning pale, and had blushed as he listened to words of praise. D'Artagnan, deceived, did him honor; but D'Artagnan, trustful and reliant, made him feel ashamed. "Are you going away?" he said, as he embraced him, in order to conceal the flush on his face.

"Yes. Duty summons me. I have to get the watch-word. It seems I am to be lodged in the king's ante-room. Where does Porthos sleep?"

"Take him away with you, if you like, for he rumbles through his sleepy nose like a park of artillery."

"Ah! he does not stay with you, then?" said D'Artagnan.

"Not the least in the world. He has a chamber to himself, but I don't know where."

"Very good!" said the musketeer; from whom this separation of the two associates removed his last suspicion, and he touched Porthos lightly on the shoulder; the latter replied by a loud yawn. "Come," said D'Artagnan.

"What, D'Artagnan, my dear fellow, is that you? What a lucky chance! Oh, yes – true; I have forgotten; I am at the **fete** at Vaux."

"Yes; and your beautiful dress, too."

"Yes, it was very attentive on the part of Monsieur Coquelin de Voliere, was it not?"

"Hush!" said Aramis. "You are walking so heavily you will make the flooring give way."

"True," said the musketeer; "this room is above the dome, I think."

"And I did not choose it for a fencing-room, I assure you," added the bishop. "The ceiling of the king's room has all the lightness and calm of wholesome sleep. Do not forget, therefore, that my flooring is merely the covering of his ceiling. Good night, my friends, and in ten minutes I shall be asleep myself." And Aramis accompanied them to the door, laughing quietly all the while. As soon as they were outside, he bolted the door, hurriedly; closed up the chinks of the windows, and then called out, "Monseigneur! – monseigneur!" Philippe made his appearance from the alcove, as he pushed aside a sliding panel placed behind the bed.

"M. d'Artagnan entertains a great many suspicions, it seems," he said.

"Ah! – you recognized M. d'Artagnan, then?"

"Before you called him by his name, even."

"He is your captain of musketeers."

"He is very devoted to **me**," replied Philippe, laying a stress upon the personal pronoun.

"As faithful as a dog; but he bites sometimes. If D'Artagnan does not recognize you before **the other** has disappeared, rely upon D'Artagnan to the end of the world; for in that case, if he has seen nothing, he will keep his fidelity. If he sees, when it is too late, he is a Gascon, and will never admit that he has been deceived."

"I thought so. What are we to do, now?"

"Sit in this folding-chair. I am going to push aside a portion of the flooring; you will look through the opening, which answers to one of the false windows made in the dome of the king's apartment. Can you see?"

"Yes," said Philippe, starting as at the sight of an enemy; "I see the king!"

"What is he doing?"

"He seems to wish some man to sit down close to him."

"M. Fouquet?"

"No, no; wait a moment – "

"Look at the notes and the portraits, my prince."

"The man whom the king wishes to sit down in his presence is M. Colbert."

"Colbert sit down in the king's presence!" exclaimed Aramis. "It is impossible."

"Look."

Aramis looked through the opening in the flooring. "Yes," he said. "Colbert himself. Oh, monseigneur! what can we be going to hear – and what can result from this intimacy?"

"Nothing good for M. Fouquet, at all events."

The prince did not deceive himself.

We have seen that Louis XIV. had sent for Colbert, and Colbert had arrived. The conversation began between them by the king according to him one of the highest favors that he had ever done; it was true the king was alone with his subject. "Colbert," said he, "sit down."

The intendant, overcome with delight, for he feared he was about to be dismissed, refused this unprecedented honor.

"Does he accept?" said Aramis.

"No, he remains standing."

"Let us listen, then." And the future king and the future pope listened eagerly to the simple mortals they held under their feet, ready to crush them when they liked.

"Colbert," said the king, "you have annoyed me exceedingly to-day."

"I know it, sire."

"Very good; I like that answer. Yes, you knew it, and there was courage in the doing of it."

"I ran the risk of displeasing your majesty, but I risked, also, the concealment of your best interests."

"What! you were afraid of something on **my** account?"

"I was, sire, even if it were nothing more than an indigestion," said Colbert; "for people do not give their sovereigns such banquets as the one of to-day, unless it be to stifle them beneath the burden of good living." Colbert awaited the effect this coarse jest would produce upon the king; and Louis XIV., who was the vainest and the most fastidiously delicate man in his kingdom, forgave Colbert the joke.

"The truth is," he said, "that M. Fouquet has given me too good a meal. Tell me, Colbert, where does he get all the money required for this enormous expenditure, –

can you tell?"

"Yes, I do know, sire."

"Will you be able to prove it with tolerable certainty?"

"Easily; and to the utmost farthing."

"I know you are very exact."

"Exactitude is the principal qualification required in an intendant of finances."

"But all are not so."

"I thank you majesty for so flattering a compliment from your own lips."

"M. Fouquet, therefore, is rich – very rich, and I suppose every man knows he is so."

"Every one, sire; the living as well as the dead."

"What does that mean, Monsieur Colbert?"

"The living are witnesses of M. Fouquet's wealth, – they admire and applaud the result produced; but the dead, wiser and better informed than we are, know how that wealth was obtained – and they rise up in accusation."

"So that M. Fouquet owes his wealth to

some cause or other."

"The occupation of an intendant very often favors those who practice it."

"You have something to say to me more confidentially, I perceive; do not be afraid, we are quite alone."

"I am never afraid of anything under the shelter of my own conscience, and under the protection of your majesty," said Colbert, bowing.

"If the dead, therefore, were to speak – "

"They do speak sometimes, sire, – read."

"Ah!" murmured Aramis, in the prince's ear, who, close beside him, listened without losing a syllable, "since you are placed here, monseigneur, in order to learn your vocation of a king, listen to a piece of infamy – of a nature truly royal. You are about to be a witness of one of those scenes which the foul fiend alone conceives and executes. Listen attentively, – you will find your advantage in it."

The prince redoubled his attention, and

saw Louis XIV. take from Colbert's hands a letter the latter held out to him.

"The late cardinal's handwriting," said the king.

"Your majesty has an excellent memory," replied Colbert, bowing; "it is an immense advantage for a king who is destined for hard work to recognize handwritings at the first glance."

The king read Mazarin's letter, and, as its contents are already known to the reader, in consequence of the misunderstanding between Madame de Chevreuse and Aramis, nothing further would be learned if we stated them here again.

"I do not quite understand," said the king, greatly interested.

"Your majesty has not acquired the utilitarian habit of checking the public accounts."

"I see that it refers to money that had been given to M. Fouquet."

"Thirteen millions. A tolerably good sum."

"Yes. Well, these thirteen millions are wanting to balance the total of the account. That is what I do not very well understand. How was this deficit possible?"

"Possible I do not say; but there is no doubt about fact that it is really so."

"You say that these thirteen millions are found to be wanting in the accounts?"

"I do not say so, but the registry does."

"And this letter of M. Mazarin indicates the employment of that sum and the name of the person with whom it was deposited?"

"As your majesty can judge for yourself."

"Yes; and the result is, then, that M. Fouquet has not yet restored the thirteen millions."

"That results from the accounts, certainly, sire."

"Well, and, consequently – "

"Well, sire, in that case, inasmuch as M. Fouquet has not yet given back the thirteen millions, he must have appropriated them to his own purpose; and with those thirteen millions one could incur four times and a little more as much expense, and make four times as great a display, as your majesty was able to do at Fontainebleau, where we only spent three millions altogether, if you remember."

For a blunderer, the **souvenir** he had evoked was a rather skillfully contrived piece of baseness; for by the remembrance of his own **fete** he, for the first time, perceived its inferiority compared with that of Fouquet. Colbert received back again at Vaux what Fouquet had given him at Fontainebleau, and, as a good financier, returned it with the best possible interest. Having once disposed the king's mind in this artful way, Colbert had nothing of much importance to detain him. He felt that such was the case, for the king, too, had again sunk into a dull and gloomy state. Colbert awaited the first words from the king's lips with as much impatience as Philippe and Aramis did from their place of observation.

"Are you aware what is the usual and

natural consequence of all this, Monsieur Colbert?" said the king, after a few moments' reflection.

"No, sire, I do not know."

"Well, then, the fact of the appropriation of the thirteen millions, if it can be proved – "

"But it is so already."

"I mean if it were to be declared and certified, M. Colbert."

"I think it will be to-morrow, if your majesty – "

"Were we not under M. Fouquet's roof, you were going to say, perhaps," replied the king, with something of nobility in his demeanor.

"The king is in his own palace wherever he may be – especially in houses which the royal money has constructed."

"I think," said Philippe in a low tone to Aramis, "that the architect who planned this dome ought, anticipating the use it could be put to at a future opportunity, so to have contrived that it might be made to fall upon the heads of scoundrels such as M. Colbert."

"I think so too," replied Aramis; "but M. Colbert is so very **near the king** at this moment."

"That is true, and that would open the succession."

"Of which your younger brother would reap all the advantage, monseigneur. But stay, let us keep quiet, and go on listening."

"We shall not have long to listen," said the young prince.

"Why not, monseigneur?"

"Because, if I were king, I should make no further reply."

"And what would you do?"

"I should wait until to-morrow morning to give myself time for reflection."

Louis XIV. at last raised his eyes, and finding Colbert attentively waiting for his next remarks, said, hastily, changing the conversation, "M. Colbert, I perceive it is getting very late, and I shall now retire to bed. By to-morrow morning I shall have made up my mind."

"Very good, sire," returned Colbert, greatly incensed, although he restrained himself in the presence of the king.

The king made a gesture of adieu, and Colbert withdrew with a respectful bow. "My attendants!" cried the king; and, as they entered the apartment, Philippe was about to quit his post of observation.

"A moment longer," said Aramis to him, with his accustomed gentleness of manner; "what has just now taken place is only a detail, and to-morrow we shall have no occasion to think anything more about it; but the ceremony of the king's retiring to rest, the etiquette observed in addressing the king, that indeed is of the greatest importance. Learn, sire, and study well how you ought to go to bed of a night. Look! look!"

CHAPTER FIFTEEN

Colbert

HISTORY WILL TELL US, or rather history has told us, of the various events of the following day, of the splendid **fetes** given by the surintendant to his sovereign. Nothing but amusement and delight was allowed to prevail throughout the whole of the following day; there was a promenade, a banquet, a comedy to be acted, and a comedy, too, in which, to his great amazement, Porthos recognized “M. Coquelin de Voliere” as one of the actors, in the piece called “Les Facheux.” Full of preoccupation, however, from the scene of the previous evening, and hardly recovered from the effects of the poison which Colbert had then administered to him, the king, during the whole of the day, so brilliant in its effects, so full of unexpected and startling novelties, in which all the wonders of the “Arabian Night’s Entertainments” seemed to be reproduced for his especial amusement – the king, we say, showed himself cold, reserved, and taciturn. Nothing could smooth the frowns upon his face; every one who observed him noticed that a deep feeling of resentment, of remote origin, increased by slow degrees, as the source becomes a river, thanks to the thousand threads of water that increase its body, was keenly alive in the depths of the king’s heart. Towards the middle of the day only did he begin to resume a little serenity of manner, and by that time he had, in all probability, made up his mind. Aramis, who followed him step by step in his thoughts, as in his walk, concluded that the event he was expecting would not be long before it was announced. This time Colbert seemed to walk in concert with the bishop of Vannes, and had he received for every annoyance which he inflicted on the king a word of direction from Aramis, he could not have done better. During the whole of the day the king, who, in all probability, wished to free himself from some of the thoughts which disturbed his mind, seemed to seek La Valliere's society as actively as he seemed to show his anxiety to flee that of M. Colbert or M. Fouquet. The evening came. The king had expressed a wish not to walk in the park until after cards in the evening. In the interval between supper and the promenade, cards and dice were introduced. The king won a thousand pistoles, and, having won them, put them in his pocket, and then rose, saying, "And now, gentlemen, to the park."

He found the ladies of the court were already there. The king, we have before observed, had won a thousand pistoles, and had put them in his pocket; but M. Fouquet had somehow contrived to lose ten thousand, so that among the courtiers there was still left a hundred and ninety thousand francs' profit to divide, a circumstance which made the countenances of the courtiers and the officers of the king's household the most joyous countenances in the world. It was not the same, however, with the king's face; for, notwithstanding his success at play, to which he was by no means insensible, there still remained a slight shade of dissatisfaction. Colbert was waiting for or upon him at the corner of one of the avenues; he was most probably waiting there in consequence of a rendezvous which had been given him by the king, as Louis XIV., who had avoided him, or who had seemed to avoid him, suddenly made him a sign, and they then struck into the depths of the park together. But La Valliere, too, had observed the king's gloomy aspect and kindling glances; she had remarked this – and as nothing which lay hidden or smoldering in his heart was hidden from the gaze of her affection, she understood that this repressed wrath menaced some one; she prepared to withstand the current of his vengeance, and intercede like an angel of mercy. Overcome by sadness, nervously agitated, deeply distressed at having been so long separated from her lover, disturbed at the sight of the emotion she had divined, she accordingly presented herself to the king with an embarrassed aspect, which in his then disposition of mind the king interpreted unfavorably. Then, as they were alone – nearly alone, inasmuch as Colbert, as soon as he perceived the young girl approaching, had stopped and drawn back a dozen paces – the king advanced towards La Valliere and took her by the hand. "Mademoiselle," he said to her, "should I be guilty of an indiscretion if I were to inquire if you were indisposed? for you seem to breathe as if you were oppressed by some secret cause of uneasiness, and your eyes are filled with tears."

"Oh! sire, if I be indeed so, and if my eyes are indeed full of tears, I am sorrowful only at the sadness which seems to oppress your majesty."

"My sadness? You are mistaken, mademoiselle; no, it is not sadness I experience."

"What is it, then, sire?"

"Humiliation."

"Humiliation? oh! sire, what a word for you to use!"

"I mean, mademoiselle, that wherever I may happen to be, no one else ought to be the master. Well, then, look round you on every side, and judge whether I am not eclipsed – I, the king of France – before the monarch of these wide domains. Oh!" he continued, clenching his hands and teeth, "when I think that this king – "

"Well, sire?" said Louise, terrified.

" – That this king is a faithless, unworthy servant, who grows proud and self-sufficient upon the strength of property that belongs to me, and which he has stolen. And therefore I am about to change this impudent minister's **fete** into sorrow and mourning, of which the nymph of Vaux, as the poets say, shall not soon lose the remembrance."

"Oh! your majesty – "

"Well, mademoiselle, are you about to take M. Fouquet's part?" said Louis, impatiently.

"No, sire; I will only ask whether you are well informed. Your majesty has more than once learned the value of accusations made at court."

Louis XIV. made a sign for Colbert to approach. "Speak, Monsieur Colbert," said the young prince, "for I almost believe that Mademoiselle de la Valliere has need of your assistance before she can put any faith in the king's word. Tell mademoiselle what M. Fouquet has done; and you, mademoiselle, will perhaps have the kindness to listen. It will not be long."

Why did Louis XIV. insist upon it in such a manner? A very simple reason – his heart was not at rest, his mind was not thoroughly convinced; he imagined there lay some dark, hidden, tortuous intrigue behind these thirteen millions of francs; and he wished that the pure heart of La Valliere, which had revolted at the idea of theft or robbery, should approve – even were it only by a single word – the resolution he had taken, and which, nevertheless, he hesitated before carrying into execution.

"Speak, monsieur," said La Valliere to Colbert, who had advanced; "speak, since the king wishes me to listen to you. Tell me, what is the crime with which M. Fouquet is charged?"

"Oh! not very heinous, mademoiselle," he returned, "a mere abuse of confidence."

"Speak, speak, Colbert; and when you have related it, leave us, and go and inform

M. d'Artagnan that I have certain orders to give him."

"M. d'Artagnan, sire!" exclaimed La Valliere; "but why send for M. d'Artagnan? I entreat you to tell me."

"**Pardieu!** in order to arrest this haughty, arrogant Titan who, true to his menace, threatens to scale my heaven."

"Arrest M. Fouquet, do you say?"

"Ah! does that surprise you?"

"In his own house!"

"Why not? If he be guilty, he is as guilty in his own house as anywhere else."

"M. Fouquet, who at this moment is ruining himself for his sovereign."

"In plain truth, mademoiselle, it seems as if you were defending this traitor."

Colbert began to chuckle silently. The king turned round at the sound of this suppressed mirth.

"Sire," said La Valliere, "it is not M. Fouquet I am defending; it is yourself."

"Me! you are defending me?"

"Sire, you would dishonor yourself if you were to give such an order."

"Dishonor myself!" murmured the king, turning pale with anger. "In plain truth, mademoiselle, you show a strange persistence in what you say."

"If I do, sire, my only motive is that of serving your majesty," replied the noble-hearted girl: "for that I would risk, I would sacrifice my very life, without the least reserve."

Colbert seemed inclined to grumble and complain. La Valliere, that timid, gentle lamb, turned round upon him, and with a glance like lightning imposed silence upon him. "Monsieur," she said, "when the king acts well, whether, in doing so, he does either myself or those who belong to me an injury, I have nothing to say; but were the king to confer a benefit either upon me or mine, and if he acted badly, I should tell him so."

"But it appears to me, mademoiselle," Colbert ventured to say, "that I too love the king."

"Yes, monseigneur, we both love him, but each in a different manner," replied La Valliere, with such an accent that the heart of the young king was powerfully affected by it. "I love him so deeply, that the whole world is aware of it; so purely, that the king himself does not doubt my affection. He is my king and my master; I am the least of all his servants. But whoso touches his honor assails my life. Therefore, I repeat, that they dishonor the king who advise him to arrest M. Fouquet under his own roof."

Colbert hung down his head, for he felt that the king had abandoned him. However, as he bent his head, he murmured, "Mademoiselle, I have only one word to say."

"Do not say it, then, monsieur; for I would not listen to it. Besides, what could you have to tell me? That M. Fouquet has been guilty of certain crimes? I believe he has, because the king has said so; and, from the moment the king said, 'I think so,'

I have no occasion for other lips to say, 'I affirm it.' But, were M. Fouquet the vilest of men, I should say aloud, 'M. Fouquet's person is sacred to the king because he is the guest of M. Fouquet. Were his house a den of thieves, were Vaux a cave of coiners or robbers, his home is sacred, his palace is inviolable, since his wife is living in it; and that is an asylum which even executioners would not dare to violate.'"

La Valliere paused, and was silent. In spite of himself the king could not but admire her; he was overpowered by the passionate energy of her voice; by the nobleness of the cause she advocated. Colbert yielded, overcome by the inequality of the struggle. At last the king breathed again more freely, shook his head, and held out his hand to La Valliere. "Mademoiselle," he said, gently, "why do you decide against me? Do you know what this wretched fellow will do, if I give him time to breathe again?"

"Is he not a prey which will always be within

your grasp?"

"Should he escape, and take to flight?" exclaimed Colbert.

"Well, monsieur, it will always remain on record, to the king's eternal honor, that he allowed M. Fouquet to flee; and the more guilty he may have been, the greater will the king's honor and glory appear, compared with such unnecessary misery and shame."

Louis kissed La Valliere's hand, as he knelt before her.

"I am lost," thought Colbert; then suddenly his face brightened up again. "Oh! no, no, aha, old fox! – not yet," he said to himself.

And while the king, protected from observation by the thick covert of an enormous lime, pressed La Valliere to his breast, with all the ardor of ineffable affection, Colbert tranquilly fumbled among the papers in his pocket-book and drew out of it a paper folded in the form of a letter, somewhat yellow, perhaps, but one that must have been most precious, since the intendant smiled as he looked at it; he then bent a look, full of hatred, upon the charming group which the young girl and the king formed together – a group revealed but for a moment, as the light of the approaching torches shone upon it. Louis noticed the light reflected upon La Valliere's white dress. "Leave me, Louise," he said, "for some one is coming."

"Mademoiselle, mademoiselle, some one is coming," cried Colbert, to expedite the young girl's departure.

Louise disappeared rapidly among the trees; and then, as the king, who had been on his knees before the young girl, was rising from his humble posture, Colbert exclaimed, "Ah! Mademoiselle de la Valliere has let something fall."

"What is it?" inquired the king.

"A paper – a letter – something white; look there, sire."

The king stooped down immediately and picked up the letter, crumpling it in his hand, as he did so; and at the same moment the torches arrived, inundating the blackness of the scene with a flood of light as bight as day.

CHAPTER SIXTEEN

Jealousy

THE TORCHES WE HAVE just referred to, the eager attention every one displayed, and the new ovation paid to the king by Fouquet, arrived in time to suspend the effect of a resolution which La Valliere had already considerably shaken in Louis XIV.'s heart. He looked at Fouquet with a feeling almost of gratitude for having given La Valliere an opportunity of showing herself so generously disposed, so powerful in the influence she exercised over his heart. The moment of the last and greatest display had arrived. Hardly had Fouquet conducted the king towards the chateau, when a mass of fire burst from the dome of Vaux, with a prodigious uproar, pouring a flood of dazzling cataracts of rays on every side, and illumining the remotest corners of the gardens. The fireworks began. Colbert, at twenty paces from the king, who was surrounded and **feted** by the owner of Vaux, seemed, by the obstinate persistence of his gloomy thoughts, to do his utmost to recall Louis's attention, which the magnificence of the spectacle was already, in his opinion, too easily diverting. Suddenly, just as Louis was on the point of holding it out to Fouquet, he perceived in his hand the paper which, as he believed, La Valliere had dropped at his feet as she hurried away. The still stronger magnet of love drew the young prince's attention towards the **souvenir** of his idol; and, by the brilliant light, which increased momentarily in beauty, and drew from the neighboring villages loud cheers of admiration, the king read the letter, which he supposed was a loving and tender epistle La Valliere had destined for him. But as he read it, a death-like pallor stole over his face, and an expression of deep-seated wrath, illumined by the many-colored fire which gleamed so brightly, soaringly around the scene, produced a terrible spectacle, which every one would have shuddered at, could they only have read into his heart, now torn by the most stormy and most bitter passions. There was no truce for him now, influenced as he was by jealousy and mad passion. From the very moment when the dark truth was revealed to him, every gentler feeling seemed to disappear; pity, kindness of consideration, the religion of hospitality, all were forgotten. In the bitter pang which wrung his heart, he, still too weak to hide his sufferings, was almost on the point of uttering a cry of alarm, and calling his guards to gather round him. This letter which Colbert had thrown down at the king's feet, the reader has doubtlessly guessed, was the same that had disappeared with the porter Toby at Fontainebleau, after the attempt which Fouquet had made upon La Valliere's heart. Fouquet saw the king's pallor, and was far from guessing the evil; Colbert saw the king's anger, and rejoiced inwardly at the approach of the storm. Fouquet's voice drew the young prince from his wrathful reverie.

"What is the matter, sire?" inquired the superintendent, with an expression of graceful interest.

Louis made a violent effort over himself, as he replied, "Nothing."

"I am afraid your majesty is suffering?"

"I am suffering, and have already told you so, monsieur; but it is nothing."

And the king, without waiting for the termination of the fireworks, turned towards the chateau. Fouquet accompanied him, and the whole court followed, leaving the remains of the fireworks consuming for their own amusement. The superintendent endeavored again to question Louis XIV., but did not succeed in obtaining a reply. He imagined there had been some misunderstanding between Louis and La Valliere in the park, which had resulted in a slight quarrel; and that the king, who was not ordinarily sulky by disposition, but completely absorbed by his passion for La Valliere, had taken a dislike to every one because his mistress had shown herself offended with him. This idea was sufficient to console him; he had even a friendly and kindly smile for the young king, when the latter wished him good night. This, however, was not all the king had to submit to; he was obliged to undergo the usual ceremony, which on that evening was marked by close adherence to the strictest etiquette. The next day was the one fixed for the departure; it was but proper that the guests should thank their host, and show him a little attention in return for the expenditure of his twelve millions. The only remark, approaching to amiability, which the king could find to say to M. Fouquet, as he took leave of him, were in these words, "M. Fouquet, you shall hear from me. Be good enough to desire M. d'Artagnan to come here."

But the blood of Louis XIV., who had so profoundly dissimulated his feelings, boiled in his veins; and he was perfectly willing to order M. Fouquet to be put an end to with the same readiness, indeed, as his predecessor had caused the assassination of le Marechal d'Ancre; and so he disguised the terrible resolution he had formed beneath one of those royal smiles which, like lightning-flashes, indicated **coups d'etat**. Fouquet took the king's hand and kissed it; Louis shuddered throughout his whole frame, but allowed M. Fouquet to touch his hand with his lips. Five minutes afterwards, D'Artagnan, to whom the royal order had been communicated, entered Louis XIV.'s apartment. Aramis and Philippe were in theirs, still eagerly attentive, and still listening with all their ears. The king did not even give the captain of the musketeers time to approach his armchair, but ran forward to meet him. "Take care," he exclaimed, "that no one enters here."

"Very good, sire," replied the captain, whose glance had for a long time past analyzed the stormy indications on the royal countenance. He gave the necessary order at the door; but, returning to the king, he said, "Is there something fresh the matter, your majesty?"

"How many men have you here?" inquired the king, without making any other reply to the question addressed to him.

"What for, sire?"

"How many men have you, I say?" repeated the king, stamping upon the ground with his foot.

"I have the musketeers."

"Well; and what others?"

"Twenty guards and thirteen Swiss."

"How many men will be required to – "

"To do what, sire?" replied the musketeer, opening his large, calm eyes.

"To arrest M. Fouquet."

D'Artagnan fell back a step.

"To arrest M. Fouquet!" he burst forth.

"Are you going to tell me that it is impossible?" exclaimed the king, in tones of cold, vindictive passion.

"I never say that anything is impossible," replied D'Artagnan, wounded to the quick.

"Very well; do it, then."

D'Artagnan turned on his heel, and made his way towards the door; it was but a short distance, and he cleared it in half a dozen paces; when he reached it he suddenly paused, and said, "Your majesty will forgive me, but, in order to effect this arrest, I should like written directions."

"For what purpose – and since when has the king's word been insufficient for you?"

"Because the word of a king, when it

springs from a feeling of anger, may possibly change when the feeling changes."

"A truce to set phrases, monsieur; you have another thought besides that?"

"Oh, I, at least, have certain thoughts and ideas, which, unfortunately, others have not," D'Artagnan replied, impertinently.

The king, in the tempest of his wrath, hesitated, and drew back in the face of D'Artagnan's frank courage, just as a horse crouches on his haunches under the strong hand of a bold and experienced rider. "What is your thought?" he exclaimed.

"This, sire," replied D'Artagnan: "you cause a man to be arrested when you are still under his roof; and passion is alone the cause of that. When your anger shall have passed, you will regret what you have done; and then I wish to be in a position to show you your signature. If that, however, should fail to be a reparation, it will at least show us that the king was wrong to lose his temper."

"Wrong to lose his temper!" cried the king,

in a loud, passionate voice. "Did not my father, my grandfathers, too, before me, lose their temper at times, in Heaven's name?"

"The king your father and the king your grandfather never lost their temper except when under the protection of their own palace."

"The king is master wherever he may be."

"That is a flattering, complimentary phrase which cannot proceed from any one but M. Colbert; but it happens not to be the truth. The king is at home in every man's house when he has driven its owner out of it."

The king bit his lips, but said nothing.

"Can it be possible?" said D'Artagnan; "here is a man who is positively ruining himself in order to please you, and you wish to have him arrested! **Mordioux!** Sire, if my name was Fouquet, and people treated me in that manner, I would swallow at a single gulp all sorts of fireworks and other things, and I would set fire to them, and send myself and everybody else in blown-up atoms to the sky. But it is all the same; it is your wish, and it shall be done."

"Go," said the king; "but have you men enough?"

"Do you suppose I am going to take a whole host to help me? Arrest M. Fouquet! why, that is so easy that a very child might do it! It is like drinking a glass of wormwood; one makes an ugly face, and that is all."

"If he defends himself?"

"He! it is not at all likely. Defend himself when such extreme harshness as you are going to practice makes the man a very martyr! Nay, I am sure that if he has a million of francs left, which I very much doubt, he would be willing enough to give it in order to have such a termination as this. But what does that matter? it shall be done at once."

"Stay," said the king; "do not make his arrest a public affair."

"That will be more difficult."

"Why so?"

"Because nothing is easier than to go up

to M. Fouquet in the midst of a thousand enthusiastic guests who surround him, and say, 'In the king's name, I arrest you.' But to go up to him, to turn him first one way and then another, to drive him up into one of the corners of the chess-board, in such a way that he cannot escape; to take him away from his guests, and keep him a prisoner for you, without one of them, alas! having heard anything about it; that, indeed, is a genuine difficulty, the greatest of all, in truth; and I hardly see how it is to be done."

"You had better say it is impossible, and you will have finished much sooner. Heaven help me, but I seem to be surrounded by people who prevent me doing what I wish."

"I do not prevent your doing anything. Have you indeed decided?"

"Take care of M. Fouquet, until I shall have made up my mind by to-morrow morning."

"That shall be done, sire."

"And return, when I rise in the morning, for further orders; and now leave me to myself."

"You do not even want M. Colbert, then?" said the musketeer, firing his last shot as he was leaving the room. The king started. With his whole mind fixed on the thought of revenge, he had forgotten the cause and substance of the offense.

"No, no one," he said; "no one here! Leave me."

D'Artagnan quitted the room. The king closed the door with his own hands, and began to walk up and down his apartment at a furious pace, like a wounded bull in an arena, trailing from his horn the colored streamers and the iron darts. At last he began to take comfort in the expression of his violent feelings.

"Miserable wretch that he is! not only does he squander my finances, but with his ill-gotten plunder he corrupts secretaries, friends, generals, artists, and all, and tries to rob me of the one to whom I am most attached. This is the reason that perfidious girl so boldly took his part! Gratitude! and who can tell whether it was not a stronger feeling – love itself?" He gave himself up for a moment to the bitterest reflections. "A satyr!" he thought, with that abhorrent hate with which young men regard those more advanced in life, who still think of love. "A man who has never found opposition or resistance in any one, who lavishes his gold and jewels in every direction, and who retains his staff of painters in order to take the portraits of his mistresses in the costume of goddesses." The king trembled with passion as he continued, "He pollutes and profanes everything that belongs to me! He destroys everything that is mine. He will be my death at last, I know. That man is too much for me; he is my mortal enemy, but he shall forthwith fall! I hate him – I hate him – I hate him!" and as he pronounced these words, he struck the arm of the chair in which he was sitting violently, over and over again, and then rose like one in an epileptic fit. "To-morrow! to-morrow! oh, happy day!" he murmured, "when the sun rises, no other rival shall that brilliant king of space possess but me. That man shall fall so low that when people look at the abject ruin my anger shall have wrought, they will be forced to confess at last and at least that I am indeed greater than he." The king, who was incapable of mastering his emotions any longer, knocked over with a blow of his fist a small table placed close to his bedside, and in the very bitterness of anger, almost weeping, and half-suffocated, he threw himself on his bed, dressed as he was, and bit the sheets in his extremity of passion, trying to find repose of body at least there. The bed creaked beneath his weight, and with the exception of a few broken sounds, emerging, or, one might say, exploding, from his overburdened chest, absolute silence soon reigned in the chamber of Morpheus.

CHAPTER SEVENTEEN

High Treason

THE UNGOVERNABLE FURY WHICH took possession of the king at the sight and at the perusal of Fouquet's letter to La Valliere by degrees subsided into a feeling of pain and extreme weariness. Youth, invigorated by health and lightness of spirits, requiring soon that what it loses should be immediately restored – youth knows not those endless, sleepless nights which enable us to realize the fable of the vulture unceasingly feeding on Prometheus. In cases where the man of middle life, in his acquired strength of will and purpose, and the old, in their state of natural exhaustion, find incessant augmentation of their bitter sorrow, a young man, surprised by the sudden appearance of misfortune, weakens himself in sighs, and groans, and tears, directly struggling with his grief, and is thereby far sooner overthrown by the inflexible enemy with whom he is engaged. Once overthrown, his struggles cease. Louis could not hold out more than a few minutes, at the end of which he had ceased to clench his hands, and scorch in fancy with his looks the invisible objects of his hatred; he soon ceased to attack with his violent imprecations not M. Fouquet alone, but even La Valliere herself; from fury he subsided into despair, and from despair to prostration. After he had thrown himself for a few minutes to and fro convulsively on his bed, his nerveless arms fell quietly down; his head lay languidly on his pillow; his limbs, exhausted with excessive emotion, still trembled occasionally, agitated by muscular contractions; while from his breast faint and infrequent sighs still issued. Morpheus, the tutelary deity of the apartment, towards whom Louis raised his eyes, wearied by his anger and reconciled by his tears, showered down upon him the sleep-inducing poppies with which his hands are ever filled; so presently the monarch closed his eyes and fell asleep. Then it seemed to him, as it often happens in that first sleep, so light and gentle, which raises the body above the couch, and the soul above the earth – it seemed to him, we say, as if the god Morpheus, painted on the ceiling, looked at him with eyes resembling human eyes; that something shone brightly, and moved to and fro in the dome above the sleeper; that the crowd of terrible dreams which thronged together in his brain, and which were interrupted for a moment, half revealed a human face, with a hand resting against the mouth, and in an attitude of deep and absorbed meditation. And strange enough, too, this man bore so wonderful a resemblance to the king himself, that Louis fancied he was looking at his own face reflected in a mirror; with the exception, however, that the face was saddened by a feeling of the profoundest pity. Then it seemed to him as if the dome gradually retired, escaping from his gaze, and that the figures and attributes painted by Lebrun became darker and darker as the distance became more and more remote. A gentle, easy movement, as regular as that by which a vessel plunges beneath the waves, had succeeded to the immovableness of the bed. Doubtless the king was dreaming, and in this dream the crown of gold, which fastened the curtains together, seemed to recede from his vision, just as the dome, to which it remained suspended, had done, so that the winged genius which, with both its hand, supported the crown, seemed, though vainly so, to call upon the king, who was fast disappearing from it. The bed still sunk. Louis, with his eyes open, could not resist the deception of this cruel hallucination. At last, as the light of the royal chamber faded away into darkness and gloom, something cold, gloomy, and inexplicable in its nature seemed to infect the air. No paintings, nor gold, nor velvet hangings, were visible any longer, nothing but walls of a dull gray color, which the increasing gloom made darker every moment. And yet the bed still continued to descend, and after a minute, which seemed in its duration almost an age to the king, it reached a stratum of air, black and chill as death, and then it stopped. The king could no longer see the light in his room, except as from the bottom of a well we can see the light of day. "I am under the influence of some atrocious dream," he thought. "It is time to awaken from it. Come! let me wake."

Every one has experienced the sensation

the above remark conveys; there is hardly a person who, in the midst of a nightmare whose influence is suffocating, has not said to himself, by the help of that light which still burns in the brain when every human light is extinguished, "It is nothing but a dream, after all." This was precisely what Louis XIV. said to himself; but when he said, "Come, come! wake up," he perceived that not only was he already awake, but still more, that he had his eyes open also. And then he looked all round him. On his right hand and on his left two armed men stood in stolid silence, each wrapped in a huge cloak, and the face covered with a mask; one of them held a small lamp in his hand, whose glimmering light revealed the saddest picture a king could look upon. Louis could not help saying to himself that his dream still lasted, and that all he had to do to cause it to disappear was to move his arms or to say something aloud; he darted from his bed, and found himself upon the damp, moist ground. Then, addressing himself to the man who held the lamp in his hand, he said:

"What is this, monsieur, and what is the meaning of this jest?"

"It is no jest," replied in a deep voice the masked figure that held the lantern.

"Do you belong to M. Fouquet?" inquired the king, greatly astonished at his situation.

"It matters very little to whom we belong," said the phantom; "we are your masters now, that is sufficient."

The king, more impatient than intimidated, turned to the other masked figure. "If this is a comedy," he said, "you will tell M. Fouquet that I find it unseemly and improper, and that I command it should cease."

The second masked person to whom the king had addressed himself was a man of huge stature and vast circumference. He held himself erect and motionless as any block of marble. "Well!" added the king, stamping his foot, "you do not answer!"

"We do not answer you, my good

monsieur," said the giant, in a stentorian voice, "because there is nothing to say."

"At least, tell me what you want," exclaimed Louis, folding his arms with a passionate gesture.

"You will know by and by," replied the man who held the lamp.

"In the meantime tell me where I am."

"Look."

Louis looked all round him; but by the light of the lamp which the masked figure raised for the purpose, he could perceive nothing but the damp walls which glistened here and there with the slimy traces of the snail. "Oh – oh! – a dungeon," cried the king.

"No, a subterranean passage."

"Which leads – ?"

"Will you be good enough to follow us?"

"I shall not stir from hence!" cried the king.

"If you are obstinate, my dear young friend," replied the taller of the two, "I will lift you up in my arms, and roll you up in your own cloak, and if you should happen to be stifled, why –

so much the worse for you."

As he said this, he disengaged from beneath his cloak a hand of which Milo of Crotona would have envied him the possession, on the day when he had that unhappy idea of rending his last oak. The king dreaded violence, for he could well believe that the two men into whose power he had fallen had not gone so far with any idea of drawing back, and that they would consequently be ready to proceed to extremities, if necessary. He shook his head and said: "It seems I have fallen into the hands of a couple of assassins. Move on, then."

Neither of the men answered a word to this remark. The one who carried the lantern walked first, the king followed him, while the second masked figure closed the procession. In this manner they passed along a winding gallery of some length, with as many staircases leading out of it as are to be found in the mysterious and gloomy palaces of Ann Radcliffe's creation. All these windings and turnings, during which the king heard the sound of running water **over his head**, ended at last in a long corridor closed by an iron door. The figure with the lamp opened the door with one of the keys he wore suspended at his girdle, where, during the whole of the brief journey, the king had heard them rattle. As soon as the door was opened and admitted the air, Louis recognized the balmy odors that trees exhale in hot summer nights. He paused, hesitatingly, for a moment or two; but the huge sentinel who followed him thrust him out of the subterranean passage.

"Another blow," said the king, turning towards the one who had just had the audacity to touch his sovereign; "what do you intend to do with the king of France?"

"Try to forget that word," replied the man with the lamp, in a tone which as little admitted of a reply as one of the famous decrees of Minos.

"You deserve to be broken on the wheel for

the words that you have just made use of," said the giant, as he extinguished the lamp his companion handed to him; "but the king is too kind-hearted."

Louis, at that threat, made so sudden a movement that it seemed as if he meditated flight; but the giant's hand was in a moment placed on his shoulder, and fixed him motionless where he stood. "But tell me, at least, where we are going," said the king.

"Come," replied the former of the two men, with a kind of respect in his manner, and leading his prisoner towards a carriage which seemed to be in waiting.

The carriage was completely concealed amid the trees. Two horses, with their feet fettered, were fastened by a halter to the lower branches of a large oak.

"Get in," said the same man, opening the carriage-door and letting down the step. The king obeyed, seated himself at the back of the carriage, the padded door of which was shut and locked immediately upon him and his guide. As for the giant, he cut the fastenings by which the horses were bound, harnessed them himself, and mounted on the box of the carriage, which was unoccupied. The carriage set off immediately at a quick trot, turned into the road to Paris, and in the forest of Senart found a relay of horses fastened to the trees in the same manner the first horses had been, and without a postilion. The man on the box changed the horses, and continued to follow the road towards Paris with the same rapidity, so that they entered the city about three o'clock in the morning. They carriage proceeded along the Faubourg Saint-Antoine, and, after having called out to the sentinel, "By the king's order," the driver conducted the horses into the circular inclosure of the Bastile, looking out upon the courtyard, called La Cour du Gouvernement. There the horses drew up, reeking with sweat, at the flight of steps, and a sergeant of the guard ran forward. "Go and wake the governor," said the coachman in a voice of thunder.

With the exception of this voice, which might have been heard at the entrance of the Faubourg Saint-Antoine, everything remained as calm in the carriage as in the prison. Ten minutes afterwards, M. de Baisemeaux appeared in his dressing-gown on the threshold of the door. "What is the matter now?" he asked; "and whom have you brought me there?"

The man with the lantern opened the carriage-door, and said two or three words to the one who acted as driver, who immediately got down from his seat, took up a short musket which he kept under his feet, and placed its muzzle on his prisoner's chest.

"And fire at once if he speaks!" added aloud the man who alighted from the carriage.

"Very good," replied his companion, without another remark.

With this recommendation, the person who had accompanied the king in the carriage ascended the flight of steps, at the top of which the governor was awaiting him. "Monsieur d'Herblay!" said the latter.

"Hush!" said Aramis. "Let us go into your room."

"Good heavens! what brings you here at this hour?"

"A mistake, my dear Monsieur de Baisemeaux," Aramis replied, quietly. "It appears that you were quite right the other day."

"What about?" inquired the governor.

"About the order of release, my dear friend."

"Tell me what you mean, monsieur – no, monseigneur," said the governor, almost suffocated by surprise and terror.

"It is a very simple affair: you remember, dear M. de Baisemeaux, that an order of release was sent to you."

"Yes, for Marchiali."

"Very good! we both thought that it was for Marchiali?"

"Certainly; you will recollect, however, that

I would not credit it, but that you compelled me to believe it."

"Oh! Baisemeaux, my good fellow, what a word to make use of! – strongly recommended, that was all."

"Strongly recommended, yes; strongly recommended to give him up to you; and that you carried him off with you in your carriage."

"Well, my dear Monsieur de Baisemeaux, it was a mistake; it was discovered at the ministry, so that I now bring you an order from the king to set at liberty Seldon, – that poor Seldon fellow, you know."

"Seldon! are you sure this time?"

"Well, read it yourself," added Aramis, handing him the order.

"Why," said Baisemeaux, "this order is the very same that has already passed through my hands."

"Indeed?"

"It is the very one I assured you I saw the other evening. **Parbleu!** I recognize it by the blot of ink."

"I do not know whether it is that; but all I know is, that I bring it for you."

"But then, what about the other?"

"What other?"

"Marchiali."

"I have got him here with me."

"But that is not enough for me. I require a new order to take him back again."

"Don't talk such nonsense, my dear Baisemeaux; you talk like a child! Where is the order you received respecting Marchiali?"

Baisemeaux ran to his iron chest and took it out. Aramis seized hold of it, coolly tore it in four pieces, held them to the lamp, and burnt them. "Good heavens! what are you doing?" exclaimed Baisemeaux, in an extremity of terror.

"Look at your position quietly, my good governor," said Aramis, with imperturbable self-possession, "and you will see how very simple the whole affair is. You no longer possess any order justifying Marchiali's release."

"I am a lost man!"

"Far from it, my good fellow, since I have brought Marchiali back to you, and all accordingly is just the same as if he had never left."

"Ah!" said the governor, completely overcome by terror.

"Plain enough, you see; and you will go and shut him up immediately."

"I should think so, indeed."

"And you will hand over this Seldon to me, whose liberation is authorized by this order. Do you understand?"

"I – I – "

"You do understand, I see," said Aramis. "Very good." Baisemeaux clapped his hands together.

"But why, at all events, after having taken Marchiali away from me, do you bring him back again?" cried the unhappy governor, in a paroxysm of terror, and completely dumbfounded.

"For a friend such as you are," said

Aramis – “for so devoted a servant, I have no secrets;” and he put his mouth close to Baisemeaux’s ear, as he said, in a low tone of voice, “you know the resemblance between that unfortunate fellow, and – ”

“And the king? – yes!”

“Very good; the first use that Marchiali made of his liberty was to persist – Can you guess what?”

“How is it likely I should guess?”

“To persist in saying that he was king of France; to dress himself up in clothes like those of the king; and then pretend to assume that he was the king himself.”

“Gracious heavens!”

“That is the reason why I have brought him back again, my dear friend. He is mad and lets every one see how mad he is.”

“What is to be done, then?”

“That is very simple; let no one hold any communication with him. You understand that when his peculiar style of madness came to the king’s ears, the king, who had pitied his terrible affliction, and saw that all his kindness had been repaid by black ingratitude, became perfectly furious; so that, now – and remember this very distinctly, dear Monsieur de Baisemeaux, for it concerns you most closely – so that there is now, I repeat, sentence of death pronounced against all those who may allow him to communicate with any one else but me or the king himself. You understand, Baisemeaux, sentence of death!"

"You need not ask me whether I understand."

"And now, let us go down, and conduct this poor devil back to his dungeon again, unless you prefer he should come up here."

"What would be the good of that?"

"It would be better, perhaps, to enter his name in the prison-book at once!"

"Of course, certainly; not a doubt of it."

"In that case, have him up."

Baisemeaux ordered the drums to be beaten and the bell to be rung, as a warning to every one to retire, in order to avoid meeting a prisoner, about whom it was desired to observe a certain mystery. Then, when the passages were free, he went to take the prisoner from the carriage, at whose breast Porthos, faithful to the directions which had been given him, still kept his musket leveled. "Ah! is that you, miserable wretch?" cried the governor, as soon as he perceived the king. "Very good, very good." And immediately, making the king get out of the carriage, he led him, still accompanied by Porthos, who had not taken off his mask, and Aramis, who again resumed his, up the stairs, to the second Bertaudiere, and opened the door of the room in which Philippe for six long years had bemoaned his existence. The king entered the cell without pronouncing a single word: he faltered in as limp and haggard as a rain-struck lily. Baisemeaux shut the door upon him, turned the key twice in the lock, and then returned to Aramis. "It is quite true," he said, in a low tone, "that he bears a striking resemblance to the king; but less so than you said."

"So that," said Aramis, "you would not have been deceived by the substitution of the one for the other?"

"What a question!"

"You are a most valuable fellow, Baisemeaux," said Aramis; "and now, set Seldon free."

"Oh, yes. I was going to forget that. I will go and give orders at once."

"Bah! to-morrow will be time enough."

"To-morrow! – oh, no. This very minute."

"Well; go off to your affairs, I will go away to mine. But it is quite understood, is it not?"

"What 'is quite understood'?"

"That no one is to enter the prisoner's cell, expect with an order from the king; an order which I will myself bring."

"Quite so. Adieu, monseigneur."

Aramis returned to his companion. "Now, Porthos, my good fellow, back again to Vaux, and as fast as possible."

"A man is light and easy enough, when he has faithfully served his king; and, in serving him, saved his country," said Porthos. "The horses will be as light as if our tissues were constructed of the wind of heaven. So let us be off." And the carriage, lightened of a prisoner, who might well be – as he in fact was – very heavy in the sight of Aramis, passed across the drawbridge of the Bastile, which was raised again immediately behind it.

CHAPTER EIGHTEEN

A Night at the Bastile

PAIN, ANGUISH, and suffering in human life are always in proportion to the strength with which a man is endowed. We will not pretend to say that Heaven always apportions to a man's capability of endurance the anguish with which he afflicts him; for that, indeed, would not be true, since Heaven permits the existence of death, which is, sometimes, the only refuge open to those who are too closely pressed – too bitterly afflicted, as far as the body is concerned. Suffering is in proportion to the strength which has been accorded; in other words, the weak suffer more, where the trial is the same, than the strong. And what are the elementary principles, we may ask, that compose human strength? Is it not – more than anything else – exercise, habit, experience? We shall not even take the trouble to demonstrate this, for it is an axiom in morals, as in physics. When the young king, stupefied and crushed in every sense and feeling, found himself led to a cell in the Bastile, he fancied death itself is but a sleep; that it, too, has its dreams as well; that the bed had broken through the flooring of his room at Vaux; that death had resulted from the occurrence; and that, still carrying out his dream, the king, Louis XIV., now no longer living, was dreaming one of those horrors, impossible to realize in life, which is termed dethronement, imprisonment, and insult towards a sovereign who formerly wielded unlimited power. To be present at – an actual witness, too – of this bitterness of death; to float, indecisively, in an incomprehensible mystery, between resemblance and reality; to hear everything, to see everything, without interfering in a single detail of agonizing suffering, was – so the king thought within himself – a torture far more terrible, since it might last forever. "Is this what is termed eternity – hell?" he murmured, at the moment the door was closed upon him, which we remember Baisemeaux had shut with his own hands. He did not even look round him; and in the room, leaning with his back against the wall, he allowed himself to be carried away by the terrible supposition that he was already dead, as he closed his eyes, in order to avoid looking upon something even worse still. "How can I have died?" he said to himself, sick with terror. "The bed might have been let down by some artificial means? But no! I do not remember to have felt a bruise, nor any shock either. Would they not rather have poisoned me at my meals, or with the fumes of wax, as they did my ancestress, Jeanne d'Albret?" Suddenly, the chill of the dungeons seemed to fall like a wet cloak upon Louis's shoulders. "I have seen," he said, "my father lying dead upon his funeral couch, in his regal robes. That pale face, so calm and worn; those hands, once so skillful, lying nerveless by his side; those limbs stiffened by the icy grasp of death; nothing there betokened a sleep that was disturbed by dreams. And yet, how numerous were the dreams which Heaven might have sent that royal corpse – him whom so many others had preceded, hurried away by him into eternal death! No, that king was still the king: he was enthroned still upon that funeral couch, as upon a velvet armchair; he had not abdicated one title of his majesty. God, who had not punished him, cannot, will not punish me, who have done nothing." A strange sound attracted the young man's attention. He looked round him, and saw on the mantel-shelf, just below an enormous crucifix, coarsely painted in fresco on the wall, a rat of enormous size engaged in nibbling a piece of dry bread, but fixing all the time, an intelligent and inquiring look upon the new occupant of the cell. The king could not resist a sudden impulse of fear and disgust: he moved back towards the door, uttering a loud cry; and as if he but needed this cry, which escaped from his breast almost unconsciously, to recognize himself, Louis knew that he was alive and in full possession of his natural senses. "A prisoner!" he cried. "I – I, a prisoner!" He looked round him for a bell to summon some one to him. "There are no bells in the Bastile," he said, "and it is in the Bastile I am imprisoned. In what way can I have been made a prisoner? It must have been owing to a conspiracy of M. Fouquet. I have been drawn to Vaux, as to a snare. M. Fouquet cannot be acting alone in this affair. His agent

– That voice that I but just now heard was M. d'Herblay's; I recognized it. Colbert was right, then. But what is Fouquet's object? To reign in my place and stead? – Impossible. Yet who knows!" thought the king, relapsing into gloom again. "Perhaps my brother, the Duc d'Orleans, is doing that which my uncle wished to do during the whole of his life against my father. But the queen? – My mother, too? And La Valliere? Oh! La Valliere, she will have been abandoned to Madame. Dear, dear girl! Yes, it is – it must be so. They have shut her up as they have me. We are separated forever!" And at this idea of separation the poor lover burst into a flood of tears and sobs and groans.

"There is a governor in this place," the king continued, in a fury of passion; "I will speak to him, I will summon him to me."

He called – no voice replied to his. He seized hold of his chair, and hurled it against the massive oaken door. The wood resounded against the door, and awakened many a mournful echo in the profound depths of the staircase; but from a human creature, none.

This was a fresh proof for the king of the slight regard in which he was held at the Bastile. Therefore, when his first fit of anger had passed away, having remarked a barred window through which there passed a stream of light, lozenge-shaped, which must be, he knew, the bright orb of approaching day, Louis began to call out, at first gently enough, then louder and louder still; but no one replied. Twenty other attempts which he made, one after another, obtained no other or better success. His blood began to boil within him, and mount to his head. His nature was such, that, accustomed to command, he trembled at the idea of disobedience. The prisoner broke the chair, which was too heavy for him to lift, and made use of it as a battering ram to strike against the door. He struck so loudly, and so repeatedly, that the perspiration soon began to pour down his face. The sound became tremendous and continuous; certain stifled, smothered cries replied in different directions. This sound produced a strange effect upon the king. He paused to listen; it was the voice of the prisoners, formerly his victims, now his companions. The voices ascended like vapors through the thick ceilings and the massive walls, and rose in accusations against the author of this noise, as doubtless their sighs and tears accused, in whispered tones, the author of their captivity. After having deprived so many people of their liberty, the king came among them to rob them of their rest. This idea almost drove him mad; it redoubled his strength, or rather his will, bent upon obtaining some information, or a conclusion to the affair. With a portion of the broken chair he recommenced the noise. At the end of an hour, Louis heard something in the corridor, behind the door of his cell, and a violent blow, which was returned upon the door itself, made him cease his own.

"Are you mad?" said a rude, brutal voice. "What is the matter with you this morning?"

"This morning!" thought the king; but he said aloud, politely, "Monsieur, are you the governor of the Bastile?"

"My good fellow, your head is out of sorts," replied the voice; "but that is no reason why you should make such a terrible disturbance. Be quiet; **mordioux!**"

"Are you the governor?" the king inquired again.

He heard a door on the corridor close; the jailer had just left, not condescending to reply a single word. When the king had assured himself of his departure, his fury knew no longer any bounds. As agile as a tiger, he leaped from the table to the window, and struck the iron bars with all his might. He broke a pane of glass, the pieces of which fell clanking into the courtyard below. He shouted with increasing hoarseness, "The governor, the governor!" This excess lasted fully an hour, during which time he was in a burning fever. With his hair in disorder and matted on his forehead, his dress torn and covered with dust and plaster, his linen in shreds, the king never rested until his strength was utterly exhausted, and it was not until then that he clearly understood the pitiless thickness of the walls, the impenetrable nature of the cement, invincible to every influence but that of time, and that he possessed no other weapon but despair. He leaned his forehead against the door, and let the feverish throbbings of his heart calm by degrees; it had seemed as if one single additional pulsation would have made it burst.

"A moment will come when the food which is given to the prisoners will be brought to me. I shall then see some one, I shall speak to him, and get an answer."

And the king tried to remember at what hour the first repast of the prisoners was served at the Bastile; he was ignorant even of this detail. The feeling of remorse at this remembrance smote him like the thrust of a dagger, that he should have lived for five and twenty years a king, and in the enjoyment of every happiness, without having bestowed a moment's thought on the misery of those who had been unjustly deprived of their liberty. The king blushed for very shame. He felt that Heaven, in permitting this fearful humiliation, did no more than render to the man the same torture as had been inflicted by that man upon so many others. Nothing could be more efficacious for reawakening his mind to religious influences than the prostration of his heart and mind and soul beneath the feeling of such acute wretchedness. But Louis dared not even kneel in prayer to God to entreat him to terminate his bitter trial.

"Heaven is right," he said; "Heaven acts wisely. It would be cowardly to pray to Heaven for that which I have so often refused my own fellow-creatures."

He had reached this stage of his reflections, that is, of his agony of mind, when a similar noise was again heard behind his door, followed this time by the sound of the key in the lock, and of the bolts being withdrawn from their staples. The king bounded forward to be nearer to the person who was about to enter, but, suddenly reflecting that it was a movement unworthy of a sovereign, he paused, assumed a noble and calm expression, which for him was easy enough, and waited with his back turned towards the window, in order, to some extent, to conceal his agitation from the eyes of the person who was about to enter. It was only a jailer with a basket of provisions. The king looked at the man with restless anxiety, and waited until he spoke.

"Ah!" said the latter, "you have broken your chair. I said you had done so! Why, you have gone quite mad."

"Monsieur," said the king, "be careful what

you say; it will be a very serious affair for you."

The jailer placed the basket on the table, and looked at his prisoner steadily. "What do you say?" he said.

"Desire the governor to come to me," added the king, in accents full of calm and dignity.

"Come, my boy," said the turnkey, "you have always been very quiet and reasonable, but you are getting vicious, it seems, and I wish you to know it in time. You have broken your chair, and made a great disturbance; that is an offense punishable by imprisonment in one of the lower dungeons. Promise me not to begin over again, and I will not say a word about it to the governor."

"I wish to see the governor," replied the king, still governing his passions.

"He will send you off to one of the dungeons, I tell you; so take care."

"I insist upon it, do you hear?"

"Ah! ah! your eyes are becoming wild

again. Very good! I shall take away your knife."

And the jailer did what he said, quitted the prisoner, and closed the door, leaving the king more astounded, more wretched, more isolated than ever. It was useless, though he tried it, to make the same noise again on his door, and equally useless that he threw the plates and dishes out of the window; not a single sound was heard in recognition. Two hours afterwards he could not be recognized as a king, a gentleman, a man, a human being; he might rather be called a madman, tearing the door with his nails, trying to tear up the flooring of his cell, and uttering such wild and fearful cries that the old Bastile seemed to tremble to its very foundations for having revolted against its master. As for the governor, the jailer did not even think of disturbing him; the turnkeys and the sentinels had reported the occurrence to him, but what was the good of it? Were not these madmen common enough in such a prison? and were not the walls still stronger? M. de Baisemeaux, thoroughly impressed with what Aramis had told him, and in perfect conformity with the king's order, hoped only that one thing might happen; namely, that the madman Marchiali might be mad enough to hang himself to the canopy of his bed, or to one of the bars of the window. In fact, the prisoner was anything but a profitable investment for M. Baisemeaux, and became more annoying than agreeable to him. These complications of Seldon and Marchiali – the complications first of setting at liberty and then imprisoning again, the complications arising from the strong likeness in question – had at last found a very proper **denouement**. Baisemeaux even thought he had remarked that D'Herblay himself was not altogether dissatisfied with the result.

"And then, really," said Baisemeaux to his next in command, "an ordinary prisoner is already unhappy enough in being a prisoner; he suffers quite enough, indeed, to induce one to hope, charitably enough, that his death may not be far distant. With still greater reason, accordingly, when the prisoner has gone mad, and might bite and make a terrible disturbance in the Bastile; why, in such a case, it is not simply an act of mere charity to wish him dead; it would be almost a good and even commendable action, quietly to have him put out of his misery."

And the good-natured governor thereupon sat down to his late breakfast.

CHAPTER NINETEEN

The Shadow of M. Fouquet

D'ARTAGNAN, STILL CONFUSED and oppressed by the conversation he had just had with the king, could not resist asking himself if he were really in possession of his senses, if he were really and truly at Vaux; if he, D'Artagnan, were really the captain of the musketeers, and M. Fouquet the owner of the chateau in which Louis XIV. was at that moment partaking of his hospitality. These reflections were not those of a drunken man, although everything was in prodigal profusion at Vaux, and the surintendant's wines had met with a distinguished reception at the **fete**. The Gascon, however, was a man of calm self-possession; and no sooner did he touch his bright steel blade, than he knew how to adopt morally the cold, keen weapon as his guide of action.

"Well," he said, as he quitted the royal apartment, "I seem now to be mixed up historically with the destinies of the king and of the minister; it will be written, that M. d'Artagnan, a younger son of a Gascon family, placed his hand on the shoulder of M. Nicolas Fouquet, the surintendant of the finances of France. My descendants, if I have any, will flatter themselves with the distinction which this arrest will confer, just as the members of the De Luynes family have done with regard to the estates of the poor Marechal d'Ancre. But the thing is, how best to execute the king's directions in a proper manner. Any man would know how to say to M. Fouquet, 'Your sword, monsieur.' But it is not every one who would be able to take care of M. Fouquet without others knowing anything about it. How am I to manage, then, so that M. le surintendant pass from the height of favor to the direst disgrace; that Vaux be turned into a dungeon for him; that after having been steeped to his lips, as it were, in all the perfumes and incense of Ahasuerus, he is transferred to the gallows of Haman; in other words, of Enguerrand de Marigny?" And at this reflection, D'Artagnan's brow became clouded with perplexity. The musketeer had certain scruples on the matter, it must be admitted. To deliver up to death (for not a doubt existed that Louis hated Fouquet mortally) the man who had just shown himself so delightful and charming a host in every way, was a real insult to one's conscience. "It almost seems," said D'Artagnan to himself, "that if I am not a poor, mean, miserable fellow,

I should let M. Fouquet know the opinion the king has about him. Yet, if I betray my master's secret, I shall be a false-hearted, treacherous knave, a traitor, too, a crime provided for and punishable by military laws – so much so, indeed, that twenty times, in former days when wars were rife, I have seen many a miserable fellow strung up to a tree for doing, in but a small degree, what my scruples counsel me to undertake upon a great scale now. No, I think that a man of true readiness of wit ought to get out of this difficulty with more skill than that. And now, let us admit that I do possess a little readiness of invention; it is not at all certain, though, for, after having for forty years absorbed so large a quantity, I shall be lucky if there were to be a pistole's-worth left." D'Artagnan buried his head in his hands, tore at his mustache in sheer vexation, and added, "What can be the reason of M. Fouquet's disgrace? There seem to be three good ones: the first, because M. Colbert doesn't like him; the second, because he wished to fall in love with Mademoiselle de la Valliere; and lastly, because the king likes M. Colbert and loves Mademoiselle de la Valliere. Oh! he is lost! But shall I put my foot on his neck, I, of all men, when he is falling a prey to the intrigues of a pack of women and clerks? For shame! If he be dangerous, I will lay him low enough; if, however, he be only persecuted, I will look on. I have come to such a decisive determination, that neither king nor living man shall change my mind. If Athos were here, he would do as I have done. Therefore, instead of going, in cold blood, up to M. Fouquet, and arresting him off-hand and shutting him up altogether, I will try and conduct myself like a man who understands what good manners are. People will talk about it, of course; but they shall talk well of it, I am determined." And D'Artagnan, drawing by a gesture peculiar to himself his shoulder-belt over his shoulder, went straight off to M. Fouquet, who, after he had taken leave of his guests, was preparing to retire for the night and to sleep tranquilly after the triumphs of the day. The air was still perfumed, or infected, whichever way it may be considered, with the odors of the torches and the fireworks. The wax-lights were dying away in their sockets, the flowers fell unfastened from the garlands, the groups of dancers and courtiers were separating in the salons. Surrounded by his friends, who complimented him and received his flattering remarks in return, the surintendant half-closed his wearied eyes. He longed for rest and quiet; he sank upon the bed of laurels which had been heaped up for him for so many days past; it might almost have been said that he seemed bowed beneath the weight of the new debts which he had incurred for the purpose of giving the greatest possible honor to this **fete**. Fouquet had just retired to his room, still smiling, but more than half-asleep. He could listen to nothing more, he could hardly keep his eyes open; his bed seemed to possess a fascinating and irresistible attraction for him. The god Morpheus, the presiding deity of the dome painted by Lebrun, had extended his influence over the adjoining rooms, and showered down his most sleep-inducing poppies upon the master of the house. Fouquet, almost entirely alone, was being assisted by his **valet de chambre** to undress, when M. d'Artagnan appeared at the entrance of the room. D'Artagnan had never been able to succeed in making himself common at the court; and notwithstanding he was seen everywhere and on all occasions, he never failed to produce an effect wherever and whenever he made his appearance. Such is the happy privilege of certain natures, which in that respect resemble either thunder or lightning; every one recognizes them; but their appearance never fails to arouse surprise and astonishment, and whenever they occur, the impression is always left that the last was the most conspicuous or most important.

“What! M. d’Artagnan?” said Fouquet, who had already taken his right arm out of the sleeve of his doublet.

“At your service,” replied the musketeer.

“Come in, my dear M. d’Artagnan.”

“Thank you.”

“Have you come to criticise the **fete?** You are ingenious enough in your criticisms, I know.”

“By no means.”

“Are not your men looked after properly?”

“In every way.”

“You are not comfortably lodged, perhaps?”

“Nothing could be better.”

“In that case, I have to thank you for being so amiably disposed, and I must not fail to express my obligations to you for all your flattering kindness.”

These words were as much as to say, “My dear D’Artagnan, pray go to bed, since you have a bed to lie down on, and let me do the same."

D'Artagnan did not seem to understand it.

"Are you going to bed already?" he said to the superintendent.

"Yes; have you anything to say to me?"

"Nothing, monsieur, nothing at all. You sleep in this room, then?"

"Yes; as you see."

"You have given a most charming **fete** to the king."

"Do you think so?"

"Oh! beautiful!"

"Is the king pleased?"

"Enchanted."

"Did he desire you to say as much to me?"

"He would not choose so unworthy a messenger, monseigneur."

"You do not do yourself justice, Monsieur d'Artagnan."

"Is that your bed, there?"

"Yes; but why do you ask? Are you not satisfied with your own?"

"My I speak frankly to you?"

"Most assuredly."

"Well, then, I am not."

Fouquet started; and then replied, "Will you take my room, Monsieur d'Artagnan?"

"What! deprive you of it, monseigneur? never!"

"What am I to do, then?"

"Allow me to share yours with you."

Fouquet looked at the musketeer fixedly. "Ah! ah!" he said, "you have just left the king."

"I have, monseigneur."

"And the king wishes you to pass the night in my room?"

"Monseigneur – "

"Very well, Monsieur d'Artagnan, very well. You are the master here."

"I assure you, monseigneur, that I do not wish to abuse – "

Fouquet turned to his valet, and said, "Leave us." When the man had left, he said to D'Artagnan, "You have something to say to me?"

"I?"

"A man of your superior intelligence cannot have come to talk with a man like myself, at such an hour as the present, without grave motives."

"Do not interrogate me."

"On the contrary. What do you want with me?"

"Nothing more than the pleasure of your society."

"Come into the garden, then," said the superintendent suddenly, "or into the park."

"No," replied the musketeer, hastily, "no."

"Why?"

"The fresh air – "

"Come, admit at once that you arrest me," said the superintendent to the captain.

"Never!" said the latter.

"You intend to look after me, then?"

"Yes, monseigneur, I do, upon my honor."

"Upon your honor – ah! that is quite another thing! So I am to be arrested in my own house."

"Do not say such a thing."

"On the contrary, I will proclaim it aloud."

"If you do so, I shall be compelled to request you to be silent."

"Very good! Violence towards me, and in my own house, too."

"We do not seem to understand one another at all. Stay a moment; there is a chess-board there; we will have a game, if you have no objections."

"Monsieur d'Artagnan, I am in disgrace, then?"

"Not at all; but – "

"I am prohibited, I suppose, from withdrawing from your sight."

"I do not understand a word you are saying, monseigneur; and if you wish me to withdraw, tell me so."

"My dear Monsieur d'Artagnan, your mode of action is enough to drive me mad; I was almost sinking for want of sleep, but you have completely awakened me."

"I shall never forgive myself, I am sure;

and if you wish to reconcile me with myself, why, go to sleep in your bed in my presence; and I shall be delighted."

"I am under surveillance, I see."

"I will leave the room if you say any such thing."

"You are beyond my comprehension."

"Good night, monseigneur," said D'Artagnan, as he pretended to withdraw.

Fouquet ran after him. "I will not lie down," he said. "Seriously, and since you refuse to treat me as a man, and since you finesse with me, I will try and set you at bay, as a hunter does a wild boar."

"Bah!" cried D'Artagnan, pretending to smile.

"I shall order my horses, and set off for Paris," said Fouquet, sounding the captain of the musketeers.

"If that be the case, monseigneur, it is very difficult."

"You will arrest me, then?"

"No, but I shall go along with you."

"That is quite sufficient, Monsieur d'Artagnan," returned Fouquet, coldly. "It was not for nothing you acquired your reputation as a man of intelligence and resource; but with me all this is quite superfluous. Let us come to the point. Do me a service. Why do you arrest me? What have I done?"

"Oh! I know nothing about what you may have done; but I do not arrest you – this evening, at least!"

"This evening!" said Fouquet, turning pale, "but to-morrow?"

"It is not to-morrow just yet, monseigneur. Who can ever answer for the morrow?"

"Quick, quick, captain! let me speak to M. d'Herblay."

"Alas! that is quite impossible, monseigneur. I have strict orders to see that you hold no communication with any one."

"With M. d'Herblay, captain – with your friend!"

"Monseigneur, is M. d'Herblay the only

person with whom you ought to be prevented holding any communication?"

Fouquet colored, and then assuming an air of resignation, he said: "You are right, monsieur; you have taught me a lesson I ought not to have evoked. A fallen man cannot assert his right to anything, even from those whose fortunes he may have made; for a still stronger reason, he cannot claim anything from those to whom he may never have had the happiness of doing a service."

"Monseigneur!"

"It is perfectly true, Monsieur d'Artagnan; you have always acted in the most admirable manner towards me – in such a manner, indeed, as most becomes the man who is destined to arrest me. You, at least, have never asked me anything."

"Monsieur," replied the Gascon, touched by his eloquent and noble tone of grief, "will you – I ask it as a favor – pledge me your word as a man of honor that you will not leave this room?"

"What is the use of it, dear Monsieur d'Artagnan, since you keep watch and ward over me? Do you suppose I should contend against the most valiant sword in the kingdom?"

"It is not that, at all, monseigneur; but that I am going to look for M. d'Herblay, and, consequently, to leave you alone."

Fouquet uttered a cry of delight and surprise.

"To look for M. d'Herblay! to leave me alone!" he exclaimed, clasping his hands together.

"Which is M. d'Herblay's room? The blue room is it not?"

"Yes, my friend, yes."

"Your friend! thank you for that word, monseigneur; you confer it upon me to-day, at least, if you have never done so before."

"Ah! you have saved me."

"It will take a good ten minutes to go from hence to the blue room, and to return?" said

D'Artagnan.

"Nearly so."

"And then to wake Aramis, who sleeps very soundly, when he is asleep, I put that down at another five minutes; making a total of fifteen minutes' absence. And now, monseigneur, give me your word that you will not in any way attempt to make your escape, and that when I return I shall find you here again."

"I give it, monsieur," replied Fouquet, with an expression of the warmest and deepest gratitude.

D'Artagnan disappeared. Fouquet looked at him as he quitted the room, waited with a feverish impatience until the door was closed behind him, and as soon as it was shut, flew to his keys, opened two or three secret doors concealed in various articles of furniture in the room, looked vainly for certain papers, which doubtless he had left at Saint-Mande, and which he seemed to regret not having found in them; then hurriedly seizing hold of letters, contracts, papers, writings, he heaped them up into a pile, which he burnt in the extremest haste upon the marble hearth of the fireplace, not even taking time to draw from the interior of it the vases and pots of flowers with which it was filled. As soon as he had finished, like a man who has just escaped an imminent danger, and whose strength abandons him as soon as the danger is past, he sank down, completely overcome, on a couch. When D'Artagnan returned, he found Fouquet in the same position; the worthy musketeer had not the slightest doubt that Fouquet, having given his word, would not even think of failing to keep it, but he had thought it most likely that Fouquet would turn his (D'Artagnan's) absence to the best advantage in getting rid of all the papers, memorandums, and contracts, which might possibly render his position, which was even now serious enough, more dangerous than ever. And so, lifting up his head like a dog who has regained the scent, he perceived an odor resembling smoke he had relied on finding in the atmosphere, and having found it, made a movement of his head in token of satisfaction. As D'Artagnan entered, Fouquet, on his side, raised his head, and not one of D'Artagnan's movements escaped him. And then the looks of the two men met, and they both saw that they had understood each other without exchanging a syllable.

"Well!" asked Fouquet, the first to speak, "and M. d'Herblay?"

"Upon my word, monseigneur," replied D'Artagnan, "M. d'Herblay must be desperately fond of walking out at night, and composing verses by moonlight in the park of Vaux, with some of your poets, in all probability, for he is not in his own room."

"What! not in his own room?" cried Fouquet, whose last hope thus escaped him; for unless he could ascertain in what way the bishop of Vannes could assist him, he perfectly well knew that he could expect assistance from no other quarter.

"Or, indeed," continued D'Artagnan, "if he is in his own room, he has very good reasons for not answering."

"But surely you did not call him in such a manner that he could have heard you?"

"You can hardly suppose, monseigneur, that having already exceeded my orders, which forbade me leaving you a single moment – you can hardly suppose, I say, that I should have been mad enough to rouse the whole house and allow myself to be seen in the corridor of the bishop of Vannes, in order that M. Colbert might state with positive certainty that I gave you time to burn your papers."

"My papers?"

"Of course; at least that is what I should have done in your place. When any one opens a door for me I always avail myself of it."

"Yes, yes, and I thank you, for I have availed myself of it."

"And you have done perfectly right. Every man has his own peculiar secrets with which others have nothing to do. But let us return to Aramis, monseigneur."

"Well, then, I tell you, you could not have called loud enough, or Aramis would have heard you."

"However softly any one may call Aramis, monseigneur, Aramis always hears when he has an interest in hearing. I repeat what I said before – Aramis was not in his own room, or Aramis had certain reasons for not recognizing my voice, of which I am ignorant, and of which you may be even ignorant yourself, notwithstanding your liege-man is His Greatness the Lord Bishop of Vannes."

Fouquet drew a deep sigh, rose from his seat, took three or four turns in his room, and finished by seating himself, with an expression of extreme dejection, upon his magnificent bed with velvet hangings, and costliest lace. D'Artagnan looked at Fouquet with feelings of the deepest and sincerest pity.

"I have seen a good many men arrested in my life," said the musketeer, sadly; "I have seen both M. de Cinq-Mars and M. de Chalais arrested, though I was very young then. I have seen M. de Conde arrested with the princes; I have seen M. de Retz arrested; I have seen M. Broussel arrested. Stay a moment, monseigneur, it is disagreeable to have to say, but the very one of all those whom you most resemble at this moment was that poor fellow Broussel. You were very near doing as he did, putting your dinner napkin in your portfolio, and wiping your mouth with your papers. **Mordioux!** Monseigneur Fouquet, a man like you ought not to be dejected in this manner. Suppose your friends saw you?"

"Monsieur d'Artagnan," returned the

surintendant, with a smile full of gentleness, "you do not understand me; it is precisely because my friends are not looking on, that I am as you see me now. I do not live, exist even, isolated from others; I am nothing when left to myself. Understand that throughout my whole life I have passed every moment of my time in making friends, whom I hoped to render my stay and support. In times of prosperity, all these cheerful, happy voices – rendered so through and by my means – formed in my honor a concert of praise and kindly actions. In the least disfavor, these humbler voices accompanied in harmonious accents the murmur of my own heart. Isolation I have never yet known. Poverty (a phantom I have sometimes beheld, clad in rags, awaiting me at the end of my journey through life) – poverty has been the specter with which many of my own friends have trifled for years past, which they poetize and caress, and which has attracted me towards them. Poverty! I accept it, acknowledge it, receive it, as a disinherited sister; for poverty is neither solitude, nor exile, nor imprisonment. Is it likely I shall ever be poor, with such friends as Pelisson, as La Fontaine, as Moliere? with such a mistress as – Oh! if you knew how utterly lonely and desolate I feel at this moment, and how you, who separate me from all I love, seem to resemble the image of solitude, of annihilation – death itself."

"But I have already told you, Monsieur Fouquet," replied D'Artagnan, moved to the depths of his soul, "that you are woefully exaggerating. The king likes you."

"No, no," said Fouquet, shaking his head.

"M. Colbert hates you."

"M. Colbert! What does that matter to me?"

"He will ruin you."

"Ah! I defy him to do that, for I am ruined already."

At this singular confession of the superintendent, D'Artagnan cast his glance all round the room; and although he did not open his lips, Fouquet understood him so thoroughly, that he added: "What can be done with such wealth of substance as surrounds us, when a man can no longer cultivate his taste for the magnificent? Do you know what good the greater part of the wealth and the possessions which we rich enjoy, confer upon us? merely to disgust us, by their very splendor even, with everything which does not equal it! Vaux! you will say, and the wonders of Vaux! What of it? What boot these wonders? If I am ruined, how shall I fill with water the urns which my Naiads bear in their arms, or force the air into the lungs of my Tritons? To be rich enough, Monsieur d'Artagnan, a man must be too rich."

D'Artagnan shook his head.

"Oh! I know very well what you think," replied Fouquet, quickly. "If Vaux were yours, you would sell it, and would purchase an estate in the country; an estate which should have woods, orchards, and land attached, so that the estate should be made to support its master. With forty millions you might – "

"Ten millions," interrupted D'Artagnan.

"Not a million, my dear captain. No one in France is rich enough to give two millions for Vaux, and to continue to maintain it as I have done; no one could do it, no one would know how."

"Well," said D'Artagnan, "in any case, a million is not abject misery."

"It is not far from it, my dear monsieur. But you do not understand me. No; I will not sell my residence at Vaux; I will give it to you, if you like;" and Fouquet accompanied these words with a movement of the shoulders to which it would be impossible to do justice.

"Give it to the king; you will make a better bargain."

"The king does not require me to give it to him," said Fouquet; "he will take it away from me with the most absolute ease and grace, if it pleases him to do so; and that is the very reason I should prefer to see it perish. Do you know, Monsieur d'Artagnan, that if the king did not happen to be under my roof, I would take this candle, go straight to the dome, and set fire to a couple of huge chests of fusees and fireworks which are in reserve there, and would reduce my palace to ashes."

"Bah!" said the musketeer, negligently. "At all events, you would not be able to burn the gardens, and that is the finest feature of the place."

"And yet," resumed Fouquet, thoughtfully, "what was I saying? Great heavens! burn Vaux! destroy my palace! But Vaux is not mine; these wonderful creations are, it is true, the property, as far as sense of enjoyment goes, of the man who has paid for them; but as far as duration is concerned, they belong to those who created them. Vaux belongs to Lebrun, to Lenotre, to Pelisson, to Levau, to La Fontaine, to Moliere; Vaux belongs to posterity, in fact. You see, Monsieur d'Artagnan, that my very house has ceased to be my own."

"That is all well and good," said D'Artagnan; "the idea is agreeable enough, and I recognize M. Fouquet himself in it. That idea, indeed, makes me forget that poor fellow Broussel altogether; and I now fail to recognize in you the whining complaints of that old Frondeur. If you are ruined, monsieur, look at the affair manfully, for you too, **mordioux!** belong to posterity, and have no right to lessen yourself in any way. Stay a moment; look at me, I who seem to exercise in some degree a kind of superiority over you, because I am arresting you; fate, which distributes their different parts to the comedians of this world, accorded me a less agreeable and less advantageous part to fill than yours has been. I am one of those who think that the parts which kings and powerful nobles are called upon to act are infinitely of more worth than the parts of beggars or lackeys. It is far better on the stage – on the stage,

I mean, of another theater than the theater of this world – it is far better to wear a fine coat and to talk a fine language, than to walk the boards shod with a pair of old shoes, or to get one's backbone gently polished by a hearty dressing with a stick. In one word, you have been a prodigal with money, you have ordered and been obeyed – have been steeped to the lips in enjoyment; while I have dragged my tether after me, have been commanded and have obeyed, and have drudged my life away. Well, although I may seem of such trifling importance beside you, monseigneur, I do declare to you, that the recollection of what I have done serves me as a spur, and prevents me from bowing my old head too soon. I shall remain unto the very end a trooper; and when my turn comes, I shall fall perfectly straight, all in a heap, still alive, after having selected my place beforehand. Do as I do, Monsieur Fouquet, you will not find yourself the worse for it; a fall happens only once in a lifetime to men like yourself, and the chief thing is, to take it gracefully when the chance presents itself. There is a Latin proverb – the words have escaped me, but I remember the sense of it very well, for I have thought over it more than once – which says, 'The end crowns the work!'"

Fouquet rose from his seat, passed his arm round D'Artagnan's neck, and clasped him in a close embrace, whilst with the other hand he pressed his hand. "An excellent homily," he said, after a moment's pause.

"A soldier's, monseigneur."

"You have a regard for me, in telling me all that."

"Perhaps."

Fouquet resumed his pensive attitude once more, and then, a moment after, he said: "Where can M. d'Herblay be? I dare not ask you to send for him."

"You would not ask me, because I would not do it, Monsieur Fouquet. People would learn it, and Aramis, who is not mixed up with the affair, might possibly be compromised and included in your disgrace."

"I will wait here till daylight," said Fouquet.

"Yes; that is best."

"What shall we do when daylight comes?"

"I know nothing at all about it, monseigneur."

"Monsieur d'Artagnan, will you do me a favor?"

"Most willingly."

"You guard me, I remain; you are acting in the full discharge of your duty, I suppose?"

"Certainly."

"Very good, then; remain as close to me as my shadow if you like; and I infinitely prefer such a shadow to any one else."

D'Artagnan bowed to the compliment.

"But, forget that you are Monsieur d'Artagnan, captain of the musketeers; forget that I am Monsieur Fouquet, surintendant of the finances; and let us talk about my affairs."

"That is rather a delicate subject."

"Indeed?"

"Yes; but, for your sake, Monsieur Fouquet, I will do what may almost be regarded as an impossibility."

"Thank you. What did the king say to you?"

"Nothing."

"Ah! is that the way you talk?"

"The deuce!"

"What do you think of my situation?"

"I do not know."

"However, unless you have some ill feeling against me – "

"Your position is a difficult one."

"In what respect?"

"Because you are under your own roof."

"However difficult it may be, I understand it very well."

"Do you suppose that, with any one else but yourself, I should have shown so much frankness?"

"What! so much frankness, do you say? you, who refuse to tell me the slightest thing?"

"At all events, then, so much ceremony

and consideration."

"Ah! I have nothing to say in that respect."

"One moment, monseigneur: let me tell you how I should have behaved towards any one but yourself. It might be that I happened to arrive at your door just as your guests or your friends had left you – or, if they had not gone yet, I should wait until they were leaving, and should then catch them one after the other, like rabbits; I should lock them up quietly enough, I should steal softly along the carpet of your corridor, and with one hand upon you, before you suspected the slightest thing amiss, I should keep you safely until my master's breakfast in the morning. In this way, I should just the same have avoided all publicity, all disturbance, all opposition; but there would also have been no warning for M. Fouquet, no consideration for his feelings, none of those delicate concessions which are shown by persons who are essentially courteous in their natures, whenever the decisive moment may arrive. Are you satisfied with the plan?"

"It makes me shudder."

"I thought you would not like it. It would have been very disagreeable to have made my appearance to-morrow, without any preparation, and to have asked you to deliver up your sword."

"Oh! monsieur, I should have died of shame and anger."

"Your gratitude is too eloquently expressed. I have not done enough to deserve it, I assure you."

"Most certainly, monsieur, you will never get me to believe that."

"Well, then, monseigneur, if you are satisfied with what I have done, and have somewhat recovered from the shock which I prepared you for as much as I possibly could, let us allow the few hours that remain to pass away undisturbed. You are harassed, and should arrange your thoughts; I beg you, therefore, go to sleep, or pretend to go to sleep, either on your bed, or in your bed; I will sleep in this armchair; and when I fall asleep, my rest is so sound that a cannon would not wake me."

Fouquet smiled. "I expect, however," continued the musketeer, "the case of a door being opened, whether a secret door, or any other; or the case of any one going out of, or coming into, the room – for anything like that my ear is as quick and sensitive as the ear of a mouse. Creaking noises make me start. It arises, I suppose, from a natural antipathy to anything of the kind. Move about as much as you like; walk up and down in any part of the room, write, efface, destroy, burn, – nothing like that will prevent me from going to sleep or even prevent me from snoring, but do not touch either the key or the handle of the door, for I should start up in a moment, and that would shake my nerves and make me ill."

"Monsieur d'Artagnan," said Fouquet, "you are certainly the most witty and the most courteous man I ever met with; and you will leave me only one regret, that of having made your acquaintance so late."

D'Artagnan drew a deep sigh, which seemed to say, "Alas! you have perhaps made it too soon." He then settled himself in his armchair, while Fouquet, half lying on his bed and leaning on his arm, was meditating on his misadventures. In this way, both of them, leaving the candles burning, awaited the first dawn of the day; and when Fouquet happened to sigh too loudly, D'Artagnan only snored the louder. Not a single visit, not even from Aramis, disturbed their quietude: not a sound even was heard throughout the whole vast palace. Outside, however, the guards of honor on duty, and the patrol of musketeers, paced up and down; and the sound of their feet could be heard on the gravel walks. It seemed to act as an additional soporific for the sleepers, while the murmuring of the wind through the trees, and the unceasing music of the fountains whose waters tumbled in the basin, still went on uninterruptedly, without being disturbed at the slight noises and items of little moment that constitute the life and death of human nature.

CHAPTER TWENTY

The Morning

IN VIVID CONTRAST TO the sad and terrible destiny of the king imprisoned in the Bastile, and tearing, in sheer despair, the bolts and bars of his dungeon, the rhetoric of the chroniclers of old would not fail to present, as a complete antithesis, the picture of Philippe lying asleep beneath the royal canopy. We do not pretend to say that such rhetoric is always bad, and always scatters, in places where they have no right to grow, the flowers with which it embellishes and enlivens history. But we shall, on the present occasion, carefully avoid polishing the antithesis in question, but shall proceed to draw another picture as minutely as possible, to serve as foil and counterfoil to the one in the preceding chapter. The young prince alighted from Aramis's room, in the same way the king had descended from the apartment dedicated to Morpheus. The dome gradually and slowly sank down under Aramis's pressure, and Philippe stood beside the royal bed, which had ascended again after having deposited its prisoner in the secret depths of the subterranean passage. Alone, in the presence of all the luxury which surrounded him; alone, in the presence of his power; alone, with the part he was about to be forced to act, Philippe for the first time felt his heart, and mind, and soul expand beneath the influence of a thousand mutable emotions, which are the vital throbs of a king's heart. He could not help changing color when he looked upon the empty bed, still tumbled by his brother's body. This mute accomplice had returned, after having completed the work it had been destined to perform; it returned with the traces of the crime; it spoke to the guilty author of that crime, with the frank and unreserved language which an accomplice never fears to use in the company of his companion in guilt; for it spoke the truth. Philippe bent over the bed, and perceived a pocket-handkerchief lying on it, which was still damp from the cold sweat which had poured from Louis XIV.'s face. This sweat-bestained handkerchief terrified Philippe, as the gore of Abel frightened Cain.

"I am face to face with my destiny," said Philippe, his eyes on fire, and his face a livid white. "Is it likely to be more terrifying than my captivity has been sad and gloomy?

Though I am compelled to follow out, at every moment, the sovereign power and authority I have usurped, shall I cease to listen to the scruples of my heart? Yes! the king has lain on this bed; it is indeed his head that has left its impression on this pillow; his bitter tears that have stained this handkerchief: and yet, I hesitate to throw myself on the bed, or to press in my hand the handkerchief which is embroidered with my brother's arms. Away with such weakness; let me imitate M. d'Herblay, who asserts that a man's action should be always one degree above his thoughts; let me imitate M. d'Herblay, whose thoughts are of and for himself alone, who regards himself as a man of honor, so long as he injures or betrays his enemies only. I, I alone, should have occupied this bed, if Louis XIV. had not, owing to my mother's criminal abandonment, stood in my way; and this handkerchief, embroidered with the arms of France, would in right and justice belong to me alone, if, as M. d'Herblay observes, I had been left my royal cradle. Philippe, son of France, take your place on that bed; Philippe, sole king of France, resume the blazonry that is yours! Philippe, sole heir presumptive to Louis XIII., your father, show yourself without pity or mercy for the usurper who, at this moment, has not even to suffer the agony of the remorse of all that you have had to submit to."

With these words, Philippe, notwithstanding an instinctive repugnance of feeling, and in spite of the shudder of terror which mastered his will, threw himself on the royal bed, and forced his muscles to press the still warm place where Louis XIV. had lain, while he buried his burning face in the handkerchief still moistened by his brother's tears. With his head thrown back and buried in the soft down of his pillow, Philippe perceived above him the crown of France, suspended, as we have stated, by angels with outspread golden wings.

A man may be ambitious of lying in a lion's den, but can hardly hope to sleep there quietly. Philippe listened attentively to every sound; his heart panted and throbbed at the very suspicion of approaching terror and misfortune; but confident in his own strength, which was confirmed by the force of an overpoweringly resolute determination, he waited until some decisive circumstance should permit him to judge for himself. He hoped that imminent danger might be revealed to him, like those phosphoric lights of the tempest which show the sailors the altitude of the waves against which they have to struggle. But nothing approached. Silence, that mortal enemy of restless hearts, and of ambitious minds, shrouded in the thickness of its gloom during the remainder of the night the future king of France, who lay there sheltered beneath his stolen crown. Towards the morning a shadow, rather than a body, glided into the royal chamber; Philippe expected his approach and neither expressed nor exhibited any surprise.

"Well, M. d'Herblay?"

"Well, sire, all is accomplished."

"How?"

"Exactly as we expected."

"Did he resist?"

"Terribly! tears and entreaties."

"And then?"

"A perfect stupor."

"But at last?"

"Oh! at last, a complete victory, and absolute silence."

"Did the governor of the Bastile suspect anything?"

"Nothing."

"The resemblance, however – "

"Was the cause of the success."

"But the prisoner cannot fail to explain himself. Think well of that. I have myself been able to do as much as that, on former occasion."

"I have already provided for every chance. In a few days, sooner if necessary, we will take the captive out of his prison, and will send him out of the country, to a place of exile so remote – "

"People can return from their exile, Monsieur d'Herblay."

"To a place of exile so distant, I was going to say, that human strength and the duration of human life would not be enough for his return."

Once more a cold look of intelligence passed between Aramis and the young king.

"And M. du Vallon?" asked Philippe in order to change the conversation.

"He will be presented to you to-day, and confidentially will congratulate you on the danger which that conspirator has made you run."

"What is to be done with him?"

"With M. du Vallon?"

"Yes; confer a dukedom on him, I suppose."

"A dukedom," replied Aramis, smiling in a significant manner.

"Why do you laugh, Monsieur d'Herblay?"

"I laugh at the extreme caution of your idea."

"Cautious, why so?"

"Your majesty is doubtless afraid that poor Porthos may possible become a troublesome witness, and you wish to get rid of him."

"What! in making him a duke?"

"Certainly; you would assuredly kill him, for he would die from joy, and the secret would die with him."

"Good heavens!"

"Yes," said Aramis, phlegmatically; "I should lose a very good friend."

At this moment, and in the middle of this idle conversation, under the light tone of which the two conspirators concealed their joy and pride at their mutual success, Aramis heard something which made him prick up his ears.

"What is that?" said Philippe.

"The dawn, sire."

"Well?"

"Well, before you retired to bed last night, you probably decided to do something this morning at break of day."

"Yes, I told my captain of the musketeers," replied the young man hurriedly, "that I should expect him."

"If you told him that, he will certainly be here, for he is a most punctual man."

"I hear a step in the vestibule."

"It must be he."

"Come, let us begin the attack," said the young king resolutely.

"Be cautious for Heaven's sake. To begin the attack, and with D'Artagnan, would be madness. D'Artagnan knows nothing, he has seen nothing; he is a hundred miles from suspecting our mystery in the slightest degree, but if he comes into this room the first this morning, he will be sure to detect something of what has taken place, and which he would imagine it his business to occupy himself about. Before we allow D'Artagnan to penetrate into this room, we must air the room thoroughly, or introduce so many people into it, that the keenest scent in the whole kingdom may be deceived by the traces of twenty different persons."

"But how can I send him away, since I have given him a rendezvous?" observed the prince, impatient to measure swords with so redoubtable an antagonist.

"I will take care of that," replied the bishop, "and in order to begin, I am going to strike a blow which will completely stupefy our man."

"He, too, is striking a blow, for I hear him at the door," added the prince, hurriedly.

And, in fact, a knock at the door was heard at that moment. Aramis was not mistaken; for it was indeed D'Artagnan who adopted that mode of announcing himself.

We have seen how he passed the night in philosophizing with M. Fouquet, but the musketeer was very weary even of feigning to fall asleep, and as soon as earliest dawn illumined with its gloomy gleams of light the sumptuous cornices of the superintendent's room, D'Artagnan rose from his armchair, arranged his sword, brushed his coat and hat with his sleeve, like a private soldier getting ready for inspection.

"Are you going out?" said Fouquet.

"Yes, monseigneur. And you?"

"I shall remain."

"You pledge your word?"

"Certainly."

"Very good. Besides, my only reason for going out is to try and get that reply, – you know what I mean?"

"That sentence, you mean – "

"Stay, I have something of the old Roman in me. This morning, when I got up, I remarked that my sword had got caught in one of the **aiguillettes**, and that my shoulder-belt had slipped quite off. That is an infallible sign."

"Of prosperity?"

"Yes, be sure of it; for every time that that confounded belt of mine stuck fast to my back, it always signified a punishment from M. de Treville, or a refusal of money by M. de Mazarin. Every time my sword hung fast to my shoulder-belt, it always predicted some disagreeable commission or another for me to execute, and I have had showers of them all my life through. Every time, too, my sword danced about in its sheath, a duel, fortunate in its result, was sure to follow: whenever it dangled about the calves of my legs, it signified a slight wound; every time it fell completely out of the scabbard, I was booked, and made up my mind that I should have to remain on the field of battle, with two or three months under surgical bandages into the bargain."

"I did not know your sword kept you so well informed," said Fouquet, with a faint smile, which showed how he was struggling against his own weakness. "Is your sword bewitched, or under the influence of some imperial charm?"

"Why, you must know that my sword may almost be regarded as part of my own body. I have heard that certain men seem to have warnings given them by feeling something the matter with their legs, or a throbbing of their temples. With me, it is my sword that warns me. Well, it told me of nothing this morning. But, stay a moment – look here, it has just fallen of its own accord into the last hole of the belt. Do you know what that is a warning of?"

"No."

"Well, that tells me of an arrest that will have to be made this very day."

"Well," said the surintendant, more astonished than annoyed by this frankness, "if there is nothing disagreeable predicted to you by your sword, I am to conclude that it is not disagreeable for you to arrest me."

"You! arrest **you!**"

"Of course. The warning – "

"Does not concern you, since you have been arrested ever since yesterday. It is not you I shall have to arrest, be assured of that. That is the reason why I am delighted, and also the reason why I said that my day will be a happy one."

And with these words, pronounced with the most affectionate graciousness of manner, the captain took leave of Fouquet in order to wait upon the king. He was on the point of leaving the room, when Fouquet said to him, "One last mark of kindness."

"What is it, monseigneur?"

"M. d'Herblay; let me see Monsieur d'Herblay."

"I am going to try and get him to come to you."

D'Artagnan did not think himself so good a prophet. It was written that the day would pass away and realize all the predictions that had been made in the morning. He had accordingly knocked, as we have seen, at the king's door. The door opened. The captain thought that it was the king who had just opened it himself; and this supposition was not altogether inadmissible, considering the state of agitation in which he had left Louis XIV. the previous evening; but instead of his royal master, whom he was on the point of saluting with the greatest respect, he perceived the long, calm features of Aramis. So extreme was his surprise that he could hardly refrain from uttering a loud exclamation. "Aramis!" he said.

"Good morning, dear D'Artagnan," replied the prelate, coldly.

"You here!" stammered out the musketeer.

"His majesty desires you to report that he is still sleeping, after having been greatly fatigued during the whole night."

"Ah!" said D'Artagnan, who could not understand how the bishop of Vannes, who had been so indifferent a favorite the previous evening, had become in half a dozen hours the most magnificent mushroom of fortune that had ever sprung up in a sovereign's bedroom. In fact, to transmit the orders of the king even to the mere threshold of that monarch's room, to serve as an intermediary of Louis XIV. so as to be able to give a single order in his name at a couple paces from him, he must have become more than Richelieu had ever been to Louis XIII. D'Artagnan's expressive eye, half-opened lips, his curling mustache, said as much indeed in the plainest language to the chief favorite, who remained calm and perfectly unmoved.

"Moreover," continued the bishop, "you will be good enough, monsieur le capitaine des mousquetaires, to allow those only to pass into the king's room this morning who have special permission. His majesty does not wish to be disturbed just yet."

"But," objected D'Artagnan, almost on the point of refusing to obey this order, and particularly of giving unrestrained passage to the suspicions which the king's silence had aroused – "but, monsieur l'eveque, his majesty gave me a rendezvous for this morning."

"Later, later," said the king's voice, from the bottom of the alcove; a voice which made a cold shudder pass through the musketeer's veins. He bowed, amazed, confused, and stupefied by the smile with which Aramis seemed to overwhelm him, as soon as these words had been pronounced.

"And then," continued the bishop, "as an answer to what you were coming to ask the king, my dear D'Artagnan, here is an order of his majesty, which you will be good enough to attend to forthwith, for it concerns M. Fouquet."

D'Artagnan took the order which was held out to him. "To be set at liberty!" he murmured. "Ah!" and he uttered a second "ah!" still more full of intelligence than the former; for this order explained Aramis's presence with the king, and that Aramis, in order to have obtained Fouquet's pardon, must have made considerable progress in the royal favor, and that this favor explained, in its tenor, the hardly conceivable assurance with which M. d'Herblay issued the order in the king's name. For D'Artagnan it was quite sufficient to have understood something of the matter in hand to order to understand the rest. He bowed and withdrew a couple of paces, as though he were about to leave.

"I am going with you," said the bishop.

"Where to?"

"To M. Fouquet; I wish to be a witness of his delight."

"Ah! Aramis, how you puzzled me just now!" said D'Artagnan again.

"But you understand **now**, I suppose?"

"Of course I understand," he said aloud; but added in a low tone to himself, almost hissing the words between his teeth, "No, no, I do not understand yet. But it is all the same, for here is the order for it." And then he added, "I will lead the way, monseigneur," and he conducted Aramis to Fouquet's apartments.

CHAPTER TWENTY ONE

The King's Friend

FOUQUET WAS WAITING WITH anxiety; he had already sent away many of his servants and friends, who, anticipating the usual hour of his ordinary receptions, had called at his door to inquire after him. Preserving the utmost silence respecting the danger which hung suspended by a hair above his head, he only asked them, as he did every one, indeed, who came to the door, where

Aramis was. When he saw D'Artagnan return, and when he perceived the bishop of Vannes behind him, he could hardly restrain his delight; it was fully equal to his previous uneasiness. The mere sight of Aramis was a complete compensation to the surintendant for the unhappiness he had undergone in his arrest. The prelate was silent and grave; D'Artagnan completely bewildered by such an accumulation of events.

"Well, captain, so you have brought M. d'Herblay to me."

"And something better still, monseigneur."

"What is that?"

"Liberty."

"I am free!"

"Yes; by the king's order."

Fouquet resumed his usual serenity, that he might interrogate Aramis with a look.

"Oh! yes, you can thank M. l'eveque de Vannes," pursued D'Artagnan, "for it is indeed to him that you owe the change that has taken place in the king."

"Oh!" said Fouquet, more humiliated at the service than grateful at its success.

"But you," continued D'Artagnan, addressing Aramis – "you, who have become M. Fouquet's protector and patron, can you not do something for me?"

"Anything in the wide world you like, my friend," replied the bishop, in his calmest tones.

"One thing only, then, and I shall be perfectly satisfied. How on earth did you manage to become the favorite of the king, you who have never spoken to him more than twice in your life?"

"From a friend such as you are," said Aramis, "I cannot conceal anything."

"Ah! very good, tell me, then."

"Very well. You think that I have seen the king only twice, whilst the fact is I have seen him more than a hundred times; only we have kept it very secret, that is all." And without trying to remove the color which at this revelation made D'Artagnan's face flush scarlet, Aramis turned towards M. Fouquet, who was as much surprised as the musketeer. "Monseigneur," he resumed, "the king desires me to inform you that he is more than ever your friend, and that your beautiful **fete**, so generously offered by you on his behalf, has touched him to the very heart."

And thereupon he saluted M. Fouquet with so much reverence of manner, that the latter, incapable of understanding a man whose diplomacy was of so prodigious a character, remained incapable of uttering a single syllable, and equally incapable of thought or movement. D'Artagnan fancied he perceived that these two men had something to say to each other, and he was about to yield to that feeling of instinctive politeness which in such a case hurries a man towards the door, when he feels his presence is an inconvenience for others; but his eager curiosity, spurred on by so many mysteries, counseled him to remain.

Aramis thereupon turned towards him, and said, in a quiet tone, “You will not forget, my friend, the king’s order respecting those whom he intends to receive this morning on rising.” These words were clear enough, and the musketeer understood them; he therefore bowed to Fouquet, and then to Aramis, – to the latter with a slight admixture of ironical respect, – and disappeared.

No sooner had he left, than Fouquet, whose impatience had hardly been able to wait for that moment, darted towards the door to close it, and then returning to the bishop, he said, “My dear D’Herblay, I think it now high time you should explain all that has passed, for, in plain and honest truth, I do not understand anything.”

“We will explain all that to you,” said Aramis, sitting down, and making Fouquet sit down also. “Where shall I begin?”

“With this first of all. Why does the king set me at liberty?”

“You ought rather to ask me what his

reason was for having you arrested."

"Since my arrest, I have had time to think over it, and my idea is that it arises out of some slight feeling of jealousy. My **fete** put M. Colbert out of temper, and M. Colbert discovered some cause of complaint against me; Belle-Isle, for instance."

"No; there is no question at all just now of Belle-Isle."

"What is it, then?"

"Do you remember those receipts for thirteen millions which M. de Mazarin contrived to steal from you?"

"Yes, of course!"

"Well, you are pronounced a public robber."

"Good heavens!"

"Oh! that is not all. Do you also remember that letter you wrote to La Valliere?"

"Alas! yes."

"And that proclaims you a traitor and a suborner."

"Why should he have pardoned me, then?"

"We have not yet arrived at that part of our

argument. I wish you to be quite convinced of the fact itself. Observe this well: the king knows you to be guilty of an appropriation of public funds. Oh! of course I know that you have done nothing of the kind; but, at all events, the king has seen the receipts, and he can do no other than believe you are incriminated."

"I beg your pardon, I do not see – "

"You will see presently, though. The king, moreover, having read your love-letter to La Valliere, and the offers you there made her, cannot retain any doubt of your intentions with regard to that young lady; you will admit that, I suppose?"

"Certainly. Pray conclude."

"In the fewest words. The king, we may henceforth assume, is your powerful, implacable, and eternal enemy."

"Agreed. But am I, then, so powerful, that he has not dared to sacrifice me, notwithstanding his hatred, with all the means which my weakness, or my misfortunes, may have given him as a hold upon me?"

"It is clear, beyond all doubt," pursued Aramis, coldly, "that the king has quarreled with you – irreconcilably."

"But, since he has absolved me – "

"Do you believe it likely?" asked the bishop, with a searching look.

"Without believing in his sincerity, I believe it in the accomplished fact."

Aramis slightly shrugged his shoulders.

"But why, then, should Louis XIV. have commissioned you to tell me what you have just stated?"

"The king charged me with no message for you."

"With nothing!" said the superintendent, stupefied. "But, that order – "

"Oh! yes. You are quite right. There **is** an order, certainly;" and these words were pronounced by Aramis in so strange a tone, that Fouquet could not resist starting.

"You are concealing something from me, I

see. What is it?"

Aramis softly rubbed his white fingers over his chin, but said nothing.

"Does the king exile me?"

"Do not act as if you were playing at the game children play at when they have to try and guess where a thing has been hidden, and are informed, by a bell being rung, when they are approaching near to it, or going away from it."

"Speak, then."

"Guess."

"You alarm me."

"Bah! that is because you have not guessed, then."

"What did the king say to you? In the name of our friendship, do not deceive me."

"The king has not said one word to me."

"You are killing me with impatience, D'Herblay. Am I still superintendent?"

"As long as you like."

"But what extraordinary empire have you so suddenly acquired over his majesty's mind?"

"Ah! that's the point."

"He does your bidding?"

"I believe so."

"It is hardly credible."

"So any one would say."

"D'Herblay, by our alliance, by our friendship, by everything you hold dearest in the world, speak openly, I implore you. By what means have you succeeded in overcoming Louis XIV.'s prejudices, for he did not like you, I am certain."

"The king will like me **now**," said Aramis, laying stress upon the last word.

"You have something particular, then, between you?"

"Yes."

"A secret, perhaps?"

"A secret."

"A secret of such a nature as to change his majesty's interests?"

"You are, indeed, a man of superior intelligence, monseigneur, and have made a particularly accurate guess. I have, in fact, discovered a secret, of a nature to change the interests of the king of France."

"Ah!" said Fouquet, with the reserve of a man who does not wish to ask any more questions.

"And you shall judge of it yourself," pursued Aramis; "and you shall tell me if I am mistaken with regard to the importance of this secret."

"I am listening, since you are good enough to unbosom yourself to me; only do not forget that I have asked you about nothing which it may be indiscreet in you to communicate."

Aramis seemed, for a moment, as if he were collecting himself.

"Do not speak!" said Fouquet: "there is still time enough."

"Do you remember," said the bishop, casting down his eyes, "the birth of Louis XIV.?"

"As if it were yesterday."

"Have you ever heard anything particular

respecting his birth?"

"Nothing; except that the king was not really the son of Louis XIII."

"That does not matter to us, or the kingdom either; he is the son of his father, says the French law, whose father is recognized by law."

"True; but it is a grave matter, when the quality of races is called into question."

"A merely secondary question, after all. So that, in fact, you have never learned or heard anything in particular?"

"Nothing."

"That is where my secret begins. The queen, you must know, instead of being delivered of a son, was delivered of twins."

Fouquet looked up suddenly as he replied:

"And the second is dead?"

"You will see. These twins seemed likely to be regarded as the pride of their mother, and the hope of France; but the weak nature of the king, his superstitious feelings, made him apprehend a series of conflicts between two children whose rights were equal; so he put out of the way – he suppressed – one of the twins."

"Suppressed, do you say?"

"Have patience. Both the children grew up; the one on the throne, whose minister you are – the other, who is my friend, in gloom and isolation."

"Good heavens! What are you saying, Monsieur d'Herblay? And what is this poor prince doing?"

"Ask me, rather, what has he done."

"Yes, yes."

"He was brought up in the country, and then thrown into a fortress which goes by the name of the Bastile."

"Is it possible?" cried the surintendant, clasping his hands.

"The one was the most fortunate of men: the other the most unhappy and miserable of all living beings."

"Does his mother not know this?"

"Anne of Austria knows it all."

"And the king?"

"Knows absolutely nothing."

"So much the better," said Fouquet.

This remark seemed to make a great impression on Aramis; he looked at Fouquet with the most anxious expression of countenance.

"I beg your pardon; I interrupted you," said Fouquet.

"I was saying," resumed Aramis, "that this poor prince was the unhappiest of human beings, when Heaven, whose thoughts are over all His creatures, undertook to come to his assistance."

"Oh! in what way? Tell me."

"You will see. The reigning king – I say the reigning king – you can guess very well why?"

"No. Why?"

"Because **both** of them, being legitimate princes, ought to have been kings. Is not that your opinion?"

"It is, certainly."

"Unreservedly?"

"Most unreservedly; twins are one person in two bodies."

"I am pleased that a legist of your learning and authority should have pronounced such an opinion. It is agreed, then, that each of them possessed equal rights, is it not?"

"Incontestably! but, gracious heavens, what an extraordinary circumstance!"

"We are not at the end of it yet. – Patience."

"Oh! I shall find 'patience' enough."

"Heaven wished to raise up for that oppressed child an avenger, or a supporter, or vindicator, if you prefer it. It happened that the reigning king, the usurper – you are quite of my opinion, I believe, that it is an act of usurpation quietly to enjoy, and selfishly to assume the right over, an inheritance to which a man has only half a right?"

"Yes, usurpation is the word."

"In that case, I continue. It was Heaven's will that the usurper should possess, in the person of his first minister, a man of great talent, of large and generous nature."

"Well, well," said Fouquet, "I understand you; you have relied upon me to repair the wrong which has been done to this unhappy brother of Louis XIV. You have thought well; I will help you. I thank you, D'Herblay, I thank you."

"Oh, no, it is not that at all; you have not allowed me to finish," said Aramis, perfectly unmoved.

"I will not say another word, then."

"M. Fouquet, I was observing, the minister of the reigning sovereign, was suddenly taken into the greatest aversion, and menaced with the ruin of his fortune, loss of liberty, loss of life even, by intrigue and personal hatred, to which the king gave too readily an attentive ear. But Heaven permits (still, however, out of consideration for the unhappy prince who had been sacrificed) that M. Fouquet should in his turn have a devoted friend who knew this state secret, and felt that he possessed strength and courage enough to divulge this secret, after having had the strength to carry it locked up in his own heart for twenty years.

"Go no farther," said Fouquet, full of generous feelings. "I understand you, and can guess everything now. You went to see the king when the intelligence of my arrest reached you; you implored him, he refused to listen to you; then you threatened him with that secret, threatened to reveal it, and Louis XIV., alarmed at the risk of its betrayal, granted to the terror of your indiscretion what he refused to your generous intercession. I understand, I understand; you have the king in your power; I understand."

"You understand **nothing** – as yet," replied Aramis, "and again you interrupt me. Then, too, allow me to observe that you pay no attention to logical reasoning, and seem to forget what you ought most to remember."

"What do you mean?"

"You know upon what I laid the greatest stress at the beginning of our conversation?"

"Yes, his majesty's hate, invincible hate for me; yes, but what feeling of hate could resist the threat of such a revelation?"

"Such a revelation, do you say? that is the very point where your logic fails you. What! do you suppose that if I had made such a revelation to the king, I should have been alive now?"

"It is not ten minutes ago that you were with the king."

"That may be. He might not have had the time to get me killed outright, but he would have had the time to get me gagged and thrown in a dungeon. Come, come, show a little consistency in your reasoning, **mordieu!**"

And by the mere use of this word, which was so thoroughly his old musketeer's expression, forgotten by one who never seemed to forget anything, Fouquet could not but understand to what a pitch of exaltation the calm, impenetrable bishop of Vannes had wrought himself. He shuddered.

"And then," replied the latter, after having mastered his feelings, "should I be the man I really am, should I be the true friend you believe me, if I were to expose you, whom the king already hates so bitterly, to a feeling more than ever to be dreaded in that young man? To have robbed him, is nothing; to have addressed the woman he loves, is not much; but to hold in your keeping both his crown and his honor, why, he would pluck out your heart with his own hands."

"You have not allowed him to penetrate your secret, then?"

"I would sooner, far sooner, have swallowed at one draught all the poisons that Mithridates drank in twenty years, in order to try and avoid death, than have betrayed my secret to the king."

"What have you done, then?"

"Ah! now we are coming to the point, monseigneur. I think I shall not fail to excite in you a little interest. You are listening, I hope."

"How can you ask me if I am listening? Go on."

Aramis walked softly all round the room, satisfied himself that they were alone, and that all was silent, and then returned and placed himself close to the armchair in which Fouquet was seated, awaiting with the deepest anxiety the revelation he had to make.

"I forgot to tell you," resumed Aramis, addressing himself to Fouquet, who listened to him with the most absorbed attention – "I forgot to mention a most remarkable circumstance respecting these twins, namely, that God had formed them so startlingly, so miraculously, like each other, that it would be utterly impossible to distinguish the one from the other. Their own mother would not be able to distinguish them."

"Is it possible?" exclaimed Fouquet.

"The same noble character in their features, the same carriage, the same stature, the same voice."

"But their thoughts? degree of intelligence? their knowledge of human life?"

"There is inequality there, I admit, monseigneur. Yes; for the prisoner of the Bastile is, most incontestably, superior in every way to his brother; and if, from his prison, this unhappy victim were to pass to the throne, France would not, from the earliest period of its history, perhaps, have had a master more powerful in genius and nobility of character."

Fouquet buried his face in his hands, as if he were overwhelmed by the weight of this immense secret. Aramis approached him.

"There is a further inequality," he said, continuing his work of temptation, "an inequality which concerns yourself, monseigneur, between the twins, both sons of Louis XIII., namely, the last comer does not know M. Colbert."

Fouquet raised his head immediately – his features were pale and distorted. The bolt had hit its mark – not his heart, but his mind and comprehension.

"I understand you," he said to Aramis; "you are proposing a conspiracy to me?"

"Something like it."

"One of those attempts which, as you said at the beginning of this conversation, alters the fate of empires?"

"And of superintendents, too; yes, monseigneur."

"In a word, you propose that I should agree to the substitution of the son of Louis XIII., who is now a prisoner in the Bastile, for the son of Louis XIII., who is at this moment asleep in the Chamber of Morpheus?"

Aramis smiled with the sinister expression of the sinister thought which was passing through his brain. "Exactly," he said.

"Have you thought," continued Fouquet, becoming animated with that strength of talent which in a few seconds originates, and matures the conception of a plan, and with that largeness of view which foresees all consequences, and embraces every result at a glance – "have you thought that we must assemble the nobility, the clergy, and the third estate of the realm; that we shall have to depose the reigning sovereign, to disturb by so frightful a scandal the tomb of their dead father, to sacrifice the life, the honor of a woman, Anne of Austria, the life and peace of mind and heart of another woman, Maria Theresa; and suppose that it were all done, if we were to succeed in doing it – "

"I do not understand you," continued Aramis, coldly. "There is not a single syllable of sense in all you have just said."

"What!" said the superintendent, surprised, "a man like you refuse to view the practical bearing of the case! Do you confine yourself to the childish delight of a political illusion, and neglect the chances of its being carried into execution; in other words, the reality itself, is it possible?"

"My friend," said Aramis, emphasizing the word with a kind of disdainful familiarity, "what does Heaven do in order to substitute one king for another?"

"Heaven!" exclaimed Fouquet – "Heaven gives directions to its agent, who seizes upon the doomed victim, hurries him away, and seats the triumphant rival on the empty throne. But you forget that this agent is called death. Oh! Monsieur d'Herblay, in Heaven's name, tell me if you have had the idea – "

"There is no question of that, monseigneur; you are going beyond the object in view. Who spoke of Louis XIV.'s death? who spoke of adopting the example which Heaven sets in following out the strict execution of its decrees? No, I wish you to understand that Heaven effects its purposes without confusion or disturbance, without exciting comment or remark, without difficulty or exertion; and that men, inspired by Heaven, succeed like Heaven itself, in all their undertakings, in all they attempt, in all they do."

"What do you mean?"

"I mean, my **friend**," returned Aramis, with the same intonation on the word friend that he had applied to it the first time – "I mean that if there has been any confusion, scandal, and even effort in the substitution of the prisoner for the king, I defy you to prove it."

"What!" cried Fouquet, whiter than the handkerchief with which he wiped his temples, "what do you say?"

"Go to the king's apartment," continued Aramis, tranquilly, "and you who know the mystery, I defy even you to perceive that the prisoner of the Bastile is lying in his brother's bed."

"But the king," stammered Fouquet, seized with horror at the intelligence.

"What king?" said Aramis, in his gentlest tone; "the one who hates you, or the one who likes you?"

"The king – of – **yesterday**."

"The king of yesterday! be quite easy on that score; he has gone to take the place in the Bastile which his victim occupied for so many years."

"Great God! And who took him there?"

"I."

"You?"

"Yes, and in the simplest way. I carried him away last night. While he was descending into midnight, the other was ascending into day. I do not think there has been any disturbance whatever. A flash of lightning without thunder awakens nobody."

Fouquet uttered a thick, smothered cry, as if he had been struck by some invisible blow, and clasping his head between his clenched hands, he murmured: "You did that?"

"Cleverly enough, too; what do you think of it?"

"You dethroned the king? imprisoned him, too?"

"Yes, that has been done."

"And such an action was committed **here**, at Vaux?"

"Yes, here, at Vaux, in the Chamber of Morpheus. It would almost seem that it had been built in anticipation of such an act."

"And at what time did it occur?"

"Last night, between twelve and one o'clock."

Fouquet made a movement as if he were on the point of springing upon Aramis; he restrained himself. "At Vaux; under my roof!" he said, in a half-strangled voice.

"I believe so! for it is still your house, and it is likely to continue so, since M. Colbert cannot rob you of it now."

"It was under my roof, then, monsieur, that you committed this crime?"

"This crime?" said Aramis, stupefied.

"This abominable crime!" pursued Fouquet, becoming more and more excited; "this crime more execrable than an assassination! this crime which dishonors my name forever, and entails upon me the horror of posterity."

"You are not in your senses, monsieur," replied Aramis, in an irresolute tone of voice; "you are speaking too loudly; take care!"

"I will call out so loudly, that the whole world shall hear me."

"Monsieur Fouquet, take care!"

Fouquet turned round towards the prelate, whom he looked at full in the face. "You have dishonored me," he said, "in committing so foul an act of treason, so heinous a crime upon my guest, upon one who was peacefully reposing beneath my roof. Oh! woe, woe is me!"

"Woe to the man, rather, who beneath your roof meditated the ruin of your fortune, your life. Do you forget that?"

"He was my guest, my sovereign."

Aramis rose, his eyes literally bloodshot, his mouth trembling convulsively. "Have I a man out of his senses to deal with?" he said.

"You have an honorable man to deal with."

"You are mad."

"A man who will prevent you consummating your crime."

"You are mad, I say."

"A man who would sooner, oh! far sooner, die; who would kill you even, rather than allow you to complete his dishonor."

And Fouquet snatched up his sword, which D'Artagnan had placed at the head of his bed, and clenched it resolutely in his hand. Aramis frowned, and thrust his hand into his breast as if in search of a weapon. This movement did not escape Fouquet, who, full of nobleness and pride in his magnanimity, threw his sword to a distance from him, and approached Aramis so close as to touch his shoulder with his disarmed hand. "Monsieur," he said, "I would sooner die here on the spot than survive this terrible disgrace; and if you have any pity left for me, I entreat you to take my life."

Aramis remained silent and motionless.

"You do not reply?" said Fouquet.

Aramis raised his head gently, and a glimmer of hope might be seen once more to animate his eyes. "Reflect, monseigneur," he said, "upon everything we have to expect. As the matter now stands, the king is still alive, and his imprisonment saves your life."

"Yes," replied Fouquet, "you may have been acting on my behalf, but I will not, do not, accept your services. But, first of all, I do not wish your ruin. You will leave this house."

Aramis stifled the exclamation which almost escaped his broken heart.

"I am hospitable towards all who are dwellers beneath my roof," continued Fouquet, with an air of inexpressible majesty; "you will not be more fatally lost than he whose ruin you have consummated."

"You will be so," said Aramis, in a hoarse, prophetic voice, "you will be so, believe me."

"I accept the augury, Monsieur d'Herblay; but nothing shall prevent me, nothing shall stop me. You will leave Vaux – you must leave France; I give you four hours to place yourself out of the king's reach."

"Four hours?" said Aramis, scornfully and incredulously.

"Upon the word of Fouquet, no one shall follow you before the expiration of that time. You will therefore have four hours' advance of those whom the king may wish to dispatch after you."

"Four hours!" repeated Aramis, in a thick, smothered voice.

"It is more than you will need to get on board a vessel and flee to Belle-Isle, which I give you as a place of refuge."

"Ah!" murmured Aramis.

"Belle-Isle is as much mine for you, as Vaux is mine for the king. Go, D'Herblay, go! as long as I live, not a hair of your head shall be injured."

"Thank you," said Aramis, with a cold irony of manner.

"Go at once, then, and give me your hand, before we both hasten away; you to save your life, I to save my honor."

Aramis withdrew from his breast the hand he had concealed there; it was stained with his blood. He had dug his nails into his flesh, as if in punishment for having nursed so many projects, more vain, insensate, and fleeting than the life of the man himself. Fouquet was horror-stricken, and then his heart smote him with pity. He threw open his arms as if to embrace him.

"I had no arms," murmured Aramis, as wild and terrible in his wrath as the shade of Dido. And then, without touching Fouquet's hand, he turned his head aside, and stepped back a pace or two. His last word was an imprecation, his last gesture a curse, which his blood-stained hand seemed to invoke, as it sprinkled on Fouquet's face a few drops of blood which flowed from his breast. And both of them darted out of the room by the secret staircase which led down to the inner courtyard. Fouquet ordered his best horses, while Aramis paused at the foot of the staircase which led to Porthos's apartment. He reflected profoundly and for some time, while Fouquet's carriage left the courtyard at full gallop.

"Shall I go alone?" said Aramis to himself, "or warn the prince? Oh! fury! Warn the prince, and then – do what? Take him with me? To carry this accusing witness about with me everywhere? War, too, would follow – civil war, implacable in its nature! And without any resource save myself – it is impossible! What could he do without me? Oh! without me he will be utterly destroyed. Yet who knows – let destiny be fulfilled – condemned he was, let him remain so then! Good or evil Spirit – gloomy and scornful Power, whom men call the genius of humanity, thou art a power more restlessly uncertain, more baselessly useless, than wild mountain wind! Chance, thou term'st thyself, but thou art nothing; thou inflamest everything with thy breath, crumblest mountains at thy approach, and suddenly art thyself destroyed at the presence of the Cross of dead wood behind which stand another Power invisible like thyself – whom thou deniest, perhaps, but whose avenging hand is on thee, and hurls thee in the dust dishonored and unnamed! Lost! – I am lost! What can be done? Flee to Belle-Isle? Yes, and leave Porthos behind me, to talk and relate the whole affair to every one! Porthos, too, who will have to suffer for what he has done. I will not let poor Porthos suffer. He seems like one of the members of my own frame; and his grief or misfortune would be mine as well. Porthos shall leave with me, and shall follow my destiny. It must be so."

And Aramis, apprehensive of meeting any one to whom his hurried movements might appear suspicious, ascended the staircase without being perceived. Porthos, so recently returned from Paris, was already in a profound sleep; his huge body forgot its fatigue, as his mind forgot its thoughts. Aramis entered, light as a shadow, and placed his nervous grasp on the giant's shoulder. "Come, Porthos," he cried, "come."

Porthos obeyed, rose from his bed, opened his eyes, even before his intelligence seemed to be aroused.

"We leave immediately," said Aramis.

"Ah!" returned Porthos.

"We shall go mounted, and faster than we have ever gone in our lives."

"Ah!" repeated Porthos.

"Dress yourself, my friend."

And he helped the giant to dress himself, and thrust his gold and diamonds into his pocket. Whilst he was thus engaged, a slight noise attracted his attention, and on looking up, he saw D'Artagnan watching them through the half-opened door. Aramis started.

"What the devil are you doing there in such an agitated manner?" said the musketeer.

"Hush!" said Porthos.

"We are going off on a mission of great

importance," added the bishop.

"You are very fortunate," said the musketeer.

"Oh, dear me!" said Porthos, "I feel so wearied; I would far sooner have been fast asleep. But the service of the king...."

"Have you seen M. Fouquet?" said Aramis to D'Artagnan.

"Yes, this very minute, in a carriage."

"What did he say to you?"

"'Adieu;' nothing more."

"Was that all?"

"What else do you think he could say? Am I worth anything now, since you have got into such high favor?"

"Listen," said Aramis, embracing the musketeer; "your good times are returning again. You will have no occasion to be jealous of any one."

"Ah! bah!"

"I predict that something will happen to you to-day which will increase your importance more than ever."

"Really?"

"You know that I know all the news?"

"Oh, yes!"

"Come, Porthos, are you ready? Let us go."

"I am quite ready, Aramis."

"Let us embrace D'Artagnan first."

"Most certainly."

"But the horses?"

"Oh! there is no want of them here. Will you have mine?"

"No; Porthos has his own stud. So adieu! adieu!"

The fugitives mounted their horses beneath the very eyes of the captain of the musketeers, who held Porthos's stirrup for him, and gazed after them until they were out of sight.

"On any other occasion," thought the Gascon, "I should say that those gentlemen were making their escape; but in these days politics seem so changed that such an exit is termed going on a mission. I have no objection; let me attend to my own affairs, that is more than enough for **me**," – and he philosophically entered his apartments.

CHAPTER TWENTY TWO

Showing how the Countersign was Respected at the Bastile

FOUQUET TORE ALONG AS fast as his horses could drag him. On his way he trembled with horror at the idea of what had just been revealed to him.

"What must have been," he thought, "the youth of those extraordinary men, who, even as age is stealing fast upon them, are still able to conceive such gigantic plans, and carry them through without a tremor?"

At one moment he could not resist the idea that all Aramis had just been recounting to him was nothing more than a dream, and whether the fable itself was not the snare; so that when Fouquet arrived at the Bastile, he might possibly find an order of arrest, which would send him to join the dethroned king. Strongly impressed with this idea, he gave certain sealed orders on his route, while fresh horses were being harnessed to his carriage. These orders were addressed to M. d'Artagnan and to certain others whose fidelity to the king was far above suspicion.

"In this way," said Fouquet to himself, "prisoner or not, I shall have performed the duty that I owe my honor. The orders will not reach them until after my return, if I should return free, and consequently they will not have been unsealed. I shall take them back again. If I am delayed; it will be because some misfortune will have befallen me; and in that case assistance will be sent for me as well as for the king."

Prepared in this manner, the superintendent arrived at the Bastile; he had traveled at the rate of five leagues and a half the hour. Every circumstance of delay which Aramis had escaped in his visit to the Bastile befell Fouquet. It was useless giving his name, equally useless his being recognized; he could not succeed in obtaining an entrance. By dint of entreaties, threats, commands, he succeeded ih inducing a sentinel to speak to one of the subalterns, who went and told the major. As for the governor they did not even dare disturb him. Fouquet sat in his carriage, at the outer gate of the fortress, chafing with rage and impatience, awaiting the return of the officers, who at last reappeared with a sufficiently sulky air.

"Well," said Fouquet, impatiently, "what did the major say?"

"Well, monsieur," replied the soldier, "the major laughed in my face. He told me that M. Fouquet was at Vaux, and that even were he at Paris, M. Fouquet would not get up at so early an hour as the present."

"**Mordieu!** you are an absolute set of fools," cried the minister, darting out of the carriage; and before the subaltern had time to shut the gate, Fouquet sprang through it, and ran forward in spite of the soldier, who cried out for assistance. Fouquet gained ground, regardless of the cries of the man, who, however, having at last come up with Fouquet, called out to the sentinel of the second gate, "Look out, look out, sentinel!" The man crossed his pike before the minister; but the latter, robust and active, and hurried away, too, by his passion, wrested the pike from the soldier and struck him a violent blow on the shoulder with it. The subaltern, who approached too closely, received a share of the blows as well. Both of them uttered loud and furious cries, at the sound of which the whole of the first body of the advanced guard poured out of the guardhouse. Among them there was one, however, who recognized the superintendent, and who called, "Monseigneur, ah! monseigneur. Stop, stop, you fellows!" And he effectually checked the soldiers, who were on the point of revenging their companions. Fouquet desired them to open the gate, but they refused to do so without the countersign; he desired them to inform the governor of his presence; but the latter had already heard the disturbance at the gate. He ran forward, followed by his major, and accompanied by a picket of twenty men, persuaded that an attack was being made on the Bastile. Baisemeaux also recognized Fouquet immediately, and dropped the sword he bravely had been brandishing.

"Ah! monseigneur," he stammered, "how can I excuse – "

"Monsieur," said the superintendent, flushed with anger, and heated by his exertions, "I congratulate you. Your watch and ward are admirably kept."

Baisemeaux turned pale, thinking that this remark was made ironically, and portended a furious burst of anger. But Fouquet had recovered his breath, and, beckoning the sentinel and the subaltern, who were rubbing their shoulders, towards him, he said, "There are twenty pistoles for the sentinel, and fifty for the officer. Pray receive my compliments, gentlemen. I will not fail to speak to his majesty about you. And now, M. Baisemeaux, a word with you."

And he followed the governor to his official residence, accompanied by a murmur of general satisfaction. Baisemeaux was already trembling with shame and uneasiness. Aramis's early visit, from that moment, seemed to possess consequences, which a functionary such as he (Baisemeaux) was, was perfectly justified in apprehending. It was quite another thing, however, when Fouquet in a sharp tone of voice, and with an imperious look, said, "You have seen M. d'Herblay this morning?"

"Yes, monseigneur."

"And are you not horrified at the crime of which you have made yourself an accomplice?"

"Well," thought Baisemeaux, "good so far;" and then he added, aloud, "But what crime, monseigneur, do you allude to?"

"That for which you can be quartered alive, monsieur – do not forget that! But this is not a time to show anger. Conduct me immediately to the prisoner."

"To what prisoner?" said Baisemeaux, trembling.

"You pretend to be ignorant? Very good – it is the best plan for you, perhaps; for if, in fact, you were to admit your participation in such a crime, it would be all over with you. I wish, therefore, to seem to believe in your assumption of ignorance."

"I entreat you, monseigneur – "

"That will do. Lead me to the prisoner."

"To Marchiali?"

"Who is Marchiali?"

"The prisoner who was brought back this morning by M. d'Herblay."

"He is called Marchiali?" said the superintendent, his conviction somewhat shaken by Baisemeaux's cool manner.

"Yes, monseigneur; that is the name under which he was inscribed here."

Fouquet looked steadily at Baisemeaux, as if he would read his very heart; and perceived, with that clear-sightedness most men possess who are accustomed to the exercise of power, that the man was speaking with perfect sincerity. Besides, in observing his face for a few moments, he could not believe that Aramis would have chosen such a confidant.

"It is the prisoner," said the superintendent to him, "whom M. d'Herblay carried away the day before yesterday?"

"Yes, monseigneur."

"And whom he brought back this morning?" added Fouquet, quickly: for he understood immediately the mechanism of Aramis's plan.

"Precisely, monseigneur."

"And his name is Marchiali, you say?"

"Yes, Marchiali. If monseigneur has come here to remove him, so much the better, for I was going to write about him."

"What has he done, then?"

"Ever since this morning he has annoyed me extremely. He has had such terrible fits of passion, as almost to make me believe that he would bring the Bastile itself down about our ears."

"I will soon relieve you of his possession," said Fouquet.

"Ah! so much the better."

"Conduct me to his prison."

"Will monseigneur give me the order?"

"What order?"

"An order from the king."

"Wait until I sign you one."

"That will not be sufficient, monseigneur. I must have an order from the king."

Fouquet assumed an irritated expression. "As you are so scrupulous," he said, "with regard to allowing prisoners to leave, show me the order by which this one was set at liberty."

Baisemeaux showed him the order to release Seldon.

"Very good," said Fouquet; "but Seldon is not Marchiali."

"But Marchiali is not at liberty, monseigneur; he is here."

"But you said that M. d'Herblay carried him away and brought him back again."

"I did not say so."

"So surely did you say it, that I almost seem to hear it now."

"It was a slip of my tongue, then, monseigneur."

"Take care, M. Baisemeaux, take care."

"I have nothing to fear, monseigneur; I am acting according to the very strictest regulation."

"Do you dare to say so?"

"I would say so in the presence of one of the apostles. M. d'Herblay brought me an order to set Seldon at liberty. Seldon is free."

"I tell you that Marchiali has left the Bastile."

"You must prove that, monseigneur."

"Let me see him."

"You, monseigneur, who govern this kingdom, know very well that no one can see any of the prisoners without an express order from the king."

"M. d'Herblay has entered, however."

"That remains to be proved, monseigneur."

"M. de Baisemeaux, once more I warn you to pay particular attention to what you are saying."

"All the documents are there, monseigneur."

"M. d'Herblay is overthrown."

"Overthrown? – M. d'Herblay! Impossible!"

"You see that he has undoubtedly influenced you."

"No, monseigneur; what does, in fact,

influence me, is the king's service. I am doing my duty. Give me an order from him, and you shall enter."

"Stay, M. le gouverneur, I give you my word that if you allow me to see the prisoner, I will give you an order from the king at once."

"Give it to me now, monseigneur."

"And that, if you refuse me, I will have you and all your officers arrested on the spot."

"Before you commit such an act of violence, monseigneur, you will reflect," said Baisemeaux, who had turned very pale, "that we will only obey an order signed by the king; and that it will be just as easy for you to obtain one to see Marchiali as to obtain one to do me so much injury; me, too, who am perfectly innocent."

"True. True!" cried Fouquet, furiously; "perfectly true. M. de Baisemeaux," he added, in a sonorous voice, drawing the unhappy governor towards him, "do you know why I am so anxious to speak to the prisoner?"

"No, monseigneur; and allow me to observe that you are terrifying me out of my senses; I am trembling all over – in fact, I feel as though I were about to faint."

"You will stand a better chance of fainting outright, Monsieur Baisemeaux, when I return here at the head of ten thousand men and thirty pieces of cannon."

"Good heavens, monseigneur, you are losing your senses."

"When I have roused the whole population of Paris against you and your accursed towers, and have battered open the gates of this place, and hanged you to the topmost tree of yonder pinnacle!"

"Monseigneur! monseigneur! for pity's sake!"

"I give you ten minutes to make up your mind," added Fouquet, in a calm voice. "I will sit down here, in this armchair, and wait for you; if, in ten minutes' time, you still persist, I leave this place, and you may think me as mad as you like. Then – you shall **see!**"

Baisemeaux stamped his foot on the ground like a man in a state of despair, but he did not reply a single syllable; whereupon Fouquet seized a pen and ink, and wrote:

"Order for M. le Prevot des Marchands to assemble the municipal guard and to march upon the Bastile on the king's immediate service."

Baisemeaux shrugged his shoulders. Fouquet wrote:

"Order for the Duc de Bouillon and M. le Prince de Conde to assume the command of the Swiss guards, of the king's guards, and to march upon the Bastile on the king's immediate service."

Baisemeaux reflected. Fouquet still wrote:

"Order for every soldier, citizen, or gentleman to seize and apprehend, wherever he may be found, le Chevalier d'Herblay, Eveque de Vannes, and his accomplices, who are: first, M. de Baisemeaux, governor of the Bastile, suspected of the crimes of high treason and rebellion – "

"Stop, monseigneur!" cried Baisemeaux; "I do not understand a single jot of the whole matter; but so many misfortunes, even were it madness itself that had set them at their awful work, might happen here in a couple of hours, that the king, by whom I must be judged, will see whether I have been wrong in withdrawing the countersign before this flood of imminent catastrophes. Come with me to the keep, monseigneur, you shall see Marchiali."

Fouquet darted out of the room, followed by Baisemeaux as he wiped the perspiration from his face. "What a terrible morning!" he said; "what a disgrace for **me!**"

"Walk faster," replied Fouquet.

Baisemeaux made a sign to the jailer to precede them. He was afraid of his companion, which the latter could not fail to perceive.

"A truce to this child's play," he said, roughly. "Let the man remain here; take the keys yourself, and show me the way. Not a single person, do you understand, must hear what is going to take place here."

"Ah!" said Baisemeaux, undecided.

"Again!" cried M. Fouquet. "Ah! say 'no' at once, and I will leave the Bastile and will myself carry my own dispatches."

Baisemeaux bowed his head, took the keys, and unaccompanied, except by the minister, ascended the staircase. The higher they advanced up the spiral staircase, the more clearly did certain muffled murmurs become distinct appeals and fearful imprecations.

"What is that?" asked Fouquet.

"That is your Marchiali," said the governor; "this is the way these madmen scream."

And he accompanied that reply with a glance more pregnant with injurious allusion, as far as Fouquet was concerned, than politeness. The latter trembled; he had just recognized in one cry more terrible than any that had preceded it, the king's voice.

He paused on the staircase, snatching the bunch of keys from Baisemeaux, who thought this new madman was going to dash out his brains with one of them. "Ah!" he cried, "M. d'Herblay did not say a word about that."

"Give me the keys at once!" cried Fouquet, tearing them from his hand. "Which is the key of the door I am to open?"

"That one."

A fearful cry, followed by a violent blow against the door, made the whole staircase resound with the echo.

"Leave this place," said Fouquet to Baisemeaux, in a threatening tone.

"I ask nothing better," murmured the latter, to himself. "There will be a couple of madmen face to face, and the one will kill the other, I am sure."

"Go!" repeated Fouquet. "If you place your foot on this staircase before I call you, remember that you shall take the place of the meanest prisoner in the Bastile."

"This job will kill me, I am sure it will," muttered Baisemeaux, as he withdrew with tottering steps.

The prisoner's cries became more and more terrible. When Fouquet had satisfied himself that Baisemeaux had reached the bottom of the staircase, he inserted the key in the first lock. It was then that he heard the hoarse, choking voice of the king, crying out, in a frenzy of rage, "Help, help! I am the king." The key of the second door was not the same as the first, and Fouquet was obliged to look for it on the bunch. The king, however, furious and almost mad with rage and passion, shouted at the top of his voice, "It was M. Fouquet who brought me here. Help me against M. Fouquet! I am the king! Help the king against M. Fouquet!" These cries filled the minister's heart with terrible emotions. They were followed by a shower of blows leveled against the door with a part of the broken chair with which the king had armed himself. Fouquet at last succeeded in finding the key. The king was almost exhausted; he could hardly articulate distinctly as he shouted, “Death to Fouquet! death to the traitor Fouquet!” The door flew open.

CHAPTER TWENTY THREE

The King's Gratitude

THE TWO MEN WERE on the point of darting towards each other when they suddenly and abruptly stopped, as a mutual recognition took place, and each uttered a cry of horror.

"Have you come to assassinate me, monsieur?" said the king, when he recognized Fouquet.

"The king in this state!" murmured the

minister.

Nothing could be more terrible indeed than the appearance of the young prince at the moment Fouquet had surprised him; his clothes were in tatters; his shirt, open and torn to rags, was stained with sweat and with the blood which streamed from his lacerated breast and arms. Haggard, ghastly pale, his hair in disheveled masses, Louis XIV. presented the most perfect picture of despair, distress, anger and fear combined that could possibly be united in one figure. Fouquet was so touched, so affected and disturbed by it, that he ran towards him with his arms stretched out and his eyes filled with tears. Louis held up the massive piece of wood of which he had made such a furious use.

"Sire," said Fouquet, in a voice trembling with emotion, "do you not recognize the most faithful of your friends?"

"A friend – you!" repeated Louis, gnashing his teeth in a manner which betrayed his hate and desire for speedy vengeance.

"The most respectful of your servants," added Fouquet, throwing himself on his knees. The king let the rude weapon fall from his grasp. Fouquet approached him, kissed his knees, and took him in his arms with inconceivable tenderness.

"My king, my child," he said, "how you must have suffered!"

Louis, recalled to himself by the change of situation, looked at himself, and ashamed of the disordered state of his apparel, ashamed of his conduct, and ashamed of the air of pity and protection that was shown towards him, drew back. Fouquet did not understand this movement; he did not perceive that the king's feeling of pride would never forgive him for having been a witness of such an exhibition of weakness.

"Come, sire," he said, "you are free."

"Free?" repeated the king. "Oh! you set me at liberty, then, after having dared to lift up your hand against me."

"You do not believe that!" exclaimed

Fouquet, indignantly; "you cannot believe me to be guilty of such an act."

And rapidly, warmly even, he related the whole particulars of the intrigue, the details of which are already known to the reader. While the recital continued, Louis suffered the most horrible anguish of mind; and when it was finished, the magnitude of the danger he had run struck him far more than the importance of the secret relative to his twin brother.

"Monsieur," he said, suddenly to Fouquet, "this double birth is a falsehood; it is impossible – you cannot have been the dupe of it."

"Sire!"

"It is impossible, I tell you, that the honor, the virtue of my mother can be suspected, and my first minister has not yet done justice on the criminals!"

"Reflect, sire, before you are hurried away by anger," replied Fouquet. "The birth of your brother – "

"I have only one brother – and that is

Monsieur. You know it as well as myself. There is a plot, I tell you, beginning with the governor of the Bastile."

"Be careful, sire, for this man has been deceived as every one else has by the prince's likeness to yourself."

"Likeness? Absurd!"

"This Marchiali must be singularly like your majesty, to be able to deceive every one's eye," Fouquet persisted.

"Ridiculous!"

"Do not say so, sire; those who had prepared everything in order to face and deceive your ministers, your mother, your officers of state, the members of your family, must be quite confident of the resemblance between you."

"But where are these persons, then?" murmured the king.

"At Vaux."

"At Vaux! and you suffer them to remain there!"

"My most instant duty appeared to me to be

your majesty's release. I have accomplished that duty; and now, whatever your majesty may command, shall be done. I await your orders."

Louis reflected for a few moments.

"Muster all the troops in Paris," he said.

"All the necessary orders are given for that purpose," replied Fouquet.

"You have given orders!" exclaimed the king.

"For that purpose, yes, sire; your majesty will be at the head of ten thousand men in less than an hour."

The only reply the king made was to take hold of Fouquet's hand with such an expression of feeling, that it was very easy to perceive how strongly he had, until that remark, maintained his suspicions of the minister, notwithstanding the latter's intervention.

"And with these troops," he said, "we shall go at once and besiege in your house the rebels who by this time will have established and intrenched themselves therein."

"I should be surprised if that were the case," replied Fouquet.

"Why?"

"Because their chief – the very soul of the enterprise – having been unmasked by me, the whole plan seems to me to have miscarried."

"You have unmasked this false prince also?"

"No, I have not seen him."

"Whom have you seen, then?"

"The leader of the enterprise, not that unhappy young man; the latter is merely an instrument, destined through his whole life to wretchedness, I plainly perceive."

"Most certainly."

"It is M. l'Abbe d'Herblay, Eveque de Vannes."

"Your friend?"

"He was my friend, sire," replied Fouquet, nobly.

"An unfortunate circumstance for you,"

said the king, in a less generous tone of voice.

"Such friendships, sire, had nothing dishonorable in them so long as I was ignorant of the crime."

"You should have foreseen it."

"If I am guilty, I place myself in your majesty's hands."

"Ah! Monsieur Fouquet, it was not that I meant," returned the king, sorry to have shown the bitterness of his thought in such a manner. "Well! I assure you that, notwithstanding the mask with which the villain covered his face, I had something like a vague suspicion that he was the very man. But with this chief of the enterprise there was a man of prodigious strength, the one who menaced me with a force almost herculean; what is he?"

"It must be his friend the Baron du Vallon, formerly one of the musketeers."

"The friend of D'Artagnan? the friend of the Comte de la Fere? Ah!" exclaimed the king, as he paused at the name of the latter, "we must not forget the connection that existed between the conspirators and M. de Bragelonne."

"Sire, sire, do not go too far. M. de la Fere is the most honorable man in France. Be satisfied with those whom I deliver up to you."

"With those whom you deliver up to me, you say? Very good, for you will deliver up those who are guilty to me."

"What does your majesty understand by that?" inquired Fouquet.

"I understand," replied the king, "that we shall soon arrive at Vaux with a large body of troops, that we will lay violent hands upon that nest of vipers, and that not a soul shall escape."

"Your majesty will put these men to death!" cried Fouquet.

"To the very meanest of them."

"Oh! sire."

"Let us understand one another, Monsieur Fouquet," said the king, haughtily. "We no longer live in times when assassination was the only and the last resource kings held in reservation at extremity. No, Heaven be praised! I have parliaments who sit and judge in my name, and I have scaffolds on which supreme authority is carried out."

Fouquet turned pale. "I will take the liberty of observing to your majesty, that any proceedings instituted respecting these matters would bring down the greatest scandal upon the dignity of the throne. The august name of Anne of Austria must never be allowed to pass the lips of the people accompanied by a smile."

"Justice must be done, however, monsieur."

"Good, sire; but royal blood must not be shed upon a scaffold."

"The royal blood! you believe that!" cried the king with fury in his voice, stamping his foot on the ground. "This double birth is an invention; and in that invention, particularly, do I see M. d'Herblay's crime. It is the crime I wish to punish rather than the violence, or the insult."

"And punish it with death, sire?"

"With death; yes, monsieur, I have said it."

"Sire," said the surintendant, with firmness, as he raised his head proudly, "your majesty will take the life, if you please, of your brother Philippe of France; that concerns you alone, and you will doubtless consult the queen-mother upon the subject. Whatever she may command will be perfectly correct. I do not wish to mix myself up in it, not even for the honor of your crown, but I have a favor to ask of you, and I beg to submit it to you."

"Speak," said the king, in no little degree agitated by his minister's last words. "What do you require?"

"The pardon of M. d'Herblay and of M. du Vallon."

"My assassins?"

"Two rebels, sire, that is all."

"Oh! I understand, then, you ask me to forgive your friends."

"My friends!" said Fouquet, deeply

wounded.

"Your friends, certainly; but the safety of the state requires that an exemplary punishment should be inflicted on the guilty."

"I will not permit myself to remind your majesty that I have just restored you to liberty, and have saved your life."

"Monsieur!"

"I will not allow myself to remind your majesty that had M. d'Herblay wished to carry out his character of an assassin, he could very easily have assassinated your majesty this morning in the forest of Senart, and all would have been over." The king started.

"A pistol-bullet through the head," pursued Fouquet, "and the disfigured features of Louis XIV., which no one could have recognized, would be M. d'Herblay's complete and entire justification."

The king turned pale and giddy at the bare idea of the danger he had escaped.

"If M. d'Herblay," continued Fouquet, "had been an assassin, he had no occasion to inform me of his plan in order to succeed. Freed from the real king, it would have been impossible in all futurity to guess the false. And if the usurper had been recognized by Anne of Austria, he would still have been – her son. The usurper, as far as Monsieur d'Herblay's conscience was concerned, was still a king of the blood of Louis XIII. Moreover, the conspirator, in that course, would have had security, secrecy, impunity. A pistol-bullet would have procured him all that. For the sake of Heaven, sire, grant me his forgiveness."

The king, instead of being touched by the picture, so faithfully drawn in all details, of Aramis's generosity, felt himself most painfully and cruelly humiliated. His unconquerable pride revolted at the idea that a man had held suspended at the end of his finger the thread of his royal life. Every word that fell from Fouquet's lips, and which he thought most efficacious in procuring his friend's pardon, seemed to pour another drop of poison into the already ulcerated heart of Louis XIV. Nothing could bend or soften him. Addressing himself to Fouquet, he said, "I really don't know, monsieur, why you should solicit the pardon of these men. What good is there in asking that which can be obtained without solicitation?"

"I do not understand you, sire."

"It is not difficult, either. Where am I now?"

"In the Bastile, sire."

"Yes; in a dungeon. I am looked upon as a madman, am I not?"

"Yes, sire."

"And no one is known here but Marchiali?"

"Certainly."

"Well; change nothing in the position of affairs. Let the poor madman rot between the slimy walls of the Bastile, and M. d'Herblay and M. du Vallon will stand in no need of my forgiveness. Their new king will absolve them."

"Your majesty does me a great injustice, sire; and you are wrong," replied Fouquet, dryly; "I am not child enough, nor is M. d'Herblay silly enough, to have omitted to make all these reflections; and if I had wished to make a new king, as you say, I had no occasion to have come here to force open the gates and doors of the Bastile, to free you from this place. That would show a want of even common sense. Your majesty's mind is disturbed by anger; otherwise you would be far from offending, groundlessly, the very one of your servants who has rendered you the most important service of all."

Louis perceived that he had gone too far; that the gates of the Bastile were still closed upon him, whilst, by degrees, the floodgates were gradually being opened, behind which the generous-hearted Fouquet had restrained his anger. "I did not say that to humiliate you, Heaven knows, monsieur," he replied. "Only you are addressing yourself to me in order to obtain a pardon, and I answer according to my conscience. And so, judging by my conscience, the criminals we speak of are not worthy of consideration or forgiveness."

Fouquet was silent.

"What I do is as generous," added the king, "as what you have done, for I am in your power. I will even say it is more generous, inasmuch as you place before me certain conditions upon which my liberty, my life, may depend; and to reject which is to make a sacrifice of both."

"I was wrong, certainly," replied Fouquet. "Yes, – I had the appearance of extorting a favor; I regret it, and entreat your majesty's forgiveness."

"And you are forgiven, my dear Monsieur Fouquet," said the king, with a smile, which restored the serene expression of his features, which so many circumstances had altered since the preceding evening.

"I have my own forgiveness," replied the minister, with some degree of persistence; "but M. d'Herblay, and M. du Vallon?"

"They will never obtain theirs, as long as I live," replied the inflexible king. "Do me the kindness not to speak of it again."

"Your majesty shall be obeyed."

"And you will bear me no ill-will for it?"

"Oh! no, sire; for I anticipated the event."

"You had 'anticipated' that I should refuse to forgive those gentlemen?"

"Certainly; and all my measures were taken in consequence."

"What do you mean to say?" cried the king, surprised.

"M. d'Herblay came, as may be said, to deliver himself into my hands. M. d'Herblay left to me the happiness of saving my king and my country. I could not condemn M. d'Herblay to death; nor could I, on the other hand, expose him to your majesty's justifiable wrath; it would have been just the same as if I had killed him myself."

"Well! and what have you done?"

"Sire, I gave M. d'Herblay the best horses in my stables and four hours' start over all those your majesty might, probably, dispatch after him."

"Be it so!" murmured the king. "But still, the world is wide enough and large enough for those whom I may send to overtake your horses, notwithstanding the 'four hours' start' which you have given to M. d'Herblay."

"In giving him these four hours, sire, I knew I was giving him his life, and he will save his life."

"In what way?"

"After having galloped as hard as possible, with the four hours' start, before your musketeers, he will reach my chateau of Belle-Isle, where I have given him a safe asylum."

"That may be! But you forget that you have made me a present of Belle-Isle."

"But not for you to arrest my friends."

"You take it back again, then?"

"As far as that goes – yes, sire."

"My musketeers shall capture it, and the affair will be at an end."

"Neither your musketeers, nor your whole army could take Belle-Isle," said Fouquet, coldly. "Belle-Isle is impregnable."

The king became perfectly livid; a lightning flash seemed to dart from his eyes. Fouquet felt that he was lost, but he as not one to shrink when the voice of honor spoke loudly within him. He bore the king's wrathful gaze; the latter swallowed his rage, and after a few moments' silence, said, "Are we going to return to Vaux?"

"I am at your majesty's orders," replied Fouquet, with a low bow; "but I think that your majesty can hardly dispense with changing your clothes previous to appearing before your court."

"We shall pass by the Louvre," said the king. "Come." And they left the prison, passing before Baisemeaux, who looked completely bewildered as he saw Marchiali once more leave; and, in his helplessness, tore out the major portion of his few remaining hairs. It was perfectly true, however, that Fouquet wrote and gave him an authority for the prisoner's release, and that the king wrote beneath it, "Seen and approved, Louis"; a piece of madness that Baisemeaux, incapable of putting two ideas together, acknowledged by giving himself a terrible blow on the forehead with his own fist.

CHAPTER TWENTY FOUR

The False King

IN THE MEANTIME, usurped royalty was playing out its part bravely at Vaux. Philippe gave orders that for his **petit lever** the **grandes entrees**, already prepared to appear before the king, should be introduced. He determined to give this order notwithstanding the absence of M. d'Herblay, who did not return – our readers know the reason. But the prince, not believing that absence could be prolonged, wished, as all rash spirits do, to try his valor and his fortune far from all protection and instruction. Another reason urged him to this – Anne of Austria was about to appear; the guilty mother was about to stand in the presence of her sacrificed son. Philippe was not willing, if he had a weakness, to render the man a witness of it before whom he was bound thenceforth to display so much strength. Philippe opened his folding doors, and several persons entered silently. Philippe did not stir whilst his **valets de chambre** dressed him. He had watched, the evening before, all the habits of his brother, and played the king in such a manner as to awaken no suspicion. He was thus completely dressed in hunting costume when he received his visitors. His own memory and the notes of Aramis announced everybody to him, first of all Anne of Austria, to whom Monsieur gave his hand, and then Madame with M. de

Saint-Aignan. He smiled at seeing these countenances, but trembled on recognizing his mother. That still so noble and imposing figure, ravaged by pain, pleaded in his heart the cause of the famous queen who had immolated a child to reasons of state. He found his mother still handsome. He knew that Louis XIV. loved her, and he promised himself to love her likewise, and not to prove a scourge to her old age. He contemplated his brother with a tenderness easily to be understood. The latter had usurped nothing, had cast no shades athwart his life. A separate tree, he allowed the stem to rise without heeding its elevation or majestic life. Philippe promised himself to be a kind brother to this prince, who required nothing but gold to minister to his pleasures. He bowed with a friendly air to Saint-Aignan, who was all reverences and smiles, and trembling held out his hand to Henrietta, his sister-in-law, whose beauty struck him; but he saw in the eyes of that princess an expression of coldness which would facilitate, as he thought, their future relations.

"How much more easy," thought he, "it will be to be the brother of that woman than her gallant, if she evinces towards me a coldness that my brother could not have for her, but which is imposed upon me as a duty." The only visit he dreaded at this moment was that of the queen; his heart – his mind – had just been shaken by so violent a trial, that, in spite of their firm temperament, they would not, perhaps, support another shock. Happily the queen did not come. Then commenced, on the part of Anne of Austria, a political dissertation upon the welcome M. Fouquet had given to the house of France. She mixed up hostilities with compliments addressed to the king, and questions as to his health, with little maternal flatteries and diplomatic artifices.

"Well, my son," said she, "are you convinced with regard to M. Fouquet?"

"Saint-Aignan," said Philippe, "have the goodness to go and inquire after the queen."

At these words, the first Philippe had pronounced aloud, the slight difference that there was between his voice and that of the king was sensible to maternal ears, and Anne of Austria looked earnestly at her son. Saint-Aignan left the room, and Philippe continued:

"Madame, I do not like to hear M. Fouquet ill-spoken of, you know I do not – and you have even spoken well of him yourself."

"That is true; therefore I only question you on the state of your sentiments with respect to him."

"Sire," said Henrietta, "I, on my part, have always liked M. Fouquet. He is a man of good taste, – a superior man."

"A superintendent who is never sordid or niggardly," added Monsieur; "and who pays in gold all the orders I have on him."

"Every one in this thinks too much of himself, and nobody for the state," said the old queen. "M. Fouquet, it is a fact, M.

Fouquet is ruining the state."

"Well, mother!" replied Philippe, in rather a lower key, "do you likewise constitute yourself the buckler of M. Colbert?"

"How is that?" replied the old queen, rather surprised.

"Why, in truth," replied Philippe, "you speak that just as your old friend Madame de Chevreuse would speak."

"Why do you mention Madame de Chevreuse to me?" said she, "and what sort of humor are you in to-day towards me?"

Philippe continued: "Is not Madame de Chevreuse always in league against somebody? Has not Madame de Chevreuse been to pay you a visit, mother?"

"Monsieur, you speak to me now in such a manner that I can almost fancy I am listening to your father."

"My father did not like Madame de Chevreuse, and had good reason for not liking her," said the prince. "For my part, I like her no better than **he** did, and if she thinks proper to come here as she formerly did, to sow divisions and hatreds under the pretext of begging money – why – ”

“Well! what?” said Anne of Austria, proudly, herself provoking the storm.

“Well!” replied the young man firmly, “I will drive Madame de Chevreuse out of my kingdom – and with her all who meddle with its secrets and mysteries.”

He had not calculated the effect of this terrible speech, or perhaps he wished to judge the effect of it, like those who, suffering from a chronic pain, and seeking to break the monotony of that suffering, touch their wound to procure a sharper pang. Anne of Austria was nearly fainting; her eyes, open but meaningless, ceased to see for several seconds; she stretched out her arms towards her other son, who supported and embraced her without fear of irritating the king.

“Sire,” murmured she, “you are treating your mother very cruelly.”

“In what respect, madame?” replied he. “I

am only speaking of Madame de Chevreuse; does my mother prefer Madame de Chevreuse to the security of the state and of my person? Well, then, madame, I tell you Madame de Chevreuse has returned to France to borrow money, and that she addressed herself to M. Fouquet to sell him a certain secret."

"A certain secret!" cried Anne of Austria.

"Concerning pretended robberies that monsieur le surintendant had committed, which is false," added Philippe. "M. Fouquet rejected her offers with indignation, preferring the esteem of the king to complicity with such intriguers. Then Madame de Chevreuse sold the secret to M. Colbert, and as she is insatiable, and was not satisfied with having extorted a hundred thousand crowns from a servant of the state, she has taken a still bolder flight, in search of surer sources of supply. Is that true, madame?"

"You know all, sire," said the queen, more uneasy than irritated.

"Now," continued Philippe, "I have good reason to dislike this fury, who comes to my court to plan the shame of some and the ruin of others. If Heaven has suffered certain crimes to be committed, and has concealed them in the shadow of its clemency, I will not permit Madame de Chevreuse to counteract the just designs of fate."

The latter part of this speech had so agitated the queen-mother, that her son had pity on her. He took her hand and kissed it tenderly; she did not feel that in that kiss, given in spite of repulsion and bitterness of the heart, there was a pardon for eight years of suffering. Philippe allowed the silence of a moment to swallow the emotions that had just developed themselves. Then, with a cheerful smile:

"We will not go to-day," said he, "I have a plan." And, turning towards the door, he hoped to see Aramis, whose absence began to alarm him. The queen-mother wished to leave the room.

"Remain where you are, mother," said he, "I wish you to make your peace with M. Fouquet."

"I bear M. Fouquet no ill-will; I only dreaded his prodigalities."

"We will put that to rights, and will take nothing of the superintendent but his good qualities."

"What is your majesty looking for?" said Henrietta, seeing the king's eyes constantly turned towards the door, and wishing to let fly a little poisoned arrow at his heart, supposing he was so anxiously expecting either La Valliere or a letter from her.

"My sister," said the young man, who had divined her thought, thanks to that marvelous perspicuity of which fortune was from that time about to allow him the exercise, "my sister, I am expecting a most distinguished man, a most able counselor, whom I wish to present to you all, recommending him to your good graces. Ah! come in, then, D'Artagnan."

"What does your majesty wish?" said D'Artagnan, appearing.

"Where is monsieur the bishop of Vannes, your friend?"

"Why, sire – "

"I am waiting for him, and he does not come. Let him be sought for."

D'Artagnan remained for an instant stupefied; but soon, reflecting that Aramis had left Vaux privately on a mission from the king, he concluded that the king wished to preserve the secret. "Sire," replied he, "does your majesty absolutely require M. d'Herblay to be brought to you?"

"Absolutely is not the word," said Philippe; "I do not want him so particularly as that; but if he can be found – "

"I thought so," said D'Artagnan to himself.

"Is this M. d'Herblay the bishop of Vannes?"

"Yes, madame."

"A friend of M. Fouquet?"

"Yes, madame; an old musketeer."

Anne of Austria blushed.

"One of the four braves who formerly performed such prodigies."

The old queen repented of having wished to bite; she broke off the conversation, in order to preserve the rest of her teeth. "Whatever may be your choice, sire," said she, "I have no doubt it will be excellent."

All bowed in support of that sentiment.

"You will find in him," continued Philippe, "the depth and penetration of M. de Richelieu, without the avarice of M. de Mazarin!"

"A prime minister, sire?" said Monsieur, in a fright.

"I will tell you all about that, brother; but it is strange that M. d'Herblay is not here!"

He called out:

"Let M. Fouquet be informed that I wish to speak to him – oh! before you, before you; do not retire!"

M. de Saint-Aignan returned, bringing satisfactory news of the queen, who only kept her bed from precaution, and to have strength to carry out the king's wishes. Whilst everybody was seeking M. Fouquet and Aramis, the new king quietly continued his experiments, and everybody, family, officers, servants, had not the least suspicion of his identity, his air, his voice, and manners were so like the king's. On his side, Philippe, applying to all countenances the accurate descriptions and key-notes of character supplied by his accomplice Aramis, conducted himself so as not to give birth to a doubt in the minds of those who surrounded him. Nothing from that time could disturb the usurper. With what strange facility had Providence just reversed the loftiest fortune of the world to substitute the lowliest in its stead! Philippe admired the goodness of God with regard to himself, and seconded it with all the resources of his admirable nature. But he felt, at times, something like a specter gliding between him and the rays of his new glory. Aramis did not appear. The conversation had languished in the royal family; Philippe, preoccupied, forgot to dismiss his brother and Madame Henrietta. The latter were astonished, and began, by degrees, to lose all patience. Anne of Austria stooped towards her son's ear and addressed some words to him in Spanish. Philippe was completely ignorant of that language, and grew pale at this unexpected obstacle. But, as if the spirit of the imperturbable Aramis had covered him with his infallibility, instead of appearing disconcerted, Philippe rose. "Well! what?" said Anne of Austria.

"What is all that noise?" said Philippe, turning round towards the door of the second staircase.

And a voice was heard saying, "This way, this way! A few steps more, sire!"

"The voice of M. Fouquet," said D'Artagnan, who was standing close to the queen-mother.

"Then M. d'Herblay cannot be far off," added Philippe.

But he then saw what he little thought

to have beheld so near to him. All eyes were turned towards the door at which M. Fouquet was expected to enter; but it was not M. Fouquet who entered. A terrible cry resounded from all corners of the chamber, a painful cry uttered by the king and all present. It is given to but few men, even those whose destiny contains the strangest elements, and accidents the most wonderful, to contemplate such a spectacle similar to that which presented itself in the royal chamber at that moment. The half-closed shutters only admitted the entrance of an uncertain light passing through thick violet velvet curtains lined with silk. In this soft shade, the eyes were by degrees dilated, and every one present saw others rather with imagination than with actual sight. There could not, however, escape, in these circumstances, one of the surrounding details; and the new object which presented itself appeared as luminous as though it shone out in full sunlight. So it happened with Louis XIV., when he showed himself, pale and frowning, in the doorway of the secret stairs. The face of Fouquet appeared behind him, stamped with sorrow and determination. The queen-mother, who perceived Louis XIV., and who held the hand of Philippe, uttered a cry of which we have spoken, as if she beheld a phantom. Monsieur was bewildered, and kept turning his head in astonishment from one to the other. Madame made a step forward, thinking she was looking at the form of her brother-in-law reflected in a mirror. And, in fact, the illusion was possible. The two princes, both pale as death – for we renounce the hope of being able to describe the fearful state of Philippe – trembling, clenching their hands convulsively, measured each other with looks, and darted their glances, sharp as poniards, at each other. Silent, panting, bending forward, they appeared as if about to spring upon an enemy. The unheard-of resemblance of countenance, gesture, shape, height, even to the resemblance of costume, produced by chance – for Louis XIV. had been to the Louvre and put on a violet-colored dress – the perfect analogy of the two princes, completed the consternation of Anne of Austria. And yet she did not at once guess the truth. There are misfortunes in life so truly dreadful that no one will at first accept them; people rather believe in the supernatural and the impossible. Louis had not reckoned on these obstacles. He expected that he had only to appear to be acknowledged. A living sun, he could not endure the suspicion of equality with any one. He did not admit that every torch should not become darkness at the instant he shone out with his conquering ray. At the aspect of Philippe, then, he was perhaps more terrified than any one round him, and his silence, his immobility were, this time, a concentration and a calm which precede the violent explosions of concentrated passion.

But Fouquet! who shall paint his emotion

and stupor in presence of this living portrait of his master! Fouquet thought Aramis was right, that this newly-arrived was a king as pure in his race as the other, and that, for having repudiated all participation in this **coup d'etat**, so skillfully got up by the General of the Jesuits, he must be a mad enthusiast, unworthy of ever dipping his hands in political grand strategy work. And then it was the blood of Louis XIII. which Fouquet was sacrificing to the blood of Louis XIII.; it was to a selfish ambition he was sacrificing a noble ambition; to the right of keeping he sacrificed the right of having. The whole extent of his fault was revealed to him at simple sight of the pretender. All that passed in the mind of Fouquet was lost upon the persons present. He had five minutes to focus meditation on this point of conscience; five minutes, that is to say five ages, during which the two kings and their family scarcely found energy to breathe after so terrible a shock. D'Artagnan, leaning against the wall, in front of Fouquet, with his hand to his brow, asked himself the cause of such a wonderful prodigy. He could not have said at once why he doubted, but he knew assuredly that he had reason to doubt, and that in this meeting of the two Louis XIV.s lay all the doubt and difficulty that during late days had rendered the conduct of Aramis so suspicious to the musketeer. These ideas were, however, enveloped in a haze, a veil of mystery. The actors in this assembly seemed to swim in the vapors of a confused waking. Suddenly Louis XIV., more impatient and more accustomed to command, ran to one of the shutters, which he opened, tearing the curtains in his eagerness. A flood of living light entered the chamber, and made Philippe draw back to the alcove. Louis seized upon this movement with eagerness, and addressing himself to the queen:

"My mother," said he, "do you not acknowledge your son, since every one here has forgotten his king!" Anne of Austria started, and raised her arms towards Heaven, without being able to articulate a single word.

"My mother," said Philippe, with a calm voice, "do you not acknowledge your son?" And this time, in his turn, Louis drew back.

As to Anne of Austria, struck suddenly in head and heart with fell remorse, she lost her equilibrium. No one aiding her, for all were petrified, she sank back in her fauteuil, breathing a weak, trembling sigh. Louis could not endure the spectacle and the affront. He bounded towards D'Artagnan, over whose brain a vertigo was stealing and who staggered as he caught at the door for support.

"**A moi! mousquetaire!**" said he. "Look us in the face and say which is the paler, he or I!"

This cry roused D'Artagnan, and stirred in his heart the fibers of obedience. He shook his head, and, without more hesitation, he walked straight up to Philippe, on whose shoulder he laid his hand, saying, “Monsieur, you are my prisoner!”

Philippe did not raise his eyes towards Heaven, nor stir from the spot, where he seemed nailed to the floor, his eye intently fixed upon the king his brother. He reproached him with a sublime silence for all misfortunes past, all tortures to come. Against this language of the soul the king felt he had no power; he cast down his eyes, dragging away precipitately his brother and sister, forgetting his mother, sitting motionless within three paces of the son whom she left a second time to be condemned to death. Philippe approached Anne of Austria, and said to her, in a soft and nobly agitated voice:

“If I were not your son, I should curse you, my mother, for having rendered me so unhappy.”

D’Artagnan felt a shudder pass through the marrow of his bones. He bowed respectfully to the young prince, and said as he bent, “Excuse me, monseigneur, I am but a soldier, and my oaths are his who has just left the chamber.”

“Thank you, M. d’Artagnan.... What has become of M. d’Herblay?”

“M. d’Herblay is in safety, monseigneur,” said a voice behind them; “and no one, while I live and am free, shall cause a hair to fall from his head.”

“Monsieur Fouquet!” said the prince, smiling sadly.

“Pardon me, monseigneur,” said Fouquet, kneeling, “but he who is just gone out from hence was my guest.”

“Here are,” murmured Philippe, with a sigh, “brave friends and good hearts. They make me regret the world. On, M. d’Artagnan, I follow you.”

At the moment the captain of the musketeers was about to leave the room with his prisoner, Colbert appeared, and, after remitting an order from the king to D’Artagnan, retired. D’Artagnan read the paper, and then crushed it in his hand with rage.

"What is it?" asked the prince.

"Read, monseigneur," replied the musketeer.

Philippe read the following words, hastily traced by the hand of the king:

"M. d'Artagnan will conduct the prisoner to the Ile Sainte-Marguerite. He will cover his face with an iron vizor, which the prisoner shall never raise except at peril of his life."

"That is just," said Philippe, with resignation; "I am ready."

"Aramis was right," said Fouquet, in a low voice, to the musketeer, "this one is every whit as much a king as the other."

"More so!" replied D'Artagnan. "He wanted only you and me."

CHAPTER TWENTY FIVE

In which Porthos Thinks he is Pursuing a Duchy

ARAMIS AND PORTHOS, having profited by the time granted them by Fouquet, did honor to the French cavalry by their speed. Porthos did not clearly understand on what kind of mission he was forced to display so much velocity; but as he saw Aramis spurring on furiously, he, Porthos, spurred on in the same way. They had soon, in this manner, placed twelve leagues between them and Vaux; they were then obliged to change horses, and organize a sort of post arrangement. It was during a relay that Porthos ventured to interrogate Aramis discreetly.

"Hush!" replied the latter, "know only that our fortune depends on our speed."

As if Porthos had still been the musketeer, without a sou or a **maille** of 1626, he pushed forward. That magic word "fortune" always means something in the human ear. It means **enough** for those who have nothing; it means **too much** for those who have enough.

"I shall be made a duke!" said Porthos, aloud. He was speaking to himself.

"That is possible," replied Aramis, smiling after his own fashion, as Porthos's horse passed him. Aramis felt, notwithstanding, as though his brain were on fire; the activity of the body had not yet succeeded in subduing that of the mind. All there is of raging passion, mental toothache or mortal threat, raged, gnawed and grumbled in the thoughts of the unhappy prelate. His countenance exhibited visible traces of this rude combat. Free on the highway to abandon himself to every impression of the moment, Aramis did not fail to swear at every start of his horse, at every inequality in the road. Pale, at times inundated with boiling sweats, then again dry and icy, he flogged his horses till the blood streamed from their sides. Porthos, whose dominant fault was not sensibility, groaned at this. Thus traveled they on for eight long hours, and then arrived at Orleans. It was four o'clock in the afternoon. Aramis, on observing this, judged that nothing showed pursuit to be a possibility. It would be without example that a troop capable of taking him and Porthos should be furnished with relays sufficient to perform forty leagues in eight hours. Thus, admitting pursuit, which was not at all manifest, the fugitives were five hours in advance of their pursuers.

Aramis thought that there might be no

imprudence in taking a little rest, but that to continue would make the matter more certain. Twenty leagues more, performed with the same rapidity, twenty more leagues devoured, and no one, not even D'Artagnan, could overtake the enemies of the king. Aramis felt obliged, therefore, to inflict upon Porthos the pain of mounting on horseback again. They rode on till seven o'clock in the evening, and had only one post more between them and Blois. But here a diabolical accident alarmed Aramis greatly. There were no horses at the post. The prelate asked himself by what infernal machination his enemies had succeeded in depriving him of the means of going further, – he who never recognized chance as a deity, who found a cause for every accident, preferred believing that the refusal of the postmaster, at such an hour, in such a country, was the consequence of an order emanating from above: an order given with a view of stopping short the king-maker in the midst of his flight. But at the moment he was about to fly into a passion, so as to procure either a horse or an explanation, he was struck with the recollection that the Comte de la Fere lived in the neighborhood.

"I am not traveling," said he; "I do not want horses for a whole stage. Find me two horses to go and pay a visit to a nobleman of my acquaintance who resides near this place."

"What nobleman?" asked the postmaster.

"M. le Comte de la Fere."

"Oh!" replied the postmaster, uncovering with respect, "a very worthy nobleman. But, whatever may be my desire to make myself agreeable to him, I cannot furnish you with horses, for all mine are engaged by M. le Duc de Beaufort."

"Indeed!" said Aramis, much disappointed.

"Only," continued the postmaster, "if you will put up with a little carriage I have, I will harness an old blind horse who has still his legs left, and peradventure will draw you to the house of M. le Comte de la Fere."

"It is worth a louis," said Aramis.

"No, monsieur, such a ride is worth no more than a crown; that is what M. Grimaud, the comte's intendant, always pays me when he makes use of that carriage; and I should not wish the Comte de la Fere to have to reproach me with having imposed on one of his friends."

"As you please," said Aramis, "particularly as regards disobliging the Comte de la Fere; only I think I have a right to give you a louis for your idea."

"Oh! doubtless," replied the postmaster with delight. And he himself harnessed the ancient horse to the creaking carriage. In the meantime Porthos was curious to behold. He imagined he had discovered a clew to the secret, and he felt pleased, because a visit to Athos, in the first place, promised him much satisfaction, and, in the next, gave him the hope of finding at the same time a good bed and good supper. The master, having got the carriage ready, ordered one of his men to drive the strangers to La Fere. Porthos took his seat by the side of Aramis, whispering in his ear, "I understand."

"Aha!" said Aramis, "and what do you understand, my friend?"

"We are going, on the part of the king, to make some great proposal to Athos."

"Pooh!" said Aramis.

"You need tell me nothing about it," added the worthy Porthos, endeavoring to reseat himself so as to avoid the jolting, "you need tell me nothing, I shall guess."

"Well! do, my friend; guess away."

They arrived at Athos's dwelling about nine o'clock in the evening, favored by a splendid moon. This cheerful light rejoiced Porthos beyond expression; but Aramis appeared annoyed by it in an equal degree. He could not help showing something of this to Porthos, who replied – "Ay! ay! I guess how it is! the mission is a secret one."

These were his last words in the carriage.

The driver interrupted him by saying, "Gentlemen, we have arrived."

Porthos and his companion alighted before the gate of the little chateau, where we are about to meet again our old acquaintances Athos and Bragelonne, the latter of whom had disappeared since the discovery of the infidelity of La Valliere. If there be one saying truer than another, it is this: great griefs contain within themselves the germ of consolation. This painful wound, inflicted upon Raoul, had drawn him nearer to his father again; and God knows how sweet were the consolations which flowed from the eloquent mouth and generous heart of Athos. The wound was not cicatrized, but Athos, by dint of conversing with his son and mixing a little more of his life with that of the young man, had brought him to understand that this pang of a first infidelity is necessary to every human existence; and that no one has loved without encountering it. Raoul listened, again and again, but never understood. Nothing replaces in the deeply afflicted heart the remembrance and thought of the beloved object. Raoul then replied to the reasoning of his father:

"Monsieur, all that you tell me is true; I believe that no one has suffered in the affections of the heart so much as you have; but you are a man too great by reason of intelligence, and too severely tried by adverse fortune not to allow for the weakness of the soldier who suffers for the first time. I am paying a tribute that will not be paid a second time; permit me to plunge myself so deeply in my grief that I may forget myself in it, that I may drown even my reason in it."

"Raoul! Raoul!"

"Listen, monsieur. Never shall I accustom myself to the idea that Louise, the chastest and most innocent of women, has been able to so basely deceive a man so honest and so true a lover as myself. Never can I persuade myself that I see that sweet and noble mask change into a hypocritical lascivious face. Louise lost! Louise infamous! Ah! monseigneur, that idea is much more cruel to me than Raoul abandoned – Raoul unhappy!"

Athos then employed the heroic remedy. He defended Louise against Raoul, and justified her perfidy by her love. "A woman who would have yielded to a king because he is a king," said he, "would deserve to be styled infamous; but Louise loves Louis. Young, both, they have forgotten, he his rank, she her vows. Love absolves everything, Raoul. The two young people love each other with sincerity."

And when he had dealt this severe poniard-thrust, Athos, with a sigh, saw Raoul bound away beneath the rankling wound, and fly to the thickest recesses of the wood, or the solitude of his chamber, whence, an hour after, he would return, pale, trembling, but subdued. Then, coming up to Athos with a smile, he would kiss his hand, like the dog who, having been beaten, caresses a respected master, to redeem his fault. Raoul redeemed nothing but his weakness, and only confessed his grief. Thus passed away the days that followed that scene in which Athos had so violently shaken the indomitable pride of the king. Never, when conversing with his son, did he make any allusion to that scene; never did he give him the details of that vigorous lecture, which might, perhaps, have consoled the young man, by showing him his rival humbled. Athos did not wish that the offended lover should forget the respect due to his king. And when Bragelonne, ardent, angry, and melancholy, spoke with contempt of royal words, of the equivocal faith which certain madmen draw from promises that emanate from thrones, when, passing over two centuries, with that rapidity of a bird that traverses a narrow strait to go from one continent to the other, Raoul ventured to predict the time in which kings would be esteemed as less than other men, Athos said to him, in his serene, persuasive voice, "You are right, Raoul; all that you say will happen; kings will lose their privileges, as stars which have survived their aeons lose their splendor. But when that moment comes, Raoul, we shall be dead. And remember well what I say to you. In this world, all, men, women, and kings, must live for the present. We can only live for the future for God."

This was the manner in which Athos and Raoul were, as usual, conversing, and walking backwards and forwards in the long alley of limes in the park, when the bell which served to announce to the comte either the hour of dinner or the arrival of a visitor, was rung; and, without attaching any importance to it, he turned towards the house with his son; and at the end of the alley they found themselves in the presence of Aramis and Porthos.

CHAPTER TWENTY SIX

The Last Adieux

RAOUL UTTERED A CRY, and affectionately embraced Porthos. Aramis and Athos embraced like old men; and this embrace itself being a question for Aramis, he immediately said, “My friend, we have not long to remain with you.”

“Ah!” said the comte.

“Only time to tell you of my good fortune,” interrupted Porthos.

"Ah!" said Raoul.

Athos looked silently at Aramis, whose somber air had already appeared to him very little in harmony with the good news Porthos hinted.

"What is the good fortune that has happened to you? Let us hear it," said Raoul, with a smile.

"The king has made me a duke," said the worthy Porthos, with an air of mystery, in the ear of the young man, "a duke by **brevet**."

But the **asides** of Porthos were always loud enough to be heard by everybody. His murmurs were in the diapason of ordinary roaring. Athos heard him, and uttered an exclamation which made Aramis start. The latter took Athos by the arm, and, after having asked Porthos's permission to say a word to his friend in private, "My dear Athos," he began, "you see me overwhelmed with grief and trouble."

"With grief and trouble, my dear friend?" cried the comte; "oh, what?"

"In two words. I have conspired against the king; that conspiracy has failed, and, at this moment, I am doubtless pursued."

"You are pursued! – a conspiracy! Eh! my friend, what do you tell me?"

"The saddest truth. I am entirely ruined."

"Well, but Porthos – this title of duke – what does all that mean?"

"That is the subject of my severest pain; that is the deepest of my wounds. I have, believing in infallible success, drawn Porthos into my conspiracy. He threw himself into it, as you know he would do, with all his strength, without knowing what he was about; and now he is as much compromised as myself – as completely ruined as I am."

"Good God!" And Athos turned towards Porthos, who was smiling complacently.

"I must make you acquainted with the whole. Listen to me," continued Aramis; and he related the history as we know it. Athos, during the recital, several times felt the sweat break from his forehead. "It was a great idea," said he, "but a great error."

"For which I am punished, Athos."

"Therefore, I will not tell you my entire thought."

"Tell it, nevertheless."

"It is a crime."

"A capital crime; I know it is. **Lese majeste**."

"Porthos! poor Porthos!"

"What would you advise me to do? Success, as I have told you, was certain."

"M. Fouquet is an honest man."

"And I a fool for having so ill-judged him," said Aramis. "Oh, the wisdom of man! Oh, millstone that grinds the world! and which is one day stopped by a grain of sand which has fallen, no one knows how, between its wheels."

"Say by a diamond, Aramis. But the thing is done. How do you think of acting?"

"I am taking away Porthos. The king will never believe that that worthy man has acted innocently. He never can believe that Porthos has thought he was serving the king, whilst acting as he has done. His head would pay my fault. It shall not, must not, be so."

"You are taking him away, whither?"

"To Belle-Isle, at first. That is an impregnable place of refuge. Then, I have the sea, and a vessel to pass over into England, where I have many relations."

"You? in England?"

"Yes, or else in Spain, where I have still more."

"But, our excellent Porthos! you ruin him, for the king will confiscate all his property."

"All is provided for. I know how, when once in Spain, to reconcile myself with Louis XIV., and restore Porthos to favor."

"You have credit, seemingly, Aramis!" said Athos, with a discreet air.

"Much; and at the service of my friends."

These words were accompanied by a warm pressure of the hand.

"Thank you," replied the comte.

"And while we are on this head," said Aramis, "you also are a malcontent; you also, Raoul, have griefs to lay to the king. Follow our example; pass over into Belle-Isle. Then we shall see, I guarantee upon my honor, that in a month there will be war between France and Spain on the subject of this son of Louis XIII., who is an Infante likewise, and whom France detains inhumanly. Now, as Louis XIV. would have no inclination for a war on that subject, I will answer for an arrangement, the result of which must bring greatness to Porthos and to me, and a duchy in France to you, who are already a grandee of Spain. Will you join us?"

"No; for my part I prefer having something to reproach the king with; it is a pride natural to my race to pretend to a superiority over royal races. Doing what you propose, I should become the obliged of the king; I should certainly be the gainer on that ground, but I should be a loser in my conscience. – No, thank you!"

"Then give me two things, Athos, – your absolution."

"Oh! I give it you if you really wished to avenge the weak and oppressed against the oppressor."

"That is sufficient for me," said Aramis, with a blush which was lost in the obscurity of the night. "And now, give me your two best horses to gain the second post, as I have been refused any under the pretext of the Duc de Beaufort being traveling in this country."

"You shall have the two best horses, Aramis; and again I recommend poor Porthos strongly to your care."

"Oh! I have no fear on that score. One word more: do you think I am maneuvering for him as I ought?"

"The evil being committed, yes; for the king would not pardon him, and you have, whatever may be said, always a supporter in M. Fouquet, who will not abandon you, he being himself compromised, notwithstanding his heroic action."

"You are right. And that is why, instead

of gaining the sea at once, which would proclaim my fear and guilt, that is why I remain upon French ground. But Belle-Isle will be for me whatever ground I wish it to be, English, Spanish, or Roman; all will depend, with me, on the standard I shall think proper to unfurl."

"How so?"

"It was I who fortified Belle-Isle; and, so long as I defend it, nobody can take Belle-Isle from me. And then, as you have said just now, M. Fouquet is there. Belle-Isle will not be attacked without the signature of M. Fouquet."

"That is true. Nevertheless, be prudent. The king is both cunning and strong." Aramis smiled.

"I again recommend Porthos to you," repeated the count, with a sort of cold persistence.

"Whatever becomes of me, count," replied Aramis, in the same tone, "our brother Porthos will fare as I do – or **better**."

Athos bowed whilst pressing the hand of Aramis, and turned to embrace Porthos with emotion.

"I was born lucky, was I not?" murmured the latter, transported with happiness, as he folded his cloak round him.

"Come, my dear friend," said Aramis.

Raoul had gone out to give orders for the saddling of the horses. The group was already divided. Athos saw his two friends on the point of departure, and something like a mist passed before his eyes and weighed upon his heart.

"It is strange," thought he, "whence comes the inclination I feel to embrace Porthos once more?" At that moment Porthos turned round, and he came towards his old friend with open arms. This last endearment was tender as in youth, as in times when hearts were warm – life happy. And then Porthos mounted his horse. Aramis came back once more to throw his arms round the neck of Athos. The latter watched them along the high-road, elongated by the shade, in their white cloaks. Like phantoms they seemed to enlarge on their departure from the earth, and it was not in the mist, but in the declivity of the ground that they disappeared. At the end of the perspective, both seemed to have given a spring with their feet, which made them vanish as if evaporated into cloud-land.

Then Athos, with a very heavy heart, returned towards the house, saying to Bragelonne, "Raoul, I don't know what it is that has just told me that I have seen those two for the last time."

"It does not astonish me, monsieur, that you should have such a thought," replied the young man, "for I have at this moment the same, and think also that I shall never see Messieurs du Vallon and d'Herblay again."

"Oh! you," replied the count, "you speak like a man rendered sad by a different cause; you see everything in black; you are young, and if you chance never to see those old friends again, it will because they no longer exist in the world in which you have yet many years to pass. But I – "

Raoul shook his head sadly, and leaned upon the shoulder of the count, without either of them finding another word in their hearts, which were ready to overflow.

All at once a noise of horses and voices, from the extremity of the road to Blois, attracted their attention that way. Flambeaux-bearers shook their torches merrily among the trees of their route, and turned round, from time to time, to avoid distancing the horsemen who followed them. These flames, this noise, this dust of a dozen richly caparisoned horses, formed a strange contrast in the middle of the night with the melancholy and almost funereal disappearance of the two shadows of Aramis and Porthos. Athos went towards the house; but he had hardly reached the parterre, when the entrance gate appeared in a blaze; all the flambeaux stopped and appeared to enflame the road. A cry was heard of "M. le Duc de Beaufort" – and Athos sprang towards the door of his house. But the duke had already alighted from his horse, and was looking around him.

"I am here, monseigneur," said Athos.

"Ah! good evening, dear count," said the prince, with that frank cordiality which won him so many hearts. "Is it too late for a friend?"

"Ah! my dear prince, come in!" said the count.

And, M. de Beaufort leaning on the arm of Athos, they entered the house, followed by Raoul, who walked respectfully and modestly among the officers of the prince, with several of whom he was acquainted.

CHAPTER TWENTY SEVEN

Monsieur de Beaufort

THE PRINCE TURNED ROUND at the moment when Raoul, in order to leave him alone with Athos, was shutting the door, and preparing to go with the other officers into an adjoining apartment.

"Is that the young man I have heard M. le Prince speak so highly of?" asked M. de Beaufort.

"It is, monseigneur."

"He is quite the soldier; let him stay, count, we cannot spare him."

"Remain, Raoul, since monseigneur permits it," said Athos.

"**Ma foi!** he is tall and handsome!" continued the duke. "Will you give him to me, monseigneur, if I ask him of you?"

"How am I to understand you, monseigneur?" said Athos.

"Why, I call upon you to bid you farewell."

"Farewell!"

"Yes, in good truth. Have you no idea of what I am about to become?"

"Why, I suppose, what you have always been, monseigneur, – a valiant prince, and an excellent gentleman."

"I am going to become an African prince, – a Bedouin gentleman. The king is sending me to make conquests among the Arabs."

"What is this you tell me, monseigneur?"

"Strange, is it not? I, the Parisian **par essence**, I who have reigned in the faubourgs, and have been called King of the

Halles, – I am going to pass from the Place Maubert to the minarets of Gigelli; from a Frondeur I am becoming an adventurer!"

"Oh, monseigneur, if you did not yourself tell me that – "

"It would not be credible, would it? Believe me, nevertheless, and we have but to bid each other farewell. This is what comes of getting into favor again."

"Into favor?"

"Yes. You smile. Ah, my dear count, do you know why I have accepted this enterprise, can you guess?"

"Because your highness loves glory above – everything."

"Oh! no; there is no glory in firing muskets at savages. I see no glory in that, for my part, and it is more probable that I shall there meet with something else. But I have wished, and still wish earnestly, my dear count, that my life should have that last **facet**, after all the whimsical exhibitions I have seen myself make during fifty years.

For, in short, you must admit that it is sufficiently strange to be born the grandson of a king, to have made war against kings, to have been reckoned among the powers of the age, to have maintained my rank, to feel Henry IV. within me, to be great admiral of France – and then to go and get killed at Gigelli, among all those Turks, Saracens, and Moors."

"Monseigneur, you harp with strange persistence on that theme," said Athos, in an agitated voice. "How can you suppose that so brilliant a destiny will be extinguished in that remote and miserable scene?"

"And can you believe, upright and simple as you are, that if I go into Africa for this ridiculous motive, I will not endeavor to come out of it without ridicule? Shall I not give the world cause to speak of me? And to be spoken of, nowadays, when there are Monsieur le Prince, M. de Turenne, and many others, my contemporaries, I, admiral of France, grandson of Henry IV., king of

Paris, have I anything left but to get myself killed? **Cordieu!** I will be talked of, I tell you; I shall be killed whether or not; if not there, somewhere else."

"Why, monseigneur, this is mere exaggeration; and hitherto you have shown nothing exaggerated save in bravery."

"**Peste!** my dear friend, there is bravery in facing scurvy, dysentery, locusts, poisoned arrows, as my ancestor St. Louis did. Do you know those fellows still use poisoned arrows? And then, you know me of old, I fancy, and you know that when I once make up my mind to a thing, I perform it in grim earnest."

"Yes, you made up your mind to escape from Vincennes."

"Ay, but you aided me in that, my master; and, **a propos**, I turn this way and that, without seeing my old friend, M. Vaugrimaud. How is he?"

"M. Vaugrimaud is still your highness's most respectful servant," said Athos, smiling.

"I have a hundred pistoles here for him, which I bring as a legacy. My will is made, count."

"Ah! monseigneur! monseigneur!"

"And you may understand that if Grimaud's name were to appear in my will – " The duke began to laugh; then addressing Raoul, who, from the commencement of this conversation, had sunk into a profound reverie, "Young man," said he, "I know there is to be found here a certain De Vouvray wine, and I believe – " Raoul left the room precipitately to order the wine. In the meantime M. de Beaufort took the hand of Athos.

"What do you mean to do with him?" asked he.

"Nothing at present, monseigneur."

"Ah! yes, I know; since the passion of the king for La Valliere."

"Yes, monseigneur."

"That is all true, then, is it? I think I know her,

that little La Valliere. She is not particularly handsome, if I remember right?"

"No, monseigneur," said Athos.

"Do you know whom she reminds me of?"

"Does she remind your highness of any one?"

"She reminds me of a very agreeable girl, whose mother lived in the Halles."

"Ah! ah!" said Athos, smiling.

"Oh! the good old times," added M. de Beaufort. "Yes, La Valliere reminds me of that girl."

"Who had a son, had she not?"[3]

"I believe she had," replied the duke, with careless **naivete** and a complaisant forgetfulness, of which no words could translate the tone and the vocal expression.

---

[3] It is possible that the preceding conversation is an obscure allegorical allusion to the Fronde, or perhaps an intimation that the Duc was the father of Mordaunt, from Twenty Years After, but a definite interpretation still eludes modern scholars.

"Now, here is poor Raoul, who is your son, I believe."

"Yes, he is my son, monseigneur."

"And the poor lad has been cut out by the king, and he frets."

"Still better, monseigneur, he abstains."

"You are going to let the boy rust in idleness; it is a mistake. Come, give him to me."

"My wish is to keep him at home, monseigneur. I have no longer anything in the world but him, and as long as he likes to remain – "

"Well, well," replied the duke. "I could, nevertheless, have soon put matters to rights again. I assure you, I think he has in him the stuff of which marechals of France are made; I have seen more than one produced from less likely rough material."

"That is very possible, monseigneur; but it is the king who makes marechals of France, and Raoul will never accept anything of the king."

Raoul interrupted this conversation by his

return. He preceded Grimaud, whose still steady hands carried the plateau with one glass and a bottle of the duke's favorite wine. On seeing his old **protege**, the duke uttered an exclamation of pleasure.

"Grimaud! Good evening, Grimaud!" said he; "how goes it?"

The servant bowed profoundly, as much gratified as his noble interlocutor.

"Two old friends!" said the duke, shaking honest Grimaud's shoulder after a vigorous fashion; which was followed by another still more profound and delighted bow from Grimaud.

"But what is this, count, only one glass?"

"I should not think of drinking with your highness, unless your highness permitted me," replied Athos, with noble humility.

"**Cordieu!** you were right to bring only one glass, we will both drink out of it, like two brothers in arms. Begin, count."

"Do me the honor," said Athos, gently putting back the glass.

"You are a charming friend," replied the Duc de Beaufort, who drank, and passed the goblet to his companion. "But that is not all," continued he, "I am still thirsty, and I wish to do honor to this handsome young man who stands here. I carry good luck with me, vicomte," said he to Raoul; "wish for something while drinking out of my glass, and may the black plague grab me if what you wish does not come to pass!" He held the goblet to Raoul, who hastily moistened his lips, and replied with the same promptitude:

"I have wished for something, monseigneur." His eyes sparkled with a gloomy fire, and the blood mounted to his cheeks; he terrified Athos, if only with his smile.

"And what have you wished for?" replied the duke, sinking back into his fauteuil, whilst with one hand he returned the bottle to Grimaud, and with the other gave him a purse.

"Will you promise me, monseigneur, to grant me what I wish for?"

"**Pardieu!** That is agreed upon."

"I wished, monsieur le duc, to go with you to Gigelli."

Athos became pale, and was unable to conceal his agitation. The duke looked at his friend, as if desirous to assist him to parry this unexpected blow.

"That is difficult, my dear vicomte, very difficult," added he, in a lower tone of voice.

"Pardon me, monseigneur, I have been indiscreet," replied Raoul, in a firm voice; "but as you yourself invited me to wish – "

"To wish to leave me?" said Athos.

"Oh! monsieur – can you imagine – "

"Well, **mordieu!**" cried the duke, "the young vicomte is right! What can he do here? He will go moldy with grief."

Raoul blushed, and the excitable prince continued: "War is a distraction: we gain everything by it; we can only lose one thing by it – life – then so much the worse!"

"That is to say, memory," said Raoul, eagerly; "and that is to say, so much the better!"

He repented of having spoken so warmly when he saw Athos rise and open the window; which was, doubtless, to conceal his emotion. Raoul sprang towards the comte, but the latter had already overcome his emotion, and turned to the lights with a serene and impassible countenance. "Well, come," said the duke, "let us see! Shall he go, or shall he not? If he goes, comte, he shall be my aide-de-camp, my son."

"Monseigneur!" cried Raoul, bending his knee.

"Monseigneur!" cried Athos, taking the hand of the duke; "Raoul shall do just as he likes."

"Oh! no, monsieur, just as you like," interrupted the young man.

"**Par la corbleu!**" said the prince in his turn, "it is neither the comte nor the vicomte that shall have his way, it is I. I will take him away. The marine offers a superb fortune, my friend."

Raoul smiled again so sadly, that this time Athos felt his heart penetrated by it, and replied to him by a severe look. Raoul comprehended it all; he recovered his calmness, and was so guarded, that not another word escaped him. The duke at length rose, on observing the advanced hour, and said, with animation, "I am in great haste, but if I am told I have lost time in talking with a friend, I will reply I have gained – on the balance – a most excellent recruit."

"Pardon me, monsieur le duc," interrupted Raoul, "do not tell the king so, for it is not the king I wish to serve."

"Eh! my friend, whom, then, will you serve? The times are past when you might have said, 'I belong to M. de Beaufort.' No, nowadays, we all belong to the king, great or small. Therefore, if you serve on board my vessels, there can be nothing equivocal about it, my dear vicomte; it will be the king you will serve."

Athos waited with a kind of impatient joy for the reply about to be made to this embarrassing question by Raoul, the intractable enemy of the king, his rival. The father hoped that the obstacle would overcome the desire. He was thankful to M. de Beaufort, whose lightness or generous reflection had thrown an impediment in the way of the departure of a son, now his only joy. But Raoul, still firm and tranquil, replied: "Monsieur le duc, the objection you make I have already considered in my mind. I will serve on board your vessels, because you do me the honor to take me with you; but I shall there serve a more powerful master than the king: I shall serve God!"

"God! how so?" said the duke and Athos together.

"My intention is to make profession, and become a knight of Malta," added Bragelonne, letting fall, one by one, words more icy than the drops which fall from the bare trees after the tempests of winter.[4]

Under this blow Athos staggered and the prince himself was moved. Grimaud uttered a heavy groan, and let fall the bottle, which was broken without anybody paying attention. M. de Beaufort looked the young man in the face, and read plainly, though his eyes were cast down, the fire of resolution before which everything must give way. As to Athos, he was too well acquainted with that tender, but inflexible soul; he could not hope to make it deviate from the fatal road it had just chosen. He could only press the hand the duke held out to him. “Comte, I shall set off in two days for Toulon,” said M. de Beaufort. “Will you meet me at Paris, in order that I may know your determination?”

“I will have the honor of thanking you there, **mon prince**, for all your kindness,” replied

---

[4] The dictates of such a service would require Raoul to spend the rest of his life outside of France, hence Athos’s and Grimaud’s extreme reactions.

the comte.

"And be sure to bring the vicomte with you, whether he follows me or does not follow me," added the duke; "he has my word, and I only ask yours."

Having thrown a little balm upon the wound of the paternal heart, he pulled the ear of Grimaud, whose eyes sparkled more than usual, and regained his escort in the parterre. The horses, rested and refreshed, set off with spirit through the lovely night, and soon placed a considerable distance between their master and the chateau.

Athos and Bragelonne were again face to face. Eleven o'clock was striking. The father and son preserved a profound silence towards each other, where an intelligent observer would have expected cries and tears. But these two men were of such a nature that all emotion following their final resolutions plunged itself so deep into their hearts that it was lost forever. They passed, then, silently and almost breathlessly, the hour that preceded midnight. The clock, by striking, alone pointed out to them how many minutes had lasted the painful journey made by their souls in the immensity of their remembrances of the past and fear of the future. Athos rose first, saying, "it is late, then.... Till to-morrow."

Raoul rose, and in his turn embraced his father. The latter held him clasped to his breast, and said, in a tremulous voice, "In two days, you will have left me, my son – left me forever, Raoul!"

"Monsieur," replied the young man, "I had formed a determination, that of piercing my heart with my sword; but you would have thought that cowardly. I have renounced that determination, and **therefore** we must part."

"You leave me desolate by going, Raoul."

"Listen to me again, monsieur, I implore you. If I do not go, I shall die here of grief and love. I know how long a time I have to live thus. Send me away quickly, monsieur, or you will see me basely die before your eyes – in your house – this is stronger than my will – stronger than my strength – you may plainly see that within one month I have lived thirty years, and that I approach the end of my life."

"Then," said Athos, coldly, "you go with the intention of getting killed in Africa? Oh, tell me! do not lie!"

Raoul grew deadly pale, and remained silent for two seconds, which were to his father two hours of agony. Then, all at once: "Monsieur," said he, "I have promised to devote myself to God. In exchange for the sacrifice I make of my youth and liberty, I will only ask of Him one thing, and that is, to preserve me for you, because you are the only tie which attaches me to this world. God alone can give me the strength not to forget that I owe you everything, and that nothing ought to stand in my esteem before you."

Athos embraced his son tenderly, and

said:

"You have just replied to me on the word of honor of an honest man; in two days we shall be with M. de Beaufort at Paris, and you will then do what will be proper for you to do. You are free, Raoul; adieu."

And he slowly gained his bedroom. Raoul went down into the garden, and passed the night in the alley of limes.

CHAPTER TWENTY EIGHT

Preparations for Departure

ATHOS LOST NO MORE time in combating this immutable resolution. He gave all his attention to preparing, during the two days the duke had granted him, the proper appointments for Raoul. This labor chiefly concerned Grimaud, who immediately applied himself to it with the good-will and intelligence we know he possessed. Athos gave this worthy servant orders to take the route to Paris when the equipments should be ready; and, not to expose himself to the danger of keeping the duke waiting, or delaying Raoul, so that the duke should perceive his absence, he himself, the day after the visit of M. de Beaufort, set off for Paris with his son.

For the poor young man it was an emotion easily to be understood, thus to return to Paris amongst all the people who had known and loved him. Every face recalled a pang to him who had suffered so much; to him who had loved so much, some circumstance of his unhappy love. Raoul, on approaching Paris, felt as if he were dying. Once in Paris, he really existed no longer. When he reached Guiche's residence, he was informed that Guiche was with Monsieur. Raoul took the road to the Luxembourg, and when arrived, without suspecting that he was going to the place where La Valliere had lived, he heard so much music and respired so many perfumes, he heard so much joyous laughter, and saw so many dancing shadows, that if it had not been for a charitable woman, who perceived him so dejected and pale beneath a doorway, he would have remained there a few minutes, and then would have gone away, never to return. But, as we have said, in the first ante-chamber he had stopped, solely for the sake of not mixing himself with all those happy beings he felt were moving around him in the adjacent salons. And as one of Monsieur's servants, recognizing him, had asked him if he wished to see Monsieur or Madame, Raoul had scarcely answered him, but had sunk down upon a bench near the velvet doorway, looking at a clock, which had stopped for nearly an hour. The servant had passed on, and another, better acquainted with him, had come up, and interrogated Raoul whether he should inform M. de Guiche of his being there. This name did not even arouse the recollections of Raoul. The persistent servant went on to relate that De Guiche had just invented a new game of lottery, and was teaching it to the ladies. Raoul, opening his large eyes, like the absent man in Theophrastus, made no answer, but his sadness increased two shades. With his head hanging down, his limbs relaxed, his mouth half open for the escape of his sighs, Raoul remained, thus forgotten, in the ante-chamber, when all at once a lady's robe passed, rubbing against the doors of a side salon, which opened on the gallery. A lady, young, pretty, and gay, scolding an officer of the household, entered by that way, and expressed herself with much vivacity. The officer replied in calm but firm sentences; it was rather a little love pet than a quarrel of courtiers, and was terminated by a kiss on the fingers of the lady. Suddenly, on perceiving Raoul, the lady became silent, and pushing away the officer:

"Make your escape, Malicorne," said she; "I did not think there was any one here. I shall curse you, if they have either heard or seen us!"

Malicorne hastened away. The young lady advanced behind Raoul, and stretching her joyous face over him as he lay:

"Monsieur is a gallant man," said she, "and no doubt – "

She here interrupted herself by uttering a cry. "Raoul!" said she, blushing.

"Mademoiselle de Montalais!" said Raoul, paler than death.

He rose unsteadily, and tried to make his way across the slippery mosaic of the floor; but she had comprehended that savage and cruel grief; she felt that in the flight of Raoul there was an accusation of herself. A woman, ever vigilant, she did not think she ought to let the opportunity slip of making good her justification; but Raoul, though stopped by her in the middle of the gallery, did not seem disposed to surrender without a combat. He took it up in a tone so cold and embarrassed, that if they had been thus surprised, the whole court would have no doubt about the proceedings of Mademoiselle de Montalais.

"Ah! monsieur," said she with disdain, "what you are doing is very unworthy of a gentleman. My heart inclines me to speak to you; you compromise me by a reception almost uncivil; you are wrong, monsieur; and you confound your friends with enemies. Farewell!"

Raoul had sworn never to speak of Louise, never even to look at those who might have seen Louise; he was going into another world, that he might never meet with anything Louise had seen, or even touched. But after the first shock of his pride, after having had a glimpse of Montalais, the companion of Louise – Montalais, who reminded him of the turret of Blois and the joys of youth – all his reason faded away.

"Pardon me, mademoiselle; it enters not, it cannot enter into my thoughts to be uncivil."

"Do you wish to speak to me?" said she, with the smile of former days. "Well! come somewhere else; for we may be surprised."

"Oh!" said he.

She looked at the clock, doubtingly, then, having reflected:

"In my apartment," said she, "we shall have an hour to ourselves." And taking her course, lighter than a fairy, she ran up to her chamber, followed by Raoul. Shutting the door, and placing in the hands of her **cameriste** the mantle she had held upon her arm:

"You were seeking M. de Guiche, were you not?" said she to Raoul.

"Yes, mademoiselle."

"I will go and ask him to come up here, presently, after I have spoken to you."

"Do so, mademoiselle."

"Are you angry with me?"

Raoul looked at her for a moment, then, casting down his eyes, "Yes," said he.

"You think I was concerned in the plot which brought about the rupture, do you not?"

"Rupture!" said he, with bitterness. "Oh!

mademoiselle, there can be no rupture where there has been no love."

"You are in error," replied Montalais; "Louise did love you."

Raoul started.

"Not with love, I know; but she liked you, and you ought to have married her before you set out for London."

Raoul broke into a sinister laugh, which made Montalais shudder.

"You tell me that very much at your ease, mademoiselle. Do people marry whom they like? You forget that the king then kept for himself as his mistress her of whom we are speaking."

"Listen," said the young woman, pressing the hands of Raoul in her own, "you were wrong in every way; a man of your age ought never to leave a woman of hers alone."

"There is no longer any faith in the world, then," said Raoul.

"No, vicomte," said Montalais, quietly. "Nevertheless, let me tell you that, if, instead of loving Louise coldly and philosophically, you had endeavored to awaken her to love – ”

“Enough, I pray you, mademoiselle,” said Raoul. “I feel as though you are all, of both sexes, of a different age from me. You can laugh, and you can banter agreeably. I, mademoiselle, I loved Mademoiselle de – ” Raoul could not pronounce her name, – “I loved her well! I put my faith in her – now I am quits by loving her no longer.”

“Oh, vicomte!” said Montalais, pointing to his reflection in a looking-glass.

“I know what you mean, mademoiselle; I am much altered, am I not? Well! Do you know why? Because my face is the mirror of my heart, the outer surface changed to match the mind within.”

“You are consoled, then?” said Montalais, sharply.

“No, I shall never be consoled.”

“I don’t understand you, M. de Bragelonne.”

“I care but little for that. I do not quite

understand myself."

"You have not even tried to speak to Louise?"

"Who! I?" exclaimed the young man, with eyes flashing fire; "I! – Why do you not advise me to marry her? Perhaps the king would consent now." And he rose from his chair full of anger.

"I see," said Montalais, "that you are not cured, and that Louise has one enemy the more."

"One enemy the more!"

"Yes; favorites are but little beloved at the court of France."

"Oh! while she has her lover to protect her, is not that enough? She has chosen him of such a quality that her enemies cannot prevail against her." But, stopping all at once, "And then she has you for a friend, mademoiselle," added he, with a shade of irony which did not glide off the cuirass.

"Who! I? – Oh, no! I am no longer one of

those whom Mademoiselle de la Valliere condescends to look upon; but – "

This **but**, so big with menace and with storm; this **but**, which made the heart of Raoul beat, such griefs did it presage for her whom lately he loved so dearly; this terrible **but**, so significant in a woman like Montalais, was interrupted by a moderately loud noise heard by the speakers proceeding from the alcove behind the wainscoting. Montalais turned to listen, and Raoul was already rising, when a lady entered the room quietly by the secret door, which she closed after her.

"Madame!" exclaimed Raoul, on recognizing the sister-in-law of the king.

"Stupid wretch!" murmured Montalais, throwing herself, but too late, before the princess, "I have been mistaken in an hour!" She had, however, time to warn the princess, who was walking towards Raoul.

"M. de Bragelonne, Madame," and at these words the princess drew back, uttering a cry in her turn.

"Your royal highness," said Montalais, with volubility, "is kind enough to think of this lottery, and – "

The princess began to lose countenance. Raoul hastened his departure, without divining all, but he felt that he was in the way. Madame was preparing a word of transition to recover herself, when a closet opened in front of the alcove, and M. de Guiche issued, all radiant, also from that closet. The palest of the four, we must admit, was still Raoul. The princess, however, was near fainting, and was obliged to lean upon the foot of the bed for support. No one ventured to support her. This scene occupied several minutes of terrible suspense. But Raoul broke it. He went up to the count, whose inexpressible emotion made his knees tremble, and taking his hand, "Dear count," said he, "tell Madame I am too unhappy not to merit pardon; tell her also that I have loved in the course of my life, and that the horror of the treachery that has been practiced on me renders me inexorable towards all other treachery that may be committed around me. This is why, mademoiselle," said he, smiling to Montalais, "I never would divulge the secret of the visits of my friend to your apartment. Obtain from Madame – from Madame, who is so clement and so generous, – obtain her pardon for you whom she has just surprised also. You are both free, love each other, be happy!"

The princess felt for a moment a despair that cannot be described; it was repugnant to her, notwithstanding the exquisite delicacy which Raoul had exhibited, to feel herself at the mercy of one who had discovered such an indiscretion. It was equally repugnant to her to accept the evasion offered by this delicate deception. Agitated, nervous, she struggled against the double stings of these two troubles. Raoul comprehended her position, and came once more to her aid. Bending his knee before her: "Madame!" said he, in a low voice, "in two days I shall be far from Paris; in a fortnight I shall be far from France, where I shall never be seen again."

"Are you going away, then?" said she, with great delight.

"With M. de Beaufort."

"Into Africa!" cried De Guiche, in his turn. "You, Raoul – oh! my friend – into Africa, where everybody dies!"

And forgetting everything, forgetting that that forgetfulness itself compromised the princess more eloquently than his presence, "Ingrate!" said he, "and you have not even consulted me!" And he embraced him; during which time Montalais had led away Madame, and disappeared herself.

Raoul passed his hand over his brow, and said, with a smile, "I have been dreaming!" Then warmly to Guiche, who by degrees absorbed him, "My friend," said he, "I conceal nothing from you, who are the elected of my heart. I am going to seek death in yonder country; your secret will not remain in my breast more than a year."

"Oh, Raoul! a man!"

"Do you know what is my thought, count? This is it – I shall live more vividly, being buried beneath the earth, than I have lived for this month past. We are Christians, my friend, and if such sufferings were to continue, I would not be answerable for the safety of my soul."

De Guiche was anxious to raise objections.

"Not one word more on my account," said Raoul; "but advice to you, dear friend; what I am going to say to you is of much greater importance."

"What is that?"

"Without doubt you risk much more than I do, because you love."

"Oh!"

"It is a joy so sweet to me to be able to speak to you thus! Well, then, De Guiche, beware of Montalais."

"What! of that kind friend?"

"She was the friend of – her you know of. She ruined her by pride."

"You are mistaken."

"And now, when she has ruined her, she would ravish from her the only thing that renders that woman excusable in my eyes."

"What is that?"

"Her love."

"What do you mean by that?"

"I mean that there is a plot formed against her who is the mistress of the king – a plot formed in the very house of Madame."

"Can you think so?"

"I am certain of it."

"By Montalais?"

"Take her as the least dangerous of the enemies I dread for – the other!"

"Explain yourself clearly, my friend; and if I can understand you – "

"In two words. Madame has been long jealous of the king."

"I know she has – "

"Oh! fear nothing – you are beloved – you are beloved, count; do you feel the value of these three words? They signify that you can raise your head, that you can sleep tranquilly, that you can thank God every minute of you life. You are beloved; that signifies that you may hear everything, even the counsel of a friend who wishes to preserve your happiness. You are beloved, De Guiche, you are beloved! You do not endure those atrocious nights, those nights without end, which, with arid eye and fainting heart, others pass through who are destined to die. You will live long, if you act like the miser who, bit by bit, crumb by crumb, collects and heaps up diamonds and gold. You are beloved! – allow me to tell you what you must do that you may be beloved forever."

De Guiche contemplated for some time this unfortunate young man, half mad with despair, till there passed through his heart something like remorse at his own happiness. Raoul suppressed his feverish excitement, to assume the voice and countenance of an impassible man.

"They will make her, whose name I should

wish still to be able to pronounce – they will make her suffer. Swear to me that you will not second them in anything – but that you will defend her when possible, as I would have done myself."

"I swear I will," replied De Guiche.

"And," continued Raoul, "some day, when you shall have rendered her a great service – some day when she shall thank you, promise me to say these words to her – 'I have done you this kindness, madame, at the warm request of M. de Bragelonne, whom you so deeply injured.'"

"I swear I will," murmured De Guiche.

"That is all. Adieu! I set out to-morrow, or the day after, for Toulon. If you have a few hours to spare, give them to me."

"All! all!" cried the young man.

"Thank you!"

"And what are you going to do now?"

"I am going to meet M. le comte at Planchet's residence, where we hope to find M. d'Artagnan."

"M. d'Artagnan?"

"Yes, I wish to embrace him before my departure. He is a brave man, who loves me dearly. Farewell, my friend; you are expected, no doubt; you will find me, when you wish, at the lodgings of the comte. Farewell!"

The two young men embraced. Those who chanced to see them both thus, would not have hesitated to say, pointing to Raoul, "That is the happy man!"

CONTINUES IN VOLUME TWO

GRANDTYPECLASSICS.COM

"If a book is well written,
I always find it too short." J. Austen

As a Man Thinketh BY J. ALLEN
Au Bonheur des Dames BY É. ZOLA
Autobiography of a Yogi BY P. YOGANANDA
Barnaby Rudge BY C. DICKENS
Ben-Hur BY L. WALLACE
Beyond Good and Evil BY F. NIETZSCHE
Billy Budd, Sailor BY H. MELVILLE
Black Beauty BY A. SEWELL
Bleak House BY C. DICKENS
Candide BY VOLTAIRE
Captain Blood BY R. SABATINI
Captains Courageous BY R. KIPLING
Common Sense BY T. PAINE
Cousin Bette BY H. DE BALZAC
Cranford BY E. GASKELL
Crime and Punishment BY F. DOSTOEVSKY
Daphnis and Chloe BY LONGUS
David Copperfield BY C. DICKENS
Dead Souls BY N. GOGOL
Devils BY F. DOSTOEVSKY
Doctor Thorne BY A. TROLLOPE
Dombey and Son BY C. DICKENS
Don Quixote BY M. DE CERVANTES

www.ingramcontent.com/pod-product-compliance
Lightning Source LLC
Chambersburg PA
CBHW020919310726
48980CB00011B/954/J

* 9 7 8 1 8 3 4 1 2 3 9 3 6 *